THE PROPHET WITCH

A NOVEL OF PURITAN NEW ENGLAND (BOOK TWO)

JAMES W. GEORGE

PRAISE FOR JAMES W. GEORGE AND
MY FATHER'S KINGDOM

"Five stars to My Father's Kingdom. It's a rare read full of stunning turns of fate and unforeseen consequences that carry this satisfying saga through to its historically accurate conclusion — the long, bloody conflict between settlers and Indians that was "King Philip's War."
-        Courtesy of The Indie View

"Five stars...Reading historical fiction like My Father's Kingdom was a great experience...If you are interested in historical fiction, My Father's Kingdom: A Novel of Puritan New England by James W. George has everything and does not disappoint."
-        Courtesy of Vernita Taylor, ReadersFavorite.com

"It's a beautiful picture of American History and the fragile nature of peace and friendship...Five Stars."
-        Courtesy of The Literary Titan

"Tormented visions, Puritanical plots, and lost love all figure into the spirited narrative that brings the book's players alive...This is a tale that will fully engage you on every level... This is high historical drama handled wonderfully by first-time author James W. George"
-        Courtesy of PublishersDailyReviews.com

"The plot, the true events on which the story is based, and the engaging writing make this a fun as well as an enlightening read...5/5 Stars."
-        Courtesy of Gisela Dixon, ReadersFavorite.com

This is my second novel, and it is dedicated to my parents, Donald and Barbara George, my brother, Michael George (USMC, RET) and his family.

Additionally, it is dedicated to my wife's family: Randall and Susan Van Quill, Lois Van Quill, and Adrienne Van Quill.

Special thanks as always to my wife, Jennifer, for her love, support, and brilliant mind.

James W. George
August 2017

TABLE OF CONTENTS

PART ONE

PART THREE

AUTHOR'S NOTES (PREFACE)

The Prophet and the Witch is a historical novel set in New England in 1675. It depicts the fascinating but catastrophic events of King Philip's War. I hope a few quick notes will clarify a few issues, and will help enhance your enjoyment of the book.

1. First, please note this book is **book two of a series**. If you were unable to read book one, "My Father's Kingdom," (or if you could use a refresher), a **summary of book one** is provided.

2. This book is historical fiction. Although there are numerous fictional characters, all of the main events you will read about are taken from the pages of history. **These events really happened**. Most Americans (and students of history from any country) are unfamiliar with the events of King Philip's War, and it is often referred to as "America's forgotten war." Approximately fifty years after the Pilgrims of Plymouth Colony befriended Massasoit and the Wampanoag people, their relationship badly deteriorated, and war erupted in the summer of 1675. The war was one of the most catastrophic events in Colonial American history. Further discussions regarding historical fact versus literary fiction are included at the end of the novel.

3. You are probably aware that the seventeenth-century Puritans did not write and speak quite like we do today (if you don't believe it, go ahead and google the journals of Increase Mather, Benjamin Church, or William Hubbard). For literary purposes, **I did not attempt to emulate this**. The only exception is I adopted the old spelling of Plymouth (henceforth known as Plimoth).

4. There are quite a few characters in this book. **A list of characters has been provided** which differentiate the historical characters from the fictional characters. Please note

the **various names for Metacomet** (the leader of the Wampanoag). When relations with Plimoth Colony were cordial in the early 1660s, Metacomet and his brother Wamsutta had English names ceremoniously bestowed upon them. Metacomet became **"Philip"**, and Wamsutta was named "Alexander." Additionally, the term **"Sachem"** is a native word similar to "Chief." Consequently, **Metacomet will be variously referred to as Philip, King Philip, and Sachem throughout the book**.

5. When we think about American history, far too often we tend to think of the Native American nations as one monolithic block of people. As you can see from the map provided, the Native Americans of seventeenth-century New England were actually a remarkable tapestry of tribes and nations. King Philip was of the Pokanoket people, which was part of the broader identity of "Wampanoag." Additionally, please note the Mohegans and the Mohawks were different nations, despite their similar-sounding names. The Mohegans were primarily from Connecticut, whereas the Mohawks were situated further west, in the Hudson River valley.

I hope these notes will prove helpful, and I hope you enjoy the novel.

SUMMARY OF BOOK ONE

MY FATHER'S KINGDOM

The Prophet and the Witch is book two of a series. It is recommended that the reader complete book one first. If that is not possible, or if a lengthy period has elapsed since reading book one, here is a brief summary.

PART ONE: SUMMER 1671

CHAPTER ONE: The year is 1671 and the setting is New England. Linto is a young man in his early twenties who is part of the Wampanoag community. He was adopted as a toddler from the Abenaki people to the north. Linto is a very curious and pensive young man, and is always wondering about the nature of God and the spiritual world. He is also fascinated by the curious ways of the English, who arrived fifty years ago.

Linto's romantic partner is Wawetseka. They are both worried about Metacomet, the Wampanoag Sachem (or "chief"). Although the Wampanoag have been allied with the English from the time they arrived in the New World, the relationship is deteriorating, and things seem to be growing worse for the Wampanoag people.

CHAPTER TWO: Israel Brewster is a twenty-seven-year-old Puritan minister in the town of Middleborough. He is virtuous, devout, and living with a devastating personal tragedy. Brewster strongly advocates a more conciliatory relationship with their Indian neighbors, and he organizes a missionary trip during the next week to help bring the light of Christ to the natives.

CHAPTER THREE: Metacomet is tormented by dreams and visions of his older brother, Wamsutta. Wamsutta assumed the role of Sachem in 1661, after the death of their father, Massasoit. Massasoit was the "Great Sachem" who forged the alliance with the English. Wamsutta, however, perished under mysterious circumstances at the hands of the English a year after he became Sachem.

Metacomet convenes a council of the Wampanoag to recount the tale of Wamsutta's last days. The tale is told by Mentayyup, a senior and powerful warrior who was with Wamsutta during his final week. Wamsutta voluntarily accompanied Josiah Winslow to Plimoth to discuss land transactions, but quickly fell ill and died within days.

Metacomet always believed his older brother was poisoned by the English, but even after nine years, he can't bring himself to forsake the alliance his father built. Tobias, one of Metacomet's trusted lieutenants, despises the English and is an advocate for immediate war. John Sassamon, a Christian Indian who is very knowledgeable of the English language and customs, strongly advocates trust, and peaceful relations with the English. Nothing is resolved, but Metacomet directs Linto to accompany him for further discussion.

CHAPTER FOUR: Brewster is depicted serving the people of Middleborough. He assists with the raising of a new home, and he conducts spiritual counseling in the evening. He is clearly enthralled with Alice Fuller, an attractive young woman in the community.

During spiritual counseling, the trials and tribulations of some residents are revealed. One individual believes Indian witchcraft is responsible for his recently deceased cow. A recently married couple, the Farwells, come for marriage counseling because she is still not with child, and he is too exhausted to be romantic. The third and final counseling session deals with death, grief, and the Puritan doctrine of predestination.

Brewster contemplates his famous grandfather, Elder William Brewster, who was a spiritual leader aboard the Mayflower. Israel Brewster is convinced his own life has been unimpressive when compared to the achievements and suffering of William Brewster and the Mayflower passengers.

CHAPTER FIVE: Israel Brewster is revealed to be a widower, who lost his beloved wife eighteen months ago. He is excited to receive a letter from the famous Reverend Increase Mather in Boston, inviting him to Boston for discussion and mentoring.

The journey to Boston is long, and Brewster borrows a horse named Brownie. He reminisces about his younger days as a militiaman, and he is fixated on a mysterious conversation he can still vividly recall. Brewster spends the night with a family in Weymouth. He is continuing to suffer from night terrors due to his recent tragedy.

Brewster enjoys the visit to Boston, as he has only been there once before. Reverend Mather conveys his thoughts that the New England colonies are awash in sin and wickedness. He believes just as the Lord utilized heathen savages to decimate the ancient Kingdom of Israel as punishment for their transgressions, the Lord will likewise use the local natives to punish New England. Mather encourages Brewster to become more active in local civic matters, such as the impending meeting of the Plimoth General Court.

CHAPTER SIX: The Plimoth General Court is in session. The key figures are Governor Prence, Deputy Governor Josiah Winslow, and Treasurer Jeremiah Barron.

The deliberative assembly discusses rumors of brewing hostility and rebellion from Metacomet and the Wampanoag. A plan is formulated to force Metacomet to face the Plimoth government in order to answer for his aggression, and to strip the Wampanoag of their firearms.

Brewster is in attendance, and in the midst of feverish outcry against the Wampanoag, Brewster advises Christian charity, patience, and ministry. Jeremiah Barron condescendingly denounces him as naïve and ill-informed, and Brewster is publicly humiliated.

CHAPTER SEVEN: Metacomet and Linto have just left the Wampanoag council at which Wamsutta's final days were recounted. Metacomet feels conflicted and indecisive regarding their alliance with the English, and he pleads with Linto for guidance. Metacomet reminds Linto that he is a special, divinely-blessed being who was miraculously delivered to the Wampanoag, and he needs to start embracing his destiny as a holy man.

The story of Linto's adoption is recounted. When Metacomet was thirteen, he and his father accompanied a diplomatic mission to the Abenaki people a few days north of the Wampanoag. They encountered an entire village decimated by the smallpox plague. Not a soul was still alive, except for Linto, who was two or three years old. Amidst all the carnage, Linto was merrily singing, and was christened *Linto,* the Abenaki word for *sing.* Massasoit and the spiritual elders declared Linto was a miracle, and his survival was a sign that the spiritual world had not abandoned the people during this time of crisis.

After the tale is recounted, Linto admits to Metacomet that despite Metacomet's pleas for guidance, Linto has no advice to offer him about the English.

CHAPTER EIGHT: Brewster once again journeys with Brownie the mare. He leads approximately two dozen members of his Middleborough congregation to Taunton for a day of missionary activities. They are joined by Reverend John Eliot, one of the leading missionaries of the era.

After some devout missionary work, Brewster engages in light-hearted wrestling matches with the natives, one of whom is Linto. Linto and Brewster subsequently have a profound discussion about the nature of God, suffering, predestination, and Christianity. Linto introduces Brewster to Wawetseka.

Brewster inquires about Metacomet's health, and Linto informs him Metacomet is still tormented by the death of his brother, Wamsutta. Brewster expresses surprise Metacomet is still grieving, since Wamsutta perished nine or ten years ago. Linto conveys that Metacomet is tormented because all the Wampanoag believe Wamsutta was poisoned by Josiah Winslow.

This revelation stuns Brewster, and he reveals an astounding, secret coincidence: Brewster was a young militiaman accompanying Josiah Winslow when Wamsutta was escorted to Plimoth. Brewster was with Wamsutta during every minute of the journey, and he was positive Wamsutta could not have been poisoned, as Wamsutta never accepted any food, drink, or medicine from his English hosts.

Additionally, Brewster was the only one who heard Wamsutta's dying words, but he had failed to grasp their significance. Wamsutta was trying to convey that he was not poisoned, and he wanted to ensure all the Wampanoag understood. Linto is overjoyed that he can finally deliver some good news to Metacomet.

Throughout the conversation, Wawetseka detects an intense sense of grief emanating from Brewster, and Linto insists Brewster permit her to perform a healing ritual for him.

CHAPTER NINE: Wawetseka and another Wampanoag woman escort Brewster deep into the forest and prepare a special tea for him. He falls into a trance and intensely relives the cause of all of his grief.

On a bitterly cold night, Brewster's wife, Sarah, was in labor with their first child. The child, however, was stillborn, which the Puritans believed was a certain sign of God's divine wrath. The ordeal physically depletes Sarah, and she perishes as well. Brewster convinces himself this is somehow divine retribution, because during his militia service eleven years ago, he escorted the accused heretic, Mary Dyer, to the gallows. Brewster feels intense remorse and shame because he obediently complied while an innocent woman was executed.

After the healing ritual, Brewster suddenly feels spiritually cleansed.

CHAPTER TEN: After a successful missionary visit, and after the miraculous healing ritual, Brewster feels invigorated. He finally has the confidence to formally court Alice Fuller, but he is stunned to discover he has a romantic rival. Reverend Phelps, a suave, handsome minister from Plimoth, is also seeking her hand.

After a few weeks of this romantic battle, Brewster once again attends the public session of the Plimoth General Court.

Reverend Phelps informs him that he is to be addressed by the authorities. Brewster assumes he will be recognized and congratulated for his missionary work.

Instead, Brewster is accused and denounced by the court, with Jeremiah Barron leading the proceedings. Brewster is reprimanded for wrestling with the savages, for procuring an herb-based aphrodisiac for a member of his congregation, for participating in the witchcraft of Wawetseka's healing ritual, and for questioning the lawful execution of Mary Dyer. He is hounded and denounced until his eyes well with tears. He is stripped of his ministry, and ordered to return in three days to stand trial.

Upon arriving at his home in Middleborough, Brewster decides to flee. He gathers his possessions and takes Brownie in a westerly direction, the opposite direction of Plimoth.

CHAPTER ELEVEN: Metacomet is mentally reliving the events of the summer. He recalls how the Wampanoag were on the brink of open warfare when Linto delivered the miraculous news that Wamsutta was never poisoned. Metacomet interpreted it as a divine sign that now was not the time for war.

Metacomet submitted to all the demands of the Plimoth government that summer. The Wampanoag surrendered their firearms, and agreed to pay restitution and annual tribute to Plimoth. They also took a loyalty oath to Plimoth, and the King of England.

Metacomet is always cognizant of how the Pequot were decimated after going to war with the English four decades prior. He feels like losing the alliance with the English would be a betrayal of his father. Metacomet convinces himself he had no choice but to acquiesce to Plimoth, but deep down he is humiliated and enraged.

PART TWO: AUTUMN 1674

CHAPTER TWELVE: Approximately three years have passed, and Israel Brewster now resides in Providence. He has fled Plimoth Colony and his old life, and he is now a cooper and a drunkard. He has kept Brownie the horse, however.

While assembling barrels in the cooperage, he is accosted by Deputy Governor John Easton, a prominent Quaker and civic leader. Easton had witnessed Brewster's drunken buffoonery in a tavern the night before, and he insists Brewster accompany him for Christian worship the next day. Brewster is highly reluctant to attend Quaker worship, but Easton won't take no for an answer, and even threatens to imprison him for his drunken antics.

CHAPTER THIRTEEN: Linto is also three years older. He is married to Wawetseka and they now have two children. His English has improved tremendously, and Metacomet has asked him to review all the legal documents between Plimoth and the Wampanoag that were previously prepared by John Sassamon.

Linto is horrified to discover Sassamon has been cheating the Wampanoag at every opportunity, and has even used the language barrier to make himself the chief beneficiary of Metacomet's will. Upon his return from Plimoth, Metacomet and the Wampanoag council confront Sassamon, who flees in a panic when his treachery is revealed.

CHAPTER FOURTEEN: Brewster grudgingly attends the Quaker worship service. He is stunned at how different and unorganized it seems when compared to the Puritan worship he is so acclimated to. Brewster is especially stunned to hear women stand up and denounce the slavery, alcohol, wickedness, and maltreatment of the Indians so pervasive in the New England colonies.

Easton invites Brewster to his home for tea after the service, and they strike a quick friendship. Brewster recounts his fall from grace in Plimoth Colony, and Easton reminds him that the light of the resurrected Christ dwells within him, and nothing the government of Plimoth Colony says or does can change that.

CHAPTER FIFTEEN: Joshua Farwell, the young man in Middleborough who received marriage counseling from Brewster in Chapter Four, is now a father of two. He is in the vicinity of Assawompsett Pond on a frigid January day, searching for quality timber to be used in his work. He is deep in thought about whether he will be a good father and provider, and he ruminates about how much he misses Reverend Brewster.

Farwell finds an abandoned hat and some fishing gear near the shore of the pond, and he is horrified to discover a man entombed under the ice. Farwell extricates him and brings the corpse two miles to Middleborough. The townspeople discover evidence of strangulation and murder, and the victim is identified as John Sassamon.

CHAPTER SIXTEEN: Metacomet is enraged to learn Plimoth Colony has arrested Tobias, one of his chief lieutenants. Tobias has been charged with the murder of John Sassamon, and Tobias' son and young friend have also been charged as accomplices.

Metacomet seeks Linto's guidance on the crisis, and conveys his fear the young Wampanoag warriors will demand war if Tobias is executed. Linto declares he will stand for the accused at Plimoth Court. He will serve as their counselor.

CHAPTER SEVENTEEN: Linto has spent weeks observing the proceedings of Plimoth Court and studying English law books. On the day of the trial, Linto is magnificent. He destroys the credibility of Plimoth's evidence and befuddles their witnesses. Linto is confident of an acquittal.

CHAPTER EIGHTEEN: Linto's brilliant performance at Plimoth Court was all for naught, as the three accused men are found guilty and sentenced to hang the next day. Linto is stunned at the gross miscarriage of justice.

Linto arranges to spend the final night with the condemned men. During the night, Linto promises Tobias he will never let Metacomet humiliate himself before the English again. In the morning, the men are led to the gallows and Linto prays for a miracle.

The three men are hung by their necks, but miraculously, the rope used to execute Tobias' son suddenly breaks. The young man is still alive, and Linto convinces the authorities that the broken rope is a sign from the Lord that this young man is not to be hung. The authorities send Linto home while they debate the issue.

Three days later, Plimoth sends their ruling via messenger. They agree the Almighty had shown his displeasure about the hanging, so the prisoner was shot dead.

CHAPTER NINETEEN: Brewster's mental and physical health have improved tremendously in the preceding weeks. Thanks to Easton's friendship and mentoring, Brewster is drinking far less, and is engaged in charitable work for the community. Although he frequently attends worship, he still does not consider himself a Quaker. Additionally, he has become romantically involved with Constance Wilder, one of the brilliant women who astonished him at his first Quaker worship service with her brilliant and articulate denunciation of the evils in their midst.

Easton briefs Brewster on the events of the past few weeks in Plimoth. Easton insists they travel to see Metacomet to try to mediate the conflict before war breaks out.

CHAPTER TWENTY: Brewster travels unaccompanied to Montaup where he is captured and accused of being an English spy. He asks to see Linto, and Linto is delighted to see him. Brewster is overjoyed to see Linto and Wawetseka again, and to meet their children.

After recounting the events since their last meeting, Brewster reveals his mission: He, Deputy Governor Easton and some men from Providence seek an audience with Metacomet to mediate the conflict. Brewster is presented to Metacomet, and he agrees to meet with the delegation from Providence. Despite Easton's best efforts, Metacomet is not persuaded. The Wampanoag submitted to an English peace treaty four years prior, and their lives grew ceaselessly worse. War is imminent, and Brewster pleads with Linto to find a way to prevent it.

CHAPTER TWENTY-ONE: That night Linto travels alone into the forest to think and pray. He feels more confused than ever about the Great Spirit, the English, Christianity, and Metacomet. Finally, he stumbles upon a brilliant deception that he believes will delay the outbreak of hostilities for a week or two.

While the warriors are dancing around the fire, Linto pretends that he has fallen into a trance and is spiritually possessed. He decrees that whomever fires the first shot in the war is accursed by the heavens, and that side will lose the war. Metacomet believes the ruse.

Metacomet goes to pay his regards to his most trusted warrior, Mentayyup, who is ill and near death.

CHAPTER TWENTY-TWO: A teen-aged English farm boy in Swansea returns home from Sunday worship to find the family farm under siege from the Wampanoag. Cattle are butchered and barns are set on fire.

He is threatened by a mysterious Wampanoag warrior who seems to have the opportunity to kill him, but instead bides his time and dances. When the warrior finally charges him, the farm boy has no choice but to shoot him dead. The mysterious warrior was Mentayyup, who suicidally fulfilled Linto's prophecy in accordance with Metacomet's wishes. King Philip's War had begun.

ALPHABETICAL LIST OF MAJOR CHARACTERS

(H) = Historical
(F) = Fictional

Anderson, Cornelius (H): A pirate enlisted to aid in the war for Massachusetts Bay. Nicknamed "Dutch."

Annawon (H): Metacomet's war captain. Annawon served Metacomet's father, and is quite advanced in years.

Ares (F): A Mohawk war captain.

Barlow, Phineas (F): The owner of a Providence cooperage and Israel Brewster's employer.

Barnstrom, James (F): A father-of-three from Middleborough serving in the militia as Captain Church's second-in-command.

Barron, Jeremiah (F): The treasurer of Plimoth Colony.

Blackbird (F): The twin sister of the Bluebird, and co-Sachem of the Nipmuc. Also known as "Chogan."

Bluebird (F): The twin sister of the Blackbird, and co-Sachem of the Nipmuc. Also known as "Chosoki."

Bradford, William (H): A major in the Puritan militia, and son of the famous Governor Bradford.

Brewster, Israel (F): A disgraced Puritan minister from Middleborough, now residing in Providence.

Brewster, Sarah (F): Israel Brewster's first wife. She perished in 1669.

Brewster, William (H): Spiritual mentor of the original Pilgrims. Sailed to America on the Mayflower and died in 1644. Israel Brewster's grandfather.

Canochet (H): The Sachem of the Narragansett.

Church, Benjamin (H): A Puritan militia captain. Sometimes known as "America's first ranger."

Cudworth, James (H): Commander of the United Colonies' expedition to Mount Hope in the summer of 1675.

Easton, John (H): The Deputy Governor of Rhode Island and prominent Quaker. A close friend of Israel Brewster.

Eliot, John (H): A Puritan clergyman known for his missionary work among the Indians. He translated the Bible into their native language.

Father Jacques (F): A French Jesuit.

Fontaine, Alain (F): A French captain serving with the military of New France.

Gookin, Daniel (H): The Superintendent of the Praying Indians for the United Colonies.

Linto (F): A young spiritual leader among the Wampanoag. Linto was adopted from the Abenaki people to the north. Metacomet believes Linto is uniquely blessed by the spirit world, and a prophet. He is married to Wawetseka.

MacTavish, Elijah (F): A Scottish sugar baron, currently residing in Bermuda.

Massasoit (H): Also known as "Ossamequin." Massasoit translates to "Great Sachem." Massasoit established the original alliance between the Wampanoag and the Pilgrims in the early 1620s. He was the father of Wamsutta and Metacomet, and he died in 1661.

Mather, Increase (H): A famous Puritan scholar and minister residing in Boston. He wrote a history of King Philip's War in 1676 and was involved in the Salem witch trials in 1692. He was the father of Cotton Mather.

Mendon (H): Metacomet's eight-year-old-son. (There is very little historical evidence, however, that his name was Mendon.)

Mentayyup (F): One of the Wampanoag's most trusted and esteemed warriors. He perished in Swansea due to the first shot of the war.

Metacomet (H): The Sachem of the Wampanoag. He is the son of Massasoit and the younger brother of Wamsutta. He assumed the role of Sachem after Wamsutta's death in 1662. He is the "King Philip" of King Philip's War.

Moseley, Samuel (H): A former privateer. He is appointed a militia captain, and is charged with overseeing a band of pirate mercenaries.

Nimrod (H): One of Metacomet's warriors.

Phelps, Peter (F): A Puritan minister stationed in Plimoth. He stole Alice Fuller away from Brewster in 1671, and took Brewster's ministry in Middleborough.

Reddington, Thomas (F): A young militiaman from Middleborough serving in Captain Church's unit. The son of a carpenter, his unusual size and strength is legendary.

Rowlandson, Mary (H): A Puritan wife and mother abducted from her home in Lancaster. She was held for ransom and released. Her subsequent journal was one of the most famous literary works of seventeenth-century Colonial America.

Sachem (H): An honorary title similar to "Chief." Massasoit, Wamsutta, and Metacomet served as Sachems of the Wampanoag.

Sassamon, John (H): A Native American Christian who, due to his excellent English skills, frequently served as the liaison between the English and the Native Americans. He betrayed Metacomet, and was found murdered in early 1675.

Tobias (H): One of Metacomet's most trusted Wampanoag advisors. He was put on trial in Plimoth for Sassamon's murder, and executed in the summer of 1675. Linto defended him at his trial.

Wamsutta (H): Son of Massasoit and older brother of Metacomet. He assumed the role of Sachem after Massasoit's death in 1661. Wamsutta perished under mysterious circumstances in 1662, and his death would always torment Metacomet.

Wawetseka (F): A young spiritual leader among the Wampanoag. She is Linto's wife, and mother of two young children.

Weetamoo (H): Former wife of Wamsutta, and Sachem of the Pocasset. She is Wawetseka's mother.

Wilder, Constance (F): A young adult Quaker residing in Providence. She is romantically involved with Israel Brewster.

Wilder, Ezekiel "Zeke" (F): A Providence fisherman and Constance Wilder's father.

Williams, Roger (H): An elderly spiritual and political leader in Providence.

Winslow, Josiah (H): The son of Mayflower passenger Edward Winslow. Josiah served as the leader of the colony's military forces, and became assistant governor in 1657. In 1673, he became governor of Plimoth Colony.

Wootonekanuske (H): Wife of Metacomet and mother of Mendon.

MAP ONE: PLYMOUTH COLONY

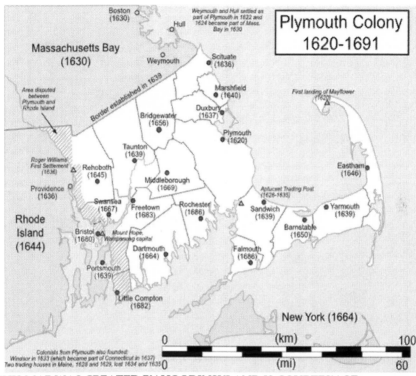

THIS MAP WAS CREATED BY HOODINSKI AND IS COURTESY OF WIKICOMMONS.

MAP TWO: NATIVE AMERICANS NATIONS

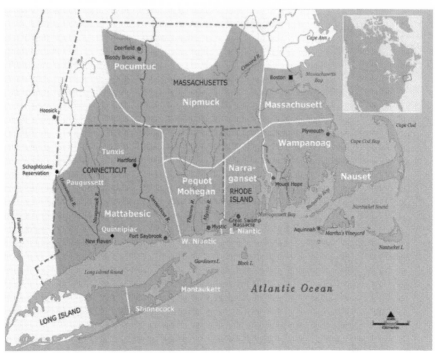

MAP COURTESY OF WIKICOMMONS.

MAP THREE: THE MOUNT HOPE REGION (MONTAUP)

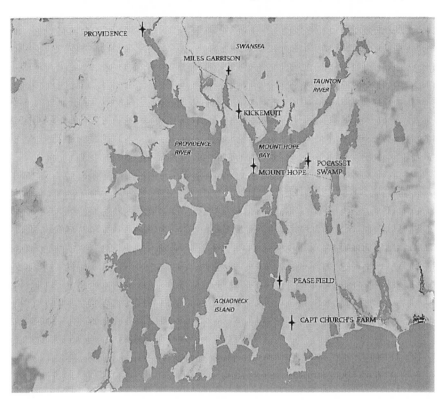

PART ONE
SUMMER
1675

"I'd had rather have a plain, russet-coated Captain
that knows what he fights for, and loves what he
knows, than that you call a Gentleman and is
nothing else"
Oliver Cromwell, 1643

CHAPTER ONE

SWANSEA

It was a glorious sign from the Almighty. Of that, there could be no doubt.

This was certainly the opinion of Major William Bradford, and few seemed inclined to question the holy assessment of the good major and his magnificent pedigree. The fact that the garrison commander, the aged and venerated James Cudworth, enthusiastically concurred with his famous underling should have eliminated any debate amongst the Puritan faithful.

Bradford, however, would take no chances, and he zealously reinforced his initial assessment. "The will of the Lord, my brothers. The will of the Lord has clearly been made manifest in the night sky. Our cause is just, and our army is righteous."

The Reverend John Miles felt obliged to speak, perhaps since it was his own Swansea home currently being used as a military garrison. "Yea, verily, hear the word of the Lord, recited for the holy soldiers of the Lord. It is certainly written in the Book of Joel, *the sun and the moon will be darkened, and the stars shall no longer shine.* And was not the death of the vile and wicked King Herod sanctified by an eclipse of the moon? Certainly, Metacomet is a vile enemy of our Lord and given to evil ways, just as King Herod. Metacomet, this odious *King Philip,* will indeed pay for his treason."

Most of the Puritan militia garrisoned in Swansea solemnly bowed their heads. Some were troubled by the sight of a lunar eclipse on this balmy June night. The more learned among them recalled their history, and knew that a partially-eclipsed moon, in accordance with prophecy, rose above Constantinople in 1453. Seven days later, the magnificent city fell to the heathen.

There were also dim mutterings about the Peloponnesian War more than a thousand years ago. Evidently, a lunar eclipse so greatly troubled the Athenians that their war vessels sat shamefully idle in the harbor. Ultimately, their enemy exploited their fear and indecision, and destroyed the fleet.

Others were certain they witnessed the image of a human scalp within the eclipse. Was it the scalp of an Indian, or an Englishman? Was there even a scalp to be seen, or was it a witchcraft-induced hallucination? The quiet ruminations within the garrison were increasingly unsettling.

The sullen deliberations continued, and their confident martial zeal was slowly eroding. Bradford could discern the consternation among his troops, and he continued his exhortation. "The savages have committed a grave sin, and the Lord has made His displeasure clear with His handiwork in the night sky. Be brave, and be of good cheer, for certainly the holy Book of Judges commands us to…"

"Pig titties."

Never before had one hundred devout Puritan men of high character witnessed such blasphemy in the face of both holy and civil authority. Major Bradford was the second-in-command of the expedition, and the respected son of the deceased and revered Governor William Bradford. Major Bradford, as usual, demonstrated a cautious temperament in the face of adversity.

"Excuse me?"

"Pig titties. Big, ugly, nasty pig titties is what I say."

The silence was astounding as all eyes gazed upon the enormous blasphemer. He was surrounded by four equally enormous mastiffs, brought along to track and corner the savages. The dogs could perceive the tension, and began to menacingly growl. Reverend Miles thought a kindly word from a servant of the Lord might restore this burly lunatic to his senses. "My son…be of good cheer. There is no need for anger or blasphemy. Although you may be fearful regarding the imminent battle with the heathens, put your trust in the Lord."

"*Fearful*? Fearful of the savages?" The blasphemer's obnoxious laughter echoed through the garrison. "Close your mealy mouth, you pathetic wretch. Close it, or I'll be wearing your jawbone around my neck. Fear? The only fear I have is my sweet dogs will consume so much flesh they will grow lazy and fat. That is my fear, *rev-er-end*."

Bradford marveled how demeaning and sarcastic the word "reverend" could be when three separate syllables were emphasized. He could feel his precious authority collapsing in an ignominious fashion. He faced the ruddy giant, who towered at least seven inches above him. "Anderson, isn't it? Dutch Cornelius? I'm surprised at the ungrateful manner in which you conduct yourself. I believe your options a mere week ago were to serve the militia, or serve the prison warden?"

Dutch Cornelius laughed so hard his beasts ceased their threatening sounds, and they now seemed to be contemplating careless slumber. "Serve? Like a tavern wench? Do you believe I'm here to *serve* you, Bradford? Damn you to hell, Bradford. You are not your father. Daddy has been buried for twenty years, and he's not here to help you." More humiliating laughter filled the room.

A sullen captain of the militia sat sulking alone in the corner, idly stroking his nine-year-old flintlock musket, seemingly lost in his thoughts. Despite his apparent demeanor, he was confident. He knew the twenty men he commanded were ready for this war. They were motivated, and rife with Puritan discipline. But the captain was suffering with grave doubts about Cornelius Anderson and this motley band of volunteers allegedly allied with their cause. To even call them volunteers was a farce. They were pirates. Some of these men had even been sentenced to hang for their crimes, but war has a way of suddenly changing everything and everyone.

There was no silencing Dutch Cornelius, and his ranting was growing more boisterous. "Are you going to say another prayer, Bradford? Or perhaps Grandfather Cudworth will discipline me after his nap. Well, listen to me, daddy's boy. I've got nothing for this whole damned assembly of Puritans and holy men, politicians and weasels. I am here to feed savages to my dogs. And the savages my dogs can't eat will line my pockets standing in chains on the slaver's wharf. So, save your holy wrath. You need me and you need Moseley's entire crew, Bradford."

Just when the assembly thought he could not be more insubordinate, Dutch Cornelius plunged deeper into his tirade. "Look at your excuse for an army, crying about the damned moon and quivering like women. Look at that pretty boy over there with tears in his eyes. I'm going to get some rum in me, and before the night's over I might be using him just like I'd use a frilly, delicate wom…"

The abomination went unfinished, as the hardened stock of a flintlock musket cracked Dutch Cornelius across the mouth. He staggered backwards as the blood spurted, and his eyes widened in disbelief as he fell to the floor. His dogs, who were on the verge on peaceful slumber, surprisingly remained uninterested.

"Shut your blasphemous mouth, pirate. You will treat the major with respect, you will treat Colonel Cudworth with respect, and you damn well will treat the reverend with respect. And if you want to finish this argument, pirate, I'm headed outside to stare at the moon." And without another word, the captain turned and was gone.

Dutch Cornelius lurched forward as if to stand, but his head was spinning, and he sank to the floor. Two of his mastiffs were licking the blood from his face, and Captain Moseley cast a glare that let him know in no uncertain terms that there would be no revenge. His obnoxious antics had caused this, and now he bore the consequences.

Outside the Miles garrison house, Captain Benjamin Church was wiping the blood from his flintlock. He marveled yet again at the eclipse and fell deep into thought. How did all of this madness happen?

THE PROPHET AND THE WITCH

A few months ago, nay, a few weeks ago, Benjamin Church was a completely content servant of the Lord. He had fashioned a homestead of sorts far from Plimoth and any tentacles of the government. At the age of thirty-three, Captain Church was certainly not young, but he knew he was walking a holy path with a bright future. He desperately missed his beautiful wife, Alice, and their adorable young son, but he was building a life of prosperity and independence, and would send for them soon. Some thought he was mad to establish an uncertain new life on a remote, dangerous frontier. Before war engulfed the colonies, Church was fashioning a marvelous homestead south of Plimoth, west of Taunton, even south of the Wampanoag sanctum of Montaup. Church was on his own in Sakonnet, on the banks of the Sakonnet River. Leaving behind a community of devout Puritan faithful, Church was delighted to embrace his new neighbors, including Baptists, Quakers, Indians, and a host of other reprobates Plimoth could never tolerate. He did good by all, and the sentiment was returned. He often wondered about his Mayflower forbears, who also chose to chart their destinies in a strange new wilderness.

But his new life on the frontier in Sakonnet was now his old life. As tensions mounted in recent weeks, Church engaged his Indian neighbors and pleaded with them not to flock to Metacomet's banner. Foremost among them was Awashonks, the esteemed female Sachem of the Sakonnet people. Church assured his friends he would travel to Plimoth, and he would help defuse this crisis.

When the drums of war were pounded, however, and English colonists were butchered, Church's destiny was clear. The call for the militia went out, and Governor Winslow promptly commissioned him as a captain. He subsequently assigned twenty Plimoth men to his command, and now, here he was. Knocking pirates to the floor and staring at the moon.

Church continued to marvel at the eclipse, but he was certain he could not discern a scalp. Unlike so many others, his confidence would not be shattered by eclipses, rumors, or whatever happened in Constantinople two-hundred years ago. Captain Benjamin Church was a member of the Lord's chosen elect, and he would fight for the community of saints. He despised the fact that Governor Winslow felt desperate enough to enlist a band of condemned cutthroats to aid in the war, but so be it. As long as they refrained from blasphemy and drunkenness, they might be useful.

Church had temporarily forgotten about blasphemous drunkards, so when he heard steps approaching from behind, he wheeled and drew his saber. He assumed Dutch Cornelius had adequately composed himself and was ready for vengeance.

"Put it down, Benjamin. Gads, there's already been enough dead Englishmen. Put it away before I change my mind and permit Cornelius to disembowel you." Moseley tried to punctuate his taunt with a friendly laugh but somehow failed.

"I'll feed his carcass to his evil beasts. Send him out, Sam. You can hold my coat."

Captain Samuel Moseley was only a year older than Church, but he carried himself with a grizzled, cynical air of a man decades older. As a Massachusetts Bay privateer, he conducted his business dealings just barely on the outskirts of the law, and when the colony needed an officer with a rough edge to control a band of condemned criminals, he was an obvious choice. Many believed Moseley's seaborne business ventures would have sent him to the stockade years ago, if not for a fortuitous marriage to the lovely Ann Addington, whose uncle just happened to be the Governor of Massachusetts Bay.

"Cornelius is staying inside. He's a drunken idiot, and he has my orders not to touch you. I told him I'd be out here giving you two pieces of the devil, so try to act frightened." Moseley lit a pipe of tobacco, a vice Church found abhorrent.

Church sighed deeply. "What in the world are we doing, Sam? Why aren't we out slaughtering the Wampanoag and the enemies of Plimoth? We should have King Philip in chains by now."

"Benjamin, your rashness impresses your young platoon of farm boys, but no one else. Certainly not me. For the love of the saints, man, you were supposed to escort the army here from Taunton, and you and your men scurried ahead like rabbits. Were you going to invade King Philip with twenty men? We're lucky no one was killed." He inhaled from his pipe in lieu of saying anything else on the matter.

Church silently stewed at the reprimand from a peer and friend, especially because he was absolutely correct. He did a poor job escorting the main body to Swansea. And now, he couldn't stand being cooped up in this garrison with drunken reprobates, seemingly waiting forever for reinforcements to arrive from Boston.

They were supposed to be the chosen people of God. They were the Puritans, and they devoted their lives to discipline, labor, and holiness. It was a mere twenty-five years ago that Cromwell and the Roundheads showed their mettle against the wicked, effete Royalists across the sea. A few decades before that, the Pequots of Connecticut felt the wrath of God's chosen elect on these very shores. And yet, here they were, a divinely sanctioned army, huddled like cowards in a garrison while whimpering about the moon.

"How long do you suspect all this will last, Benjamin?"

Church pondered the question as he peered into the dark night. He could barely discern two young militiamen sent to draw water from the well fifty yards outside the fence. He wondered why he couldn't see the sentries who should be accompanying them, and he rubbed his weary eyes.

"One month? Maybe two, if we spend our days meekly huddled in garrisons? I hope we'll be home in time to get the harvest in. I met with my friend Awashonks not long ago, and she and her warriors want no part of Metacomet's lunacy. We'll force our way onto the peninsula this week, crush any resistance at Montaup, and drag Metacomet back in chains. And then I can finish building my barn. I'll probably sell some pigs before winter and buy some..."

The sentence went unfinished as two shots pierced the night, and once again the sickening war cry of the enemy echoed through Swansea.

CHAPTER TWO

PROVIDENCE

"But I say unto you, that ye resist not evil; but whosoever shall smite thee on thy right cheek, turn to him the other also."

Israel Brewster calmly contemplated the blessed words while he sipped his milk. Truth be told, Brewster despised milk, and his mind wandered to a recipe for Scottish ale. Reddington the carpenter introduced him to it in Middleborough, but that was long ago.

Brewster knew his silence created the impression that her words from the Gospel of Matthew were resonating. He formulated his reply. *"And when the Lord thy God shall deliver them before thee; thou shalt smite them, and utterly destroy them; thou shalt make no covenant with them, nor shew mercy unto them."* Her hazel eyes smoldered as he punctuated his recitation. "Deuteronomy. Chapter Seven. Verse…" Brewster hoisted his mug of milk to his lips as he muttered, "verse twoee," as he could not recall whether it was verse two or three. He wondered if he was trying to be cute, or genuinely deceptive.

Constance Wilder rose and stood at attention, fully showcasing her remarkable height of five feet and eight inches. Her glorious red hair caught the shadows cast from the fireplace, and she resembled a magnificent and beautiful oracle of holy scripture.

"Ye have heard that it hath been said, thou shalt love thy neighbour, and hate thine enemy." Her voice, melodious yet authoritative, was growing louder. *"But I say unto you, love your enemies, bless them that curse you, do good to them that hate you, and pray for them which despitefully use you, and persecute you, that ye may be the children of your Father which is in heaven.* Matthew, Chapter Five, verse forty-three."

Brewster was really thinking about that Scottish ale now. Although he occasionally partook of wine and ale, he did his best to avoid doing so in the home of Constance and her father, so as to not offend their Quaker sensibilities. Brewster was gradually coming to the conclusion that not only was he not winning this debate, he was in imminent danger of losing, and he was not accustomed to such a thing.

Israel Brewster and Constance Wilder were sitting in the kitchen of the Wilder home in Providence. Actually, Brewster was sitting, and she was now standing. They were debating the imminent war with the Wampanoag Indians, and the Quaker doctrine of pacifism. Brewster was uncertain if he was inclined to participate in the defense of the United Colonies of New England, but as a former militiaman, he could not rule out the possibility. Constance was horrified at the notion, and was fortifying her arguments with her impressive knowledge of scripture.

He beckoned to her father, Ezekiel, rocking silently by the fire with a cup of tea and a heavy volume of Milton's *Paradise Lost*. "Have you no assistance to offer a humble cooper, Ezekiel Wilder? Willst thou not protect me from thy verbal condemnations of thy offspring?"

Zeke took his time and methodically sipped his tea. He smacked his lips with exaggerated delight, and noisily returned the cup to the saucer. He even turned a page, lest Brewster's yammering distract him from his beloved Milton. Finally, Ezekiel Wilder, the curt and boorish owner of three Providence fishing vessels and father of one beautiful daughter, imparted his wisdom.

"Good luck, youngster."

Brewster solemnly shook his head in mock despair. He sighed. *"When thou goest out to battle against thine enemies, and seest horses, and chariots, and a people more than thou, be not afraid of them: for the Lord thy God is with thee. Deuteronomy..."*

Constance was growing so passionate she cared not for Brewster's reference of chapter and verse. That was indeed fortunate, as he could not recall it, and didn't want to drink any more milk and engage in additional, pathetic subterfuge. She knew, however, that she could not keep pace with his astounding memory, and she quickly seized the holy scriptures from the mantle above the fireplace. Brewster marveled at her grace and beauty as she swept across the room.

She found her desired passage in the book of Romans and read so loudly Brewster wondered if the neighbors could hear. *"Recompense to no man evil for evil. Provide things honest in the sight of all men. If it be possible, as much as lieth in you, live peaceably with all men. Dearly beloved, avenge not yourselves, but rather give place unto wrath: for it is written, vengeance is mine; I will repay, saith the Lord!"* She actually stomped her foot for punctuation.

Brewster paused to gather his thoughts. He considered formulating a reply from the book of Joshua, but instead, he rose from the table. Unexpectedly, he declared, "Forgive me, dear Constance. I shall take a brisk walk and contemplate these issues deliberately. I shall be back soonest." What followed was a very rare episode of silence from Constance, and Zeke paid him no mind as he walked out the door.

Providence was buzzing with activity, and Israel Brewster absorbed the sights and sounds of the city. After months if not years of imminent war with Metacomet and the Wampanoag, there was no more imminence. Warriors had attacked and butchered farms in Swansea, and English blood had been spilled. Providence, though rife with pacifism and Quakers, radiated a sense of wartime energy. Merchants and tradesman worked tirelessly, wagons of goods rolled in and out of the city, and someone somewhere always seemed to yelling.

Within minutes, he arrived at his destination. Despite the bustling crowd, he soon found a seat in the tavern, ordered an ale flavored with dried peas and chine root that was indigenous to this particular establishment, and agonized about the world around him. More accurately, he agonized about *his* role in the world.

The twists of fate that had bedeviled Israel Brewster in recent years were astounding. The year was 1675, but a mere seven years ago, his life was very, very different. Seven years ago, Israel Brewster was a devout Puritan minister serving the congregation of Middleborough in Plimoth Colony. He revered his spiritual elders and mentors, especially his famous grandfather of Mayflower fame, Elder William Brewster.

Seven years ago, Israel Brewster was married to Sarah, the love of his life. They held hands, they wrote sonnets, and they made a child. But the birthing of the child was so excruciating that both Sarah and baby Patience went to be with the Lord on that frigid night, and Israel would be tormented by agonizing night terrors for months to come.

And then there were the Indians. Once, the illustrious Reverend Increase Mather of Boston told Brewster that the Lord would use the Indians as His means of divine punishment for the sins and wickedness so prevalent in the New England colonies, just as He used Godless heathen to punish and destroy the Kingdoms of Israel and Judah for their sins. Was Mather being proven right this summer?

Brewster's relationship with the Wampanoag was especially complicated, due to his almost miraculous friendship with a young Wampanoag man named Linto. Linto was approximately five years younger than Brewster, and they met during a Christian missionary service Brewster was leading. On that day, Linto's future wife, the beautiful and mysterious Wawetseka, performed a native spiritual healing ritual on Brewster that remarkably brought his night terrors to an end.

Israel Brewster felt reborn in those weeks. His agonizing grief had finally subsided thanks to Wawetseka's work, and he was courting the loveliest girl in Middleborough, the delightful Alice Fuller. But fate is a cruel and bizarre master. Israel Brewster was humiliated and defrocked in front of the Plimoth assembly on a host of absurdly exaggerated claims stemming from his association with Linto and Wawetseka. Rather than face trial, Brewster absconded to the west with his meager possessions, and a purloined, slow, flatulent, insubordinate mare named Brownie.

THE PROPHET AND THE WITCH

Brewster stumbled into the coopering profession after arriving in Providence, and stumbled was a very appropriate term. Although he took to his new profession with admirable zeal, Brewster fell horrifically into drink during those days. His spiritual being, and perhaps his very life, was saved by the friendship and outreach of Deputy Governor John Easton and his Quaker ways.

He had grown very close to Easton in recent months, and it was at Quaker worship where he met the beautiful Constance Wilder. They were growing increasingly inseparable, as perhaps Brewster was the only man in all the colonies who could match the intellect and virtue of Miss Wilder.

Brewster could not, however, fully embrace the Quaker devotion. He did not abstain from ale and wine, but this was a minor matter in the eyes of Constance and Zeke. The true division in their lives was the doctrine of pacifism. There was a war erupting in the New England colonies, and Israel Brewster had no idea what role he should be playing, if any. He served in the militia of the United Colonies as a young man, but he was thirty-three-years-old now. Despite his disgrace in the eyes of Plimoth, he could not stand the thought of sitting idly while his neighbors, relatives, and former congregation members were under attack. Constance, however, incessantly bombarded him with the tenets of her Quaker pacifism.

Conversely, the thought of fighting the Wampanoag was repellent. Brewster had ministered to countless Wampanoag, and led dozens to Christian baptism. He would always have very special feelings for Linto and Wawetseka. Brewster and Easton even tried to mediate the war a few weeks ago, and they sailed to Montaup to confer with Metacomet. The visit was fruitless, however, and Metacomet's grievances against Plimoth were so passionate and articulate that Brewster genuinely wondered which side of the conflict he was truly on.

He was so deep in thought on that June evening that he had scarcely touched his ale. *Who was Israel Brewster?* What did he want in this world? He slowly sipped his refreshment, oblivious to the usual din and rabble of the tavern. At that moment, however, Israel Brewster knew exactly what he wanted. He blinked repeatedly, and marveled at the epiphany. He turned and fled the tavern with his barely-touched mug left upon the table, much to the delight of the drunkard seated next to him.

Brewster stormed back into the Wilder residence in a breathless state, and he picked up the debate where it had left off. It was almost as if he had never left. *"For thou hast girded me with strength unto the battle: thou hast subdued under me those that rose up against me."*

If Constance was peeved by his departure, she revealed nothing. She enthusiastically jumped back into the fray. *"A new commandment I give unto you, that ye love one another; as I have loved you, that ye also love one another."*

Brewster refrained from sitting and he looked her in the eyes. *"Beloved, if God so loved us, we ought also to love one another."* Constance stepped back and eyed him suspiciously. She did not understand this new approach to the debate, and she wondered how much money he spent at the tavern. She thumbed methodically through the worn Bible.

"Therefore if thine enemy hunger, feed him; if he thirst, give him drink…"

Brewster regained his breath. *"Who can find a virtuous woman? For her price is far above rubies…"*

"Speaking of drink, what was this errand of yours, Israel Brewster? Did you leave any ale for the rest of Providence?"

He fell to one knee and gazed up at her. *"Whoso findeth a wife findeth a good thing, and obtaineth favour of the Lord."* Proverbs. Chapter Eighteen, verse…"

"Are you mad? Father, has our friend the heretic cooper gone mad? Should we send for his filthy horse to carry him off to the sanitarium?"

Brewster took her hand and remained on his knee. He gazed adoringly at her as the shadows fell across his enormous blue eyes. "Constance Wilder, I implore you to join me in holy Christian matrimony."

She stood wordlessly with her mouth agape. She had no idea what to say, and wondered if they should be asking her father for his permission. "Father?"

"My goodness, daughter. Don't let him get away. Every other man in these colonies is completely terrified of you."

"But he's…he's…"

"An ex-drunkard, ex-minister, ex-Puritan with no money and a flatulent horse? I know, I know. Who could resist something like that? Still, if nothing else, reliable barrels are notoriously hard to find these days, and with a special family discount…"

"YES! Yes, Israel Brewster! Get off the floor! YES, YES, YES!"

CHAPTER THREE

SWANSEA

After the shots rang out, Church and Moseley seized their firearms and rallied their men. Dozens assumed tactical positions behind the stockades and methodically prepared their matchlock muskets for action. Church and Moseley, however, sprinted to the probable scene of the gunfire, which seemed to emanate from Reverend Miles' well. Seventeen men from random companies accompanied them.

Halfway to their destination, they were greeted by a gruesome spectacle that was almost overlooked in the darkness. It was now sadly apparent to Church why he couldn't locate the two sentries who should have been accompanying the soldiers to the well. They were lying face-down in their own blood, apparent victims of a stealth ambush.

Upon reaching the scene, four enormous buckets were found empty and abandoned. There was no sign of the two militiamen, but once torchlight was applied to the scene, the evidence of their abduction was obvious. A trail of blood led east toward the bridge that spanned the Palmer River. The bridge led to the peninsula where the Wampanoag maintained their stronghold at Montaup. Scattered remnants of the Englishmen's presence were evident, including a belt-buckle and a hat.

Captain Church sprang into action. Calling back to the garrison, he gave the order for his twenty men to rally at the well. Major Bradford had finally arrived via horseback, and Church construed the fifty-yard journey on saddle as a senseless and vain attempt to bolster his authority.

Church was pleased, however, at the timely opportunity to address Bradford and Moseley simultaneously. "Two men abducted, Major. I'd wager they're still alive. Let's move out in two vertical columns. I'll take my men to the south side of the bridge, reconnoiter the scene and lie in wait. Send Moseley's pirates in a northerly column twenty minutes later. If the situation is too daunting, I'll whistle a signal code, and we'll rally back at the well and assemble a daybreak assault. We'll take two physicians from…"

Bradford remained mounted and shook his head solemnly. "Too risky, Captain. Your energy is infectious, but Colonel Cudworth will not permit any Englishman to cross that bridge until the Massachusetts Bay companies arrive. We'll not spill more English blood tonight for two men."

"Four men, Major." Church somberly pointed his saber in the direction of the fallen sentries. Bradford sighed and had no reply.

Moseley felt the need to break the awkward silence. "Major Bradford, let us confer with the commander. Those two men are almost certainly alive. Surely, in the name of English virtue and honor, we can be afforded the opportunity to mount a rescue. Church and I could…"

"We have our orders, Captain Moseley. Colonel Cudworth has been extremely explicit. No English boots march across that bridge, or set foot on King Philip's peninsula, until the reinforcements arrive. Do I have to repeat myself, Captain Moseley? Captain Church?"

The young captains stood forlornly, and Bradford continued. "Let's get those sentries prepped for Christian burial. I'll notify Reverend Miles. And double the watch tonight." He galloped off without another word.

"Remember I said this would all be finished in two months, Sam? It's doubling by the minute."

"Let's head back, Benjamin. There's nothing more to be done."

Church spent a sleepless night in an agitated state. No matter where his thoughts led, he was consumed by anger and disbelief. He was infuriated he would be fighting beside men of such character as Dutch Cornelius. He was appalled that the enemy could find their way to the garrison house completely undetected, and effortlessly assassinate their sentries. Cudworth and Bradford's refusal to permit a rescue operation while two young Englishmen were almost certainly being tortured was incomprehensible. And a garrison full of tentative, uncertain militia refusing to trust in the Lord and their own God-given strength repelled him.

He rose an hour after daybreak and was fortunate to procure a half-loaf of bread and an egg. In a few hours, the sun shone directly overhead, and Church was enthralled by the sight of the Massachusetts Bay companies on the horizon. Certainly, with hundreds of battle-ready troops in position, the assault on Montaup (or "Mount Hope" as the English preferred to call it) could finally commence.

If the Miles garrison house seemed rife with uncertainty and caution last night, the addition of more than three hundred newcomers brought a palpable sense of energy and vigor. The garrison was absolutely bursting with men, and even Reverend Miles tacitly hoped they would soon spring to action, so his family home could return to its previously peaceful, unmolested state.

The new day brought a new sense of exuberance to Colonel Cudworth, and he radiated an energy that belied his years. He mingled among the troops with Reverend Miles at his side, and was quick to convey a quip, witticism, or reprimand. "Look sharp, men. There will be no shoddiness here…the Lord is with us…are you getting enough to eat, boys…God help me, I almost pity King Philip…just look at this army of the Lord…shine that helmet, young man…stand tall, lads."

Church welcomed the renewed sense of purpose and circulated throughout the companies. The Massachusetts Bay men certainly seemed better equipped than his company. Almost all were issued a regal-looking "lobster tail" helmet, many of which were probably relics from the Roundhead triumphs in the mother country, now three decades past. Most had armor of one fashion or another, while barely half of Church's men even owned "buff coats," the protective garments fashioned from ox hide. Additionally, many were equipped with impressive looking pikes. They were at least twice the height of the men who wielded them, and Church genuinely wondered how they intended to employ them. Did they intend to throw them at the enemy?

What intrigued Church the most, however, was the evident reliance on the arquebus. The arquebus was a heavy matchlock musket mounted on a tripod, and it was used with great impact during the English Civil War. European tactics permitted the slow, methodical employment of this manner of weapon. Church had no doubt, however, that the savage adversary they were now facing would not be employing the plodding, deliberate tactics of the English royalist forces, and Church's men would wisely rely on the mobility and speed afforded by their flintlock muskets. Church silently shook his head in disbelief. Massachusetts Bay could keep their stationary tripods, unwieldy matchlocks and cumbersome pikes. They seemed ready to fight the last war, but Church knew Metacomet's tactics here in Plimoth would be quite different than King Charles' tactics in England.

Ultimately, however, he was quite pleased with the twenty men under his command. As his commission came directly from Josiah Winslow, the governor of Plimoth Colony, his men also were the product of Plimoth. They seemed to represent almost every corner of the colony.

Captain Church appointed James "Jemmy" Barnstrom to serve as his second. His rank was officially "cornet," the lowest rank of an officer. Church frequently reminded him of the service of Cornet George Joyce during the Civil War. Serving with Cromwell's Roundheads, Cornet Joyce aggressively seized Charles the First from parliament's custody when he suspected the Presbyterians would mount a rescue attempt. Church told Cornet Barnstrom that was the kind of independent, decisive action that would be required in this conflict. He refrained, however, from telling him about Joyce's fervent property speculation, Cromwell stripping him of his commission, and his ultimate imprisonment. Motivation was a delicate thing, indeed.

Middleborough would also be proud of its other contribution to Church's unit. Thomas Reddington was the seventeen-year-old son of a carpenter, and in addition to being the youngest member of Church's charge, he was physically one of the most impressive specimens in the United Colonies. He stood a remarkable six feet and three from head to toe, and he frequently entertained his comrades with his demonstrations of inconceivable strength.

Other members of the unit hailed from Taunton, Bridgewater, and Rehoboth. All hailed from boroughs far to the west of Plimoth, and all grew up in close proximity to the Wampanoag. These men from the frontier needed little explanation of what was at stake in this war, as almost all of their families had abandoned their homesteads for their own safety. Some families would opt for life in a garrison, and others would relocate further east to reside with relatives.

As far as Church was concerned, any further delay in taking the fight to the enemy's inner sanctum was now unconscionable. Hundreds of fresh, well-supplied men were now in position, and the summer New England weather was delightful. But yet, there was no talk of a planned assault, and Church continued to silently stew throughout the day while tactfully keeping his distance from Dutch Cornelius and his brood.

That evening, he sat by the fire in the courtyard and devoured one of the many ducks his men had shot that morning. If this was the life of the soldier, he thought, he had little to complain about. He was warm, well fed, and quite safe despite the leering eyes of Moseley's cutthroats. But Benjamin Church did complain, albeit in a tacit manner. The boredom and lack of action would soon drive him mad.

He was pleasantly surprised when John Gill and Andrew Belcher, two of the designated quartermasters of the militia, joined him by the fire in an effort to trade salted bacon for duck.

Church contemplated his surplus of fire-roasted duck and seized upon the good deal while he could.

Gill did not let a mouth crammed with bacon and duck delay his remarks. "God bless the Reverend Miles, Benjamin. His house makes a delightful fortress and his pigs are delectable."

Belcher smiled and opened his canteen. "If only he had some daughters. Wine, my brothers?"

"He would need at least five hundred, Belcher. Well, perhaps four hundred and ninety-nine. Benjamin is a married man."

"I'm not even sure Benjamin craves the company of women, Mr. Gill. Isn't that why he left Duxbury to live alone in God-forsaken Indian country?"

Church ignored the barbs and consumed a hearty swig. "Just keep plying me with bacon and wine, and I'll be content. Bacon, wine, and some savages to kill."

Belcher grinned at Gill and lowered his voice. "We knew you were our man, Benjamin. We're planning some action for the morrow. Will you take the lead?"

"Action?"

"We'll be crossing that damned bridge and having our way with the heathen. We'll only need a dozen of us or so. As long as they're fine and righteous men. Any more, and we'll lose the element of surprise."

"And who has endorsed this alleged mission? Reverend Miles' pigs?"

"Old man Cudworth."

"You are jesting."

"We briefed the notion to him just now. Billy Hammond agreed to serve as scout. He's good, Benjamin. One of the best horsemen in the colony. Bradford was there and nodded like a whirligig."

"Cudworth and Bradford have authorized you to cross the bridge with a dozen men?"

"Yes. I believe his outlook has changed immensely now that the Massachusetts Bay men have arrived. He even shared an ale with Moseley tonight."

"Remarkable."

"So, you're in?"

"I don't know. How much more bacon do you have?"

"Hilarious. Tomorrow night, an hour after sunset."

"How many of my men should I…"

"Just you, Benjamin. We want to be mobile and nimble. You'll be the twelfth man."

"So be it. Blessings to heaven. Finally, some action."

The next day was another balmy summer delight. Church spent the day preparing his flintlock, resting, and praying. He was infused with manic energy and had to force himself to eat. The sun could not set soon enough.

The cool of the evening was welcome as the twelve men gathered. It soon became apparent the mission was far from secret, and their incursion into hostile territory would soon devolve into a spectator sport, as the bridge was less than four hundred yards from the garrison. Much to Church's fury, their surreptitious departure was accentuated with whoops, huzzahs, and borderline mockery from Dutch Cornelius and his rabble.

Church refused to succumb to distraction, however, and he earnestly prayed. He knelt and quietly prayed that he may be able to do his duty for Plimoth Colony, his friends and family, and for the Almighty. He arose and peered through the darkness. Despite the sudden array of dark clouds, a sliver of summer light remained, and Church thought he could spot Hammond scouting ahead. Hammond paused before crossing the bridge, dismounted, and crouched in the shadows.

The evening was remarkably quiet now that the whoops of encouragement had died away. Hammond thought he could discern the "chacker chacker chacker" chattering of an earthbound collection of starlings. He listened carefully to ensure the sounds emanated from some harmless birds, and were not a cunning signal among enemy assassins.

After at least ten minutes, Hammond was satisfied, and he signaled for his comrades to proceed. As they closed to within fifty yards, he took to the saddle and gingerly crossed the bridge spanning the Palmer River. He was apprehensive, yet exhilarated. The queasiness in his stomach had subsided hours ago. He heard the melodic call of the starlings once again, and it would be the second-to-last sound his mortal senses would ever hear.

The roar of gunfire was everywhere, and the projectiles seemingly came from all directions. The deceased William Hammond slumped in the saddle. Gill and Belcher were close behind, riding their horses across the bridge. They randomly pointed their weapons and shot at everything, yet they shot at nothing. How could this enemy maintain such numbers, yet remain so concealed?

Gill cried out in pain and instantly knew he was hit in the stomach. He turned to rally the troops, and was horrified to discover at least eight were running back to the garrison without hesitation.

Church was appalled at the spectacle. He watched as Belcher's horse was shot from under him, and grimaced as the beast collapsed on his leg, trapping him in a hail of gunfire. Church angrily called after the fleeing men. *"Damn you! Where is your pride? Turn around!"* He may as well have been calling after the starlings.

He surged forward to Hammond's horse, now staggering about in a sickening, directionless display as its lifeless rider slumped across it. He could not even attempt to avoid the musket fire, as it continued to torment him from every direction. He contemplated getting a shot off in hopes of felling at least one savage, but there was no time.

Church felt like his heart would explode in his chest as he somehow transferred Hammond to his own horse. There were no signs of life, but Church had no time to tend to him. Another barrage of gunfire found Hammond's leg, but unsurprisingly, there was no response from the mortally wounded man.

When Church was certain the situation could not become any more difficult, a flash of lightning illuminated the sky. If his enemy had any doubts about Church's position, they were certainly settled as the catastrophic scene was illuminated in bright light. The inevitable crash of thunder followed, which Church found more unnerving than the musket fire.

He cupped his hands to his mouth and futilely screamed in the direction of the garrison. "Bring your weapons! The enemy is upon us!" Church wasted no more time in that pointless endeavor, and the rain began to fall.

Church somehow extricated Belcher from under his horse. He could hear the chants and cries of his enemy growing louder, and he thought of his wife and child. He contemplated how ignominious his death would be, and wondered what would become of his Sakonnet homestead. Where the devil was Gill? Belcher was sobbing uncontrollably as Church placed him atop his horse next to Hammond's corpse.

"Savages! The devil take you, you Godless heathen!" Church's rambling cries went unheard as another bout of thunder rumbled ominously, and the rain intensified. Thankfully, the rain seemed to subdue the enemy fire, and he finally spotted Gill thirty yards behind the bridge. Gill had drawn a pistol, but seemed delirious and lost.

The thunder was now instilling terror in the horses. Hammond's mount sprinted east toward the enemy. Church employed all of his horsemanship in his efforts to keep his mount calm while transporting himself and two casualties. He diverted his eyes from Belcher's mangled leg for fear of vomiting.

Somehow, he directed himself and Gill through the darkness and back to the garrison. The rain was unrelenting, and he was stunned to return to applause and hoots of acclamation. Upon dismounting, he quickly identified the source. Dutch Cornelius was leading his band in a despicable, sarcastic ceremony.

Cornelius had his sword drawn in a position of salute. "All hail Captain Church and his glorious victory! God be praised! This pinnacle of Puritan virtue hath vanquished the savages! If only he left some enemy for us to fight. We salute you, Captain Church!" The laughter was sickening. Church drew his sword and was planning to silence the giant pirate for an eternity. At least one savage would meet his just reward tonight.

"Not another step, Benjamin." Bradford had seized him from behind by his collar, and the soaked, defeated Church collapsed to the floor with exhaustion and disgust. Cornelius whooped with delight, only to be interrupted by a scene he found even more entertaining.

A teenaged militiaman from Bridgewater had been sitting morosely in the corner, rocking and sobbing. He now ranted pathetically as the thunder shook the garrison, and he loudly wailed for all to hear. "We are cursed! Lord God have mercy, we are cursed by witchcraft. God has abandoned us! It was the moon. I saw our deaths in the moon. *Have mercy on me, Lord!* Forgive my wickedness! I do not wish to be butchered by savages!"

Cornelius could scarcely control his laughter as he thanked the youngster for his display of typical Puritan bravery and manhood.

Church remained on the ground, speechless and aghast. How was this possible? They were the sovereign, holy army of the Almighty Lord. They were God's spear, to be employed mercilessly against the wicked heathen. And they couldn't cross a bridge. They were soaked, humiliated, and defeated.

Who would answer the prayers of such a miserable, cowardly rabble?

CHAPTER FOUR

PROVIDENCE

John Easton appeared impressive and dignified as he stood in the meeting house with the Society of Friends. "Frankly, Israel, I didn't believe this day would ever come."

"You never thought I'd marry again? You must have known I would, John."

"I did, but I never dreamt any woman would have you. I thought you'd be marrying your smelly horse."

"I considered it, but she won't tolerate my singing."

"You've never seen Miss Wilder's expression during your Puritan psalmody?"

"No, why?"

"Umm. No reason. Stand tall, Israel, here she comes."

The meeting house was sticky and uncomfortable on this balmy Sunday. Brewster knew Constance would accept nothing but a Quaker wedding at the local meeting house, and he complied with her wishes. After all, the wedding day was all about the bride.

A Quaker wedding, as an outsider might surmise, was conducted with minimal fanfare. There was technically no minister to conduct the service, for as Quaker theologian George Fox had written a mere six years prior, *"For the right joining in marriage is the work of the Lord only, and not the priests' or the magistrates'; for it is God's ordinance and not man's; and therefore, Friends cannot consent that they should join them together: for we marry none; it is the Lord's work, and we are but witnesses."*

In fact, such minimal fanfare was ascribed to the event that it transpired within the confines of a normal worship service. Congregation members prayed silently, occasionally interrupted by a devotee standing to give their testimony. When the prospective couple decided the time was right, they would stand, hold hands while reciting their vows, sign a certificate, and sit back down.

Despite Mr. Fox's thoughts on the matter, Deputy Governor Easton opted for a more formal role, and seemed to be orchestrating the ceremony as a traditional clergyman. Perhaps as an homage to Brewster's Puritan sensibilities, Easton stood before the congregation and read some verses from Corinthians and Proverbs. Brewster stood by his side, and soon Constance Wilder made her way to the front.

Unsurprisingly, she appeared stunning. With her scarlet hair and porcelain skin, she radiated vitality and beauty. Her gown appeared most unfortunate, however, as she insisted on wearing her mother's dress. Her mother, Vivian Wilder, had perished from influenza on a dark winter's morning nine years ago. Vivian was four inches shorter than Constance and at least twenty-five pounds heavier, but Constance could scarcely bear to alter the dress in any tangible fashion.

If the Society of Friends were to pass judgement, however, the ill-fitting dress was hardly the focus of their concerns. Constance's beloved, Israel Brewster, was a marginal Quaker at best. As a fallen Puritan, he never quite conformed to all the practices of the Quaker faith. Additionally, her father Ezekiel was accompanying her to stand with the groom, which was a practice foreign to their wedding traditions, and some deemed it an unseemly extravagance.

If anyone was truly bothered by these issues, however, they certainly offered no outward appearances of disapproval or ill will. This was a joyous day. Most of the congregation remembered shedding their tears with Ezekiel and fifteen-year-old Constance on the bitter day they buried Vivian. Through the years, they watched with glee but increasing consternation as one male suitor after the other slinked away from Constance, inevitably overwhelmed by her fierce independence, intellect, and intolerance for spiritual indolence. As they watched her romance blossom with Israel Brewster, and watched Easton preside over Brewster's rapid redemption from misery and drink, the congregation gave thanks to the Lord.

Easton could not contain his mirth and grinned merrily. Even Zeke seemed delighted at the prospect of this addition to his family. He bowed his head as Easton recited scripture.

"And the Lord God caused a deep sleep to fall upon Adam, and he slept: and he took one of his ribs, and closed up the flesh instead thereof; and the rib, which the Lord God had taken from man, made he a woman, and brought her unto the man. And Adam said, this is now bone of my bones, and flesh of my flesh: she shall be called Woman, because she was taken out of Man. Therefore, shall a man leave his father and his mother, and shall cleave unto his wife: and they shall be one flesh."

Easton knew it was probably time to recite the vows, lest the ceremony degenerate into some kind of Roman Catholic frippery fit for the royal court of France. "Take each other's hands please, and recite your vows."

"In the presence of God and before these, our families and friends, I take thee, Constance, to be my wife, promising with divine assistance to be unto thee a loving and faithful husband so long as we both shall live."

"In the presence of God and before these, our families and friends, I take thee, Israel, to be my husband, promising with divine assistance to be unto thee a loving and faithful wife so long as we both shall live."

Easton seemed to wipe away a tear, though he steadfastly attested it was a bead of sweat rolling down his cheek on this stifling day. He presented the certificates of marriage, and Mister and Missus Israel Brewster signed them accordingly. And they were husband and wife. Of course, all those present would also sign the certificate to attest to the holy union.

Brewster and his wife returned to their seats along with Easton and Zeke. The worship service would continue with more silent prayer and spontaneous testimony.

An elderly widow rose to speak. "I thank the Lord for this man and woman, and pray that they remain steadfast, fruitful, and holy." She resumed her seat.

After ten minutes passed, a middle-aged father of five stood to speak. "God bless Israel and Constance. They are two of the finest people in all of Providence. Imagine how brilliant their children will be."

There was some quiet, subdued singing, and the sweat began to roll down Brewster's forehead. He wondered when Easton would dismiss the congregation. Another parishioner, a hunched, elderly man, rose to speak.

"I wish to take this opportunity to pray for peace in this land, and to denounce this war that is ceaselessly spreading like a disease. I denounce the wickedness and violence inherent in our nature, and I condemn the governments of Plimoth and Massachusetts Bay for making war on unenlightened natives when they should be instead bringing them the holy light of Christ. Frankly, the thought of the entire enterprise fills me with revulsion."

He took his seat and the congregation remained silent. Brewster was certain he could hear his own breathing. Although he did not wish to contemplate such serious and depressing matters on the day of his marriage, he felt compelled to say something. He was, until quite recently, an ordained minister in Plimoth Colony. A mere four years ago, he was a spiritual and civic leader in the bustling hamlet of Middleborough. Certainly, he should think of something to say.

He rose to speak. "Blessings be upon this holy assembly. I convey my humble gratitude for the thoughts and prayers for my beloved and I. I pray for the continued peace and prosperity of Providence and the people present." Brewster paused because his inadvertent alliteration had made him feel silly, and he hoped no one misinterpreted it as a preordained attempt to sound pompous and pretentious. What? More P's?

Brewster shook his head vigorously, and many were subsequently perplexed.

"Blessings upon Deputy Governor Easton. One of the most noble undertakings I have ever participated in was our journey to Montaup to visit Metacomet and mediate the conflict. I am saddened our journey was unsuccessful, and I pray for a rapid end to the hostilities, and for peace with our neighbors. All of our neighbors."

He ruminated on the notion that four years ago, while addressing a congregation assembled for worship, he would have spoken for at least sixty minutes with nary a pause for water. He was learning the virtue of brevity.

The peaceful stillness resumed, and Brewster went to prayer. He earnestly implored the Lord that he would be a good and faithful husband. He prayed he would be diligent provider, and he thought about the future in an age of calamity and war.

The silence was soon broken as a young woman, certainly no older than fourteen years, stood upright and began singing. Her voice was unique and wonderful, and Brewster was captivated. He soon recognized her words as the 128th Psalm:

"Blessed is every one that feareth the Lord; that walketh in his ways.
For thou shalt eat the labour of thine hands: happy shalt thou be, and it shall be well with thee.
Thy wife shall be as a fruitful vine by the sides of thine house: thy children like olive plants round about thy table.
Behold, that thus shall the man be blessed that feareth the Lord.
The Lord shall bless thee out of Zion: and thou shalt see the good of Jerusalem all the days of thy life.
Yea, thou shalt see thy children's children, and peace upon Israel"

Peace upon Israel, indeed, thought Brewster. He knew it was a very special contribution, as the Quaker faith typically shunned Brewster's beloved psalmody as an insincere and unspontaneous parroting of words. They had made this day very special for the fallen Puritan in their midst.

At this time Easton rose, and dismissed the congregation with a blessing. He reminded them that a sumptuous lunch would be served at the Wilder home, and all would be welcome. Brewster took his wife's hand, and stepped into the sunlight. It was a magnificent day.

Easton had suggested hosting a reception at his impressive home, but Zeke would have none of it. Several of the most trusted men of his three-boat fishing fleet were currently in his home making preparations, along with wives and daughters. Brewster wondered how many guests would appear, and he wondered if he might get to witness a modern-day miracle of loaves and fishes. Upon arriving back at the four-room clapboard house, however, he realized no miracle would be necessary, unless the size of the congregation had quintupled that morning. Brewster was stunned by the sight.

The kitchen burst at the seams with every manner of the Atlantic's bounty. The cod was too numerous to count, of course, and the lobster was so plentiful they almost appeared as a sinister invasion of diabolical, pinching creatures. There was haddock, clams, bread, stews, and there was even Zeke's secret delicacy: A mincing of crabmeat, eggs, and dried bread roasted over a fire that he called his "cake of crabs." All were delightfully complimented with fruit, vegetables, and puddings.

Well-wishers were plentiful, and Brewster was overwhelmed. Unsurprisingly, the modest home soon overflowed, and the affair filled the street. Equally unsurprisingly, there was not a drop of ale or wine to be found.

Brewster reflected on the fact that despite the hordes of well-wishers, he and his bride had only one family member present. If not completely sad, it was quite remarkable, as most families in New England boasted upwards of six or seven children. He reminisced on the marriages he had performed in

Middleborough, rife with dozens of siblings, cousins, aunts, uncles, and grandparents.

In addition to her widowed father, Constance had two older brothers who were making a new life in the south. There were currently rumblings among the Society of Friends that their future prosperity lay far, far away from the Puritans of New England and the royalists of England, and a better New World awaited them south of New Amsterdam, on the western frontier of Jersey. The community of dissenters was led by a remarkable Englishman named William Penn, who hailed from a well-to-do family. There was fervent talk among the faithful that Penn was on the verge of procuring an extraordinary tract of land for Quakers to live and worship without persecution. Constance's brothers, Henry and Oliver, were now men of the wilderness, given to exploring the uncharted territory of west Jersey while building cordial relationships with the local Indians.

As the grandson of the famed Mayflower leader, Elder William Brewster, Israel Brewster had more relatives in New England than he could even track. Any communication with family and friends in Plimoth Colony, however, ceased abruptly when he was ignominiously reprimanded and defrocked in front of the Plimoth General Court four years ago. Since fleeing to Providence, he had made no attempt at correspondence, which was probably just as well, since he felt confident they could not abide the shame and humiliation associated with consorting with his ilk.

Brewster peered across the packed kitchen and was delighted to see his employer, Mister Barlow, wolfing down yet another cake of crabs. Barlow took a chance on Israel Brewster when, as a mysterious stranger with no coopering experience, he appeared at his door four years ago. Barlow's risk was rewarded, and Brewster had proven to be a reliable cooper and associate.

Barlow approached and extended his hand. "Such a feast, Izzy. Clearly my wages are far too generous."

"You should marry a girl whose father owns three fishing vessels."

"Hmm, that is good advice. Does he need any more barrels for all these leftovers? I hope you're not offering any unauthorized discounts."

"Have you seen this crowd eat, Mr. Barlow? There shan't be a scrap left over, I presume."

"There won't be any of this crabmeat remaining, I trust. Why did the ale run out so quickly? Are you to blame?" Barlow managed two jibes at once, teasing Brewster about his prolific alcohol consumption during the first years in his employ, and his teetotaler Quaker associates.

"I have a few bottles in Brownie's saddle bag."

"Are you going to..."

"Joking, Mr. Barlow! Joking!"

"Oh yes, of course. So was I. Umm, Izzy..."

"Yes?"

"When can I expect you back at the cooperage?"

"I don't know if I'll ever be back. I seem to have enough food for two lifetimes." Barlow's eyes grew wide at the prospect, and Brewster guffawed.

"My, you are gullible today. I'll refrain from telling you the bizarre things Zeke puts in his secret crab recipe for fear you might believe me." Barlow eyed the concoction suspiciously but resumed eating.

"Well, come back next week, Izzy. Monday. We have to discuss your future."

"My future?"

"How old do you think I am, Izzy?"

"Nine hundred and sixty-nine!" Brewster leapt at the opportunity to reference scripture and Methuselah.

"How dare you ridicule your employer. You'd be doing tavern tricks for bread crusts if it weren't for me. I'm sixty-two, Izzy. Sixty-two! Oh, how my hands ache. Who is going to take this cooperage from me whilst I sit by the fire with my memories?"

"The cooperage? What of your son?"

"Captain Barlow? He's in Ireland fighting for crown and country. What kind of cooper would he be? You can't shoot or stab a barrel."

"Are you proposing giving it to me?" Brewster could scarcely contain his shock.

"Oh heavens, no. Give it away? What would I have to eat as I rock in front of the fire? What comely lass wishes to associate with a destitute old man with achy hands? Come, come Izzy. But certainly, we could reach some kind of credit arrangement. I have no doubt Ezekiel, the king of the seas, would stake his newest son. Aren't you Quakers savvy with your business dealings?"

Brewster wasn't certain how he felt about being addressed as "you Quakers." He took a breath. "My goodness, Mr. Barlow. That is a lot to think about. Will you deduct your meal today from the cost?"

"Everyone loves a funny, disgraced minister." He peered at the table behind Brewster and changed the subject. "What kind of stew does Zeke do with clams?"

"I don't know."

"Well, I'm about to find out. Think about my words, young man. Let's discuss it more when you get back. You can't support a family with sarcasm and psalmody."

"Thank you, Mr. Barlow." He now refrained from sarcasm. "God keep you, and thank you for being here."

As Barlow went in search of his next free delicacy, Brewster took in his words. Imagine. *Owning* a cooperage. Could it be done? Why not? He had no doubt Zeke would support him in this venture. He went in search of his beautiful bride.

Brewster feared with such a feast offered up for the masses, he might be cursed with wedding guests until all hours of the night. Perhaps it was the lack of wine and ale, or good Quaker manners, or Zeke's gentle prodding, but by three in the afternoon, the house was once again on the verge of peace and emptiness. Zeke's associates had removed the astounding quantity of remaining food, to be given away to the poor and indigent. Of course, much would remain for Israel and Constance and their post-wedding bliss. The family felt weary, blessed, and delighted as they bade farewell to their last guest.

Zeke Wilder, in addition to being an outstanding commercial fisherman, would prove himself in the ensuing week to be an outstanding father-in-law. He fondly reminisced about the days after his nuptials all those decades ago, and he had made arrangements to take his fleet back to sea for the week. The newlyweds extended their heartfelt love and devotion.

"I don't know why you're back out to sea, Zeke. There can't be any more fish left in the ocean."

"You're right, Israel. I've changed my mind. I'll unpack."

"NO, father! That won't be, um…we'll manage without you, somehow." Constance smiled joyfully and embraced him. "Thank you for the feast, father. God be with you at sea."

"Blessings upon you daughter. I am so very proud."

Brewster awkwardly sidled forward. "Zeke," he exclaimed, offering his handshake.

Zeke would have none of it. He pulled Brewster into a suffocating hug. "Be well, son." He finally ended the embrace and whispered his parting thoughts. "Grandchildren, son. Big, strapping grandchildren named Ezekiel. Fishermen. Even the girls."

Without another word, he was out the door.

CHAPTER FIVE

SWANSEA

The torrential rains were increasingly perceived as yet another manifestation of the Almighty's displeasure.

Hundreds of men seemed to spend every waking and resting hour pursuing no other meaningful activity except staying dry. And they consistently failed. Men huddled together in close quarters on the porch, in a leaky barn, under makeshift lean-tos, or they even shivered underneath the main house while keeping a watchful eye on the rats.

Even the consumption of food was a daunting task as the rains cascaded from the heavens. Reverend Miles led numerous voluntary prayer services seeking the Lord's blessed sunshine so His chosen people could administer justice to the savages. Few if any attended, at least until their officers taught them the true meaning of the word "voluntary" in the militia. Their enthusiasm became even more intense when they realized the services would be in the main house and out of the rain.

It had been thirty-six hours since the failed raid on the bridge, and morale was dismal. Benjamin Church was very confident that one of two things was destined to transpire in the next few days. The rain would stop, and the militia would finally seize the pagan stronghold at Mount Hope, or Church would abandon this sorry rabble and return to his homestead at Sakonnet.

Colonel Cudworth was certainly not oblivious to the wretched morale, and he was almost as enthused about their next military venture as Captain Church. Even during wartime, news traveled fast in Plimoth Colony, and there were already whispers among the governor's staff that Cudworth was too feeble, too cautious, too old, and the army of the Lord would be best served if Governor Winslow himself simply commanded the expedition. Cudworth knew there had been enough dawdling and enough dead Englishmen. The time for action was upon them.

Finally, that afternoon, the sun blessedly appeared. Cudworth and Bradford attributed the fortunate development to Reverend Miles' entreaties, whereas Dutch Cornelius said a strong westerly wind deserved the credit. No matter who or what received the praise, this army would be on the move in the morning.

The skies were clear, and signs of life were gradually returning. Men drank wine, battled one another in tests of strength, and sang bawdy songs when they were adequately out of earshot of their watchful Puritan leaders.

> *"Be merry my hearts, and call for your quarts,*
> *And let no liquor be lacking*
> *We have gold in store, we purpose to roar*
> *Until we set care a-packing!*
> *Then hostess make haste, and let no time waste*
> *Let every man have his due*
> *To save shoes and trouble, bring in the pots double*
> *For he that made one, made two"*

Church had kept a careful eye on his men. He inspected flintlocks and reviewed the hand-to-hand combat drills they had mastered in the previous week. The men had learned Church's techniques well: Stay low, never move in a predictable trajectory, dive and roll when faced with a drawn bow, rely on your trusted saber, and finally, there is no diversion more effective than tossing your musket at your befuddled adversary while striking low. Most of his men also had daggers in addition to their sabers. He ensured they were well fed, and he led the evening prayers. Oddly enough, that night Church enjoyed one of his best slumbers since he arrived at the garrison.

The men were roused not long after sunrise by the lone drummer assigned to the expedition. Diego the Spaniard, one of Moseley's band, promptly found the youngster responsible for the noise, stared deep into his eyes until the poor boy quivered, threw the drumsticks at least thirty yards in opposite directions, and returned to sleep. Moseley subsequently forced him to retrieve the sticks and even scrub the mud from them. Diego returned the implements of noise-making to their rightful owner, and he even patted the boy on the head as the quivering subsided. Moseley could not discern if Diego was being genuinely remorseful or theatrically sarcastic.

After devouring an apple, Church reported in to the reverend's sitting room for the final briefing. Cudworth was agonizing over a makeshift map spread across the reverend's desk, and Bradford nodded incessantly. Moseley appeared somber but confident.

Despite Church's persistent efforts to dissuade him, Cudworth would not relent on his decision that Moseley's band would lead the charge across the bridge. Church silently contemplated whether this was a glaring condemnation of his failure on the previous night, or an unspoken acknowledgement that the first assault would, once again, meet brutal resistance, and Moseley's men were more dispensable. Of course, Bradford would phrase the decision as "better suited to unconventional combat at close quarters."

Church was initially dismayed that his men were merely tasked to protect the left flank of the main body, but at this point any tasking would be preferable to his current, sour idleness. He was attentive as the officers reviewed the intelligence reports. After fighting their way across the bridge, the army would turn south and proceed approximately ten miles through heavy enemy resistance. Their objective was King Philip's capital at Mount Hope, strategically situated on the peninsula bordered by the Providence River to the west and Mount Hope Bay to the east.

After a brief prayer, Reverend Miles blessed the officers with a recitation of the eleventh psalm.

"In the Lord put I my trust: how say ye to my soul, Flee as a bird to your mountain?
For, lo, the wicked bend their bow, they make ready their arrow upon the string, that they may privily shoot at the upright in heart.
If the foundations be destroyed, what can the righteous do?
The Lord is in his holy temple, the Lord's throne is in heaven: his eyes behold, his eyelids try, the children of men.
The Lord trieth the righteous: but the wicked and him that loveth violence his soul hateth.
Upon the wicked he shall rain snares, fire and brimstone, and a horrible tempest*: this shall be the portion of their cup.*
For the righteous Lord loveth righteousness; his countenance doth behold the upright."

Church listened devoutly. He surmised the Wampanoag were making ready their arrows upon their strings, but he was ready to rain a horrible tempest upon them.

The army gathered and proceeded east without further fanfare. Moseley's band made a fearsome sight indeed, with their savage tattoos, piercings, and outlandish attire. Cornelius and his mastiffs led the charge. They sauntered across the bridge as if they were merely enroute to a strange new tavern. They were enthusiastic, confident, but vigilant in the face of unexplored territory.

Church evaluated the merits of assaulting the bridge in broad daylight, and was surprised to witness at least a dozen enemy combatants across the river. They were making no effort to conceal themselves, and were even shouting insults at Moseley's platoon. Their English was so poor their insults were marginally effective, but Church was certain he could discern "skunks...women...gowns."

Whatever they intended to convey, it was more than enough, for Moseley and his platoon pursued the savages with wild abandon as they disappeared into a nearby swamp.

This was the moment when the brunt of New England's military might would finally engage the enemy head-on. This would be no skirmish. This would be a glorious battle that could very well decisively end this hideous rebellion. The brave and hearty assembly of English Puritans cast their eyes upward to the heavens, superstitiously anticipating one final manifestation of the Lord's approval. And Benjamin Church could not believe what he was seeing.

It was raining again.

It was not mere rain, and once again he was suffering the wrath of a vicious downpour as thunder rumbled over the horizon. The bulk of the army was across the bridge, and the lead element was at least a mile into enemy territory. There was no sign of Moseley and his pirates.

And then the shooting began.

Church's eyesight was legendary, but he could not discern any enemy activity in the torrential rain. The young man charged to bear the colors dropped to the ground in terror when a musket ball harmlessly pierced his hat. The flag remained shamefully on the ground, as no other volunteers were inclined to hoist it.

The sound of musket fire was now deafening, but Church still did not see any enemy activity. Frankly, he wasn't even certain anyone was shooting at them. As he watched the young volunteers point their muskets and fire in any conceivable direction, he was increasingly convinced they themselves were a bigger threat to their safety than the enemy.

The army had now proceeded two miles closer to Mount Hope, and the rain was unrelenting. Cornelius' dogs scampered from the swamp, with Moseley's platoon not far behind. The wind was now howling, and Moseley reported in to Major Bradford.

"I think we gunned down five or six of the savage bastards, Major. The rest knew what was best for them and fled south."

"Well done, Captain. I've just conferred with Colonel Cudworth, and he is pleased with the day's progress. We've shown King Philip our resolve, but this blasted weather is not conducive to campaigning today. Prepare your men."

Church was flabbergasted when the news reached him. They were going back to the garrison.

He spent the rest of the afternoon in a state of numb disbelief. Was this army ever going to fight? Was their mission somehow cursed with the Lord's disapproval? He quietly agonized as he performed what seemed to be his primary duty in this conflict: He huddled under a lean-to and stayed dry.

Any potential rage on his part was mitigated by Cudworth's directive that, weather permitting, they would seize Mount Hope tomorrow. Additionally, Church was very impressed with the way Moseley's men acquitted themselves, and he bitterly wondered if they wouldn't do better to replace half of the Puritans in the ranks with pirates. He secretly questioned, however, their claim to have felled six enemy combatants.

Although the rains blessedly ceased shortly after midnight, Cudworth was still skittish about the endeavor, and the army milled around the garrison all morning. By lunchtime, men were removing their white linen shirts to bask in the sunlight, and a few casks of wine were being tapped. Bradford gently encouraged his superior officer to make a decision, and he tactfully invoked Cudworth's increasingly overdue report to the Plimoth government. Cudworth had heard enough and once again, the army was reassembled, fed, blessed, briefed, blessed again, and led across the bridge.

Even the most reluctant warrior in the army knew there would be no excuses today. There was no resistance at the bridge, not even a rabble gleefully hurling insults. The weather was magnificent, and despite the previous heavy downpours, their footing was adequate. Yea, there would be no monsoons or eclipses today. There was nothing to stand in the way of the Lord's army, and they progressed at a rapid clip. Nothing would deter them or sway their righteous confidence.

They were now four miles south of the garrison and on the neck of King Philip's peninsula. They were rapidly approaching the humble English settlement of Kickemuit, and the Puritan forces were eager to instill hope and confidence in a terrorized citizenry unnerved by the suddenness in which a trusted ally embraced treasonous rebellion. There would, however, not be any hope given, or confidence instilled at Kickemuit.

Kickemuit no longer existed.

Even Moseley's cutthroats seemed horrified at the scene. More than a dozen homes lay abandoned and burned to their foundation. Three barns and a meeting house lay in ruins. And all of it paled in comparison to the further desecration they witnessed.

Half-burned, smoldering scraps of books and parchment were scattered everywhere. Some were adequately intact to read. Baptism certificates. Marriage licenses. Hand-written love sonnets and letters to the mother country were no more than charred tatters. But most despicable of all, the holy scriptures lay torn, burnt, and desecrated. Pieces fluttered hauntingly in the breeze, like a revulsive, blasphemous snow shower.

When Church's contempt for the enemy was inflamed beyond measure, his men discovered the ultimate desecration. Human bodies lay tortured and butchered in the courtyard of the meeting house. A precise body count was difficult, as the savagery was so total. Heads stood mounted on poles, with hands neatly stacked on top of them. A partially intact Bible was desecrated, blanketed with a blood-soaked scalp. Severed feet were aligned in a perfect row, and Church stopped counting at eleven.

Identification of the victims was a daunting task at best, but with careful scrutiny, the men could discern man from woman, and old from young. Adding to the grim horror permeating the assembly, the fate of the two missing sentries was no longer a mystery.

Church did everything in his power to avoid vomiting, or even worse, fainting in front of his men. As if he had not already been overwhelmed by the satanic atrocities in their midst, the torture of the sentries was a unique mode of savagery. Clearly, their manhood had been butchered away, and fastened somehow to the hideous, bloody emptiness were the tails of skunks.

"What in holy creation have they done? Sam, what is that? *Why would they do such a thing?*"

"Damned if I know, Benjamin. I think I'm going to be ill."

Bradford maintained an aura of calm focus. "A message, gentlemen. For Governor Winslow."

"Winslow?"

"It's their foul, disgusting name for the governor. We learned it from our informants." Bradford paused. If he was inviting guesses, no one was playing the game.

"They call him Skunk Genitals, gentlemen. That's the heathen name for our governor." Bradford's solemn explanation was shamefully interrupted by Cornelius and Diego laughing hysterically.

"Skunk Genitals?"

Bradford immediately regretted his explanation.

"Governor Skunk Genitals Winslow!" Every man within fifty yards could hear Cornelius struggle to contain his laughter. "I'm liking these heathens more and more! I don't know if I'll take King Philip's head, or if I'll take him drinking with me in the taverns! Perhaps I'll do both. Skunk Genitals, indeed! Did you hear that Diego? I only wish I'd thought of it first!"

Church felt certain there would now be a repeat of his previous encounter with the giant Dutchman. He took a step in his direction but was apprehended by Moseley. "Benjamin…not here."

Colonel Cudworth had finished surveying the catastrophe and dismounted. "Gentlemen, never forget what you have seen here today." Most of the men were removing their hats and solemnly bowing their heads. "Never underestimate the butchery and savagery of these Godless heathen. Bear witness to what you have seen here today, and follow me to Mount Hope for righteous vengeance. Now, let's prepare these tragic souls for Christian burial."

Church donned his hat and noted this might be the first time he heard Cudworth actually inspire the men. Yet, he could not help noting, it seemed like all the enemy ever did was kill English colonists, and all the English ever did was prepare them for Christian burial.

That fact notwithstanding, after the funeral arrangements, Church could feel his passion intensifying. They were now only five miles to the stronghold at Mount Hope. How many savages would be awaiting them there? Three hundred? Seven hundred? Intelligence reports placed their numbers at five hundred, and the armies would most likely be evenly matched. Accurate figures were hard to formulate, however, as no one knew how many warriors from other nations had joined Metacomet's rebellion. Prior to reporting to Governor Winslow, Church spent the week near his Sakonnet homestead trying to persuade the great female Sachems Weetamoo and Awashonks to at least remain neutral, and resist Metacomet's treasonous aggression. He was uncertain if he was successful.

Five hundred, six hundred, one thousand savages. It no longer mattered. He and his men had endured enough delay, enough English death, and enough humiliation. No obstacle or resistance would deter them from their objective. One way or another, they would capture Mount Hope today. One way or another, Metacomet would be drawn and quartered.

Church's heart was pounding as he led his men south. He was apprehensive, but delirious with frenzied energy. He would tolerate no fear, for he was a soldier in the service of the Lord. Five miles turned to four, and four miles became three.

Where was the resistance? Where were the sentries, and where was the withering fire from Metacomet's archers?

He paid it no mind and focused on encouraging his men. They were guarding the flanks of the main body, and proceeded cautiously. Ambushes could spring from almost anywhere, but his men would be ready. He had trained them, he had motivated them, he had corrected them, he had inspired them. By the will of the great Jehovah, they would be ready.

Church had to be careful not to stray too far from the main body. Moseley's pirates were guarding the western flank, and Church had lost sight of them long ago. He still maintained marginal visual contact with Bradford and the four hundred men in the main assault. Church still heard nothing, however. No gunfire, no cries of the wounded, no arrows soaring through the air.

Mount Hope was situated on the eastern side of the peninsula, and soon the three components of the assault would be merging. Church's men encountered a village on the eastern shore, but unsurprisingly, it was abandoned. Despite some weak protests, he knew they had no time for treasure-hunting or torching of homes and crops. Mount Hope was their objective.

They were gradually rendezvousing with the main body for the final mile. Moseley's men would come in from the west, and possibly even get behind the enemy fortifications. Church tried to put himself in Metacomet's shoes and ascertain his strategy. Mount Hope would be a veritable fortress, fortified with fences, archers, flintlock muskets, and mounted cavalry with long, deadly hatchets. He mentally tried to predict the English casualties. Two hundred men? Three hundred?

Church could barely speak as Mount Hope began to come into view. He had to force his men to stop for water, since they could anticipate incessant, draining, hand-to-hand combat. His heart was racing, and he was mentally praying for the Lord's hand to give him strength. He could now clearly make out his objective, and the sight was so stunning, he stopped in his tracks.

He squinted and tried to assure himself his eyes were deceiving him. Although the sight was at least half a mile away, he was certain he could discern Moseley's brigands kneeling on the ground and bowing! They were actually bowing! In the center of their assembly, with his back turned, was Metacomet, sporting a magnificent ceremonial headdress that was unmistakably regal. While remaining on their knees, the pirates rose and fell, physically conveying their awe and allegiance.

Church knew it. He absolutely knew this traitorous gallery of rogues could not be trusted. How on earth did they reach the objective so quickly? How many hundreds of warriors did Metacomet have stashed to the south? What were the Plimoth authorities thinking when they enlisted the service of these villainous reprobates?

His men were drawing closer to the hideous spectacle, and they could hear the disgusting chanting. "All hail, King Philip! All hail, Metacomet, the great and wise victor! All hail, King Philip!" They continued to bow like pagans engaged in some cultish ritual.

Church knew he was ready to kill someone, perhaps anyone. He raised his musket. Could he get a shot at Metacomet? How many of Moseley's traitors could he kill? How much treasure was expended to buy their allegiance? And where the devil was Moseley? Church surmised that Moseley's loathsome brood probably murdered him long ago.

And at that very moment Metacomet, who was much more enormous in stature than Church had ever suspected, turned to face the arriving party of Puritan warriors. He was attired in an ill-fitting, odd assortment of English and Wampanoag apparel.

"What took you bastards so long?"

Dutch Cornelius roared with delight, removed his ceremonial headdress, and flippantly tossed it to Diego. The

Spaniard dramatically donned it like it was a jewel-encrusted crown of the Habsburg empire.

Metacomet wasn't there. The Wampanoag weren't there. There was not a single enemy combatant on the entire peninsula. The English had spent almost two weeks formulating the courage and resources to assault an enemy stronghold that didn't even exist.

The enemy was gone, and once again, Church felt ridiculous and ashamed.

CHAPTER SIX

POCASSET

Linto knew there was only one thing in the world he was undoubtedly certain of: He was absolutely a complete idiot.

The longer Linto contemplated this sentiment, however, the less certain he became. The first problem with his truism was there were many *other* things in the world he was certain of. He was certain he loved his wife, Wawetseka, and he was certain he loved and adored their two young children. Linto was also certain he loved and revered the Sachem of his people, and he would continue to obey and serve Metacomet to the best of his abilities. He was certain he despised this war against the English, and he had been praying constantly for it all to somehow end. So, to say that there was only one thing in the world he was certain of was clearly and completely false.

Additionally, as he probed deeper into the issue, he could not even be certain he was an idiot. Linto was one of the most brilliant men in the history of the Wampanoag people. But every time he put his gifts to good use in the service of his adopted people, the results were dismal, if not catastrophic.

Linto was now twenty-six summers old, and he was the product of a miraculous event. When he was two summers old, his Abenaki village was visited by a Wampanoag delegation. The delegation was led by the great Sachem Massasoit, and he was accompanied by his teen-aged son, Metacomet.

When the delegation arrived at Linto's village, they were horrified to discover an odious sea of death. The English plagues had so thoroughly decimated the village that not a living soul was found. Except one. Under a filthy blanket, a toddler was smiling and singing. Massasoit and his spiritual elders declared the child a divine miracle, and a sign the spirit world had not abandoned them in an age of desolation. Massasoit christened the child as "Linto," the Abenaki word for "sing." Surely, the child was delivered to the Wampanoag for a divine purpose. And Linto lived his entire life trying to fulfill this mystical destiny.

Four years ago, prior to the outbreak of this war, Metacomet was tormented with visions and nightmares about his older brother, Wamsutta. Wamsutta preceded Metacomet as Sachem, and died mysteriously at the hands of the English. Metacomet and the Wampanoag suspected he was poisoned, and the visions seemed to be an overdue cry for vengeance from the spirit world. Metacomet agonized between maintaining the cherished alliance with the English that his father forged, or going to war to avenge Wamsutta and crush the English wickedness.

Just when it seemed like war was imminent, there was a miraculous coincidence. While discussing religion with an English minister at a missionary service, Linto discovered this minister was present with Wamsutta during his last days, and could absolutely attest he was not poisoned. He could even recount Wamsutta's dying words that absolved the English of his death, words that would be forgotten and misinterpreted if not for Linto. Linto rushed the news to Metacomet, and war was averted. **Linto was brilliant**.

But it was all for naught. Four years later, Linto and the Wampanoag were now at war with the English.

A mere six months ago, Linto discovered that John Sassamon, the Christian Indian who served as counselor to Metacomet and as the liaison to the English, had been incessantly betraying Metacomet and his people. Sassamon was using his mastery of the English language to manipulate and alter legal documents, shamelessly enriching himself in the process.

After Sassamon was dismissed from Metacomet's service, he was promptly found murdered, with his strangled corpse entombed under a frozen pond near the English village of Middleborough. The English arrested Tobias, who was one of Metacomet's closest associates, along with Tobias' son and friend. They put them on trial for murder, which infuriated Metacomet and drove the Wampanoag to the brink of war. But once again Linto, the wise and divinely blessed Linto, stepped into the void and served as counselor to the accused. Linto used his remarkable mastery of the English language and his intellectual acumen to befuddle the learned Englishmen and expose their treachery. Their evidence was pathetic and woefully inadequate. Even more, they had no business intervening in an Indian affair in the first place. In the name of justice, the men had to be acquitted. **Linto was brilliant**.

But it was all for naught. The three accused men were found guilty and sentenced to die.

When Linto stood before the gallows and witnessed the executions, he prayed relentlessly for divine intervention. He prayed and prayed for some holy sign, some miraculous event that would validate his faith in the spirit world.

And then...the hangman's rope broke, and Tobias' young son somehow survived the execution. Linto leapt into action. He convinced the Plimoth authorities that this was a sign from the Almighty, and the English God had clearly conveyed his displeasure that the accused was sentenced to hang. **Linto was brilliant**.

But it was all for naught. Plimoth shot the young man after he survived the hanging.

Linto the magnificent, however, intervened one final time in an attempt to stop the war and save his people. The blessed and holy Linto, the supernatural prophet to the Wampanoag, made one more desperate effort. Since the truth had previously failed him on every occasion, he lied. He crafted a spectacular lie and sold it magnificently to Metacomet. Linto pretended to be in a spiritual trance, and he prophesized that whichever side fired the first shot and drew the first blood in this war would be cursed. The aggressors would wind up losing the war. Metacomet believed every word, and Linto knew he had a brief reprieve so he could orchestrate some kind of peace. **Linto was brilliant**.

But it was all for naught. Metacomet sent his dying friend, the brave and solemn Mentayyup, to terrorize and threaten an English farm boy until he drew the first shot. Mentayyup was killed, and the war had begun.

So, on that summer day in Pocasset, Linto was not in the mood for spiritual communion, or divine prophecy, or holy oracles. But he knelt on the cool ground of the forest and earnestly prayed, because he didn't know what else to do.

Linto's prayers were brief, because he knew Metacomet would be ready for his daily Bible lesson. Metacomet was obsessively studying the English Bible, not because he had any interest in worshipping the English God and His Gentle Son, but because he was convinced nothing could give him better insight into the plans, strategy, and mindset of the English. So far, the approach seemed to be working.

"Linto! Linto the prophet! Don't keep us waiting!" Metacomet motioned to Linto to join him under an enormous elm tree. Metacomet was with Annawon, and he was finishing his early afternoon meal of beans and corn meal, a paltry meal indeed for the Sachem of the Wampanoag.

Metacomet sat and used the tree for support. Although the events of the spring were indeed horrific, Metacomet showed little strain or fatigue. He remained amazed and thankful for Linto's divine prophecy about the first shot. Since the English drew the first blood, Metacomet was now confident victory for the Wampanoag had been ordained by the heavens.

Annawon remained standing and crossed his arms. Linto did not see him take food, and he wondered if he had ever seen Annawon eat. Annawon was a mystery, indeed.

He was a remarkable age, but was unable to recall with any certainty how many winters he had survived. Annawon could remember being a young child when the first English arrived at Patuxet, and he could also remember Massasoit debating the significance of the event.

He was short in stature, but wielded unrelenting strength from his enormous arms and hands. Mentayyup was the only one who could match him in the wrestling arena, but the victories often left Mentayyup exhausted for hours. Metacomet had ceased wrestling Annawon years ago in order to avoid the lost prestige associated with his inevitable defeat. (There was no tradition of permitting the Sachem to win, and no one seemed inclined to start such a tradition, despite Metacomet's encouragement.) Annawon had been very close to Mentayyup, and though filled with grief, he knew his duty now was to replace Mentayyup as Metacomet's war captain to the best of his abilities.

"Come and sit down, Linto, you scrawny little prophet. Make haste or I'll pick you up and throw you like a spear." Annawon flashed a smile.

Linto stood toe-to-toe with Annawon and gazed down at his scalp. Linto must have been two heads taller, and Annawon laughed merrily. For an old man who had known decades of suffering, disease, and death, he was always in good spirits.

"So let's see, Linto...I believe you are Gotial, and I'm Davin? Shall I get my slingshot? Isn't that what you taught us last night?"

Linto chuckled appreciatively. "I am Goliath, Annawon. Go-LIE-uth. And that makes you DAY-vid. But it's still not a fair fight. David couldn't throw Goliath like a spear."

Even Metacomet was laughing by now, and he climbed to his feet. "Teach us, Linto. What of the English God and His devotees? What does the big book teach us today?"

Linto was enjoying his role as counselor to the Sachem. Comprehending and predicting the ways of the English seemed by far the most useful thing he could be doing for the Wampanoag. He certainly would make a poor warrior. Still, he prayed incessantly for a speedy end to the war, and secretly prayed for minimal loss of life on both sides.

"Sachem, I was reading about the Midianites last night. I believe the tale will give the English confidence in deploying fewer soldiers."

"Fewer soldiers? What do you mean, Linto?"

"I was reading their book of Judges last night, and studying one of the warriors of their God. His name was Gideon, and he was tasked to defeat the Midianites."

Annawon grunted. "Gid-yonn. What an odd name."

"Yes, but a fascinating story. The English God tasked Gideon to defeat the Midianites, an enemy that lived south of Israel. The Midianite army had one hundred and thirty-five thousand warriors."

Metacomet looked perplexed. "Is that a lot? How many is that?"

"It would be like…" Linto thought carefully. "If each finger was all of the Wampanoag and Narragansett, and there were ten fingers…"

"Impossible."

"This was a strange land, Sachem. A very long time ago, and far across the sea. So, Gideon raised a big army, but he only had one fourth as many men as the Midianites. But the English God did not want Gideon to have even that many warriors. He told him to send some home. So, he did."

"Send them home? Why?"

"Evidently, God wanted to take all the credit for the victory, and he was afraid that if Gideon had a big army then He wouldn't get the credit."

Annawon blinked repeatedly. "Are you sure you're reading this correctly, Linto? None of this makes any sense to me."

"No, I am certain I'm correct. So, Gideon sent many men home, and then he only had ten thousand men."

"*Only ten thousand*? What I would give for ten thousand warriors. The English would all be sailing home in a week."

"Yes, Sachem, but remember the Midianites had more than ten times as many. But the English God said it was still too many, and He told Gideon to give the men a test. They all went down to a river to drink, but any man who failed to keep his eyes open for enemy activity while drinking was dismissed."

"Clever."

"Yes, but now Gideon only had three hundred warriors."

"Three hundred?   To fight one hundred...five hundred...thousand..."

"One hundred and thirty-five thousand warriors, Sachem."

Annawon was so amazed, he began grinning. "This is unbelievable. What kind of weapons did the three hundred have?"

Linto paused and perused the scripture. "It says they had lamps and horns."

Annawon loudly guffawed. "Lamps and horns! You're reading that wrong, you skinny little twig."

A somber baritone joined the conversation. *"Ridiculous."* The voice almost made Linto jump in the air with fright.

Nimrod had stealthily joined the three men and had been standing behind Linto for who knows how long. Nimrod was Metacomet's deputy war captain, and he chilled Linto to the bone.

Linto, in his twenty-six summers, had known many prominent warriors and leaders, among both the Wampanoag and English. He had been intimidated by most of them.

He thought of Tobias, Metacomet's lieutenant and confidante. Tobias was always drinking rum and scowling at Linto. He despised the English, and Linto was frightened of him. But Linto did his duty and defended Tobias when the English put him on trial for murder. During his last night in this world, Linto sang and prayed with Tobias, and Tobias demanded Linto make a promise. Linto promised Tobias, who would be hung by his neck in a matter of hours, that he would never let Metacomet humiliate himself in the face of the English again. Although he was once afraid of him, Linto now missed Tobias terribly.

Linto was also once afraid of Mentayyup. Mentayyup was a huge, unsmiling warrior who would have never harmed a hair on Linto's head. Mentayyup was also gone to the spirit world, the victim of Linto's false prophecy. And Linto missed him terribly.

THE PROPHET AND THE WITCH

Linto was afraid of Metacomet. He had seen the full range of Metacomet's emotions through the years. He had known the sadness and grief in Metacomet's heart when he discussed his deceased brother, Wamsutta. Linto had seen the hatred and rage in Metacomet's heart when he spoke of Josiah Winslow, whom he referred to as "Skunk Genitals." But Linto also knew Metacomet loved him, and would always regard him as a holy, divinely blessed being. Linto also knew how Metacomet agonized about leading the nations into this war.

But Nimrod. Cruel, vicious Nimrod. He absolutely radiated hatred, violence, and bloodlust. His hair was completely shaven, and his face almost completely tattooed. He wore a necklace of human and animal bones that seemed to be ceaselessly growing through the years. His skill with every manner of weaponry was unmatched. And he hated the English and the Christian Indians so intensely it made Linto shudder. He would always be completely terrified of Nimrod.

Metacomet greeted his deputy war captain. "Nimrod! Finally! How was the journey? The Kickemuit mission is complete? You chased the English away? Tell me they have all packed up and left."

"Sachem, you have my word there are no more English settlers or militia in Kickemuit." Nimrod hoped he was not grinning. He fulfilled his mission to the letter. The additional desecration was merely Nimrod taking the initiative, and sending a special message to the English. He remembered laughing when he decorated the corpses with skunk parts. Metacomet did not need to know any details. The Sachem had enough on his mind.

"Wonderful. Well done. Come, listen to Linto the prophet. Continue, Linto."

Linto felt uneasy as Nimrod's steely eyes met his. "Well, um, Sachem. Gideon's weapons were, um...lamps and horns."

"And this worked? They defeated their enemy with lamps and horns?"

"Evidently so. They snuck into the enemy camp while they were sleeping. Gideon blew his horn and revealed his lit lamp. His men all did the same. They blew their horns and shone their lamps and the enemy became so confused that they woke up and began slaying each other."

Metacomet was captivated. "And Gideon won the battle? He defeated that enormous army?"

"Yes, Sachem."

Metacomet now paced quickly and haphazardly as he was prone to do when deep in thought. "Do you think it was magic, Linto? Do you think the English God will give the Plimoth men magic horns?"

Linto answered cautiously. "I don't know, Sachem. I don't think so. I have never seen the Englishmen work any kind of magic here. I think miracles like this only happened in their holy land, thousands of years ago."

"But Winslow the Father cured my father with Christian magic." Metacomet was referring to the fateful day almost fifty years ago, when his father, Massasoit, was dying. Edward Winslow immediately arrived from Plimoth, scraped his father's tongue, and provided medicinal herbs.

"I'm not so sure, Sachem. I think that was just good medicine. And your father was very strong."

Metacomet grimaced, and yearned to fully understand these mysteries. "So, what does it all mean, Linto? What will the English do next?"

"I think the lesson to be learned, Sachem, is the English will not be afraid to attack with a very small force. They believe their God performs miracles, as long as they believe in Him. I believe they will send a very small force in pursuit of us, like Gideon."

Metacomet nodded thoughtfully, seemingly impressed. The four men remained awkwardly quiet for a lengthy period.

"I liked the story." Nimrod's cold, intimidating baritone broke the silence, much to everyone's surprise.

Annawon blinked with curiosity. "You liked it, Nimrod?"

"The message is a much smaller army can defeat a much larger army, provided the larger army is very, very stupid. And that is why we will destroy the English. Behold! *Here is my lamp!*" Nimrod held his long knife high in the air, which was still coated with the slaughter of his recent victims. No one thought to ask him where the blood came from.

Metacomet refrained from acknowledging Nimrod's gesture, and he began pacing again. He was lost in thought, and did not speak for several moments. Finally, he addressed the trio. "Excellent. Very good. Thank you, Linto. You are all dismissed. I wish to meditate now, as there is much to ponder. I will see you in the evening."

Linto respectfully nodded and scurried away from Nimrod as quickly as possible. In no time, he was in the slender, delicate arms of Wawetseka.

The travails of the preceding months did not seem to be inflicting a toll on Linto's beautiful wife. She seemed to be growing more stunning with age. Even more so, her powers of prophecy and healing were growing increasingly remarkable. Linto often felt like a spiritual fraud in her presence. Their two young children clung innocently to her cloak, and stared wide-eyed at their father.

Evacuating all of Montaup, and moving that many Wampanoag across the bay was a tremendous undertaking. There was obviously now a shortage of almost any implement of comfort. Food, shelter, clothing, and blankets were all in scarce supply. But, they had done it. They had avoided the hideous carnage that would have resulted from a head-on confrontation with the enemy. They had moved their warriors and their loved ones into Pocasset. They were gathering allies, and they were now free to plot their next moves.

"You are certain the Sachem suspects nothing, Linto?"

"No, my beloved, I'm not. I don't know what I'm certain of anymore."

CHAPTER SEVEN

PROVIDENCE

For a relatively young man who had been celibate for six long years, Israel Brewster didn't seem to be rushing things.

The last guest had bid his farewell at least two hours ago, and Zeke departed not long after that. Brewster was cautious about the possible arrival of tardy guests, or, considering how splendid the meal was, guests returning to hungrily clamor for more of the Atlantic's splendor. When he was reasonably certain they could finally be alone, they joined hands and laughingly collapsed into a sturdy oak settle in front of the hearth. Though the afternoon heat was still formidable, a small fire continued to burn, and it kept a cauldron of halibut stew warm and inviting.

The settle was accentuated with a soft quilt and was quite comfortable. Zeke maintained a splendid collection of furniture in the home. Brewster gazed fondly at a chair in the far corner. It was an elaborate wooden chair boasting ornate spindles and two high posts in the back. He recognized the chair immediately, and it triggered profound memories. As if he needed any further reminder of his lineage, the chair was increasingly known in the colonies as the "Brewster chair," due to Elder William Brewster's fondness for that particular style.

He reminisced about his grandfather, and he thought back to forgotten friends and relatives from Plimoth Colony. Although his contempt for the government that scorned him had scarcely diminished, he would always miss the people and things he left behind, especially his pulpit in Middleborough.

Constance held his hand tighter and gazed into his eyes. Alone at last. They were finally united in holy wedlock in a union no mortal could tear asunder. He earnestly hoped his thoughts would not wander to Sarah, but soon her dark eyes came drifting back. Would she be ashamed of him? Would she be surprised he waited six years to remarry? How mortified would she be to see him wed to a Quaker heretic?

Constance released his hand and sauntered to the shelf of books above the mantle. She selected a leather-bound volume, removed her shoes, and returned to his side. Her words were slow, deliberate, and tender.

> *Forbear dark night, my joys now bud again,*
> *Lately grown dead, while cold aspects did chill*
> *The root at heart, and my chief hope quite kill,*
> *And thunders struck me in my pleasures' wane*
>
> *Then I alas with bitter sobs, and pain,*
> *Privately groan'd, my Fortunes present ill;*
> *All light of comfort dimm'd, woes in prides fill,*
> *With strange increase of grief, I griev'd in vain.*
>
> *And most, when as a memory too good*
> *Molested me, which still as witness stood,*
> *Of those best days, in former time I knew:*
>
> *Late gone as wonders past, like the great Snow,*
> *Melted and wasted, with what, change must know:*
> *Now back the life comes where as once it grew*

Brewster recognized the recitation as the work of Lady Mary Wroth. She was the niece of Sir Phillip Sidney and was a literary pioneer for her gender. The fact that she was a woman and composing secular and romantic poetry fifty years ago was relatively scandalous, but she enjoyed the support and admiration of beloved scholars such as Ben Jonson and George Chapman. Brewster was delighted by the reading, and he closed his eyes.

Constance seemed to read his thoughts, and she knew the words had resonated. "All light of comfort dimmed...now back the life comes." Where there was previously darkness in his life, there was now light. His suffering had truly turned to joy. The nightmares of his departed Sarah tormented him no longer, due to a mystical Wampanoag healing ceremony performed by the beautiful Wawetseka. The anguish he felt after being humiliated and dismissed from his pulpit no longer compelled him to wallow in a bottle. He had been embraced by this community, by this family, and by this woman.

She had now removed her coif and was gently manipulating her hair. It fell below her collar and Brewster marveled at how beautiful her mane of thick, scarlet locks truly was. She resumed her seat and stretched her lithe, graceful legs, and her bare feet. She smiled and stroked his hair.

"Two Ponds, my husband." She giggled. "I shall be known as Constance Two Ponds." Brewster had previously confided the name awarded him at a missionary service by a young Wampanoag man who was in awe of his enormous blue eyes. She found the name delightful.

"I believe, Mister Two Ponds the cooper, two adults lawfully wed in holy matrimony can certainly get better acquainted." She leaned forward and gently kissed him on the mouth.

And Israel Brewster was terrified.

He had fervently hoped not to be this apprehensive on this blessed evening, but it was not to be. *Six years*! Six years since he had basked in the glorious comfort of a woman's delicate touch. Would he be pleasing to her? What if she did not share the same joys and pleasures that he and Sarah did? Would he be secretly comparing her intimate features to his previous wife?

She stood and removed the hideously-fitting wedding dress. Always pragmatic, she methodically ensured it was carefully stowed away, in deference to her mother's memory. Brewster obviously knew little of women's underthings, as his beloved Sarah had only worn the most basic of smocks underneath her attire in accordance with her Puritan sensibilities. Constance, however, was attired in a dark whalebone corset, with a delicate ruffled petticoat covering her long legs. Brewster had heard the corset also referred to as a "stay" when tawdry subjects arose in the tavern. He was absolutely mesmerized, and he knew his hands were trembling. Whenever Brewster felt anxiety, he knew there was one resource that could allay his fears.

He mentally went to scripture.

"Behold, thou art fair, my love; behold, thou hast doves' eyes."

Brewster knew his bride was an extraordinary beauty, but he was still astounded. She removed his formal white shirt, and massaged the muscles in his chest. Her hands felt silken but unyielding.

"How beautiful are thy feet with shoes, O prince's daughter! The joints of thy thighs are like jewels, the work of the hands of a cunning workman. Thy navel is like a round goblet, which wanteth not liquor: thy belly is like a heap of wheat set about with lilies…Thy two breasts are like two young fawns that are twins…"

Brewster had taken her firmly in his arms and was passionately kissing her. He longed to hold her forever. She seemed so very slender and fragile, but he could sense the power in her body. The perspiration began to build on his taut chest. Soon, they were completely unclothed and walking hand-in-hand to her bed.

"Set me as a seal upon thine heart, as a seal upon thine arm: for love is strong as death; jealousy is cruel as the grave: the coals thereof are coals of fire, which hath a most vehement flame. Many waters cannot quench love, neither can the floods drown it: if a man would give all the substance of his house for love, it would utterly be scorned."

There could be no more tempering of their love and passion. Brewster thought he might cry tears of joy as they became one on the bed. Time seemed to race and stand still all at once. Her cries of delight filled the room, and the sweat relentlessly poured from his brow. The culmination of their pleasure was so intense, he was certain he lost consciousness for a second or two. He collapsed next to her, unable to slow his labored breathing.

The sunlight of the afternoon was still radiating into the home, and Brewster held his beloved. His breathing had finally slowed, and the waves of joy were still rushing over him. Joy. There would be joy in his life again. He had been delivered from the wilderness. He had known death and terror, disgrace and despair, but now he only knew joy.

Constance marveled how quickly the feverish passion returned, and soon the room was filled once again with the carnal sounds of their mutual delight. Brewster was astounded when his bride, strong and willful in all her affairs, forcefully assumed a position on top of him that he would have normally deemed illicit and unspeakable. For a second time, he was so consumed by pleasure and emotion that he briefly lost consciousness.

And so, it went the next day, and the day after that. Incomparable joy, passion, and pleasure accentuated with English sonnets, horseback rides atop Brownie, walks in the rain, and the gourmet pleasures of their bustling seaport. Strangers on the street grinned and waved as they passed, instinctively absorbed in the bliss the young couple seemed to radiate.

Brewster was delighted by the natural intensity of their physical pleasures, and was awestruck by the frequency. He wondered if he might compensate for six years of celibacy in a single week. Maybe Zeke could stay out for a second fishing voyage.

That night, he lay awake and was entranced by the hypnotic motion of her breathing. He was transfixed. His mind wandered back to his days as a minister in Middleborough, and all the marriage counseling he led. The temptation and mystery of the flesh was mystifying, indeed. Young couples came to him frequently with embarrassing questions that baffled them. Was it normal that they made love once a year? Was it normal that they made love twice a day? Was it normal that a young man's passion should be complete before his wife even removed her bodice?

Brewster sighed and almost laughed. Marriage was one of the Lord's greatest gifts. Was it preordained that he would experience so much happiness, suffer so intensely, and then experience so much happiness again? Was anything preordained in this world at all?

He knew one thing that was preordained: Israel Brewster was not going anywhere. The more he thought about Barlow's proposal, the more excited he became. He could easily run the cooperage, and he could run it more profitably than Barlow ever had. Zeke would certainly stake him, if for no other reason but to get him out from under his roof, and into a home of their own.

A home of their own. He closed his eyes and tried to picture it. Brewster would make reliable barrels all day, and he and his bride would make beautiful children all night. Failing that, Brewster would make beautiful barrels, and together they would make reliable children. No matter what, they would be together and happy, and Plimoth Colony's sanctimonious government could go to the devil.

Actually, the whole lot of his self-righteous, Puritan neighbors could go to the devil. They provoked this horrific war, and now they could reap the consequences. Brewster and Easton had done their duty. They went to Metacomet and begged him to negotiate and compromise. Brewster even risked his life by wandering unarmed and alone to Mount Hope to summon Metacomet. Now Plimoth and Massachusetts Bay were at war, and Brewster wanted no part of it. His life was right here. He sighed again, smiled, and closed his eyes for slumber.

Israel Brewster was a man finally at peace.

CHAPTER EIGHT

MOUNT HOPE

"All hail, great and mighty chief!"

Moseley's troops were now taking turns donning the ceremonial headdress, standing upright in the middle of the assembly, and reveling in the mock adulation. Diego had broken out the rum, and soon the festivities intensified as the men danced in circles while whooping and bellowing their profane war cries.

Church could scarcely compel himself to lower his flintlock. He stood motionless in front of his men with his mouth agape. How could this Puritan army be so oblivious to the movements and tactics of their adversary? He couldn't even formulate a response when Jemmy Barnstrom cautiously approached.

"Good news indeed, Captain? Shall I assemble the men?" Barnstrom was still learning the art of discerning Church's thoughts and moods, and his captain merely shook his head in disbelief.

Bradford directed pilots and assorted scouts to explore the southern and western extremes of the peninsula to ensure the enemy was still not fiendishly assembled somewhere. His pessimistic but sensible mindset envisioned a mass attack while his army was celebrating like drunken, papist buffoons. In almost no time at all, however, horsemen returned from every direction with the glorious news: There was not an Indian man, woman, or child to be found on the peninsula.

Bradford knew what had to be done next. Setting his musket on the rocky ground, he knelt and went to prayer. "Dear Lord Almighty, we give you thanks for our glorious victory…" Hundreds of soldiers voluntarily knelt in unison. "Our enemy is wicked and dreadful, and we have witnessed the satanic works of their hand. Truly, the evildoers have fled in the face of the Lord's holy army, and their stronghold is ours. Blessed be thy holy name. Amen."

Even Moseley's rabble ceased their shenanigans long enough for a dignified prayer of gratitude to transpire. Church could not conceal his consternation, and discreetly caught Moseley's ear.

"Glorious victory? Is he kidding us? Sam, this is madness!"

"All I know is a few hours ago we were burying mangled corpses, and now Mount Hope is ours. And without a shot or another…"

"Christian burial?"

"Exactly."

"Sam, this is no victory. This was a brilliant ruse. I guarantee King Philip is east of here right now, drawing allies to this rebellion."

"That may very well be, but for now, it looks like we've been summoned. Look sharp, Benjamin."

Colonel Cudworth assembled his officers at a hauntingly beautiful assemblage of quartz rock. Officers who had dealings with Metacomet before the hostilities began recognized it as "King Philip's Seat," the ceremonial sanctum of the Wampanoag people.

Cudworth seemed elated. "Gentlemen, well done. My compliments to you and your men. This army, God be praised, moved through this terrain like lightning. It is little wonder the heathen dare not face us. Our resolve is without question."

His praise was greeted with ebullient "huzzahs" and various exclamations of jubilation. The colonel was in his element, and he continued.

"Clearly, the next task before the army of the Lord is to construct a fort. We have seized this heathen stronghold, and as long as there is strength in my body, we shan't yield an inch of it back to the enemy. Major Bradford, here is my vision for the palisades. I'm envisioning a sixty-yard stretch of varying heights, culminating in a…"

"*A fort?* You can't be serious, Colonel. *A fort?*"

Bradford almost gasped at the level of insolence demonstrated by one of his captains. "Hold your tongue, Church! How dare you address the colonel in such a manner?"

"Forgive my outburst, sir. But a fort? It will take us weeks to build, while the enemy circumnavigates the bay and terrorizes the entire colony. They don't care about Mount Hope. They care about burning English farms and villages."

"*Captain…*"

"We need to be taking this fight to the enemy, Colonel. This wasn't a victory. This was planned. They're across the water, laughing at us. King Philip will merge his forces with Weetamoo, and there will be no luring her back to a neutral stance. They will be planning and scheming…"

"*Captain Church…*"

Moseley noticed his comrade seemed lost in passionate thought, and was failing to notice Bradford's increasingly dire tone. "*Benjamin!*" His curt whisper also fell on deaf ears.

Oblivious to the situation, Church continued his tirade. "We should be planning our assault on Pocasset right now, before King Philip heads west to merge his force with the Nipmucs! We need transport ships, as many as possible. Let my men take a beachhead on the southern point, and I may be able to persuade Awashonks to provide food and supplies. Major Bradford can take two hundred men with matchlocks and pikes, and he can seal their escape at the Fall River. We can end this bloody business before harvest, and…"

At that moment, it was difficult to describe the exact hue of Major Bradford's face. Some would call it maroon, but Moseley would later attest that it was magenta. "*Captain Church, I have heard enough insubordination! You will learn to conduct your affairs as an English officer, or I will have you dismissed from my service! Don't you ever embarrass this officer corps in the presence of the colonel again! You may leave us now, so you can compose yourself, Captain. **Immediately.***"

Church had finally heard something besides his own thoughts. No one had ever seen Major Bradford this impassioned, not even in the face of Dutch Cornelius' ridicule at the garrison. Church hung his head and was suddenly cognizant and ashamed of his outbursts. "Forgive me," was all he could utter, and he left without another word.

Church wandered to the east. He stood alone and gazed out over Mount Hope Bay. Quickly forgetting his rebuke, he focused on the matter at hand. He knew Metacomet had moved his forces across the water, and it was a brilliant, strategic maneuver. Metacomet could have elected to make a stand on this isolated peninsula, and with careful fortifications, he no doubt would have rendered horrific casualties on any invading army. But even if Metacomet could hold Mount Hope, victory would be fleeting. The English would inevitably overpower his entrenched forces with their superior numbers, and perhaps, they would even mount an assault by sea.

By tactically retreating across the water, however, Metacomet declared in no uncertain terms he would not be fighting this war on the terms of the English. The English were about forts and garrisons, but the Indians were about mobility. The English were obligated to protect farms and villages, but the Indians were acclimated to life in the wilderness. The English were slow and methodical, whereas the Indians already demonstrated how quickly they could strike. The English, with their United Colonies that frequently were not very united, were prone to dissension and bickering. The Indians?

Church pondered the question. The English genuinely did not know how many allies Metacomet had persuaded to join this rebellion. Church also wondered how many Indian nations would ultimately join the English, in order to settle ancient scores with Metacomet and the Wampanoag.

His reverie was interrupted as the officers' council adjourned, and Moseley found him. "What the devil, Benjamin? Dutch Cornelius despises you, Major Bradford despises you, Cudworth despises you, and the war hasn't even begun yet. What do you have to say for yourself?"

"A fort, Sam. Have you ever heard of anything so idiotic? Metacomet could be on the outskirts of Boston before we even finish building it."

"I know that, Benjamin. But even a reformed pirate like me knows when to keep his mouth shut. What kind of army did you think you were joining?"

"One that occasionally finds the enemy and fights him."

"Quiet, you fool. Here comes Bradford."

"Major Bradford, I do hope you will accept my apology. It's just that in the heat of battle, or the lack of battle...it's just..."

"I get it, Captain Church. I'm no dunce. Do you think you're the only man here who can't wait to string up King Philip? When I think of this act of betrayal..." Bradford's voice was rising, and Church thought he could detect tears forming. "He has betrayed Governor Winslow. He has betrayed my father. He's betrayed his own father, Massasoit. He has betrayed Plimoth and all the brotherhood we have shown in these fifty years of friendship. All of it gone, utterly destroyed."

Bradford took a breath and continued. "But we conduct ourselves like officers, Church. We conduct ourselves like Englishmen, and above all, Christians. We'll see no more public outbursts from you."

Bradford's articulate, dignified passion made Church feel even more ashamed. "Yes, sir." He was barely audible.

"Still, Colonel Cudworth is the forgiving type, Benjamin. To show there is no malice or retribution, we've even mustered a new assignment for you. Something uniquely suited to your skills. We need a high-energy, passionate officer for this position."

Finally. Church shuddered with anticipation. Would it be a delicate reconnaissance operation or a surreptitious, nighttime raid? Perhaps an abduction of an enemy Sachem?

He couldn't wait to see his men in action. They would be overjoyed by the news. "Sir, I'm more than ready to volunteer."

"Excellent, Captain Church. As I understand it, our commissary general has taken ill and will be returning to Plimoth. I know you will be a most suitable replacement."

"Forgive me, sir? Have I misheard?"

"Commissary General, Church. It's a very prestigious posting. Someone needs to be charged with ensuring this army is fed. There will be supplies to procure, inventories to manage, complaints to adjudicate…we will need someone energetic and passionate."

Church blinked repeatedly and launched another outburst. "Major, do you mean to tell me, that with the enemy only miles away, my only responsibility…" His voice was feverishly rising. "My only responsibility WILL BE TO ENSURE THAT…THAT…MMMPHH…"

Any ensuing words were muffled and indistinguishable, as Moseley had firmly secured his hand around Church's mouth. Bradford sauntered away and conveyed his parting thoughts.

"Well done, Captain Moseley. Well done, indeed."

CHAPTER NINE

BOSTON

Jeremiah Barron glared disapprovingly at the men assembled in the well-appointed room. He rolled his bulbous eyes and wiped the sweat from his pasty brow. Barron tried and failed to get comfortable in his firm oaken chair, and he emitted a peculiar sound somewhere between a gasp and a grunt. Governor Winslow tried to ignore him.

As the treasurer of Plimoth Colony, Jeremiah Barron was a man with numerous problems. He was now forty-six years old, and always seemed the victim of ill health. Summer was an especially difficult time as the heat was often unbearable, even in these relatively temperate colonies of New England.

Now that war was suddenly and irrevocably upon the colonies, Barron was under enormous strain. The expenditures associated with feeding and supplying the militia were staggering, and Governor Winslow did not take kindly to excuses. The other members of the United Colonies of New England, namely Massachusetts Bay and Connecticut, were not nearly as forthcoming with men and money as they should be, and they continued with their adversarial delusions that this war was exclusively the fault of Plimoth. In a holy war between God's chosen elect and savage heathen, it seemed apparent to Barron that there could be no ambivalence.

In addition to his chronically ill health and monumental professional responsibilities, Barron was now dealing with an unforeseen personal complication. Eliza, his nineteen-year-old African servant girl, was now pregnant, and in a matter of weeks there would be no hiding it. Barron was now ruminating carefully about the blasphemers and heretics currently facing execution in Plimoth, so one could be blamed for this unseemly deed. Eliza would require careful coaching in the matter, but he had no reason to question her obedience, or her powers of deception.

Barron and Governor Winslow had made the grueling journey from Plimoth to Boston, which they found demeaning and time-consuming. Although Plimoth had certainly taken the lead role in suppressing King Philip and the treasonous Wampanoag nation, Massachusetts Bay would never cease their domineering ways. They were the largest colony with the most men and money, and they would ensure Plimoth never overlooked that fact.

The assembly was currently engaged in prolonged, intense prayer, led by Reverend Increase Mather. His exhortations had lasted at least twenty minutes. He implored the Almighty to forgive the people of New England for their sinful nature, and to temper the violent wrath of the savages sent to punish them. As twenty minutes turned to thirty, Jeremiah Barron increasingly wondered if New England seemed to have more than enough devout Puritan ministers, and not nearly enough prosperous, patriotic merchants.

In addition to Barron and Winslow, the Deputy Governor of Massachusetts Bay, Samuel Symonds, was in attendance. The Plimoth men were dismayed Governor Leverett did not see fit to appear, and casually delegated his responsibilities to his deputy. Leverett frequently behaved in a very troublesome manner as far as Barron was concerned. Rumor had it that the governor even tolerated Baptists openly worshipping in Boston, which was hopefully an irresponsible falsehood carelessly promulgated by some reckless trouble maker.

If there were any genuine trouble makers in these United Colonies, however, Barron was now maliciously glaring at two of them. Reverend John Eliot and Superintendent Daniel Gookin sat side-by-side as they were wont to do. Birds of a feather, thought Barron.

Reverend John Eliot was one of the foremost missionaries to the Indians in all of New England. He even translated the Holy Bible into their native tongue, an astoundingly difficult undertaking which Barron regarded as useless and unprofitable. Despite their different approaches to the natives, however, Barron and Eliot frequently saw eye-to-eye on many of the heresies that plagued New England in these previous decades. In fact, Jeremiah Barron was merely a young boy when Reverend Eliot led the righteous authorities in the prosecution of Anne Hutchinson. How could Eliot be so right-minded in the face of a depraved woman's blasphemy, yet so compliant and misguided in the face of heathen aggression?

Just as King Charles had his Prince Rupert to inflict malice upon God's chosen people, John Eliot had his Daniel Gookin. Barron found his character as unpleasant and bizarre as his name. Gooo-kin. Gookin.

Despite his hailing from Massachusetts Bay instead of Plimoth Colony, Barron believed there was some virtue and usefulness in Daniel Gookin's life. Gookin had been a military captain, a representative to the General Court in Boston, and a selectman appointed to serve the good people of Cambridge. An educated and worldly man, he frequently alternated his time between Boston and London.

And yet, Gookin now squandered his valuable time as the officially appointed Superintendent of the Praying Indians. His role was to ensure the safety and welfare of the native Christian converts. Barron noted that Gookin accentuated his useless title with an equally useless book, *The Historical Collections of the Indians in New England*, published last year. Gookin had dedicated a remarkable quantity of energy and labor to the local natives over the last decade. But now? Now the savages were in full-scale rebellion throughout the colonies.

Governor Winslow was giving an account of military preparations and actions to date. There was a growing sense of impatience throughout all the colonies due to a lack of results, and Barron knew the doddering old fool Cudworth was the wrong choice to lead this undertaking. Barron surmised it was just a matter of time before Winslow himself would have to take charge of the militia and finally win a campaign.

Thirty minutes became forty minutes, and Reverend Mather still showed no sign of bringing his jeremiad to a close. "...and we humbly beseech Thee, Lord of our world, granter of our salvation, to assure our blessed covenant with thy holy Father, so we may gather our strength and smite the wicked heathen in our midst. We have been sinful and wicked in Your holy sight, and we implore Your forgiveness in this blessed new Israel in this strange new land, and..."

"Amen."

There was only one man in the room with the authority and temerity to unceremoniously terminate the lamentations of Reverend Mather, and all eyes turned to Governor Winslow. "Thank you, Reverend Mather. Your prayers and blessings are most inspirational. I fear we must, however, get to business." Barron mentally noted the colonies had an entire *day* dedicated to fasting and praying a few weeks ago. There could be no doubt which side the Lord was on in this conflict.

Mather was unaccustomed to interruptions in any way, shape, or form, and he pensively evaluated the appropriate response. Eliot took advantage of the lull to ask a question, even though he knew the answer.

Eliot stood and extended his hand to the meticulously dressed stranger lurking alone in the corner of the room. "My friend, we have not had the pleasure! Reverend John Eliot. Blessings upon you and your family."

The stranger's Scottish accent was apparent by the first word. "Aye, and 'tis a pleasure to be meeting all of ye. Elijah MacTavish, at your service."

"Ahh. Mr. MacTavish? And you hail from...?"

"Inverness, good sir. Inverness. Of course, Bermuda is where I serve now. I've traded one island for another."

Eliot knew exactly who he was addressing, but he maintained the charade. "How lovely! Are you an agent of his majesty's government?"

"Oh, no. No, no, no. I am a gentleman planter, Reverend. Sugar is my vocation."

"Ahh. Indeed. I am delighted to make your acquaintance, but I am curious what interest a faraway sugar baron has with the deplorable conflicts of these humble colonies."

Jeremiah Barron had heard enough. He was prepared to address the room for the first time. Barron was renowned, however, for his screeching, cacophonous voice, which earned him the unfortunate moniker of the "screech owl." The screech owl was glaring at the assembly, alertly on guard for any signs of levity or amusement when he spoke.

"Mr. MacTavish is an honored guest of Plimoth Colony and Governor Winslow! Financing this endeavor is a challenging undertaking, and Mr. MacTavish has been generous enough to provide a stake in our affairs!"

"Ahh. Indeed. From the goodness of his heart, no doubt." Eliot was biting his lower lip.

Barron was growing increasingly irate. "For the goodness of these United Colonies, for England, and for our holy faith! Mr. MacTavish is a man of means who has the ability to assist these colonies during these desperate times. He is a gentleman, he is worldly, he is connected to London merchants, he is a…"

"**He is a slaver.**" Gookin was a man of few words, but his words were almost always impactful. Even Gookin himself, however, could not anticipate the outburst of screeching triggered by his four simple words.

"*I would ask, nay, I DEMAND that the superintendent treat our guests with Christian decorum and respect!*" Barron had quickly lapsed into an emotional fury, and consequently, the screech owl was on display in all its glory for all to witness.

"*And what responsibilities do YOU bring to this table, Captain Gookin? I am charged with the responsibility of financing this war!*" The screeching was quickly escalating, and Barron's high-pitched ranting was now in that bizarre spectrum of speech where the distinction between fury and comedy rapidly blurs. "*While you have spent your days lavishing affection on pagans, pagans who are at this very instant burning English settlements, I have undertaken the grave responsibility of paying for this war! How dare you, you miscreant! I move that...that..."*

Even Barron's staunch ally, Governor Winslow knew when enough was enough. He may have even discreetly covered his smile with a sheet of parchment when Barron's cacophony reached its fervid climax. "Thank you, Mr. Barron. Superintendent Gookin, Reverend Eliot, Mr. MacTavish is present at my invitation, and I would thank you to pay him the respect you would pay me. Now gentlemen, if our introductory prayers and bickering are complete, perhaps we can turn our attention to the enemy?"

Deputy Governor Symonds spoke for the first time. "I heartily concur. This situation is indeed grave, gentlemen. This rebellion has been more sudden and ferocious than we could have anticipated, and the enemy has us on our heels. Towns throughout Plimoth Colony are being put to the torch, and I fear Massachusetts Bay is also vulnerable. I had hoped this madness would be confined to Philip and his Wampanoag, but it is increasing clear the Nipmuc have joined his cause. Governor Winslow, how would you assess the loyalties of the Indian nations?"

"Obviously, we are at war with the Wampanoag and the Nipmuc. Fortunately, the Mohegan nation has remained loyal. I have it on good authority that Sachem Uncas' son Oneco is leading men in pursuit of Philip."

Symonds inadvertently muttered under his breath. "At least someone is pursuing Philip."

Winslow had already seen enough dissension in this council, and he diplomatically chose to ignore the audible ridicule of Cudworth's incessant delays. He continued. "Mr. Elmer, what news of the Pequot?"

The colony of Connecticut was represented by Edward Elmer. Although not a military man, he was one of the original founders of Hartford. He was advanced in years, and spoke with an aura of gravitas and dignity.

"We are confident in the continuing allegiance of the Pequot, Governor Winslow."

Barron could not resist another opportunity to shriek. "They have never forgotten the lesson of 1637! Of course, they will remain loyal!" He was referring to the Pequot Wars of four decades ago, when approximately five hundred Pequot were mercilessly incinerated at the Battle of Mystic Fort.

MacTavish couldn't resist chiming in. "Hear, hear! Huzzah!"

Symonds interjected. "But what of the Narragansett?" The Narragansett nation was centered in Rhode Island, and had traditionally been the bitter rivals of the Wampanoag.

Reverend Eliot was surprised the issue was even raised. "The Narragansett? They want no part of this madness. They will remain neutral."

Barron vehemently disagreed. "Do not be so naïve, Reverend! For decades, the Wampanoag were our loyalist of allies! And then what? Massasoit perishes, and his son becomes a hateful lunatic! Now they are burning our villages and farms. I do not trust the Narragansett in the least. There can be no *neutral* in this matter, Reverend. The savages are either battling Philip, or they are our enemy."

Once again, Gookin's words were concise and impactful. "We have enough enemies right now, Barron. We don't need to be creating them in places they don't exist."

The shrieking inevitably began, and Barron's bulbous eyes seemed to become increasingly red and swollen. *"How dare you! How dare you question my assessment! I demand that..."*

The assembly was relieved when Governor Winslow intervened. "Jeremiah, your point is taken. Superintendent Gookin, I must concur with Mr. Barron. Although their allegiances are increasingly mysterious, the Narragansett are the greatest threat to our security. I know Philip has been incessantly meeting with them these past months. There is increasingly word that the Narragansett are harboring the women and children of neighboring tribes. I believe we need to carefully assess the situation before taking action."

For the first time since the assembly was called to order, there was a pensive silence. Everyone seemed to be deep in thought about the Narragansett, and whether the United Colonies could successfully deter the Wampanoag, the Nipmuc, AND the Narragansett. Ultimately, it was MacTavish who broke the silence.

"And what of the Praying Indians?"

Gookin's reply dripped with malice. "And what of them?" As the Superintendent of the Praying Indians, he knew it was a matter of time before the families under his jurisdiction would be unfairly maligned.

"What do we really know of their loyalties, Governor?"

Eliot answered the question instead. "We know their loyalties are to our Lord and savior, the resurrected Christ, God be praised."

MacTavish was unimpressed. "Yes, yes. And I believe we have King Philip's signature from four years ago, attesting to his loyalty to Plimoth Colony and the English crown. Do we not have that, Governor Winslow? Did you receive your wolf head this year, Governor?" MacTavish was sarcastically referring to a term of the Wampanoag treaty of 1671, in which Philip was to bring Plimoth Colony a wolf's head every year as a token of friendship.

Winslow did not answer, and he stared at the crossed swords decoratively hung on the oak paneling across the room. There was only so long Barron could stand to remain silent, however.

"I, for one, counsel vigilance and security in this matter. It is bad enough our frontiers are rife with treasonous animals seeking to destroy our way of life. But how many of these traitors are housed right in our midst, in these villages of "*Praying* Indians?" Never had two syllables been uttered with such sarcasm and contempt.

Gookin successfully reined in his fury, and he stood. His eyes were fixed on Governor Winslow. "Gentlemen, if nothing else, we are above all, *Christians*. Our parents and grandparents left the mother country for this wilderness so we could worship the Almighty without tyrants, kings, and popes. If nothing else, cast your eyes upon the great seal on the wall."

He resumed his seat and let the words resonate. The Great Seal of Massachusetts Bay hung on the wall behind Deputy Governor Symonds' chair. It depicted a shirtless Native American holding a bow and an arrow, and uttering five words. Gookin recited the words slowly and intensely.

"Come over and help us."

CHAPTER TEN

MOUNT HOPE

"One hundred and forty-three eggs, thirty-seven chickens, one-hundred and fifty-eight apples…"

"Captain Church? Are you sure this pork is still good? It kind of looks funny."

"Private, just get it ready for lunch. The men should be grateful for this much pork. If anyone complains, send them my way. Now then. One hundred and thirty-seven apples…forty-three chickens…"

The line of farmers and traders with wares to sell extended eight deep. Captain Benjamin Church, recently and unceremoniously appointed as Commissary General, was in delicate negotiations with Josiah Franklin, a crooked-nosed, impatient farmer from Middleborough.

"Thirty-seven chickens, Captain. Can't you keep count? I have thirty-seven chickens."

Church was interrupted again. "Captain, I can't have the men plucking chickens today because they're hauling timber for the south palisade. Why do they have to do fort duty AND commissary duty? And why aren't Moseley's men helping drag timber?" Cornet Barnstrom sounded increasingly agitated as he doffed his cap to wipe away the sweat of another July day.

"Jemmy, how long can it take to pluck a damned chicken?" Foul language was uncharacteristic for Captain Church, but he was clearly growing more profane the longer he was separated from his gentle, well-mannered wife in Duxbury.

"Captain, why can't Moseley's men pluck the chickens while our company drags the timber? All they do is sit around all day and drink."

"Because they have sentry duty, Cornet Barnstrom. And they drink because we don't want nervous, unhappy sentries.

At least that's the way Moseley explains it. Have you built the fire yet?"

"What fire?"

"For lunch! For the pork!"

"We have pork? Where did we get pork?"

"Are you daft, Jemmy? It's right over there!"

Cornet Barnstrom inspected it cautiously. "Are you sure that's pork Captain? It doesn't look right."

"Just build the fire, Jemmy."

Church loudly sighed, and Josiah Franklin sternly reminded him of the business at hand. "My chickens, Captain? I'm to be compensated for twenty-seven chickens." Church was too frazzled to question the count. "I believe thirty pine shillings is fair compensation."

"Thirty shillings? For *these* chickens?"

"There's not a farm operating within twenty miles of here, Captain. Did you know there's a war going on?"

"Thank you, Farmer Franklin, I've heard about the war."

"You should be grateful to even have twenty-two fine chickens for a mere thirty-two shillings each."

"Yes, about the shillings…"

"Let me guess, Captain. Plimoth scrip?"

"Indeed, Farmer Franklin. Indeed. You just take this promissory note to Mr. Jeremiah Barron in Plimoth, treasurer of the colony, and you will be well compensated."

"Ahh. Jeremiah, the screech owl."

"Hoot, hoot. There you are. With my official signature, and official Commissary General stamp. You will have no problems being reimbursed."

"Very well. Let me get your eighteen chickens out of the wagon, Captain. Or should I call you General? General of the Commissary?"

Jemmy Barnstrom had returned. "Captain, how big did you want the fire? What kind of wood should I…Franklin? Josiah Franklin? You're a sight for weary eyes!"

"Barnstrom! What a blessing! Look how thin you are! Where's Reddington?"

"He's off dragging timber, of course. Strong as an ox, you know."

"And almost as smart. Can you fetch him here?"

"He's a mile away, I'm afraid. How is your family, Josiah?"

"All are healthy and strong, God be praised. Alice Phelps gave birth to a girl last week. Reverend Phelps was overjoyed. And your family is doing quite well, Jemmy. But your youngest had a bit of a rash last week. I can't recall her name..."

"Margaret."

"Of course. Margaret the beauty. Well, the line to negotiate with the Commissary General is growing longer, and I must make Middleborough by nightfall. Be a good boy, and bring us back King Philip, would you? I'd like to cut him up and feed him to my hogs."

"Wouldn't we all. Farewell, Josiah."

Barnstrom went off to build the fire in accordance with Church's guidance. Church resumed his negotiations, but seemed more frazzled than ever. He had been the Commissary General for eight days now, with each day seemingly more challenging. On the third day, the entire army went virtually unfed. On the fifth day, Captain Church learned that roasting fish for five hundred men is much more difficult that preparing fish for five men, and the hungry garrison of Mount Hope was treated to dry, bitter, and burnt scraps.

Church applied his usual zeal to the task at hand, however, and was convinced that one way or another, he would ensure this army of the Lord was properly fed. Today's lunch of pork, apples, and wheat-cakes would hopefully instill a fresh sense of confidence in his abilities.

Jemmy Barnstrom was also optimistic with their progress. He was fortunate enough to be within earshot of Colonel Cudworth after the colonel had his first bite of the day's midday feast. The colonel's eyes widened, and he looked positively astonished. Jemmy was elated. The colonel had barely finished swallowing, when he whispered to his attendant. Jemmy was certain he overheard Colonel Cudworth mutter, "Get Bradford over here, right now." Finally, some well-deserved accolades would be coming their way.

Captain Church had no inkling his duties at the Mount Hope garrison would be suddenly changing once again when Major Bradford approached at a furious pace. He was accompanied by Captain Fuller, or more accurately, he thought he was accompanied. Captain Fuller was at least ten paces behind and breathing heavily. Fuller was only four or five years younger than Colonel Cudworth, and at least thirty pounds heavier than...anyone.

Major Bradford did not look well. His expressions alternated between rage, nausea, anxiety, and disgust. He spoke slowly and deliberately, well aware that vomiting was a distinct possibility.

"Church, I must be brief, as I am quite dizzy and need to lie down. First and foremost, you are hereby relieved as Commissary General, and will be turning in your stamp immediately. Secondly..." Bradford closed his eyes and waited for the wave of nausea to subside. "Secondly, you and your men are now in the stead of Captain Fuller. Follow his orders to the letter. And finally, do not let me see your face for at least..." Bradford was now covering his mouth and scampering away. "Seven days!"

Captain Fuller had finally caught up and was sweating profusely. He wiped the sweat away as he watched Bradford's sudden departure. "Frankly, Benjamin, I didn't think lunch was that bad."

Church blinked repeatedly and focused his eyes on Captain Fuller. He tried to ascertain how much lower he could sink in this army. His efforts to lead an assault on the Palmer River bridge with Gill and Belcher were disastrous. His outbursts in front of Colonel Cudworth were so excessive he was forced into the wretched position of Commissary General. He proved so bad at that demeaning task that he was just ignominiously relieved. And now? Now he had to answer to this aged, bloated, appalling excuse for a soldier.

"Say, Benjamin? Are there any more rations to be had? I'd take an apple or two if you could oblige me."

Church faced his now superior officer and vacantly gawked. "No, Captain Fuller. I'm afraid not."

"Pshaw. Call me Matthew. Well, come now. I guess we should get back to work on the fort, Benjamin."

Church despairingly hung his head. "I suppose so, Matthew."

The next two days were spent engaged in tedious labors working to build a useless fort as part of a pointless venture Church was ashamed to be associated with. Metacomet's forces would no doubt be solidifying their advantages on the other side of Mount Hope Bay. They were planning their offensive, they were gathering allies and supplies, they were training for close-quarter combat, and Captain Benjamin Church was dragging timber.

During a mid-afternoon lull, as sentry tower number five was nearing completion, Fuller was in the mood for conversation. "Benjamin, I must confess. I was quite appalled by your outbursts with Colonel Cudworth about this fort. Frankly, I think it's coming along magnificently. Look at those towers."

Church felt the urge to wrap his hands around Fuller's beefy, sagging neck. Instead, he elected to pursue cordial diplomacy for a change. He attentively watched Reddington tote a ninety-pound piece of lumber with ease, while he patiently formulated his thoughts.

"Frankly, Matthew, I feel simply awful about everything that transpired. My behavior was unseemly, and I hope to restore myself in the colonel's good graces."

"I am pleased to hear that, Benjamin. James and I go back decades together, and I assure you he was most angry."

"You know the colonel that well, Matthew?"

"Oh, my goodness. We're old enough to remember the Pequot War. I've known him for decades."

Church was increasingly intrigued. "It's just that I'm so damn anxious for this war to be over, Matthew. That's my home right across the water."

"Is it, indeed?"

"Oh, yes. I was finishing my homestead on the southwestern corner over there. Before the fighting began, I was in deliberation with my friend Awashonks of the Sakonnet people."

"Your friend you say? The female sachem?"

"Yes. She was most disheartened about the events of this year and was most uncertain about an alliance with Philip. I told her to remain neutral as best able, and I'd be back to see her as soon as possible. But now? I fear Philip and his savages are across the water in Pocasset, enlisting Awashonks and destroying my home. Who knows where they'll go next? But...my work is here. I have a fort to build." He cupped his hands to his mouth to project his voice. "Look lively, Reddington! This fort's not going to build itself!"

Reddington effortlessly lifted the enormous beam even higher in the air. "Yes, Captain Church."

"Anyway, Matthew. That's why I'm so impulsive. I just wish I had some way of getting across that water to find Awashonks, and to get a sense of Philip's next move. But, what's done is done." He casually scanned the day's progress. "Do you think the towers should be taller, Matthew?"

"No, no, they're fine. You know...Benjamin? Something has crossed my mind."

"Yes, Matthew?"

"I am dining with the colonel tonight. If you are genuinely contrite and remorseful for your actions, I could explore the possibility of a reconnaissance party."

"A reconnaissance party? Why, Matthew! That sounds like a brilliant idea."

"Oh, pshaw." He removed his hat to mop up his profuse sweat, and scanned his surroundings for a place to sit. "But something small. Twenty or thirty men. I think James would authorize something like that."

"I'm intrigued, Matthew. But do you think the fort could do without my company's efforts?"

"I suppose so. But make haste over in Pocasset, and bring back Reddington. The man is a beast."

"Indeed. So, you will address the colonel tonight?"

"Oh yes. You and your twenty men. Three or four days, tops."

Church was freshly energized, and against his better judgement, he confided to Barnstrom that some action might be afoot. Barnstrom quietly began procuring powder and rations, but kept the notion secret. The men continued their labors on the fort uninterrupted.

That night Church rendezvoused with Captain Fuller, and Church immediately knew all was not well. Fuller appeared devastated, and his defeated glare gave the impression that not only was the mission disapproved, but he was heartily reprimanded for even suggesting it. He looked so shaken Church feared he may begin to sob.

"The colonel did not think highly of the idea, Matthew?"

"Oh, he readily endorsed it, Benjamin. He was very enthusiastic. Very, very enthusiastic."

"Then why so downcast? This is wonderful news!"

"Because I am to lead the mission, Benjamin."

CHAPTER ELEVEN

POCASSET

If there had to be a war in New England, then July was the month to be fighting it.

This mundane sentiment resonated with Captain Fuller, Captain Church, and the thirty-six men who awoke that morning in Pocasset. They had traveled by boat the previous night, sailing two miles south across Mount Hope Bay to Aquidneck Island. After procuring some additional supplies, they moved east across the Sakonnet River and camped for the night. This was familiar terrain to Captain Church, and he awoke less than ten miles from his farm.

His company of twenty men were in generally good spirits. The weather was beautiful, and the trip by boat was so leisurely it was almost recreational. He knew, however, that he had to remain focused. The success of his mission depended on one task above all others. If he failed in this particular pursuit, failure was all but assured.

He had to get rid of Fuller.

Fortunately, he had ample opportunity to contemplate the matter, and he quickly engaged his objective.

"A beautiful morning, indeed! Praise be to the Lord. Will you be leading us in morning prayers, Matthew?"

"Oh, yes I will, Benjamin. It is indeed a most beautiful morning. Have you...um...have you considered our reconnaissance plan for the day?"

"Well, frankly, it seems logical to partition our forces into two independent bodies. Certainly, we can cover much more ground in far less time that way. Wouldn't you agree, Matthew?"

"That is, um, one possibility. But there is, um, a certain strength in numbers, and perhaps we shouldn't be so rash."

Fuller was blinking furiously and sweating profusely, though the sun had barely begun its daily ascent.

"Hmm. You could very well be right, Matthew. This will require careful thought. I believe our first objective should certainly be to the south. I know from experience the area is heavily fortified with Indian forces. If Philip has truly enlisted the Sakonnet, then this will be very gruesome terrain, indeed."

Fuller's eyes grew wider as Church continued. "Of course, we will have to also get a good understanding of any activity to our north. I know for a fact the terrain there tends to be quite open, and as such, the local Indians shun it as being too difficult to defend. I highly doubt we'll encounter any enemy activity there. I suppose we could initially proceed south for two or three days, and then double back and explore the north. Well, we'd best get an early start. Have you chosen a theme for morning prayers?"

Captain Fuller's response was as predictable as the tides. "Well, now…let's think about this logically, Benjamin. With so much terrain to cover, maybe it will be more expedient if we partitioned our forces. Let's say you take your company of twenty men, and I'll lead these other sixteen men to the…oh, I don't know. I suppose we'll take the northerly trek. The easier terrain will be much more suitable to my gout, I suppose."

"Captain Fuller, you are commanding these forces. If you think it best to partition them…"

"Yes. Absolutely. Our obligation is to cover as much ground in as timely a manner as possible. Let's get ready for morning worship and then brief the men."

"Yes, sir."

Morning worship was called to order. Captain Fuller led a recitation of the thirty-first psalm.

"*Blessed be the LORD: for he hath shewed me his marvelous kindness in a strong city. For I said in my haste, I am cut off from before thine eyes: nevertheless thou heardest the voice of my supplications when I cried unto thee. O love the LORD, all ye his saints: for the LORD preserveth the faithful, and plentifully rewardeth the proud doer. Be of good courage, and he shall strengthen your heart, all ye that hope in the LORD."*

Church suppressed his urge to smile as Captain Fuller led his company away to the north. Cornet Barnstrom whispered his farewell. "Finally. Thank the heavens. They won't go a hundred yards without stopping for rest."

Reddington overheard the jest. "Request permission to change commanders, sir."

A smile finally did arrive as Church replied. "Denied, Reddington. Who's going to carry me when I grow weary?"

The unit proceeded south along the shore of the Sakonnet River. The breeze was cool, and the waterfowl were abundant. One hour of patrol became two, and two became three. Barnstrom felt like this was as good an opportunity as any to ask his commander the question that had been plaguing him these last few days.

He cautiously drew near and spoke in a low mutter. "Captain. Permission to ask you a question, sir?" Church said nothing and did not take his eyes from the horizon. Barnstrom interpreted the silence as consent. "Captain Church, the men and I were wondering if...you...well, if you...if you intentionally had yourself relieved as the Commissary General, sir. You know. So we could fight. Sir."

Church still remained silent and ignored the question for what seemed to be an entire minute. The day was growing warmer, and he was surprised and disappointed they had not encountered any of Awashonk's forces. He turned to his second-in-command.

"Permission denied, Cornet Barnstrom."

As if Jemmy's question was not irritating enough, Reddington had now grown weary of the dull lack of activity. "Where are the Indians, Captain Church? You said there would be Indians. I could be finishing the sixth sentry tower on the fort by now." Barnstrom tried to cast an intimidating glare to silence Reddington. There was, however, only so much intimidation he could convey with his rank of cornet, especially when his underling seemed to be twice his size.

"If it's Indians you want, Reddington, I suspect you will be seeing them soon enough. Just pray that they are friends from Awashonks, and not savages from Philip. Stay sharp, lads. Never let your guard down."

As if magically on cue, pandemonium consumed half the company as Barnstrom's right foot inadvertently brushed up against a timber rattle-snake coiled up in the dense undergrowth. The serpent viciously lunged at his unsuspecting prey, narrowly missing Barnstrom, but instilling terror in the men. Captain Church attempted to restore order with wry commentary.

"Barnstrom, would you quit dawdling? Catch up, and quit playing with the wildlife."

The men were not amused. "Captain, how many snakes are on this trail? Maybe we should choose a different path."

Church abruptly halted in his tracks. "Fine. Do you want to fight Indians, or serpents?"

The reply seemed to be unanimous and simultaneous. "*Indians!*"

"Very well. Let's go this way, instead."

Church surmised they would encounter fewer serpents if they remained to the west within visual range of the shore. This route led them to a strip of land jutting into the Sakonnet River known as Punkatees Neck. Church knew he could almost run to his homestead from here, and the terrain became very familiar. This was an area farmed by the Almy family. But where was Awashonks? Where were the Sakonnets?

After their brief encounter with a timber rattlesnake, the men were delighted to find a cultivated area, and what seemed to be a field of peas. The men quickly began to gather them, as food of any kind was a precious commodity. Church had reservations about procuring peas from the Almy family without permission, but at that moment he found what he had been looking for.

Two Sakonnet men were wandering out of the field.

Some of his men dove to the ground in an effort to conceal themselves, but Church recognized the futility in that. He called to the men to get their attention, but upon noticing Church and his white-shirted platoon of Englishmen, the two Sakonnets sprinted toward the woods.

Church sprinted after them and waved his hands furiously in the air. "Stop! Talk! Make talk to Awashonks!" He felt increasingly silly and racked his faculties for the Sakonnet word for "friend." The two young men continued to flee until they leaped over one of the Almys' numerous wooden fences.

Then, they turned to Church and began shooting.

Their aim was highly suspect, and none of the musket fire drew near Church. Reddington, who had obviously embraced his commander's directive to be ready for anything, promptly returned fire, and his aim was not suspect. The wounded cry of a young Sakonnet burned in their ears.

Church reflexively led his platoon into the woods in pursuit. They were quickly immersed in the darkness, and their zeal began to subside. Their nervous eyes darted from the ground to the treetops, eagerly searching for a trail of blood, enemy ambushes, or even worse, timber rattlesnakes. Church raised his hand to halt their progress. He did not wish to appear adversarial by stalking the duo through the woods, and he maintained a fragile hope that the shooting was all a misunderstanding.

The fragile hope, however, was soon shattered.

The dark forest suddenly roared to life in a deafening thrash of musket fire. The assault seemingly came from every possible direction, and the Englishmen returned fire in an unorganized, ineffective fashion. Church couldn't believe it. He had foolishly stumbled into a trap.

He anticipated at least three or four fatalities among his men, and directed them all to retreat back to the open space of the field where they would hopefully be out of range. He furiously searched the forest floor for his fallen soldiers, and grew agitated as he was unable to find them. Realizing he was the last Englishman in the forest, he abandoned his search and followed his men into the clearing as musket volleys rained down upon him.

They reached the wooden fence where the hostilities originally commenced. Barnstrom directed six men to hide behind the fence and be prepared to return fire as three, independent, two-man teams. The others had reached the field, where Reddington was aggressively procuring the pea crop.

Church tried to breathe, but was uncertain if he was succeeding. The forest had resumed its inviting silence, and he monitored it closely. Perhaps his enemy was content to remain ensconced and invisible in their natural fortress, and had no appetite to engage more than a dozen Englishmen in open-field combat. He turned to face the river, regained his composure, and tried to count the men who made it out of the woods.

He was delighted and stunned to discover that no matter how many times and how many ways he counted, he was with twenty men. Miraculously, they did not lose a single man in the vicious ambush. The catastrophic situation was rapidly stabilizing, and he patiently evaluated the enemy stronghold.

The dense, wooded area would be very difficult to assault. He envisioned five columns of four men, with each column separated by at least twenty yards. The terrain rose rapidly from the field, and he assumed there would be sentries perched in the trees. He stared intently at his objective, and grew concerned that the midday sun was inducing an undue amount of fatigue. Was he hallucinating? He rubbed his eyes, took a drink of water, and looked again. The forest now seemed to be almost alive, teeming with incessant and unsettling movement. Church finally understood what he was seeing.

Once again, musket fire was everywhere. This time, the Englishmen could clearly see the enemy. At least fifty Indians had emerged from the woods, and the situation was now catastrophic. Most of his men turned and ran back toward the river, and few if any were able to return fire. But then, as if by divine providence, they found what they so desperately needed: A magnificent stone wall.

Reddington was the first to notice it, and soon, every man was safely in position behind it. They were finally able to return fire in a methodical and deliberate fashion, and at least two assailants were felled. Church tried to count the enemy forces, but gave up after seventy. There were actually more than one hundred, and more seemed to be pouring out from the forest by the minute. What's more, what initially seemed to be a magnificent bulwark of stone was proving to be the unimpressive remnants of a wall long ago left uncompleted. Church silently cursed the Almy family and their lackluster efforts.

The noise was deafening as he tried to collect his thoughts. What a fool he was. What an arrogant, careless, pathetic excuse for a leader. How foolhardy and obnoxious he was to so callously manipulate Fuller. Church had no doubt Fuller's men were not fighting for their lives behind a sad, decrepit wall. Benjamin Church was a fool, and the men entrusted to him were now hopelessly trapped.

If he was condemned to die in such an ignominious fashion, then he would do so with bravery and dignity. He commanded five men to gather up the loose stones that were scattered behind the wall and could be safely procured. They began furiously fortifying and expanding their stone bulwark while their enemies shrieked at them. He coordinated the manner in which his forces would return fire. Three men would shoot methodically but unpredictably, while three other men would aim but hold their fire. These men would focus their attention on any invaders who dared to approach their makeshift fortress. Meanwhile, the remaining nine men would reload and prime their muskets, and enter the rotation after the other men shot.

His heart raced furiously, and he struggled to make himself heard. He surveyed the Sakonnet River immediately behind them. If they had any prayer of surviving this ordeal, it would be evacuation by boat. He knew what had to be done next.

"Strip to your shirts, gentlemen! White, white, white! If we're to be spotted by boat, they have to know we're Englishmen! Show them your white shirts!" It was an act of desperation, but almost no one in New England was more desperate at that moment than Church's men.

Church expected the enemy to mass for an assault and storm the wall at any moment. Even if they only sent fifty men (and they seemed to have hundreds), Church knew his men could realistically stop five or six, and then it would be gruesome, hand-to-hand combat against a far superior force.

"Cornet Barnstrom, I just realized something important."

"Really, Captain?" Barnstrom was quite sarcastic in his tone, and Church could not fault him.

"I never answered your question."

"What? *My question*?" Barnstrom's hands trembled as he poured his precious black powder.

"About the commissary position. The answer is no."

Barnstrom's jaw dropped. He was busy trying not to think about his wife and three young children in Middleborough. "No? The answer? *What*?" He was increasingly enveloped by the surreal, dream-like sensation of randomness and insanity. The musket fire was terrifying as it ricocheted off the stone, and the trees in the forest chanted some ghastly, rhythm-less insult. The pale blue sky seemed to be spinning.

"I wasn't trying to get fired. I really was that bad of a commissary officer."

Barnstrom was uncertain whether to laugh, console his captain, or promptly take command since Church had lost his faculties. "Thank you, Captain. Now I know."

Church estimated they had been huddled and returning fire for approximately thirty minutes. He cut the long-range offensive fire by two thirds in order to conserve powder. He knew he should be inventorying their powder and musket balls to assess how long they could maintain this defensive posture, but frankly, he was afraid of the answer. He undertook another act of desperation.

He cupped his hands around his mouth and extended his head as far he could dare beyond the stone. *"I am Church! I...am...friend of Awashonks! I...am...friend of Sakonnet!"* He repeated his plea at least ten times, but the incessant pace of the musket fire left no doubt his adversaries did not care what he had to say. What's more, he genuinely did not know if he was facing the Sakonnet or Philip's Wampanoag.

Captain Church turned to his rear, and obsessively scanned the river. There was not a boat in sight. What was in sight, however, was the enormous Reddington, who was hunched on the ground and was delicately extracting peas from his ill-gotten stockpile of pods, and was distributing each one as if it was a roasted side of salted beef. The sight was so pathetic and ridiculous that Church could not contain his laughter, and soon the other men joined in the folly.

"Eat well, gentlemen. Try not to gorge yourself. I need you at your best." Soon the laughter subsided, and Church grew serious. "Trust in the Lord, men. Put your trust in the Lord and He shall never forsake you. For as the Proverbs teach us..." A musket ball ricocheted off the stone and grazed his shoulder. Unfazed, he continued. *"Trust in the Lord with all thine heart; and lean not unto thine own understanding. In all thy ways acknowledge him, and he shall direct thy paths."*

Most closed their eyes and bowed their heads. "Amen."

Though he undoubtedly trusted in the Lord, Cornet Barnstrom knew their situation was growing more dire by the minute, as their stocks of powder were slowly whittled away. He lowered his voice to a whisper.

"Captain, what about a run for it? We're all fit and healthy. Straight north, up the coast."

"Not a chance, Jemmy. Look at them, hiding in the trees up there. They're aligned a hundred yards in each direction."

"So, we just stay here?"

"It's the Sakonnet River, Jemmy. There's got to be a boat along shortly."

As if by heavenly intervention, one of the youngest men with the best vision spotted a sloop coming in from the north. The men cried out with exclamations of "Huzzah," and Church felt like he could finally take a genuine breath. It took at least thirty minutes for the craft to navigate within earshot, during which time Church was certain the enemy would mount their assault, so as to prevent their escape. Yet, no assault came.

Instead of focusing their wrath on the stone wall, the enemy combatants now directed their wrath at the incoming sloop. The boat was surrounded by projectiles splashing through the warm water, and the pilot quickly realized this rescue attempt was not going to plan. He gestured to the men ashore that the scene was too turbulent, and he would be going back the way he came.

Two of the younger men in the platoon felt the panic building, and they shouted as loudly as they could. "Don't leave us, for we will be dead men! We are running out of powder and shot! Do not leave us for the savages, our situation is hopeless! We can barely return fire!"

Church and Barnstrom did their best to silence them, but the damage was done. He had no doubt that with hundreds of Indians within earshot, at least one of them heard and understood. Church was relearning his lesson from the Palmer River bridge: No situation is so disastrous that it can't get even worse.

The men were severely demoralized after the aborted rescue. They were running out of powder. A rescue by boat proved nearly impossible. Making a run for it was suicidal. The sun was setting. The enemy knew of their desperate straits. And, perhaps worst of all, Church thought sarcastically to himself, they were out of peas.

If nothing else, he thought, they would live their remaining hours with dignity. They would fight and perish like New

England men. They would trust in the Almighty, and they would give these heathens all they could handle.

Church directed his men to bow their heads with him. He thought about his family back in Duxbury. How would he be honored? Would he go down in history as a brave, patriotic, devout man of the New England frontier? Or would he be eternally remembered as the impulsive, self-absorbed fool who dragged twenty fine men to the grave? He focused intently on his favorite Psalm, the one Psalm he felt he had adequately committed to memory through the years. He was pleased how accurately he could recite it despite the circumstances.

"Deliver me from mine enemies, O my God: defend me from them that rise up against me.

Deliver me from the workers of iniquity, and save me from bloody men. For, lo, they lie in wait for my soul: the mighty are gathered against me; not for my transgression, nor for my sin, O Lord. They run and prepare themselves without my fault: awake to help me, and behold. Thou therefore, O Lord God of hosts, the God of Israel, awake to visit all the heathen: be not merciful to any wicked transgressors. They return at evening: they make a noise like a dog, and go round about the city. Behold, they belch out with their mouth: swords are in their lips: for who, say they, doth hear? But thou, O Lord, shalt laugh at them; thou shalt have all the heathen in derision. Because of his strength will I wait upon thee: for God is my defense. The God of my mercy shall prevent me: God shall let me see my desire upon mine enemies. Amen."

He revamped their tactics as the situation dictated. There would obviously be no more offensive musket fire. His men were ordered to let the enemy approach in small numbers, and once they'd closed to within twenty yards, to unleash a barrage of accurate fire.

The tactic was highly effective. As the previously deadly activity behind the wall gave way to mysterious silence, the bravest of the enemy cautiously approached. They would be convinced the Englishmen were cowering and defenseless, and then the enemy would collapse in a hail of sudden, deadly fire.

This went on for at least an hour, and Church remained stunned the enemy did not unleash a full-scale assault.

By then, the sun had almost finished setting, and Jemmy Barnstrom was wondering what he would say to his wife if he could speak to her one last time. Would he wipe away her tears and tell her to be brave? Or would he be too terrified by his imminent death to speak? Should he now tell the men how proud he was of what they had done today? Or was that Captain Church's job?

Church was whispering under his breath and staring at the river. "Goulding, you have been sent by the Lord. God bless you, Roger." Barnstrom saw nothing and was not surprised that Church had started to hallucinate and ramble. He was probably stricken with dehydration, and the prospect of imminent death affected even the bravest men in odd ways.

But then, he saw it, too.

"Captain?"

"Yes, Jemmy, yes. Goulding. Roger Goulding from Newport. I'd recognize that hideous sloop from five miles. He's a man of action and won't cower in the face of the enemy."

Goulding had been previously briefed by the defeated sloop, and came prepared. He had eight armed men ready to return fire. Rather than anchoring within range of the enemy, he remained far off-shore and sent a small canoe to the stone wall. Although the canoe could only evacuate two men at a time, the plan was working brilliantly. The enemy could not seem to hit the small vessel, and the diminishing light was making their aim even worse.

Church was still utterly amazed the enemy did not charge the wall, but perhaps the musket fire emanating from the sloop unnerved them. Like God's creatures boarding the ark, his men went two by two to the sloop. Church ensured he was the very last man to leave the stone wall, but after rowing twenty yards by canoe, he had to turn around and return to the scene.

He had forgotten his hat.

As he boarded the sloop and embraced Goulding, he could see the woods still brightly alive with musket fire and war cries. He was in a state of disbelief. His poorly-supplied twenty men held hundreds of savages at bay for at least six hours, without suffering an injury. He had led them, motivated them, reassured them, and inspired them.

Though the ordeal was harrowing indeed, Captain Benjamin Church somehow felt invigorated. He was physically exhausted, famished, and dehydrated, but he was spiritually renewed. His prayers had been answered, and his spiritual mentoring had been rewarded. Hundreds of Godless, war-crazed savages had just spent six hours trying to harm Church and end his life, but the Lord would not permit it. Finally, it had happened. Finally, at the age of thirty-three and in the face of extreme peril, he had received his blessed assurance.

Benjamin Church was one of the Lord's chosen people. He was undoubtedly one of the elect.

CHAPTER TWELVE

POCASSET

Linto squinted at Tobias in the dark, musty cell. Although it was the middle of the night, the heat was almost unbearable. Linto knew he was perspiring profusely, and he hoped he wasn't quivering.

He studied every detail of Tobias' hardened face. It conveyed no trace of anger, fear, or sadness. Linto would describe it as peaceful resignation. Linto wondered what his own expression would convey if he was the one to be executed in mere hours.

Tobias' son was loudly sobbing, and Tobias finally elected to simply let him be. A somber, intense expression now fell over him, and his eyes pierced the darkness.

"Promise me something, Linto."

Linto had been here before. Linto lived this exact moment in this exact place approximately four weeks ago. He knew exactly what was coming, and yet, he was still frightened.

"Grant a dying man his wish, Linto, and promise me something." Linto closed his eyes and braced for the impact of the words. "Promise me you will never let Metacomet humiliate himself before the English again."

Linto nodded. "Yes, yes, I promise, Tobias. I promise."

This was precisely as the conversation transpired on that fateful night, and Linto was mysteriously able to relive it. But now, he needed more. Linto needed Tobias' blessing.

"But Tobias, so much has happened in the weeks since you left us. The war has started. I tried to stop it, Tobias. I thought I had the perfect plan, but it failed miserably, and Mentayyup died for nothing. It's all my fault, Tobias."

Tobias was motionless and silent. Linto had an increasingly difficult time making out his features in the darkness. He could no longer hear Tobias' son sobbing, and Linto hoped he had drifted off to sleep.

"I've kept my promise, Tobias. At least, I think I have." Linto wiped the sweat from his face, and inadvertently lowered his voice to a whisper. "Please tell me I've kept my promise."

The condemned man remained stone-faced and speechless. Linto was growing agitated.

"Metacomet hasn't been humiliated, Tobias. He hasn't. Not at all. We've just been very…strategic in our ways. That's the word Annawon uses. We are being strategic." Linto could no longer discern Tobias' features, and he could not be sure he was still speaking with anyone.

"If we keep moving, Tobias, the English will tire of the hunt. We can negotiate a peace. They will get tired of the war."

Darkness. Darkness and silence.

"This is the best way, Tobias. No one is being humiliated. We can have peace again. But we can't fight them, Tobias. There's too many Englishmen. We have to keep avoiding the battlefield." Linto's voice was rising as he became increasingly uncertain Tobias was there. He reached out to grab him, but only felt the thick, summer air.

Linto was sobbing now. "Tell me I'm not a coward, Tobias. Tell me I kept my promise. Please talk to me, Tobias. Aren't you there? Are you with me, Tobias? *Tell me I'm not a coward!*"

The light was now surging into the prison cell, and Linto surmised dawn had broken. The sunrise was unusually fast and intense, and soon everything was bathed in nourishing, wonderful sunlight. He reached out to grab Tobias, and was relieved to feel the warmth of another human being. Tobias' shoulders were delicate, warm, and soft.

"Tobias! Speak to me!"

Linto opened his eyes and saw his quivering hands grasping Wawetseka's shoulders. The vision was over. He groaned, and she lovingly stroked his hair.

"Were we successful, my love?"

Linto rubbed his eyes and forced himself to sit up. He tried to process his surroundings.

"Did you see Tobias, Linto?"

"Yes."

"Did you speak to him? Did he reassure you?"

"I spoke to him. There was no reassurance. Nothing has changed."

Wawetseka appeared downcast. She knew how important this undertaking was. "I'm sorry, my love. The spirit world can be very unyielding sometimes."

Linto held her embrace and listened to her breathing. The children were playing games, oblivious to all the fear and suffering in their midst. Once again, her powers proved both astounding and unsettling. With a combination of boiled herbs, prayers, and delicate caresses, Wawetseka transported him to a painful event in his past. The English ministers and naysayers would say he was dreaming, but he knew better. He was there. Tobias was still alive, and Linto was in the cell with him. She conducted a similar ritual four years ago with their English friend, and she achieved great success. On that day Wawetseka completely eradicated Israel Brewster's night terrors and painful torments.

"There is another war council this afternoon. I must collect my thoughts."

'What will you tell them today, my love?"

"I don't know. Forgive me my darling, but I have no idea."

"The Sachem loves and trusts you, Linto. And so do I."

Linto embraced her and headed for his destination. He stared at the blue sky and tried to recall when he last ate. The war was barely a few weeks old, and food was already becoming a problem. Most of the men spent all their spare time fishing, as the game was increasingly limited in the swamps of Pocasset.

What was the next move of the Wampanoag? A few weeks ago, Linto counseled the Sachem with the false prophecy that whoever fired the first shot would lose the war. Then he counseled that the wisest course would be to abandon Montaup, and flee to the east. What would they do now that the English scouting parties had found them, and were preparing another invasion? The English certainly couldn't spend the rest of their days building forts. They would soon cross Mount Hope Bay to pursue Metacomet and his warriors.

The council met on a ridge overlooking the bay. The visibility was superb, and Metacomet cast his eyes west toward his beloved Montaup. He desperately longed to be reunited with the ancestral home of his forefathers. Metacomet had strong reservations about abandoning their home without a fight, but Linto had no doubts, and Annawon could see the merits as well. The plan seemed to be paying dividends, as the Wampanoag were now united with Weetamoo and her Pocasset warriors, as well as Awashonks and her Sakonnet.

Linto and the Wampanoag could discern conflicted loyalty from these two female Sachems. When the English took Wamsutta away and he perished under mysterious circumstances, Weetamoo would have burned Plimoth to the ground if she could. But that was an astounding thirteen summers ago, and her enthusiasm for this rebellion seemed to have waned dramatically. Awashonks also seemed a grudging ally, and rumors abounded that in recent months she had formed a special kinship with an English officer who settled in her midst. Now that Metacomet and hundreds of other Wampanoag warriors had arrived at Pocasset, however, cautious neutrality was no longer an option for Weetamoo and Awashonks.

Metacomet now had allies, and he had warriors. But what was their next move? The enemy were certainly coming to Pocasset, and they needed a strategy. Nimrod built a fire, and the members of the war council stared pensively as the flames rose higher.

Metacomet was satisfied with the fire. He turned and faced Linto. "You have done it again! Linto the prophet! You told us the English would arrive with very few warriors, and you were exactly right! They sent less than forty warriors after us! Just like Gideish. Brilliant, Linto! You are brilliant!"

"Gideon, Sachem. Gideon was the character in the English Bible. Thank you for your kind words, Sachem." Linto marveled at his good fortune, and he thought he could see Nimrod repressing his fury.

Weetamoo surveyed Linto from head to toe, and seemed to beam with pride. "Father of my grandchildren, and holy man of the Wampanoag. Just yesterday, you and Wawetseka were but children." Linto grinned awkwardly as his mother-in-law lavished him with praise. "Metacomet tells me your wisdom is priceless." Nimrod seemed to be biting his tongue.

Metacomet continued. "But, I fear the English have learned their lesson. Awashonks' warriors drove their tiny invasion force back into the bay. They are already assembling their next assault. And they will bring hundreds this time."

Nimrod grunted. "And now, we kill them. Finally. A battle."

Weetamoo looked concerned. "Is now the right time? Should we meet them in the open field?"

"Absolutely. Our combined forces are powerful." Nimrod spoke passionately and convincingly. "We destroy them here, and then we cross the bay to destroy that hideous fort and all who dwell within it."

Metacomet looked pensive, and he reserved judgement. "What do you think, Annawon?"

"Nimrod makes a lot of sense. We may even outnumber the invaders. A decisive victory here would mean everything to the rebellion."

Nimrod nodded and pointed west. "On the beaches. That's where we destroy them. We drive them back into the bay, and there will be no stone wall to protect them. We slaughter them here and now. Then, we march to Plimoth and drive them back into the ocean!"

Weetamoo still appeared unconvinced. "I only have seventy battle-ready warriors. Many have already gone west to fight with the Nipmuc. I think we should do the same. If we can merge with the Nipmuc, we can meet any English army in direct combat."

"We scurried away once, and that was enough." Nimrod's voice was growing louder. "Sachem, it is time to fight."

Nimrod grimaced as Metacomet uttered the inevitable words. "Linto, what are your thoughts? Is there a prophecy to be found here? Have you prayed on this?"

And once again, Linto had his opportunity. Once again, he had no doubt his influence on Metacomet would be almost unquestionable. And once again, he would do everything in his power to avoid bloodshed.

His mind raced, and he formulated his plan. He would have to devise yet another deception. "Sachem, I believe the spirit world is speaking to us about this. This morning, as I communed with the spirits, I asked them to send us a sign. Almost instantly, my head was filled with images of the English big book. I could not dispel the images, and they stayed with me all morning. Finally, I sat under an oak tree and opened the book. I read the first passage I saw."

Metacomet was mesmerized, and Linto continued. "Once again, I found the chapter called Judges with the stories of ancient battles and wars. In the fourth part of the chapter, there was the tale of a commander named Barak. Barak's people were living in fear of a people called the Canaanites because the Canaanites had nine hundred chariots made out of iron. There was, however, a priestess named Deborah. She told Barak that the Lord commanded them to attack their enemy, and their nine hundred chariots."

Nimrod was incensed. "But the English don't have chariots!" Metacomet's poisonous glare conveyed that further interruptions would not be tolerated.

"Yes, Nimrod, but there is a lesson to be found. Barak drew the nine hundred chariots to a river called the Kishon.

And their God made it rain so hard that the nine hundred chariots were trapped in the mud. They were useless, and even though their army was tremendous, the Canaanites were defeated."

Nimrod theatrically threw his arms in the air. "So, the lesson is to attack the enemy!"

"Perhaps. But when I read the tale, what captivated me the most was the mud. The image of hundreds of powerful, lethal chariots left absolutely useless. A strong enemy rendered helpless by mud."

Weetamoo understood instantly. "The swamps."

Linto nodded. "Exactly. The English have the soldiers, and the guns, and the horses, but they will never understand the swamps as we do. They will get discouraged, then disgusted with their failure, and they will leave us alone. We withdraw into the swamps."

Nimrod could not mask his fury. "Retreat again! Run away again! This is ridiculous! Sachem, I beg you. Let us fight our enemy!"

Metacomet had turned away and was looking out across the bay. "But you believe this message to be divinely inspired, Linto?"

Linto was increasingly unsettled by how easily new deceptions were forthcoming. Once he had lied one time, why not lie three times? Why not ten times? "Yes, Sachem. There has to be a reason I opened to that page. The English cannot match us in the swamps."

Linto knew his Sachem, and he knew what was coming. Whether intentionally or not, he moved a little closer to Annawon for protection, and he stealthily monitored Nimrod's reaction to Metacomet's decree.

"We will withdraw to the swamps. Let it be done."

CHAPTER THIRTEEN

POCASSET

After the war council dispersed, Linto returned to Wawetseka. He was still fatigued due to the physical and mental strain of his mystical rendezvous with Tobias. Most of all he was, as usual, filled with uncertainty and self-loathing. Was there any limit to his falsehood and deception? Would Metacomet eventually lose his faith in "Linto the prophet?" Was Linto genuinely serving the best interests of his family and the Wampanoag, or was he simply afraid? Finally, Linto contemplated the bitter wrath of Nimrod.

Wawetseka could see his distress, and she knelt on the ground beside him. She held his hand, and they stared into the sky. "Was anything resolved, my love?"

"Yes."

"For the best, I hope?" Linto remained silent and gripped her hand tighter. She lowered her voice to a whisper. "More contrived prophecy, my love?" She could not bear to utter the word "false."

"Yes."

"What will we do now?"

"We will slip away into the swamps. I don't think the English can fight us there."

"And then what?"

"I don't know. I haven't received any guidance from the spirits yet." She was uncertain if he was being flippant, and she refrained from forcing a laugh.

"Was she there?"

"Yes."

"Will she visit?"

"She didn't say. I expect she will."

Linto and Wawetseka had much in common. They were both young, slender, and attractive. They were both spiritual leaders among the Wampanoag. Linto's adoption was a miraculous event, and Wawetseka's mysterious powers were increasingly awe-inspiring. Finally, neither of them truly had parents, and they both felt like Metacomet and his wife Wootonekanuske raised them from adolescence to adulthood.

Unlike Linto, however, Wawetseka knew exactly who her parents were: Wamsutta and Weetamoo. She was the daughter of a Sachem and a *Sunksquaw*, a female Sachem. Wawetseka was nine years old when the English took her father away. He would never return, and his younger brother Metacomet became Sachem. After Wamsutta perished, English poison was suspected. Weetamoo raged and shrieked for vengeance, but Metacomet did nothing. His grief and subsequent guilt would torment him for years until, one miraculous day four years ago, Linto met the remarkable Englishman who was with Wamsutta during his final days, and could attest he was not poisoned.

After Wamsutta's death, mother and daughter drifted apart. As the Sunksquaw of the Pocasset, she was obligated to marry for security and alliances. She subsequently married Quequequanachet of the Nipmuc, but he seemed to love rum more than her. She did not grieve when he perished in a canoe on a winter's morning. Next, she married Petonowit of the Sakonnet. Petonowit was enamored with Plimoth and all things English. Although they enjoyed some happy years together, as the specter of war drew closer, she had to bid farewell to Petonowit and his English sympathies.

As a thrice-remarried Sunksquaw of the Pocasset, Weetamoo was estranged from Wawetseka, and had only seen her twice since Wamsutta perished. After nine children with four husbands, (Wamsutta was her second), Weetamoo frequently could not even be certain how many grandchildren she actually had. Twenty-nine? Thirty? She would, however, take this opportunity to reconnect with Wawetseka and Linto, who still ranked among the favorites in her enormous family.

"Children of the Wampanoag! Wawetseka, my beautiful child! And my beautiful grandchildren! Come close, and let me hold you all."

Wawetseka hoped she was not shedding tears. "Mother. Sunksquaw. You are so regal and magnificent." Weetamoo truly was magnificent, and she was never modest. She ostentatiously painted her face with a bold, horizontal, violet stripe that spanned from ear to ear. Her eyelids conveyed the image of a bird's wings, with white feathers soaring across her forehead. Additionally, she was adorned with an impressive array of jewelry from every corner of New England, including the finest from Boston.

Linto joined in the embrace. "And a free woman again, ready for a new husband! As if this war was not creating enough turmoil in these lands!"

Weetamoo lovingly patted his back. "The gift of prophecy AND a funny man. No wonder you married the most beautiful woman of all the Wampanoag."

"She would be the second most beautiful woman if her mother was still among the Wampanoag."

"Prophets should only speak the truth, Linto."

Linto blinked and almost stammered. He was relatively certain Weetamoo was merely engaged in good-natured banter, but the words still made him reel. He could not gauge her facial expression, as she was now tickling the children.

Their mischievous son had now seen two summers, and their adorable daughter was experiencing her first. They were both healthy, and they were both remarkably attractive like their parents. The boy was named Ahanu, meaning "he laughs." He was cheerful and precocious. His younger sister was named Kanti, the Wampanoag word for "sings." It was Wawetseka's choice, and an obvious homage to Linto. It grieved Linto that their formative childhood years would be nothing but a whirlwind of violence, hunger, and hatred.

"Daughter, you are all too thin. Just look at this husband of yours. Didn't I tell you to marry into the wolf clan? These turtle men are nothing but skin and bones."

Despite Weetamoo's attempts at levity, once again, there was a sad truth to her words. "I fear we will all be thinner than we can imagine by winter's end, Mother."

"Stay positive, daughter. Linto has once again been blessed by the spirit world, and I think the course of action he preaches is absolutely correct. We know how the English stumble like drunken buffoons through the swamps. They will bring their horses and their ridiculous spears that are longer than three men. They will quickly get discouraged."

Wawetseka was not comforted. "And then?"

Both women turned their eyes to Linto, who wanted to crawl away. Who could know? But if they fought the English in the manner Nimrod demanded, Linto knew hundreds would die.

Weetamoo recognized the awkward moment as a good opportunity to take her leave. "I must go and inspect my forces. We have to ensure we're well supplied for the siege. Just know I will be with you in the weeks ahead, and our time together is a blessing." There was another embrace, and she was gone.

Linto and Wawetseka also began collecting their meager belongings to prepare for their new sanctuary. During this time, a second visitor came to see them, and this visit would be much more unpleasant than the first.

Linto was hunched over and rolling a blanket when he was startled by the deathly baritone. As usual, it emerged from behind him with no warning. "A word, if we may, Linto?" Nimrod maliciously glared at Wawetseka. He increasingly considered them both as adversaries, but the more he witnessed Wawetseka's powers, the more cautious he became in her presence. "A word in private, please?" His hideous necklace reflected the afternoon sun.

"Yes, of course, Nimrod." Linto escorted him far from his family, but he did his best to remain within Wawetseka's visual range. They climbed a small hilltop, and faced each other.

"Do you take me for a fool, Linto? Is the Sachem a fool?"

Linto did not need prophecy to know where this conversation was going. Regardless, he would have to proceed carefully. "I would never take you or Metacomet as fools, Nimrod."

"Prophecy. English Bibles. Fairy tales. Giddyup, Barat, and Devvro! Nonsense!"

Linto wisely ascertained that correcting Nimrod's pronunciation of Gideon, Barak, and Deborah would probably not pay dividends. He opted to remain silent.

"You magically opened the big book, and you magically read a story about armies getting stranded in the mud? You always have Metacomet fooled, and Annawon is old and gullible, but not me! You are a fraud, Linto. Everything you ever say or do results in us not fighting our enemy! Are you in their pay? Are you an English, Christian spy, like Sassamon? You two certainly spent enough time together!"

Linto could barely get a word in. Nimrod was quivering with rage. "Nimrod, please hear me…"

"It stops now, do you understand? We will scurry away and hide in the swamps tonight. But after this, there is no more prophecy! There are no more lies, there is no more cowardice. So, help me, Linto. Metacomet loves you and thinks you're holy, but I am not blind. If you betray us and keep us from fighting, I will…" Nimrod's hand was tightly gripping his hatchet for dramatic effect.

Linto felt like he could actually smell the aroma of violence and fear in the air. As the scent lingered in his nostrils, he was increasingly sure of it. There *was* an odd aroma wafting across the hilltop. And now, there were bizarre sounds permeating his ears. There seemed to be a foreign, hypnotic chant in the air. Linto then realized how easily she had snuck up on them.

Just as Nimrod had stealthily made his own approach, Wawetseka had also arrived silently and mysteriously. She was waving a smoldering collection of herbs in the air as they burned in an eerie vessel of some sort. The chanting continued, and she had Nimrod's attention.

"*Eee, akky tohm. Eee, akky tohm. Ehnt, wish ul. Ehnt, wish ul.*" The aroma was powerful and unsettling.

The blood seemed to drain from Nimrod's face, and he looked horrified. He stepped away from Linto in a backwards manner, never permitting his eyes to leave Wawetseka. When he felt assured he had established a safe zone of separation, he turned and scurried down the hillside.

Rather than watch his adversary flee, Linto stared at the ground. He knew Wawetseka's words were nonsense, and the herbal mixture was concocted to treat nausea in children. And Linto ruminated on his eventful day.

Earlier, Linto was spiritually reunited with Tobias, and he begged Tobias to tell him he wasn't a coward. He then crafted yet another unforgivable deception, and he formulated the battle strategy of the combined forces of the Wampanoag, Pocasset, and Sakonnet people. After a pleasant reunion with his mother-in-law, the leader of the Pocasset, he was threatened with imminent death because he was a fraud and a liar. He was then shamelessly rescued by his wife, like a helpless child.

He sighed deeply, embraced Wawetseka, and gathered their belongings. That evening, they journeyed to safety in the forbidding cedar swamp.

Life in the swamp wasn't much more different or uncomfortable. The darkness grew tedious, and the food was carefully rationed, but for the most part, all was well. Most importantly, Linto's greatest fear was quickly allayed. His plan was working perfectly.

Annawon and Nimrod each led teams of seven men. Their objective was simple: Taunt the English, and lure them into the darkness. It was almost too easy.

Just like the skirmishes at the bridge north of Montaup, the English assaults seemed to be consistently led by the unusually dressed, profane men with the enormous dogs. They were certainly not Puritans, but they were English all the same. If anything, they seemed much more aggressive and ready for combat.

They were, however, utter fodder for Metacomet and his forces. Their dogs, though loud and intimidating, were unable to track anything through the muck. As Annawon and Nimrod's forces seemed to effortlessly glide across the swamps while barefoot, the English seemed mired and cursed, like the chariots in Linto's tale. Their thick, leather boots routinely became submerged in the mud, and they were often a comical sight as they tried to extricate themselves. One Englishman would try to extend a hand, only to find himself dragged into the brackish sludge as well. If the English thought they heard howls of laughter from the treetops, they were not mistaken.

The English also heard musket fire from the treetops, and lots of it. Within three days' time, at least thirty soldiers from Cudworth's army were slain by the enemy, and many more were victims of friendly fire. Metacomet and Linto could often get close enough to eavesdrop on their leaders, and Metacomet laughed with glee as Linto translated every profane outburst:

"Control your men, Moseley... discipline them, damn you...How can those enormous dogs be so bloody useless...they eat more than we do...what do you expect to do with a matchlock mounted on a tripod, Captain...put down the damned pike, and pick up a sword...what do you mean your men got lost again?"

Metacomet and Linto strolled back through the swamp, and Metacomet could not stop grinning. The prophecy was coming to fruition. The English fired the first shot, and they were cursed.

They had finally met the enemy, and the enemy was absolutely pathetic.

CHAPTER FOURTEEN

BOSTON

Jeremiah Barron grimaced and scratched his pasty shins. The heat of the summer was still raging, and there was little comfort in sight. The war was going miserably. The United Colonies of New England appeared feeble, confused, and very vulnerable.

During the first War Council of the United Colonies of New England, Barron would have never dreamt they could be in this position. King Philip was nowhere near capture, and the geriatric Cudworth appeared increasingly lost and confused. Every week seemed to bring a new report of another English village, township, or garrison house raided, and burnt to cinders. The Nipmuc were proving to be an even deadlier threat than the Wampanoag. Assistance from the mother country was meager at best, and any provisions were appallingly slow to arrive. And now, perhaps most unpleasantly of all, he would have to endure another War Council.

Barron knew all too well what the day would entail. The blustery, sanctimonious blathering of Increase Mather. The smug condescension of Massachusetts Bay. The apathetic uselessness of Connecticut. The adversarial sniping of those two Indian-lovers, Gookin and Eliot. And the impatient, disappointed glowering of Elijah MacTavish.

If only Barron's professional responsibilities could be managed as easily as his personal responsibilities. The unpleasantness associated with his servant girl's pregnancy was now well in order. Barron had no difficulty persuading a twenty-two-year-old son of a heretic to confess to the criminal act of lustful fornication with Eliza. In exchange, his mother's execution was commuted, and the entire family was exiled west. Of course, Plimoth Colony would seize their home and farm, and as the treasurer, Barron would have to ensure the windfall was properly disbursed. After all, Eliza's child would have to be properly raised, and Barron would indeed have plans for the child.

"Lord, during these dire and frightful times, we beseech Thee for divine guidance…" Mather had begun his prayerful jeremiad, so Barron knew he could be alone with his thoughts for at least another thirty minutes. Why were his shins so irritated? Shouldn't his silk stockings alleviate this aggravation? Eliza had caressed his shins with a balm from London earlier in the week, and yet they were still swollen and itchy. He noticed she had intermittently vomited during the caressing, and he increasingly wondered how much of an inconvenience this pregnancy was going to be.

"And we solemnly confess to our sinful nature and wickedness…" Barron cast his attention upon Elijah MacTavish. Though MacTavish piously bowed his head during the first ten minutes of prayer, he was now focused intently upon his fingernails. Refined men such as MacTavish tended to be delicately groomed, and Barron made it a point to emulate his appreciation for the latest fashion from London. Barron knew, however, MacTavish's goodwill was a finite commodity. He expected to see a return on his investment, and was not in the mood to hear any more reports of doddering, blundering militia commanders.

"Through Thy holy power and righteous strength, Thy will shall be done by your chosen people. Amen." Opening prayers were finally concluded, and the council could attend to business. Even Barron noticed that in light of the events of the past few months, Mather's prayers had taken on a tone of even greater humility and apprehension. How could this war be going so poorly for the Lord's chosen people?

Deputy Governor Symonds opened the discussions, which Barron perceived as a slight. Symonds was only a deputy governor. Certainly, Governor Winslow should have been the first to speak. It was just another example of Massachusetts Bay exerting their power and influence.

"Gentlemen, what news? How is it possible that all the resources of these United Colonies cannot track and execute one simple Indian reprobate? Where, pray tell, is King Philip?"

Winslow's voice was subdued. "That is a question that I'm afraid…remains unanswered."

"More importantly, gentlemen…" Symonds' condescending tone infuriated Barron, and he stewed silently. "How have our townships and garrisons proven so vulnerable? Swansea, Deerfield, Northfield, Dartmouth, and Lancaster? Town after town falls prey to heathen wrath. West, south, north, Nipmuc, Wampanoag, Pocasset. Citizens of these colonies are actually being turned away as they flee to the east." Symonds was now pounding the enormous oaken table for effect. "I actually have citizens demanding an enormous palisade to protect Boston. How is this possible? Gentlemen! What is to be done?"

Winslow increasingly resented the notion that he had to answer to Symonds, but the questions were all valid. "These setbacks have been unfortunate, indeed. We are, however, adapting our tactics. We are employing our native allies to a greater extent, and we are integrating them into our operations. Additionally, I propose it's time to eradicate the real threat."

Gookin seemed perplexed. "King Philip? We've been chronically failing in that venture, I'm afraid."

Winslow rose to his feet, and his eyes were blazing with contempt. "The Narragansett."

Superintendent Gookin also rose to his feet, and glowered at Winslow. "The Narragansett? Governor, what madness is this?"

Barron, as expected, noisily admonished Gookin. "You will not speak out of turn! Resume your seat and afford the governor the proper respect!" Winslow, as usual, closed his eyes as Barron ranted, as if trying to ward off a malady of the cranium.

Winslow spoke calmly and methodically. "There is no madness afoot. The Narragansett are the most numerous and powerful enemy nation in our midst. They are the ones who maliciously sent my father a parcel of arrowheads fifty years ago. They have always been a threat, and there can be no true victory until they're eradicated."

Reverend Eliot finally spoke. He was patient and dignified. "Governor Winslow, surely you know the Narragansett have been the Wampanoags' adversaries since before an Englishman set foot on this land. Our missionaries report they have been very unreceptive to Philip's misguided rebellion. They are not fighting this war."

Barron squinted as he cast his dispersion upon Eliot. "And yet, they give aid and succor to the Wampanoag women, children, sick, and elderly!" Winslow resumed his seat and massaged his temples as Barron continued. "They have taken them in! They have signed a treaty in which they have committed themselves to turn over hostile members of the Wampanoag and Pocasset, and they have failed to do so! Their hostility is crystal clear!"

Gookin shook his head in disbelief. "Governor, will there ever be a time in which the United Colonies of New England seek out friends and allies instead of enemies?"

Barron was livid, and demonstrated that he also knew how to pound a table. "Be silent! Silence, I say! We will not tolerate your defeatist treachery! I dare say, your love and zeal for the savages exceeds the devotion you show to your own countrymen! You and Eliot!"

Even Winslow had heard enough of Barron's screeching. He spoke tactfully, and demonstrated how he had ascended the ranks of leadership so quickly. "Thank you, Jeremiah. But it is urgent we address all dissent in this matter. I welcome the input of everyone in the room, especially Reverend Eliot and Superintendent Gookin. Their connections to the Indians of these lands, both social and spiritual, are noteworthy and commendable. But I pray that they may come to see reason in these matters."

Winslow rose again and was now pacing through the assembly. "I know our strategic situation momentarily appears grim, but these are but temporary setbacks. I have no doubt with the right leadership, the United Colonies will soon dispatch King Philip, and bring the Nipmuc to heel. But what of the Narragansett? While it is true their Sachem, Canochet, has negotiated with us and signed a treaty of non-hostility, these matters change quickly. If they are truly friends and not foes, why have they been so reluctant to surrender the enemy sympathizers they've been harboring?"

"Why, indeed? Hear, hear!" The subject of incarcerating hostile Indians was near and dear to MacTavish, and he shouted his approval. "It's insubordination, I dare say. They are compelled to turn over these belligerents!"

Gookin was stunned. "Belligerents? Combatants? They are housing women, children, and the elderly. Turning them over would be the ultimate betrayal!"

"The ultimate betrayal is acting in a manner contrary to the interests of Plimoth Colony!" Barron had moved beyond table-pounding and was now stomping his feet. "Providing sanctuary to any individual in a state of rebellion against Plimoth and England is an abomination! An abomination, I say!"

Winslow remained composed. "Mister Barron speaks the truth. They have violated their sacred obligations to these United Colonies. Their defiance sends a clear message. Gentlemen, I ask you. Are you confident in our ability to defeat the Wampanoag AND the Nipmuc AND the Narragansett? It would be a daunting task, indeed."

"Then don't attack the Narragansett. It is not complicated."

"Ah, a noble sentiment, Superintendent Gookin. But it shows a naïve lack of strategic thinking. Our optimal course of action is to eliminate the Narragansett threat with one fell swoop, and then we can confidently focus our attention on our other adversaries."

Gookin was still aghast. "What have we been doing for all these weeks and months, Governor, if not *confidently focusing our attention*?"

Barron seethed at Gookin's insolence, and was mentally ridiculing his name again. Gooo-kin. Goo-gookin. Goo. The superintendent's fortitude and devotion to New England was nothing but *goo*.

As always, Winslow would not be deterred. "Your point is, once again, acknowledged, Superintendent Gookin. But, speaking as a military man with decades of service to these United Colonies, I am clearly convinced this is the only logical course of action. I will lead the assault myself."

MacTavish was delighted with that revelation, and he enthusiastically cheered. "Huzzah! Huzzah, I say!"

"Deputy Governor? What say you, sir?"

Symonds had been contemplative and silent during the deliberations. He had his doubts about the merits of the plan, but Winslow was certainly one of the greatest military minds in the United Colonies. What's more, any military incursion that would take the fighting far to the west, and far from the outskirts of Boston, was commendable in his eyes. "How many men are you considering, Governor?"

"The Narragansett fortress is of great renown. They boast hundreds of warriors, and will prove to be a challenging adversary. I advocate the largest expeditionary force seen to date in these colonies. Gentlemen. Grant me a thousand well-equipped men of virtue, and I will eliminate the loathsome threat of the Narragansett." MacTavish was now applauding.

Symonds' eyes were wide, but he could not contest Winslow. He sighed deeply. "Very well, it is agreed. One thousand men, proceeding west to Narragansett country."

Gookin was so furious his hands were trembling, and his teeth were clenched. "This is the most misguided venture in the history of warfare. You can't capture Philip, so you have to create a new enemy."

All eyes turned to Barron, and the council members braced themselves for the screeching. Mister Elmer from Connecticut seemed to actually have his fingers in his ears. Surprisingly, Barron was polite and reserved. He curiously unfurled a sheet of parchment, and dipped his quill in his ink jar.

"I see, Superintendent Gookin. And how many men will you be providing for this next phase of the war? Hmm? What's that you say? Absolutely none? No matter. How much specie or monetary notes can you contribute? Will you be providing muskets and armor? Come, come, sir. At least some dried biscuit, or bandages? Speak up, please. I can't hear you." MacTavish could not conceal his snickering.

Gookin maintained his Christian decorum. "You know of the bravery of the Christian Indians, Mister Barron. You know they are resolute, devout, and ready to fight. They know and understand the tactics of our adversary, and you do not. And yet, you keep them bottled up in their Praying Villages like criminals."

"Why, Superintendent! What a fortuitous segue!" Barron spread his arms as if giving a sermon. "Now that our military campaign is resolved, I suspect it is time to address the other glaring issue in our midst. What... to do...with... the Praying Indians?" He sarcastically paused intermittently as if Gookin was a dim-witted child.

"They are free Christians and citizens of England. They are not yours to do anything with."

"Ah, yes. Very interesting, Superintendent. As you're well aware, however, these extraordinary times of peril compel the United Colonies to take extraordinary measures to ensure our security. **Every day**! Every day, Governor Winslow and I field the same questions! Governor, my farm and home were burnt to the ground by savage Indians! Mister Barron, a horde of depraved heathen slaughtered my children and burned down our town. Why, pray tell, do we tolerate them living and congregating in our midst? Congregating and scheming all the while to rape and pillage English settlers?" Barron could only suppress the screeching instinct for so long, and he unleashed the shrill cacophony. *"What do I tell them, Superintendent? Indians! Indians living unscathed and untouched ten miles west of Boston in Natick! And Pukapong! Savages residing fifteen miles southwest of Boston!"*

"Punkapog, Mister Barron. It is pronounced Punkapog." Gookin's calmness and civility were an almost comical contrast to Barron's ranting.

"I pronounce it as enemy territory! And I thank the Almighty the authorities of these United Colonies have seen fit to act!"

Reverend Eliot appeared horrified, and was in no mood to commiserate with Barron. "Act? Governor, what is he speaking of?"

Governor Winslow's eyes darted to the floor and Barron continued. "Exile, of course! We will no longer tolerate these depraved wretches in our community while their brothers burn our homes! It is intolerable. Beginning immediately, these Praying Indians will be exiled to Deer Island. It is for the good of the United Colonies, as well as their own good."

"Their own good? Governor, tell me this a sad joke! Who would order such a thing?"

Governor Winslow finally spoke with an aura of gravitas and regret. "Gentlemen, I am no longer confident we can assure the safety of the Praying Indians. Their Christian faith is not guaranteed to protect them from the wrath of their neighbors."

Eliot's eyes were wide as he turned to his fellow clergyman, Reverend Mather. "Increase! My brother in Christ! This is lunacy! Who will provide for these Christian souls on Deer Island? How will they eat?"

Mather ignored the question, and remained motionless with his head bowed. His silence devastated Reverend Eliot. Eliot rose to his feet, dramatically elevated his right palm high in the air, and opened his mouth to condemn this vile, unchristian plan for the Praying Indians.

Before he could say a word, Winslow rose to his feet and brought the meeting to a close. "Well, seeing as there's no further commentary...Gentlemen. I must bid you, Good Day. I have an army to assemble."

Eliot's hand remained raised, and his mouth remained open as Winslow, Barron, and MacTavish haughtily strode from the room.

CHAPTER FIFTEEN

PROVIDENCE

Frankly, the entire spectacle was absolutely pathetic, yet Brewster was enjoying every moment.

Once again, he was a militiaman. Only this time, instead of serving the holy and righteous United Colonies of New England, he spent his days in the service of Providence. Well, three days to be exact. Three days in the past three weeks.

War had come to New England, and even unruly, unorthodox Providence had to meet its responsibilities. It would be difficult to organize a militia from a community of pacifist Quakers, rebellious Baptists, and Jewish immigrants. Additionally, the city was renowned for its scores of unsavory merchants, whose convictions did not extend past their monthly balance sheets.

Regardless of their lack of Calvinist uniformity and Puritan zeal, however, Providence would have a militia. Additionally, every militia required a commander, and Brewster's commander was certainly…unique. If nothing else, he was experienced. Extremely experienced. He may have been the most "experienced" man in New England. More than that, his fame preceded him, although Massachusetts Bay would say his infamy preceded him.

"Company! Stand at the ready!"

Brewster almost giggled as he tried to stare straight ahead while standing at attention. He used his peripheral vison to peer at the ranks. When they drilled last week, they had approximately forty men. The week prior, they had sixty men. Brewster was now trying to determine if he could count twenty-five men, and it appeared fewer than fifteen of those even carried firearms.

"Ready arms!" It was astounding such an elderly man could still bellow with such volume and authority. He held his sword aloft, imbuing the proceedings with an element of martial élan. The men who had firearms pointed them. The men who did not, like Brewster, pointed imaginary weapons. Their flintlocks were due to arrive from Hartford next week.

"Fire!" The sword came crashing down and there was a deafening din of…something. At least four muskets failed to fire due to procedural errors. Three were only simulating gunfire due to powder rationing, and their clicking noises seemed sad, yet comical. And the others who were actually issued gunpowder and managed to load their muskets correctly seemed to hit…nothing. Brewster thought he heard profane muttering in a language he suspected was Hebrew.

Zeke knelt behind the ranks on one knee. As a Quaker noncombatant, he was armed with bandages and splints. As a cranky fisherman, he was armed with sarcasm and disdain. "Praise heaven! Have we vanquished our foe?" Captain Williams did not appear to be amused.

Brewster could still scarcely fathom the fact that his militia captain was one of the most famous men in the entire New World. Roger Williams was a remarkable seventy-one years old, and he was organizing and leading a military assembly. Additionally, he seemed to be more energetic and enthusiastic than the vast majority of his company.

Brewster wondered if there was anyone in New England, or Old England for that matter, who was not aware of Roger Williams. He certainly had to be the most famous man in Brewster's current colony of residence.

Williams immigrated to Boston in 1631 with his wife, Mary. Like so many others, he quickly became embroiled in religious controversies, and was soon ostracized by the Puritan authorities. He took strong public positions regarding freedom of worship, positions which inevitably led to his exile. He subsequently purchased the land they were standing on from the Narragansett, and named his new settlement Providence. He even served as governor two decades ago.

His relations with the Indians, especially the Narragansett, would continue to be strong. When Plimoth summoned Metacomet for questioning in 1671, Williams offered himself as a hostage to ensure his safe return. Few Englishmen were as trusted and revered among the Indians, and rightfully so.

Brewster had deep regrets that during his four years in Providence, he never previously made Williams' acquaintance. It was remarkably disappointing, as they were (despite their age difference) absolutely kindred spirits. They were both exiled and reviled by Puritan governments. They both were disillusioned with the manner in which the United Colonies treated the native people of New England. They both were unenthused about military ventures, but they knew a strong defense to be an unfortunate and necessary part of life. And finally, they were both devout Christians who didn't seem to fit into any particular denomination.

The militia drills continued, with Captain Williams leading the company in some ill-conceived formation marching. The summer heat was rendering the situation even more unpleasant, and two men had to fall out to compose themselves. The militia activities concluded with demonstrations of close-quarter combat, with birch rods serving as sad approximations of sabers.

The day's affairs were ultimately a bizarre mix of absurdity and tragedy. Watching this esteemed septuagenarian desperately try to mold this disparate, unenthused, and slovenly assortment of locals into some semblance of military force was the absurdity. The reality that a horrific, brutal war was unfolding to their north, and there was now talk of evacuating the women and children to Aquidneck Island, was the tragedy.

It would be difficult to find an English colony more ambivalent about this conflict than Providence. Many of its denizens felt an almost shameful joy in any misfortune that befell their sanctimonious Puritan neighbors. An undercurrent of Quaker pacifism seemed prevalent in any quarter of the city.

The citizens knew first-hand of the capricious injustices of Plimoth, and they harbored deep sympathies for their Indian neighbors. Yet, Captain Williams persevered. The city would be ready for any foe.

The militia assembly mercifully came to an end at three in the afternoon. Brewster was delighted that he would not have to appear at the cooperage, as today was a day for drilling. Mister Barlow had recused himself from any militia obligations due to his age, and Brewster considerately refrained from pointing out the age of their devoted militia captain.

Brewster and Zeke began the journey home. Constance would be preparing supper, and another evening of marital bliss awaited.

"An entire day away from the cooperage, Son? I hope Mister Barlow doesn't feel too ill used."

"It's for the common good, Zeke. I stand ready to defend every bucket and barrel from any savage aggression. I dare say no one in the colony wields a birch rod with as much confident swagger as I." Brewster thrashed his sword hand through the air in a mock battle.

"I fear the only savage aggression in this land is coming from Plimoth. They should all come to the table and end this madness."

"You're an optimistic man, Zeke."

"It comes with the profession. Pessimistic fishermen tend to starve."

"What about pessimistic coopers?"

"I have no idea what happens to pessimistic coopers. I suspect oafish Puritan coopers tend to do well for themselves, however. I might even stake one to buy his own cooperage if I can find a trustworthy one."

"I can't speak for all the other oafish Puritans, but this one wouldn't let you down, Zeke."

"I know that. And the way things are going, this war might never end. If you can't sell buckets and barrels during wartime, you're doing something very wrong." Zeke stopped and faced Brewster.

"I'm very glad to have you in this family, Israel. I never thought Constance could be this happy. I'll say it again and again: You two need to be making tiny little fishermen together. Good-looking, tall lads, with red hair and enormous blue eyes. Make sure they're not nearly as smart as their parents. Otherwise, they'll never do as they're told."

"Count on it, Zeke. And thank you."

CHAPTER SIXTEEN

POCASSET

After the English disasters in the swamps of Pocasset, the victorious joy among Metacomet and his followers quickly dissipated.

It was easy for the warriors to laugh as the English stumbled through the inhospitable terrain, equipped with their enormous pikes, lost dogs, frightened horses, and useless matchlocks. It was easy to feel triumphant as the enemy casualties mounted, and they pathetically bickered amongst themselves. It was easy to heap accolades upon Linto for his brilliant prophecy, and it was easy to ridicule the English predilection to once again waste valuable time constructing a lumbering, unwieldy fort.

But, the sense of victory was fleeting.

As Cudworth and the English abandoned the idea of more catastrophic incursions into the swamp, they sensibly sealed a perimeter around it. Annawon, Nimrod, and hundreds of battle-ready warriors waited with tense anticipation for the opportunity to cut down more enemy soldiers, but none came. They were triumphant, but they were trapped.

By day, they heard the endless "thud thud thud" as trees were felled, and soon, another English fort rose from the ground. By night, they huddled around fires and told sagas of Massasoit, while trying to ignore their hunger. Metacomet repeatedly asked Linto if there were any new revelations from the spirit world, but Linto morosely replied that there were not.

After seven nights had passed, the situation was growing intolerable. Nimrod clamored for a direct assault on the enemy, but by now their fort had taken shape, and they were too well entrenched. A direct confrontation would be devastating.

What should they do? They no longer had the boats or the means to head west across the bay, toward Montaup. Even if they did, their ancestral home was now an English stronghold. They could head south, back to where they deterred the enemy invaders who cowered behind a stone wall. But then what? They would just be wandering further from their allies, closer to forbidding bodies of water, and further from their true objective: The despised government of Plimoth Colony.

They had to find a way to move west and join the Nipmuc. But how? As the nights passed, the notion of directly assaulting the English fort seemed increasingly likely. But Weetamoo, who knew this territory like none other, offered a different plan.

"We can escape by foot. We can head to the north, away from the enemy, and then travel west."

Annawon was perplexed. "But how? There is nothing to the west but an enormous river flowing into the bay. Are you hiding boats somewhere?"

Weetamoo conveyed a sense of confidence. "It can be done. We can move undetected under cover of darkness. When the tides are right, the river can be crossed. We will need rafts for the sick and the children, but we can do it. The water will be no deeper than a man's chest. I've seen it before."

Metacomet was intrigued. "But there will be more enemy forces across the river."

Annawon's enthusiasm was building. "I'm not so sure. I think they are all fortifying Montaup, or they are here fortifying this new fort. And what of Tuspaquin?"

"My sister's husband? He has been wreaking havoc in the Nemasket region. Near the English towns of Tawn-tawn, and..." Metacomet pensively rubbed his chin. "Linto, what do the English call Nemasket?"

"Middleborough, my Sachem."

"Yes, yes. So, it can be done. The English can play with their fort in Montaup. They can play with their new fort here in the swamps. They will be chasing my brother-in-law through Nemasket. We could conceivably reach Menameset and the Nipmucs unmolested."

Nimrod grunted. "We are traveling with hundreds of women and children. They will slow us down, and we will have to fight at a place of the enemy's choosing. Let us fight on our terms. Let us lure more victims into our swamp."

Annawon stood and began pacing. "We've been trying to lure them back for days. I fear they have learned their lesson. And we've seen the fort. I can't imagine assaulting it."

No one spoke, and Linto tended the fire. The loud but comforting sounds of the swamp echoed around them in a nocturnal chorus of crickets, owls, frogs, and birds. The fire crackled, and Linto's face was aglow.

Finally, Metacomet broke the repose. "What do you think, Linto?" Linto seemed so lost in the fire that he didn't respond. "Linto?"

"I think Weetamoo's plan is sound, Sachem."

Metacomet's eyes widened. "Has there been a revelation?" Even by firelight, Nimrod's glare was unmistakably poisonous.

"No, my Sachem. There is no prophecy. I just think it's the right thing to do."

Metacomet tried to conceal his disappointment. "Annawon?"

"It is the most logical course, Sachem. It gives us the opportunity to merge unscathed with the Nipmuc. If we are intercepted, then we fight. If we don't undertake this, our options are assaulting a fort or starving to death."

Metacomet closed his eyes and tried to hear his father's voice. He focused on the familiar call of a boreal owl, but he could not commune with his father's spirit. He was growing anxious and impatient. He had started this rebellion, and he owed his followers a victory. It was true that he and his allies had been outsmarting the English and destroying their settlements throughout the land. But the reality, however, was the English were now comfortably housed in a fort built on Metacomet's home, while his followers were cowering in a cedar swamp. He owed them a renewed sense of purpose. Metacomet owed them hope.

"We move tomorrow night."

Sunlight came early the next morning. Annawon led reconnaissance parties of Pocasset warriors. This was their home, and they seemed to know every stream, ridge, and tree. They moved silently and unbeknownst to their adversaries.

The English positions were predictable. Although the fort was nearing completion, they still had far too many men dedicated to its construction, and far too few performing sentry duties away from the fort. Metacomet's forces would have ample opportunity to slip away under cover of darkness.

Linto and Wawetseka spent the day praying and preparing. Once again, they would abandon whatever semblance of a home they had, and they would become as mobile as possible. Food, medicine, weapons, clothing, and even children's toys were evaluated and prioritized. They made agonizing decisions, and Linto increasingly grew to resent the size of the English Bible.

Weetamoo pleaded with them to permit her some time alone with the children. Perhaps it was a mother's intuition, but it was exactly what the exhausted parents needed. The couple slipped away to a remote enclave, delightfully obscured by all manner of natural camouflage. They held hands. They embraced. They made love, and caressed one another as the birds sang. Despite their momentary euphoria, they both had to suppress their urge to weep. What would become of them, and what would become of their children?

They could have stayed nestled in their secret hideaway for days, but they knew Weetamoo's responsibilities would be considerable. Many of the Pocasset were very ambivalent about even joining this rebellion, and they continued to view it as a mere squabble between Metacomet and Winslow. Now that their home had been invaded and they were preparing to flee, they needed her leadership more than ever.

The sun was setting, and preparations were being finalized. Linto had no doubt that three hundred healthy warriors could flawlessly execute this mission. They were, however, on the move with hundreds of women and children. Additionally, some of the sickest and most elderly would have to remain behind, and Linto prayed for their safety. They would hopefully be able to reach Canochet and the Narragansett, who were sheltering refugees from the war.

The expedition set out to the east. Linto was awestruck by the discipline. Even toddlers seemed soundless and agile. They effortlessly traversed terrain that would drive the English to madness. The moon was a perfect sliver, providing just enough light to maintain their awareness, but not enough to be detected.

After a mile of travel, they crossed the tiny river the English called the Fall River. The water came to Linto's knees, and the expedition had no difficulty carrying children and supplies across the cool, slow-moving water. Linto carried Ahanu on his shoulders, and Wawetseka effortlessly cradled Kanti. Due to the limited moonlight, he could not be certain, but Wawetseka seemed to be smiling as she waded through the refreshing coolness.

Although he could not be certain if his wife was smiling, Linto knew that he was. Reaching and crossing the river was perhaps the most treacherous part of their journey. They would soon be miles from the English fort, and detection was growing increasingly improbable. They were succeeding.

They headed approximately five more miles in a northerly direction. The terrain was grueling, and progress was slow. If they had escaped the deadly threat of the English forces, however, they were soon face-to-face with another cruel enemy: The Taunton River.

The Fall River would be a pleasant summer splash compared to the Taunton. Weetamoo was guiding them to its narrowest point, but it would still be a fearsome undertaking. They would have to spend the remaining hours of the night constructing makeshift rafts, but it was just as well. They would wait until the first rays of daylight to attempt the crossing.

Fabricating rafts in a stealthy manner was another difficult challenge, but the expedition continued to exceed even their own expectations. Utilizing driftwood and timber from the ground to the greatest extent possible, they minimized any noise generated by toppling trees. Linto warily noticed Nimrod was maintaining a healthy distance from him, or more accurately, between himself and Wawetseka.

Metacomet and Wootonekanuske circulated among all of them, offering cheer and encouragement. She had sweet berries for the youngsters, and their eight-year-old son, Mendon, maintained a brave face as well. As a new July morning emerged on the horizon, Annawon was the first to take to the river.

He swam to the deepest point and maintained his position so he could rescue anyone in trouble. Hundreds of men, women, and children utilized any implement of floatation they could manage. Linto pushed the children merrily along on their raft, and fought the urge to sing. Weetamoo had planned the crossing perfectly, and most of the adults were able to keep their feet on the river bottom.

One by one, they emerged on the other side as the summer sun rose behind them. They had done it. Hundreds of them had escaped undetected across the Taunton River, while the English foolishly maintained their fortress and guarded nothing. They could conceivably arrive at their destination long before their adversary even knew anything was amiss.

It was a triumph. And it didn't require a lie, a deception, or any manner of false prophecy.

CHAPTER SEVENTEEN

NIPSACHUCK

If there was one constant in Linto's life, it was this: Seemingly miraculous events were often the precursor to bitter, devastating disappointment.

The fact that hundreds of men, women, and children could so easily defy the clutches of the English warriors seemed miraculous. The manner in which they slipped away under cover of darkness was a testament to their skill and bravery. The humiliation the English must have felt when they realized they were besieging a swamp devoid of enemy combatants must have been staggering.

So, Linto was in a grateful mood when he rose early to pray that morning. According to the English calendar, that particular day was different than the prior day, because it was now a new month.

Yesterday was part of a month dedicated to the memory of a great warrior and emperor named Julius. Evidently, Julius had died long before the Gentle Son was miraculously born of a virgin. Today, however, was a new month, and it was named for a nephew of Julius. This nephew was so impressive even his name meant that he was sacred and revered.

Linto was often perplexed that the English would name their months after self-absorbed emperors who believed they were gods. What was even stranger was these emperors seemed to despise the Gentle Son and His Father. The Father's chosen people lived in a place called Judea, and these emperors conquered and ridiculed them. Why on earth would the English calendar commemorate the enemies of their God?

Linto decided to quit obsessing about such meaningless things, and he embraced the beautiful August morning. Metacomet had led his army across the Taunton River, past the town of Swansea, across the Palmer River, across the Seekonk

River, around the city of Providence, and finally, to yet another swamp. The exhausted expedition camped, and slept blissfully. Even Kanti, Linto's restless daughter, slept without stirring.

The sun had now completely risen, and Weetamoo had sent men out to forage for food. Linto knelt next to an ancient oak tree and communed with the Great Spirit. Although he was deeply saddened the war still persisted, he knew the events of the last month had been relatively tolerable. Battle casualties among the Wampanoag were few, if any. He was still united with Wawetseka and the children. Metacomet had gathered allies, and had perplexed the befuddled English at every turn. Linto still retained the Sachem's unwavering trust, and he prayed a diplomatic solution to the crisis was still possible.

His tranquility was violently shattered when Weetamoo's men tore past him, screaming in terror. Linto understood instantly, and the roar of the muskets echoed through the swamp, punctuated by cries of "**Mohegan, Mohegan!**"

In the future, Linto would look back on that day's tragedy in the Nipsachuck Swamp and wonder. Were they remarkably naïve to think hundreds of them could travel so far through enemy territory and remain undetected? Were they arrogant to believe such a venture could be successful? Or were they simply extremely unlucky that an English clergyman sighted them crossing the Seekonk Plain, and mustered every combatant within a day's march to descend upon their peaceful camp, including the bloodthirsty Mohegans?

Linto dove behind the mammoth oak tree and cowered in stunned silence. After watching the English stumble through the Pocasset swamp like blundering cattle, the Mohegan were a terrifying sight to behold. Their heads were shaven, and their faces were adorned with crimson, blood-like stripes. Their shirtless figures glistened in the morning sun, and their chest and shoulders were caked with the same horrifying, bloody hue. Soon, they came upon their quarry and undertook their business with devastating efficiency.

Arrows soared through the air and found their targets with sickening ease. The English soon arrived as well. Instead of their enormous, cumbersome spears, they wielded lightweight, deadly swords. Metacomet's warriors were roused from their slumber, but instantly lapsed into a state of confused panic. They could scarcely mount a defense, and dozens of them fell victim to the wrath of the Mohegans. Still, Linto cowered behind the tree.

The Sachem's elite inner circle of warriors had now surrounded him, and Metacomet stood poised for combat. Women and children fled deeper into the swamp, and the sound of their terrified cries merged with the triumphant whoops of the Mohegan.

Nimrod emerged from the shadows and echoed his enemy's war cry. He unsheathed his hatchet and moved with chilling fearlessness through the English ranks. One man after another fell in a bloody heap as Nimrod whirled, kicked, swung, and clubbed his way through their midst. Their depleted ranks were quickly backfilled with their Indian allies, and Nimrod vanquished any Mohegan that stood in his path with equal fury.

"*Lackey! Traitor! English boot-licker!*" Nimrod seemed to hiss a new insult for each of his victims. His adversaries seemed initially hypnotized by his ghastly necklace, then fatally wounded in the midst of their distraction.

Linto marveled at the awe-inspiring display of skill and bravery. After seemingly eliminating two young Mohegan warriors with one astounding stroke of his hatchet, Nimrod seemed to pause to revel in his dominance. He leaned back and stared at the heavens. He cried out like a crazed animal spirit and closed his eyes. He dropped his hatchet and extended both arms high into the air. And he collapsed to the earth as the blood poured from his mouth.

Nimrod grasped his chest and tried to breathe. His vision was growing cloudy, but he scanned the battlefield for one more opportunity to kill an English lackey. He watched arrows soaring through the air in a graceful arc, magnificently framed by the clear blue sky before streaking forward on their lethal journey. He fumbled blindly for his hatchet, and then felt a shadowy figure place the hatchet in his right hand, and close his grip. He reached up, and he touched Linto's face to ensure he was real.

Linto desperately wished Wawetseka was by his side. He had no idea what to do for a man who had been shot in the chest with an arrow. He pressed his hands to the wound in an effort to stop the blood, but nothing happened. He tugged gently at the arrow, only to trigger shrieks of agony.

Nimrod was dying.

Nimrod's vision was now failing, and he was coughing blood. He struggled for the energy to speak. "Aren't you frightened, my...my..." The coughing was degenerating into a pathetic gurgling sound. "Aren't you frightened, turtle clan?"

Musket fire sailed five feet above Linto's head. "Yes. I am always frightened. I wish I was more like you, Nimrod." Linto removed his tunic, and was using it to apply as much pressure as he could to the wound. He hunched lower in case the next round of fire was more accurate.

Nimrod stared intensely into Linto's eyes. He was growing disoriented, but his expression conveyed an inconsolable sadness. He had finally gotten his battle against the English, and now he was dying. Nimrod had threatened to kill Linto mere days ago, and now Linto desperately tried to save his life while enemy gunfire flew past his head. Nimrod's voice was now more gurgles than words, and Linto strained to hear.

"I wish...sometimes...I was more like you, Linto." His right hand gripped his hatchet desperately, while his left hand clung tenaciously to Linto's shoulder, as if he could not depart this world as long as he maintained his grip. The ground seemed to spring to life ten feet in front of them, as a musket ball ricocheted in the dirt. "I've done...such terrible things, Linto. I am nothing but...hate. How I hate...there can never... never be peace for me." His breaths were growing fewer and more labored. "Promise. Take care...take...take care of...him. Never...leave him. Promise...Metacomet..."

Linto's wet tears fell on Nimrod's blood-soaked chest. "I will." Nimrod was gone, and Linto had made yet another promise to a dying man.

Although Linto was grief-stricken, he still had the self-awareness to flee. The enemy was closing from all directions, and the fact that he was not slaughtered while tending to Nimrod felt like divine intervention. Linto sprinted faster than any man should conceivably be able to. He had to find Wawetseka. He had to find Metacomet.

Deeper and deeper he staggered into the swamp, and soon the vegetation grew so thick he could not walk. He crawled, he waded, and he climbed. Soon the sound of musket fire subsided, and Linto found the refugees of the battle.

The extent of the catastrophe was becoming increasingly evident. At least two dozen warriors were dead, and Annawon sobbed like a child when he received news of Nimrod. They were once again isolated and struggling for survival in a forbidding, inhospitable swamp. They had no food or powder for their muskets. The women and children seemed to almost outnumber the warriors. And the enemy was certainly planning their final, unstoppable assault.

Exhausted and numb, Metacomet tried to prepare his forces for one final defensive stand. Their muskets were almost useless, but they had arrows. They had clubs and hatchets. They had the swamp, and their spirit would be unbreakable.

And yet, no assault came. The sun rose high in the sky and then began descending. Reconnaissance parties came back with the stunning news. The Mohegan were still pilfering the remains of the camp, and the English were inexplicably idle. They had no intention of any more combat.

And once more, Metacomet and his advisors schemed and planned for another escape. Once again, they would outfox the English, who were stunningly languishing in camp and waiting for reinforcements.

The Sachem of the Wampanoag directed Linto to commune with the spirit world to try and ascertain what went wrong. He ordered Annawon to assemble patrols to plan the optimal route of escape under cover of darkness. Metacomet's son Mendon, who was as frightened, exhausted, and famished as everyone else, had now begun wailing, and the mood turned ashen.

Linto did not have the courage to speak. As the wailing finally subsided, Weetamoo addressed her brother-in-law. "Metacomet, there has to be a new way."

"We were caught by surprise by the Mohegan. They have always been Skunk Genital Winslow's lap dogs. But, I will personally seal their fate after Plimoth lies in ashes. Nothing changes, Weetamoo. We join the Nipmuc, and our combined forces will drive east, and push the English back into the ocean. They can swim to their *mother country*."

The boy's cries burst forth again as his father raised his voice. Metacomet sent him off with his mother, and Annawon cautiously approached. "Sachem, I'm not sure we can fight and still protect the children. Look at how quickly the Mohegan found and assaulted us. It was devastating. They're not traveling with hundreds of helpless children. We have to secure them somehow."

"The Narragansett." All eyes turned to Weetamoo. "The Narragansett will give us safe harbor. Canochet and his mighty fortress."

Metacomet did not meet her eyes. "My father's enemies. We have to beg them to save our families. It is a disgrace."

Annawon tried to offer solace. "It is the wisest course of action, Sachem. They have already provided sanctuary to our youngest and sickest. Their safety will be guaranteed, and we can redouble our efforts. We need to consider this."

Weetamoo continued. "I have seen their fort, Metacomet. It is astounding. It is in the middle of a swamp and can't be assaulted."

Linto liked what he was hearing, and he tried to formulate a prophecy or sign that it was the right thing to do. Failing that, he merely nodded as Metacomet caught his glance. Linto noticed, however, that the lieutenants of the Sakonnet and Pocasset were grimly whispering amongst themselves, and finally, the tallest one stepped forward.

"It is well that you bring your women and children to Canochet and his people. For we are done with you, Metacomet, and we are done with this rebellion of yours. We were promised new wealth, and a land free of English tyranny. And what have you given us? Hunger. Retreat. Swamps. Defeat. More retreat. We have served you for forty sunsets, and you have delivered nothing. We are going home."

Metacomet unsheathed his hatchet, and Annawon wisely jumped between them. He knew this horrific situation could quickly get worse. Annawon turned to face the mutineers. "Are you warriors? Or are you men of comfort? What manner of man does this? You pledged your honor to Metacomet, son of Massasoit, the greatest Sachem of lands near and far. And now, what? Things are difficult? You are afraid?" Annawon held his longbow aloft, high in the air. "Follow me, and I will show you how to humiliate our enemies!"

Annawon's inspirational tirade seemed to fall on deaf ears, and another mutineer stepped forward. "My own brother lies dead in a field of Mohegan slaughter. He is dead! And the fault lies with *you*, son of Massasoit! This rebellion is a fool's errand! You have no plan, and you've accomplished nothing!"

Metacomet clutched his hatchet tighter, and would have hacked the insubordinate coward to pieces if Annawon's powerful grip was not preventing him. Metacomet knew this scoundrel was a Praying Indian, and he feverishly wondered if the other Praying Indians in his ranks could be trusted. He tried to remember the coward's name. *Allerman…Holdermon…*whatever it was, he knew it reminded him of *Sassamon.*

The leader of the budding mutiny was not impressed by Metacomet's fury, and the wailing of frightened children was growing louder. "There was never a warrior more fearsome than Nimrod, and he was cut down today. The Mohegan are with the English! How many other nations fight for Plimoth? We did not join to fight Mohegan. We did not join to huddle in swamps and starve to death. We are leaving, and have nothing to apologize for. Whatever happened to the prophecy?" He stepped forward, and he was close enough to Metacomet that his finger almost touched his face when he pointed at him. "You should apologize to **us**! You are nothing but a failure!"

There was nothing left to do as the warriors stormed out of camp. First, a few dozen left. Then a dozen more downcast men stared at Metacomet, turned, and left. And three dozen more followed. Several hundred warriors ultimately lost their faith in the rebellion on that day, and they abandoned Metacomet. He was left broken and defeated, the warlord of no more than fifty loyal men. Somehow, they had to find the Nipmuc and fight on.

And their families would go south, and would beg the Narragansett for sanctuary.

CHAPTER EIGHTEEN

NIPSACHUCK

When Linto became resigned to the reality of this war, he was prepared to face any hardship in the service of his Sachem. He knew there would be grave peril. There would be hunger, there would be violence, and there would be loss of life. Although he despised this war, Linto was prepared to face almost any challenge for Metacomet and his people. Now, however, he had to endure the one thing he was not adequately prepared for.

He had to send Wawetseka and the children away.

The massacre and subsequent mutiny at Nipsachuck dramatically altered the fortunes of Metacomet and the Wampanoag. The day prior, they were a formidable force of hundreds of warriors that were deceiving and outsmarting their adversary at every turn. Now, they were a humbled and wretched band of no more than sixty warriors. They now confronted an uncontestable fact: There was no way they could continue to support hundreds of women and children and hope to remain a viable fighting force.

Metacomet required no further persuasion. Weetamoo and her trusted warriors would lead the beleaguered non-combatants due south to take refuge with the Narragansett and their impregnable fortress. Metacomet and his loyal soldiers would proceed north to rendezvous with the Nipmuc. Wherever Metacomet went, Linto was duty-bound to follow, and so the event he dreaded was upon them.

It had been a morning of grief, a morning of loss, and a morning of tears. Fathers and mothers embraced, and children sobbed uncontrollably. Linto hoisted his son upon his shoulders, and he tightly embraced his wife and daughter. His cheeks were hot and wet, and his hands were still marred with Nimrod's blood.

"This will pass, my love." Wawetseka was always stronger than Linto during times of crisis. "We will pray, and the spirits will know our cry. Soon the Englishmen will grow tired. They love their homes and things too much, and they won't endure any more villages burned away. The English will give us peace."

Ahanu squirmed and cooed, oblivious to the strife enveloping them. Linto could not take his eyes from his beloved. He wished her words reassured him, but they didn't. "The English will not crave peace after today. The Mohegans were like blood-thirsty animals. We have to find our way with the Nipmuc." Their son was growing so rambunctious Linto took him down from his shoulders. "I fear I don't know how to guide Metacomet anymore. The warriors are losing faith. Where were the spirits during this morning's slaughter?"

"Be strong, and be faithful, Linto. You will do what needs to be done. You are his guide and his conscience, and you are like a son."

Soon, the leadership was assembled, and there was a debate about whether they should await nightfall before evacuating. Their best course of action was apparent, however. English reinforcements from Pocasset could arrive at any minute, and the time to escape was now.

Linto solemnly prepared for their departure. He embraced Wawetseka, and prayed their kiss would not be their last one. She caressed his chest, and she whispered the words she had used to greet him during their courtship four summers ago. Four summers ago, there was no war, and they felt like care-free children.

"Linto, Linto, Linto. Staring at the sky again."

He refrained from tears as he watched Weetamoo lead the caravan of woman and children south. It was time to prepare for his next journey.

Escaping from their newest swamp enclave was relatively easy, even in the daylight. The Mohegan and English were still idle, and seemed oddly uninterested in pursuit. As a band of sixty warriors, they were agile and nimble, and they made tremendous progress on their northwesterly journey. Whereas two days ago, they were imbued with a spirit of rebellion and achievement, they were now saddled with feelings of resignation and defeat.

As Sachem, Metacomet would not part with Wootonekanuske and Mendon. Some perceived it as a gesture of confidence and faith, but others saw selfishness in his actions. Linto felt envious yet anguished as he watched Mendon sprint ahead to be with his father. He was jealous the Sachem was still united with his loved ones, but he and Wawetseka had faith in their decision. Linto's loved ones would be safe in Canochet's fortress, and Linto would fight on. He would try to find a way to end this nightmare.

Linto was pretending to be more fatigued than he was, and he lingered in the rearguard, far from Metacomet. Was there any limit to his deceptions these days? He loathed the thought of his next council with the Sachem. What advice could he possibly offer? Was there any spiritual guidance for a dispirited, exhausted shell of an army?

If there was any joy to be had, it was derived from the natural splendor of the land. As they proceeded northwest into Nipmuc territory, the gently rolling terrain was growing steeper. The cinnamon ferns were growing denser, and their telltale reddish stalks seemed to be ubiquitous. The sweet pepperbushes were approaching their late-summer peak, and as Linto breathed deeply, he was soon soothed by the unique fragrance. He daydreamed about napping under an enormous grove of chestnut trees, but he knew that was not to be.

Their pace was methodical yet grueling. Scouts scoured every direction for signs of the English and their depraved Mohegan underlings. Linto knew they would see at least two more sunrises on this arduous journey, and he tried to suppress his hunger.

During the second night of the journey, they camped on the southern tip of Quaboag Pond. After a meager excuse for a meal, Linto was assigned sentry duty on the northeast side of the water, approximately one mile away. He carried a dilapidated hatchet and little else. The forest was partially illuminated by clear skies and a beautiful moon. Linto climbed an ancient oak tree, and prepared himself for a long, lonely night.

Soon Linto's apprehension was eclipsed by drowsy boredom. Linto knew he had to stay occupied and alert, and he gazed at the moon. It was a sliver when they left Pocasset, but now it was growing. He opted to recite all the moons he was taught as a child in order to pass the time.

He knew this was the month of Augustus on the English calendar, named for the old King of Rome, and so far, he didn't like this new month one bit. The moon, however, was the green corn moon, and last month was the full thunder moon. It certainly adhered to its reputation, as the July rains were incessant. Linto knew there would be very little green corn to nurture during this summer.

Next month would be the full corn moon, and the thought filled Linto with grim resignation. Would any of them even be alive to see the new moon? Would there be corn to harvest anywhere, or would the English put all of their crops to the torch?

Assuming they could stay fed and stay alive, the next month would be the hunter's moon. Would they be the hunters or the hunted? With minimal crops to rely on, their hunting skills would be more crucial than ever. Afterwards, winter would be upon them, and the beaver moon would be shining in the sky. Linto knew there would be few if any beaver traps this year, and winter would be a brutal ordeal.

Winter. Inevitable, brutal winter. After the beaver moon came the long night moon, and then the full wolf moon. The notion of wolves reminded Linto of the cruel dangers lurking in every shadow. He closed his eyes and listened intently for footsteps, whispers, or the menacing growl of a four-legged English beast of war. The silence was reassuring but eerie.

Could he hear himself breathing? Was that the sound of his heart?

Linto resolved to focus on the task at hand. After the full wolf moon would come the full snow moon. How would they survive the full snow moon? Would this war stop when the snow was above a man's waist? The mere thought made Linto shiver, even on this balmy August night.

Assuming he survived the full snow moon, spring would finally be lurking, and they would be greeted by a full worm moon, and the joyous return of the robins. It would then be followed by the full pink moon, and then the delight of the full flower moon.

Linto thought deeply about the full flower moon, which the English called May. Why did they call it May? Was there a King of Rome named May? There was Julius and Augustus. Was there a Maius? Or a Juneus? When were they the Kings of Rome? Linto thought more about this, and he was saddened by the fact he would probably never get the chance to ask the question. Sassamon knew all of these things, but he was murdered and entombed in a frozen pond, perhaps rightfully so. Linto reminisced about John Eliot, the Englishman, who would bring his translated Bibles and his funny lip hair to the missionary services. He would certainly know the answer, but Linto knew there would be no more missionary services for the Wampanoag. And Two Ponds. Two Ponds would know all about the Kings of Rome. Would he ever see Two Ponds again?

He tried to divert his attention to happier thoughts, and he thought of the full flower moon. He thought of that spring day four years ago, when Wawetseka snuck up on him.

"Are you dreaming, my love?"

Would Wawetseka and the children be safely ensconced with the Narragansett by now? No, that would be impossible. It would take at least three sunrises with all the children in tow. He wondered what Wawetseka was doing right now. Was she huddled by a fire? Was she caressing the children's backs and singing songs for them? Was she thinking about him?

Did he recite all of the moons? Oh, yes. The strawberry moon. How could forget the strawberry moon? Everything seemed to trigger a poignant memory on that evening, and strawberries reminded him of the day Two Ponds showed up alone and unannounced at Montaup. He wanted Metacomet to talk with the Quaker men in hopes of preventing the war, and Linto gave him strawberries on that day. What would Linto be doing right now if Metacomet listened to the Quaker men and there was no war? He wouldn't be up in a tree, alone with his thoughts, and desperately afraid of the Mohegan. He would be in his wetu at Montaup, eating venison and beans, and making a third beautiful child with his beautiful wife.

Linto closed his eyes again and listened more intently than ever. The low murmur of the forest may have well been silence. He patiently tried to distinguish the sound of a comrade to help him while away the hours of solitude. He was delighted to hear the song of a lone mockingbird in the dead of night, and he closed his eyes and focused on the soothing rhythms. *"Ta-tuh. Ta-tuh. Ta-tuh. Ta-tuh. Hoo-hoo-hoo-hoo."* It wasn't long before his nocturnal friend was joined by a screech owl. *"Wooo-buh-buh-buh."* For some reason, the screech owl made him reminisce about his day in Plimoth court, and the angry man with the bulbous eyes presiding over the affair.

Why could he only hear mockingbirds and screech owls in the dead of night? Why wouldn't the spirit world call out to him? He was the lone survivor in an Abenaki sea of death and disease, but no matter how he pleaded, the spirit world was silent. He thought of Samuel in the English Bible, who didn't have to do anything. He was just a child, and yet the voice of God called out to him. Linto's mind then turned to the Gentle Son, and how He left the distractions of the world for forty days so He could go to the desert to pray. The Gentle Son even heard the call of the wicked spirit, who tried to tempt Him with wealth and power. Linto wondered how he himself would respond if he was tempted with such things. What good would wealth and power do? All Linto wanted now was to be with his family, and to see the killing stop.

Linto opened his eyes and peered through the darkness. He thought about Nimrod, and how frightened he looked at the moment he died. Nimrod had lived a life full of hatred and terrible, violent deeds. How would the spirit world receive him? Sassamon used to say the Gentle Son had the power to forgive sins. Did He forgive Sassamon for all of his wickedness and theft? If Sassamon was a disciple of the Gentle Son, how could he be so greedy? Why were the English so greedy? Didn't they have enough wonderful things?

Linto closed his eyes again and focused on the sound of his breaths. Even his winged friends had gone strangely silent. He now heard a low moan in the distance, and it seemed to be growing louder. Did he hear laughter? Linto's heart almost stopped when he thought he discerned a blood-curdling scream in the distance. Was this it? Was this a revelation from the spirit world?

He sat up straight in the tree and opened his eyes. There was a mysterious, glowing illumination in the distance, and although they were almost inaudible, Linto thought he could understand some of the words he heard. *"Lord, have mercy...Run...God, deliver us."* What did the strange words mean? Was he hallucinating?

The glowing grew brighter, and soon the unmistakable aroma of burning wood filled his nostrils. The screams were more frequent and piercing. There was a ghastly shriek of a war cry, followed by cries of terror.

Linto leapt from the tree and began running. He ran due south, and he ran as quickly away from the screams as he possibly could.

CHAPTER NINETEEN

QUABOAG POND

Linto felt faint. He gasped for breath, and as his vision blurred, he wondered if he was about to lose consciousness.

He had done his duty. He was the sentry of the north, and he had been vigilant and alert. Due to his lack of breath, his report was terse. There was a village being ravaged a few miles from their position, and the victims were almost certainly English. The aroma was beginning to waft south. Usually associated with comfort and warmth, the smell of burning wood exuded an aura of hideous suffering on this evening.

"We must hurry. There will be an opportunity for prisoners." Annawon responded as a good war captain should. He was ready for action, and he prepared to organize an assault.

Metacomet morosely shook his head. "No. We stay and fortify our camp. The situation is completely unknown. Linto heard English cries of suffering, but what else do we know? There could be five hundred Englishmen enroute."

"Or Mohegans." Linto instantly regretted his comment. He should have been instilling confidence in the warriors, and not fear.

Annawon was not easily deterred. "Sachem, think of the opportunity. Tonight, our warriors can be redeemed with English blood. We are desperate for a genuine victory."

"No. Not tonight. Look at our ranks, Annawon. How many more casualties can we endure? We do not go on the offensive unless we know the opponent we are facing. Tonight, we remain on guard and ready for anything. In the morning, we proceed on our journey."

And Linto surreptitiously breathed a sigh of relief.

No one expected sleep that night. Sentries scattered, and men assumed camouflaged, tactical positions. Fires were extinguished, and whispers mingled with the symphony of the forest. Metacomet and Wootonekanuske huddled with Mendon, and Metacomet requested Linto's company.

Linto suspected Mendon was now reaching his ninth summer. It was an awkward age even under the best of circumstances, and Linto sympathized with the plight of such a child during this cataclysm. By eight or nine summers, a child is acutely aware of everything that is transpiring. He was old enough that, as a child of a Sachem and member of the wolf clan, he would be expected to show bravery in the face of adversity. But no matter what, children are children, and Mendon was frequently found in the arms of his mother.

"Once again, Linto, the spirits have placed you in the right place at the right time."

Linto peered through the darkness and suspected Metacomet was smiling. "I was merely the first to hear the turmoil, Sachem. I am sorry I brought so little information."

"Nonsense. You are an outstanding sentry. And a blessed prophet." Linto, as usual, was growing uncomfortable when this subject was discussed. He repositioned his legs so he was sitting cross-legged, and Metacomet continued. "Tell me about Nimrod's final moments. Annawon said you were there."

Conversing in the darkness was becoming increasingly eerie. Linto wished he could light a fire. "I was alone, and engaged in morning prayers, Sachem. And then the Mohegan came. They came out of nowhere. I was unarmed, and…and…I was not brave. I hid behind a tree." Linto shamefully hung his head.

"You are of the turtle clan. You are not a warrior, Linto."

"I wish I could have done more. I sat there like a coward as Nimrod tore through the enemy. He was ferocious, and the spirits were with him. I didn't think he could be…stopped."

"But you were with him at the end."

"I tried to do something, Sachem, but the wound was devastating. I hope I provided some comfort before he left for his journey. Wawetseka knows so much more about healing. I wish I…"

"I know, Linto. I know." Metacomet strained to hear any sound from his warriors, but the deathly still was undisturbed. He could sense his son's growing discomfort, and he hoped to lighten the mood.

"Tell us a story, Linto. Tell us a tale from the big, English book."

Linto was secretly relieved, as he had no desire to speak of Nimrod, deathbed promises, or prophecies from the spirit world. He turned and faced Mendon, but he could not discern his expression in the darkness. "Would you like to hear about the time the English God got so mad, He made it rain non-stop for more than an entire moon? And then there was only one boat left…"

Mendon lightly chuckled. "We all know that! There was a husband and wife of every kind of animal! They had to start everything all over again. There are all kinds of wild animals across the ocean."

Linto smiled. "Yes. They have enormous animals over there. One has a big, long nose. Eliot the Englishman told me they are called elephants. They weigh more than fifty men!"

"Then how did they fit two of them on the boat?" Linto merely smiled. "And what about the bugs, Linto? Were there two of each bug?"

"I don't know, Mendon. Eliot never said. Maybe the bugs all flew away?"

The familiar story of the flood was boring Metacomet. "Tell us a tale we haven't heard before, Linto. Tell us something from the second book."

"The Gentle Son?"

"Yes. Tell us about the Gentle Son."

Linto closed his eyes to concentrate. He quickly selected a story. "Sometimes, the Gentle Son wasn't always gentle. Sometimes, he got really angry."

"He did? When?"

"Well, when he was alive, there was a really big church. Really big. It was made of stone, and the ceilings were made of cedar. There were many rooms, but Eliot said there was one room that was so holy, that only their best holy man could go into it."

"Was the Gentle Son allowed to go there? Wasn't he their best holy man?"

Linto wrinkled his brow. "I'm not sure. I would think so. Sometimes, though, they didn't seem to like him very much. They thought he was causing too much trouble."

Mendon was enjoying the tale. "So, they killed him! They nailed him to a piece of wood!"

"Yes, but that came later, Mendon. Right now, we're talking about the story of the money changers. Now, the people all called this big church the temple. It was really special. They killed animals, especially birds and cows, and they presented them there so the English God wouldn't get mad."

"God wants dead animals? Didn't he create the animals? Why would he need them?"

Linto wrinkled his brow again. This was more confusing than he thought. He wished Eliot or Two Ponds was here to explain these things. Sometimes he even wished he could have spent more time with Sassamon. Sassamon knew all these things. How could Sassamon have been so smart, yet so rotten? Why did he have to betray them the way he did?

"I don't know, Sachem. This is what the people did back then. They sacrificed animals to their God. Eliot said they were called the Hebrews. The Hebrews had a big, big church to honor God, but they had a lot of people trading outside."

"Trading? Like furs and knives?"

"Well, no. It was mostly money. They exchanged money."

"They traded money for money? What was the point of that?"

Linto was growing increasingly discouraged. He regretted his choice of tales and wondered if it was too late to discuss Lazarus and the tomb. He should have paid more attention when Eliot taught him the lesson of the money changers. "I think some of the money was bad. It was from the Kingdom of Rome. They needed their own Hebrew money for the temple."

"The English God doesn't take Kingdom of Rome money?"

"Well, it is confusing, Sachem. I guess I'm not explaining things very well. But the point is, the Gentle Son got angry and chased everyone away. He said the big church should have been only about his Father in heaven, but the Hebrews at the temple were making it all about money."

"Ahh. So, the Hebrews were bad. That's why they're not allowed in Plimoth Colony? Do I have that right, Linto?"

Linto remained silent because he remembered when Reverend Eliot explained that the Gentle Son was a Hebrew. His ancestor was King David, who killed Goliath, and then became King of the Hebrews. How could the Hebrews be bad? Why couldn't they live in Plimoth Colony?

Linto was relieved when Mendon grew weary of the unimpressively told tale and whispered to his mother that he was hungry. She had some grasshoppers and worms stashed away, and she took him away for his pitiful midnight meal. She hoped he would fall to slumber soon thereafter.

After they were out of earshot, Metacomet lost interest in the money changers. "I know Annawon believes me wrong, but we have no business joining someone else's fight tonight, Linto. We are too depleted. Our path is certain. We will join the Nipmuc, and I will lead the combined forces."

Linto was considering how much he would enjoy some grasshoppers and worms at that moment. He nodded, and was uncertain if Metacomet could see his silent assent in the darkness. Linto knew Metacomet's dreaded question was now coming, and Linto had spent the last few days trying to avoid it.

"Did you foresee any of these terrible events, Linto? Why are things suddenly so bad?" Linto didn't have an answer, and Metacomet persisted. "Was the spirit world silent? You've given us so much until this disaster."

"Forgive me, Sachem. I can't control the visions. I pray and I pray for guidance, but sometimes my cries go unanswered." He paused, mistakenly believing a sentry was approaching, but it was only a small woodland animal, rustling in the distance. "But this might be divine will. Look at the Hebrews. Look how King David was tormented and reviled by King Saul before he became king. David had to hide and be patient."

"Hide. How I despise that word. It's little wonder so many warriors have left us. But they're fools, Linto. They don't understand the prophecy."

Linto mentally prepared himself to ask a difficult question of his own. He had promised Metacomet victory with his false prophecy, but he wanted to genuinely understand what Metacomet thought was real, and what he thought was impossible. "Sachem, what do you believe will happen by the next strawberry moon?"

"Strawberry moon? Something will happen?"

"I mean...next summer. Will the war still be going on?"

"Aren't you the prophet? What kind of holy man are you?" Linto was uncertain whether to smile or wince, so he did nothing. He thought Metacomet was smiling, but again, there was the darkness.

"I'm not a fool, Linto. We have our prophecy, but they have the numbers. We like to talk about driving them all back into the sea, but there are thousands and thousands of them. And across the sea in England...how many more?"

Metacomet now stood and tried to keep his voice to a whisper. "We will wear them down, Linto. We will join with the Nipmuc, and burn villages and slaughter cattle. We will hide, and ambush their noisy soldiers. We will steal their supplies. We will push the English further and further east, and their families across the sea will not want to come here anymore. They will grow weary and tired, and they will give us peace. They will give us land. How much? I don't know. Before the strawberry moon? Probably not. It may take two or three winters. They are stubborn people, Linto. But do not be discouraged. The day of victory will come. We have already sacrificed so much, but the day of victory will come."

The Sachem decided it was time to join his family for a few hours of slumber. Linto resumed a sentry position not far from camp, but within minutes, he too had succumbed to exhaustion, and soon daylight was blessedly upon them. The warriors quickly assembled and resumed their northwesterly trek.

Annawon led the expedition around the southern tip of Quaboag Pond, then north across the Quaboag River. Quacumquasit Pond was immediately to their south, and the sunlight glistened spectacularly across its cool water. A few hours later, the sun was almost at its zenith when three arrows sailed high over Annawon's head in quick succession. He interpreted the gesture correctly, and his voice was deafening.

"Metacomet seeks counsel with the Nipmuc! The warriors of the Wampanoag have arrived!"

They were immediately greeted by two sentries of the Nipmuc. They were both tall and shirtless, and their arms were adorned with tattoos and armbands denoting their warrior status. The one with the most armbands grinned broadly and spoke.

"I told you, Askook. I told you the Wampanoag were fighting in this war that they started. It's only been two moons, and here they are!"

Askook did not seem to be fond of sarcasm. He embraced Annawon. After scanning the expedition, he seemed puzzled. "Where are your warriors?"

Annawon grimly replied, "These are the warriors. These are the loyal warriors of the Wampanoag."

Askook appeared stunned. "Fifty? Sixty? How is this possible? Are the others on a mission? Why did you split your forces?" Askook inferred by Annawon's silence that there were no other warriors, and he was in no mood to discuss the issue.

"Come, Annawon. Come. You must be hungry. The sisters are anxious to see you. Where is Metacomet?"

182 | P a g e

"He is in the rearguard. With his wife and son."

The aroma of burnt wood still seemed to linger in the air as they proceeded three miles north. They soon arrived in the Nipmuc village of Menameset. Hundreds of Nipmuc were diligently attending their business. Warriors were skirmishing in hand-to-hand combat training, women were husking corn and preparing fish, and spiritual elders were singing war songs. Linto was astonished. Mendon burst into a sprint when he saw the corn, and Metacomet beamed with delight.

Askook disappeared for a short time, but returned with two ceremonial drinking vessels. Carved from oak, they were wide, short, and round. They were unimpressive, save for the spectacular handles carved into the likeness of a wolf. The drinking vessels were charged with fresh water, and laced with a variety of berries. "The sisters are ready for you. They will see you and Annawon, but no one else."

He escorted them into one of the most enormous wetus Metacomet had ever seen. Deep inside, two young women sat on wooden benches piled with furs, and seemed to be attended to by a host of underlings. Metacomet awaited the invitation to sit, but it never came.

"Ah. Metacomet. Son of Massasoit. Son of the greatest Sachem of the nations, and the greatest English lackey." Her derision was met with muted laughter. "Drink your berry water. Have you travelled far?"

Metacomet stewed silently at the disrespect. "We have arrived from Pocasset, where we slaughtered the clumsy English in the swamps. We strategically withdrew under cover of night, but were ambushed by the Mohegan three days southeast of here. The Mohegan are the true lackeys of the English."

"*Sachem Chogan!*" Askook was quick to anger. "You will address her as Sachem Chogan!"

Throughout the years, Metacomet had become acclimated to condescending behavior from Plimoth, but this lack of respect was new and unwelcome. He gritted his teeth. "Sachem Chogan."

Chogan was now smiling. "Strategically withdrew? Is that what they call cowardice in Montaup these days?" This time, the laughter was less subdued. "Oh, forgive me. Montaup is now an English fortress."

Metacomet was struggling to control his temper, and spoke in a slow, deliberate fashion. "Sachem Chogan. Our ranks have been depleted due to a vicious assault from the Mohegan. Grant us warriors. Grant us a hundred fine Nipmuc warriors, so I may lead them into battle. Let us restore the grand alliance of our fathers. United, the Nipmuc and Wampanoag will prove unstoppable."

An uneasy silence descended on the wetu. Chogan had closed her eyes, and was now holding hands with the other woman seated beside her. At first glance, they appeared to be radically dissimilar in appearance. The other woman had shaven her head, and painted her entire visage a deep black color. She did not wear a tunic of any fashion, but five or six heavy, ornate necklaces concealed her bare breasts. She did not speak a word.

Later, Metacomet would come to understand their relationship. Daughters of the great Sachem of the Nipmuc, they ruled the nation in unison. Not only were they daughters, but they were identical twins. They were Chogan the Bluebird, and Chosoki the Blackbird. Before reaching womanhood, Chosoki took vows of silence and celibacy. From that day, she did not speak, and she would not lie with a man. She was the bride of the spirit world, and Chogan attested she could communicate with her sister by silently holding her hand, and listening intently.

After what seemed to be an eternity, Chogan released her gentle grip. "The Blackbird's thoughts are clear, and I agree. Putting fighting men in your care would be madness. You come here with your army decimated, and you plead for more men? This is **your** war, *King Philip*. You started this. You told the nations to rise up and rebel. You said together, we would cast off the English yoke. And what have you done since then? You've abandoned your ancestral stronghold. You've hidden away in a swamp. Your forces were slaughtered like fattened hogs at Nipsachuck. And you come to us because you are a leader who should have more warriors?"

Metacomet shifted his gaze to the floor as she continued. "Where were our Nipmuc warriors last night? They were torching the English village at Quaboag! What did the English call it, Askook?"

"Brookfield, Sachem Chogan."

"Brookfield! North field, south field, deer field, this field, that field! No matter! It is gone! With plenty of food and plunder for the people! And, where were you? You had to be near. Where was the mighty King Philip of the Wampanoag?"

Metacomet gently rested his hand on Annawon's shoulder. He could tell Annawon was ready to snap at the provocation. Fortunately, the Bluebird did not await the embarrassment of a response.

"You are here now, Metacomet. In the spirit of our fathers, your meager forces may join us as we cast off the English yoke. You may accompany us on our raids, and who knows? You may even kill your first Englishman. But do not come to our lands with the intention of "leading" us, or commanding us. That is final. Now, make sure your men get plenty to eat. I anticipate more combat this week. You are dismissed now."

Metacomet and Annawon slowly made their exit. The men assembled in the wetu were dignified enough to remain silent. Metacomet was twenty paces outside the wetu when he turned to Annawon.

"This is not our destiny, Annawon. This is not our destiny at all."

CHAPTER TWENTY

PROVIDENCE

There were countless examples of the Lord's breathtaking artistry in this world.

Brewster thought long and hard about this topic as he concentrated on his third barrel of the morning. More precisely, he was laboring on a kilderkin, with only half the capacity of a barrel. The staves were already complete, set upright, and ready for the hoops. Brewster was delighted as he forced the first hoop into position. The symmetry was remarkable, and Brewster could hardly wait to behold the finished product.

Brewster set aside his own handiwork and stepped outside into the autumn chill to admire the Lord's handiwork. He inhaled deeply and smiled. It had been a glorious season of natural beauty. The leaves of northern red oaks had transitioned from a bold red to a muted orange, and then to a warm dark brown. The beech trees had started the season with a golden hue, but were now a deep bronze. The foliage on the sumac trees behind Zeke's house had turned such an intense shade of red that they were practically purple. And the sugar maple trees across the street from the cooperage were a cavalcade of reds, oranges, and yellows. The warm, gentle fires in the chimneys of Providence rendered a delightful aroma that wafted past the cooperage. The season was truly a gift from the Almighty.

"You there!"

As always, when Easton came to visit Brewster in the cooperage, he commemorated their first eventful meeting with a condescending "you there." Brewster knew he could never tire of it, but he detected an aura of melancholy caution in Easton's voice.

"I thought coopers were known to do some work and not spend their days staring at trees."

"Perhaps I'm deep in thought about procuring timber for my labors. Do not underestimate me, John Easton."

"Harrumph. As the deputy governor, I am authorized to underestimate you, overestimate you, and then ignore you. And that's just before lunch." Easton seemed his usual jovial self, but he also seemed to somehow be dreading the visit. "Can we sit down, Israel?"

Brewster guided him to an unusual bench outside the cooperage that was crafted four years ago from the remnants of his early coopering failures. At the time Mister Barlow thought long and hard if he had committed a grievous error by taking a mysterious stranger from Middleborough into his employ. Brewster's work improved tremendously, however, and the bench was somehow still standing four years later.

"How fares the militia?"

"I suspect we could successfully defend Providence against an onslaught of rabbits and squirrels. If they ally themselves with an aggressive pack of beavers, however, then all is lost."

"That bad? Even with Captain Williams at the helm?"

"We could have Lord Protector Cromwell at the helm, and the small, furry, woodland creatures would still inflict terror in our midst."

"The militia is a serious matter, Israel."

"I know that."

There was a long, awkward pause and Easton stared at his shoes. "Where is Brownie today? I noticed a lack of foulness immediately."

"Zeke took her out to deliver food to some widows south of town." Sometimes, Brewster wondered if the horse jokes were getting a little tiresome. Clearly, his friend Easton had arrived with unpleasant news and was dawdling.

"I've never seen the sugar maples look so sharp. I dare say I can see three different shades of orange. I remember a maple tree from my youth I used to climb. Every spring it would..."

"John, why have you come?" Brewster hated to be so terse, but the procrastination was making him uncomfortable.

Easton sighed deeply and rose to his feet. "Israel, I know how you've detached yourself from Plimoth Colony."

"They certainly make it easy."

"Well, you may know the war is not going well."

"That depends on your perspective."

Easton was surprised and a bit dismayed at Brewster's callousness. "They've been trying to capture King Philip for months, and I dare say he's slipped through their grasp again. They think he's with the Nipmuc now, but he's badly weakened." Easton could not meet Brewster's gaze, and he continued to admire the sugar maples.

"And yet, Providence is safe, and the cooperage grows more prosperous. As you reap, so shall you sow, Governor."

"But you know of Philip's allies, Israel? You know of the Black Sachem? Tuspaquin?"

"From the Nemasket? Isn't he kin to Philip?"

"He married Philip's sister."

"What of him?"

"He's been leading raids throughout the colony, Israel. Dartmouth..." Easton resumed his seat and finally faced Brewster. "Middleborough..."

Brewster remained silent, and Easton finally noticed how loud the cooperage could get. Inside, workmen noisily indulged in their craft. Outside, the wind was steadily picking up, and colorful, fiery leaves were being carried aloft.

Brewster rose to his feet and rubbed his face. "Middleborough?"

"I'm afraid so. The reports are pouring in. There can be no mistake."

He was now pacing. "A few homes? The mill?"

"The reports claim everything was decimated."

"Everything? Including the..."

"Yes. The meeting house is gone. Your old home is no more. Everything."

Brewster's face felt hot, and he wanted to wipe his moist eyes. He hated the next question. How much death and misery had he already witnessed in his short life?

"Casualties?"

"Not as horrific as you'd think. The citizens seemed to have ample warning, and almost all fled to Plimoth. I'm afraid five adults and an infant were caught in the inferno of the meeting house." Easton had the names via written correspondence, but felt like it was inappropriate to recite them. His hands gently quivered as he handed the parchment to Brewster.

> To my brothers in Christ,
>
> It is with a grave and heavy heart that I must report the catastrophic and wanton destruction of Middleborough in Plimoth Colony at the hands of the heathen Tuspaquin, known to some as the "Black Sachem." All structures and homes destroyed by torch and flame. Praise God, all citizens safely secure in the fortifications of Plimoth, save six saints who were trapped while serving the Lord in the meeting house: Isaac Stewart, carpenter, Susanna Stewart, wife and mother, Martha Leister, widow, and tragically, the Reverend Peter Phelps and his beloved Alice, parents of one infant.
>
> Plimoth once again calls on their brethren in these Christian, God-fearing colonies of New England to provide brave men, weapons, supplies, and succor, and to stand united against the treasonous onslaught of the savages. Most importantly, we implore each and every one for prayers and blessings, and to grieve in Christian spirit with the families of the vanquished.
>
> Blessings upon you
> Captain T. Prentice, Plimoth Colony

Brewster read the letter three more times, and wiped away the tears. Middleborough. Home of his ministry. Home of his beloved Sarah and daughter Patience, now with the Lord for so many years. And Alice. He knew her as Alice Fuller, the loveliest flower in Middleborough. Brewster was certain she was to be his wife until she was brazenly purloined by the dashing Reverend Phelps. Now, suddenly, they were both at peace and with the Lord.

He scanned the letter one final time, and had no doubts he did not know the Stewarts. Sometimes it was easy to forget he had not set foot in Middleborough (or Plimoth Colony) for at least four years. He did, however, know Martha Leister, and he was pained by the memory.

Brewster closed his eyes and tried to recall the summer night Missus Leister came to his Middleborough home for grief counseling. He could picture her red, anguish-stricken face as she relived her torment. Her husband and only child had recently been taken from her, as they became lost and disoriented in a blizzard.

How she agonized about her fate. Brewster could recall every detail of their conversation, and the stark, unsettling questions she asked. Was her life unpleasing to the Lord in some manner? As an upstanding citizen among God's chosen people, was she not among the saints? Why should a righteous woman be made to suffer so? But now, Martha Leister, along with her husband and son, was also at peace. Brewster prayed she found some solace during her final years, and had embraced her blessed assurance before her hideous demise. He cursed his sad inability to truly provide comfort on that evening.

Easton roused him from the past. "I'm sorry, Israel. I know this is unbearable." Easton clutched Brewster's slumped shoulder in a fatherly gesture. *"And ye now therefore have sorrow: but I will see you again, and your heart shall rejoice, and your joy no man taketh from you."*

Israel's face was in his hands. "The Gospel of John, chapter sixteen…" His thoughts trailed off as he gently closed his eyes. He didn't finish his reference.

Easton began his own frantic pacing. "We tried to stop this, Israel. Who marched alone into Montaup? Who has done more than you or I?" His words were scant comfort, as Brewster knew he had heard them before.

Brewster kept his eyes closed and tried to picture the calamity. He pictured the merciless flames consuming the home where Sarah suffered so horribly while giving birth. He imagined the ghastly smoke pouring from the meeting house as frightened children ran to their parents, and invaders whooped with triumph. How many sermons had he given there? How many prayers had he led?

"I'm sure Mister Barlow will give you your leave today. Let us be with Constance, and we will pray."

Brewster recalled very little of the journey home. His grief was obvious, and Constance tenderly embraced him. She knew that despite living lives of pacifism far from Plimoth, sooner or later, in some painful manner, the war would come to haunt and torment them.

They sat in the front room, and Zeke arrived soon thereafter. He made tea, and the quartet spent the afternoon with prayer and scripture. Brewster was numb and said little. He finally excused himself, and decided to take Brownie on a ride through the city.

As the afternoon wore on, the gentle breeze of the autumn morning gradually gave way to howling winds. Trees bent and swayed, and the Lord's colorful handiwork was torn asunder. The skies turned gray, and the mysterious horseman kept his head down while plodding through the dirt streets. Upon recognizing him, urchins threw apple cores in his direction and scampered, knowing they'd usually get a jovial, mock reprimand, and Brownie would happily find a morsel or two. Even Brownie, however, seemed morose and uninterested.

The rains inevitably came, and Brewster was without any warm attire. Brownie snorted, and their pace slowed to a crawl. Brewster forced his eyes open, for fear of being tormented by images of Middleborough parishioners being enveloped by flames. Still, he was haunted by Martha Leister. Her voice echoed in his mind as the rains intensified.

"Do you ever wonder, Reverend? Wonder about..."

"Do I wonder...about what, Mrs. Leister?"

"About the Almighty. And suffering. Our destinies, Reverend. Was my husband, Bartholomew, predestined to die? What manner of wickedness have I manifest, so that my child, Peter, should suffer so? Was I not pleasing to the Almighty in manner of thought and deed?"

Brewster had no idea how much time had elapsed. He was thoroughly soaked. His eyes peered forward, and he was stunned to be back at his home. Brownie seemed to know when he shouldn't be alone any longer.

Easton had never left, and he didn't say a word. He took Brownie's mount, and prepared her food. Brewster lumbered speechlessly into the home, positioned himself by the hearth, and spent the rest of the evening staring intensely into the flames.

CHAPTER TWENTY-ONE

PROVIDENCE

Brewster awoke before dawn. The rain and wind were tormenting the white pine shingles, and slumber was increasingly difficult.

He reinvigorated the fire and sat quietly once more. There was a kettle of samp left simmering from the previous evening, and Brewster was famished. Samp was a traditional local dish of cornmeal, blueberries, and walnuts adopted from the Wampanoag, who knew it as "nasaump." Brewster devoured the entire contents of the kettle, and felt remorse for his gluttony.

The sun was trying to rise, but it would spend the day obscured on this overcast autumn day. The flames roared to life, and once more, Israel Brewster was hypnotized.

What was his destiny? Did the Lord truly have a plan for him? Why should he agonize so intensely about anything that happened in Plimoth Colony? Their government reviled and humiliated him. They tried to put him on trial. Who knows what manner of torture he may have endured if he didn't flee west to Providence?

Didn't Israel Brewster deserve the joy that had embraced him these last few months? Hadn't he suffered enough? Suffering. How he had grown to despise that word.

"What manner of wickedness have I manifest, that Peter should suffer so?"

How many hideous images were now burned into Brewster's consciousness? He could picture Mary Dyer's lifeless, innocent body tortured under the noose, because he was there fifteen years ago. He willingly helped facilitate her shameful execution. How many times would he relive the bitterly cold night in Middleborough, when his tender wife, exhausted and devoured by the rigors of childbirth, and pathetically cradling their tiny, stillborn daughter, turned to him and whispered her final mortal words?

"How blessed I have been."

And now, he could picture even more suffering. Although he wasn't there, he could picture the sheer panic and terror in the meeting house. He could picture Alice's delicate features, and how she must have cradled her tender infant as the flames consumed them. What prayer would she and her husband have recited when the end drew near? Or did they bravely sing psalmody through the hideous ordeal?

Brewster shifted his gaze from the flames and stared at the wooden floor. He cradled his head in his hands, and massaged his throbbing temples. *Was he one of the Lord's chosen elect?* If so, what was his destiny in this horrific conflict? Was he destined to craft barrels, march to and fro with a pathetic excuse for a militia, and make glorious love with his beautiful bride in the evenings? Or was he called upon to do something more?

Somberly and earnestly, he went to prayer. He meditated on the final verses of the Book of Ecclesiastes. *"Let us hear the conclusion of the whole matter: Fear God, and keep his commandments: for this is the whole duty of man. For God shall bring every work into judgment, with every secret thing, whether it be good, or whether it be evil."*

Brewster now stood up and began furiously pacing. He felt like the Almighty was calling him. But to do…what? Could he serve once again with the militia of the United Colonies? Perhaps he could serve as a chaplain. How he had debated these issues with Constance and Zeke, time and time again. But somehow, after the incineration of the community he worked so hard to nurture and build, everything had changed. Even as he sat in comfort and devoured his morning samp, the enemies of New England could be terrorizing another village.

It was time to serve. And he could not serve while pointing imaginary muskets with the Providence militia. Israel Brewster had to find a way to serve, and that meant he had to leave the family and the home he loved.

Constance had risen, and the late autumn winds continued to wail. The shingles stood true, however, and the house remained warm and dry. Wordlessly, she sat next to him and held his gently trembling hand. Her Bible was opened and resting in her lap.

"The eyes of the Lord are upon the righteous, and his ears are open unto their cry. The face of the Lord is against them that do evil, to cut off the remembrance of them from the earth. The righteous cry, and the Lord heareth, and delivereth them out of all their troubles. The Lord is nigh unto them that are of a broken heart; and saveth such as be of a contrite spirit.

"Many are the afflictions of the righteous: but the Lord delivereth him out of them all. He keepeth all his bones: not one of them is broken. Evil shall slay the wicked: and they that hate the righteous shall be desolate. The Lord redeemeth the soul of his servants: and none of them that trust in him shall be desolate."

A lone tear rolled down his cheek, and she gripped his hand tighter. "You will be comforted, Israel. Blessed are they that mourn, for they shall be comforted."

He released her hand and stood up. He meticulously tended the fire, and then he stared out the window. "I need to leave. Forgive me, but I am called."

How many times had they been here? How often had they debated the issue? She was certain this turmoil was behind them, and their days would be a sea of domestic tranquility. Her face reddened, and she wasn't sure if she could speak. Her eyes moistened, and she nodded rapidly. Without a word, she retreated back to their bed where she felt she could sob with abandon.

What a fool he was. What was he doing? Did he even have a plan? Brewster wondered where he would even go. Would the army be making camp for the winter? Should he ride north to Brookfield? Perhaps he should go east to Taunton. How much hardship could he endure? What's more, how much could Brownie endure?

Zeke emerged from the far room and cast a grim glare at Brewster. "It would appear my daughter is sobbing."

"So am I, Zeke. So am I."

Zeke sat in front of the fire, and restlessly stirred. "I suppose yet another theological debate is out of the question? May I recite chapter six of the gospel of Luke yet again?"

Brewster resumed his seat. *"And unto him that smiteth thee on the one cheek offer also the other; and him that taketh away thy cloak forbid not to take thy coat also."*

"What do you intend to accomplish, Israel?"

"I don't know. I just know I can't be idle while these colonies burn."

"Will you kill the Indians? Will you point a musket and shoot them dead?"

"I don't know. I just know I will do something."

And now it was Zeke who was fighting to keep his face dry. "At least let me find you a real horse."

Brewster almost smiled. "We've been through too much together. Maybe we're inseparable."

"A man and his wife are inseparable."

The words were painful. "I have a duty, Zeke. Somehow, somewhere, I have a duty. I will put my faith in the Lord."

Zeke made no effort to dry his eyes. "Then do it well, my son. Do your duty well."

PART TWO

WINTER
1675 – 1676

"Summer's lease hath all too short a date."
Shakespeare

CHAPTER TWENTY-TWO

TAUNTON

"Have you seen him today?"

"Of course not. He is off prancing and gallivanting with his holiness, Governor Winslow."

"I wonder if he even remembers our names, Jemmy."

Cornet Barnstrom paused to consider his words. He eyed Corporal Thomas Reddington with envy. Even in the frigid November weather, he gleefully went about his business with no coat. When other men huddled with hunger and cold, Reddington always appeared to be a vigorous picture of health, as if he was ready to take down a tree with his bare hands.

"He's certainly come far from Mount Hope. Four months ago, he was the worst commissary officer in all of his majesty's domain. Now he's the governor's right-hand man."

"I guess he deserves it, Jemmy. He certainly knows how to fight."

"A welcome change from old man Cudworth. They certainly put him out to pasture."

"About ten years too late, I surmise."

Barnstrom rubbed his hands together and blew on them in an effort to stay warm. Although there was no snow on the ground, the temperatures consistently remained low, and the ponds were frozen or in the process of freezing.

Although he was now the de facto commander of Church's company, Barnstrom remained on a casual basis with the men, especially Reddington. They both felt an acute sense of loss at the destruction of their homes in Middleborough, but they gave thanks to the Lord that their families were spared. They contemplated a leave of absence from the war, but ultimately deemed it pointless. Everything they owned was gone, their families were safe in Plimoth, and most pointedly, they were certainly not the only men in the militia to see their hometowns razed in recent months.

They were joining up with other militia companies in Taunton to form an enormous expeditionary force, almost certainly the largest ever assembled in New England. Rumor had it there would be at least a thousand men, and they would be marching somewhere west, but details were scant.

"Do you think we'll be chasing King Philip, Jemmy?"

"I heard he's very far north, even north of Deerfield. Everyone says he's far, far away. I wager we're going to assault the Nipmuc. Probably across the mountains in Brookfield."

"No one thought this bloody affair would last so long."

"No one ever does, Corporal Reddington. No one ever does. Look! Is that him?"

Across the field, they could see Governor Winslow, now General Winslow, mounted on a chestnut pacer that was almost fifteen hands tall. Captain Church, his new aide-de-camp, rode behind him, and as usual, wore a face of grim concern. He was scanning the assembly and mentally counting. General Winslow would occasionally make a sidelong remark, and Church would solemnly nod.

In the preceding week, the militia encamped at Taunton was able to recruit seventy more men. Since most of the able-bodied fighting men had enlisted months ago, the more recent batch tended to be an odder assortment of young and old, eccentric, and sick. Cornet Barnstrom now had four additional men under his command, and new applicants had diminished to three or four per day.

New recruits were easy to find due to their lost and helpless demeanor, and Barnstrom was certain he was currently watching one. A tall man in his thirties approached on a brown mare, and Barnstrom was amused at the horse's slow, obstinate manner. He now found himself inexplicably staring, and he didn't notice General Winslow making his approach.

"And this was your company, Benjamin? Superb. All Plimoth men, I hope and presume. Who's in charge here?"

"General, may I introduce Cornet Jemmy Barnstrom. He's a Middleborough man. None finer, General. None finer, indeed. Absolutely unshakable at the Battle of Pease Field."

Seemingly impressed, Winslow nodded. "Young man, how did you manage to hold off hundreds of savages with twenty men and a stone wall?"

Barnstrom was almost too intimidated to address General Winslow. "P-prayer, sir. Lots of p-prayer. And Captain Church."

Winslow beamed with pride. "I almost take pity on the savages. With men like these, Benjamin, I almost take..."

The sentence went unfinished, and Winslow seemed suddenly distracted. Now *he* was also engrossed by the unfamiliar newcomer on the brown mare who was now dismounted and discussing his pending enlistment. Without a word, Winslow spurred his pacer forward and developed a look of astonishment.

"My Lord. This cannot be."

A bewildered general was not a pleasing sight for an aide-de-camp, and Church sprang into action. "Sir? What concerns you, sir?"

"That man. That man with the horse. He is a...he's a...that man is a criminal."

"A *criminal?*"

"He should be in prison. He...Plimoth...Jeremiah Barron...he...he is a blasphemer. Reverend Phelps, bless his memory, told me he committed blasphemy with the heathen. He is...Elder Brewster's grandson. He..."

Finally, Jemmy Barnstrom understood his previous fixation. "*Israel Brewster!*"

Winslow's eyes went wide at the mention of his name. "Yes! Church! Seize that man!"

Church dismounted, and soon a stunned Israel Brewster was dragged by his collar to face Winslow, who glared down from his pacer like a mighty colossus. Brewster had only been back in the militia for five minutes, and he was already catastrophically in trouble.

"Reverend Israel Brewster of Middleborough! How could you show your face in Plimoth Colony? How could you show your face at a time like this? Are you here to demoralize the militia with your love of the savages and your Quaker heresy?"

Brewster could not comprehend what was happening. Five minutes. He affixed his signature and swore an oath five minutes ago, and he was already cowering before the mighty Josiah Winslow. He desperately formulated a reply. "I'm here to fight for my home, Governor."

Winslow actually chuckled in a sinister fashion. "Your home? *Your home?* And where is your home, Reverend Brewster? Is it in Providence, with the Quakers, Baptists, and Hebrews? It certainly can't be Middleborough, which you abandoned four years ago, and is now lying in ashes due to Indian lovers of your ilk. Where is your home, Israel Brewster?"

Brewster stood silently, but ruminated on the Book of Luke. *"Foxes have holes, and birds of the air have nests..."* He uttered not a word as he mentally pictured the beautiful home he left. He pictured the hearth and the sumptuous seafood feasts. He pictured the cooperage and reminisced about the intoxicating aroma of shaven wood. He imagined the countless taverns of Providence, bustling with exotic newcomers from every corner of Europe and the New World, serving intriguing ales from the most unique of recipes. And then he could see Constance. His beautiful, scarlet-haired delight. Brewster imagined her pale, creamy skin and her haunting eyes. How was she occupying herself at this very moment? What a fool he was. He was the most wretched of creatures. If only...

"BREWSTER! *Answer the governor! You are being addressed!*" Church's tone was sharp and impatient. He noticed Barnstrom and Reddington huddled together, excitedly discussing something in hushed tones as they spied the proceedings.

"Forgive me, Governor. I am currently residing in Providence. I make my living as a humble cooper. I didn't think this war to be my business until...until I got news."

"News of *what*?" Church was unsympathetic, as the notion of this war not being any business of an Englishman was inconceivable to him.

It was General Winslow who responded with somber resignation. "Middleborough." Brewster merely gazed at his shoes. Brownie had caught up, and was standing cautiously behind him.

Church was still contemptuous. "And what skills do you bring to this militia? Are you here to build barrels?" In only a few weeks as an aide-de-camp, Church seemed to be increasingly adopting the haughty condescension of General Winslow.

"I...I am a militia man. I have served before. As a young man." Brewster gazed up at Winslow, hoping he might be triggering memories of escorting Wamsutta to Plimoth all those years ago. It appeared as if Winslow was seated twenty feet in the air on a horse of marble. He gazed off in the distance and seemed to be ignoring the conversation.

Finally, General Winslow gave an order in a calm, methodical voice. "Captain Church, take this man into custody, and prepare him for transport to Plimoth. He is a blasphemer who consorts with our Wampanoag enemy and Quaker heretics. He is a fugitive who should have stood trial four years ago."

"Aye, sir. Reddington, fetch us some manacles. You can accompany the prisoner and his ugly beast to Plimoth, provided the pathetic creature can make it that far without keeling over. Leave the creature there to be recycled into something useful."

Winslow's tone was now dripping with contempt. "Ensure he is delivered into the custody of Jeremiah Barron. He will see to a prompt trial. Justice has been delayed, but the judgement of the righteous will now be sure and swift."

THE PROPHET AND THE WITCH

Brewster's eyes had not left his shoes. He was now absent-mindedly stroking Brownie's long nose. Plimoth's contempt for him wasn't enough. Their hatred even extended to his horse. Why did he choose to return? He had to be the most foolish man in all of these colonies. Four years spent rebuilding his broken spirit, nurturing his soul, and for what?

He felt compelled to speak. He was so mortified he could scarcely formulate a coherent thought, but finally he said something. He couldn't bear to raise his eyes. "I told them, Josiah." If he was destined for the rack, he felt little need for formalities. "Their hearts were filled with hatred, and I gave them the truth. I told them."

Church was aghast. *"You are to address the governor accordingly, prisoner Brewster. And if I were in your shoes, I would remain silent!"*

Winslow held up his hand in a seemingly magnanimous gesture. "Thank you, Captain. Brewster, what on earth are you yammering about? Is this some kind of depraved Quaker filth?"

"Wamsutta, Governor. Four years ago. I told the Wampanoag the truth, and it may have prevented the war. They all thought you poisoned Wamsutta, but I knew as a Christian man you would never do that. I told them the truth. Wamsutta never took a morsel from you. He perished of his own sickness. I spoke the truth when they slandered you."

Church had heard enough. "Reddington, let's get moving. Where are those leg irons?"

"No."

"Excuse me?"

"No, Captain Church."

Captain Church was, to say the least, not acclimated to underlings disobeying his orders under any circumstances, and certainly not in the presence of the governor. "Are you daft, man? Go and get the shackles! You heard the governor! This man is dangerous."

Reddington shook his head. "This man is the most righteous Christian I have ever known. He has elevated and comforted my family during every manner of pain and hardship imaginable. My father accompanied him on missionary trips to the Indians, and he swore Israel Brewster was the finest man he ever met. He actually sobbed when he disappeared."

"Barnstrom! You have one moment to rectify this insubordination! What madness is this?"

Cornet Jemmy Barnstrom was not nearly as bold and outspoken as Reddington. "Captain Church, this is..." He lowered his voice and removed his hat. "This is Reverend Brewster, Captain. Of Middleborough. He's done so much for us. He helped raise our home four years ago, Captain. He hauled timber and lifted joists and he gave God's blessing."

"And my father supervised the construction." Reddington's emotions were not abating.

"Captain, what crime did he commit? He is the most devout man I know." Jemmy's voice was rising. "Please, Captain, there must be another way. Let's just send him back to Providence."

"If he is dragged away in shackles, then make sure you fit me for a pair, Captain." Reddington was now standing perfectly rigid, and placed his hands on his hips so his hulking arms could not be missed.

Winslow knew it was time to defuse this potentially catastrophic situation. "Men! Stand silent!" He then trotted forty feet away where he could be alone with his thoughts.

Was he being too impulsive? Was he so stunned to see Brewster make an appearance that he acted irrationally? What exactly were his crimes? It was all so long ago. Wasn't there something about drinking tea? Didn't Barron say it was witchcraft tea? And wasn't there something about wrestling with the Wampanoag? *Wrestling?* Didn't Reverend Phelps say Brewster's conduct was unacceptable for a minister? Wasn't

Phelps dead now? Didn't he perish in the flames of Middleborough?

Winslow stared back to the congregation of men. Barnstrom and Reddington were hugging Brewster and offering their meager rations. He noted they were now praying with their heads bowed, and even Church seemed to be increasingly cordial to his prisoner. Winslow thought back to that day twelve years ago…or was it thirteen? The teen-aged militiaman Brewster accompanied Winslow to escort Wamsutta to Plimoth. He almost laughed when he pictured Brewster's shaking hands and frightened manner.

As the governor, Winslow thrived on cold, objective calculations. The United Colonies needed every able-bodied man that they could muster in this war, and Brewster clearly buoyed the spirits of the men who so recently lost their homes. Barron had enough to be concerned with, and he did not need the rigors of another trial for heresy. Finally, what good could come of tangling with that beast, Reddington? They would have to shoot him three times before they could get him in shackles.

General Winslow trotted back with his pacer. If nothing else, he would ensure to maintain the proper aura of authority and sure-handedness his position demanded. "Gentlemen, I have thought this matter through, and my position has evolved."

Church appeared alarmed, but respectfully remained silent as Winslow continued. "First and foremost, we will need every able-bodied man for this expedition. As such, I have the authority to pardon any crimes against Plimoth Colony. Provided you take an oath of allegiance to Plimoth, Israel Brewster, your transgressions are absolved."

Winslow dismounted, approached Barnstrom, and continued. "You two men are on half rations for a week due to your insolent conduct. I am, however, commuting your punishment due to the emotional turmoil you've suffered due to the loss of your homes. My prayers are with the people of Middleborough."

Winslow now turned and faced Brewster. "Oh, and Brewster. It is imperative you remember your role in this militia. You are not a chaplain or an ordained minister. If I get any inkling that you are spreading Quaker heresy in our midst, I will send for the shackles. You are not an officer, and you are not a gentleman. You are the lowest ranking member of the company, and you will obey all the orders of your superiors. Cornet Barnstrom? This recruit is now your personal responsibility."

Flurries of snow were now gently cascading from the dull, gray sky. Winslow stared Brewster in the eye. "Congratulations, Brewster. Thirteen years later, I am the Governor, and you are once again a private in the militia. Your grandfather would be so proud."

Winslow climbed aboard his magnificent steed. "Let's go, Benjamin. We have troops to inspect. And Brewster? Keep that filthy animal of yours downwind, won't you?"

CHAPTER TWENTY-THREE

SCHAGHTICOKE

Was his hand trembling?

Linto tried to pay it no mind, but he knew his hand was trembling intensely. What's more, he knew that despite the seasonally cool weather, he was sweating profusely and could not stop. Was his hand trembling *and* sweating? How long could this possibly go on?

He had been with the Nipmuc at Menameset for at least three entire moons. During these months, Annawon had led the Wampanoag warriors on raids and skirmishes that, while certainly not altering the course of the war, boosted their depleted morale. English convoys were ambushed, muskets were seized, and storehouses of grain were emptied. Now that winter was approaching, they showed no sign of slowing their activity.

Linto, meanwhile, had been summoned on this particular day to the grandiose wetu of the two sisters. They had heard much of Metacomet's skinny prophet, and they wished to know more. They wanted to hear the tale of the miraculous day Massasoit found Linto as a toddler. They yearned to hear his thoughts on the Great Spirit, the English God, and the divine implications of this war. Above all, they were most eager to hear every detail of the prophecy, and Linto recounted in excruciating detail the fateful moment he revealed it to Metacomet and the warriors.

"I have been fasting and meditating, and the Great Spirit has blessed me with a holy vision. We are ready for war with a vile and despicable enemy, but the Great Spirit demands we truly reveal their evil nature for all to see. Therefore, it has been blessedly revealed to me, that whomever fires the first shot of the war and slays the first man, is accursed, and their side will taste defeat! Victory shall be awarded to the nation that is restrained and disciplined, and does not fire the first shot in anger! It has been spoken, it has been revealed!"

The Bluebird's interrogation was indeed unsettling, but it paled in comparison to his time with the Blackbird. They sat silently with their eyes closed, and he held her delicate, frigid hand. The minutes seemed to be hours. Was she reading his thoughts? What powers did she really have? How long did he have to endure this?

The Blackbird finally inhaled deeply, opened her eyes, and released his hand. She exhaled, and cast her eyes on her twin sister. The Bluebird answered the summons and reached for her sister's hand. She closed her eyes and nodded vigorously. In less than a minute, the ritual was complete.

"Sachem Chosoki, the Blackbird, was able to peer deep inside your soul, Linto. She could not discern any supernatural powers. The spirit world has no interest in you, Linto of the Abenaki. Therefore, there can be no validity in the prophecy."

Linto blinked and stood dumbfounded. What was he to say? What was he to do? The Bluebird witnessed his awkward helplessness, and mercifully dismissed him.

"You are dismissed, ordinary Linto of the Abenaki. Perhaps you may find something useful to do in this conflict. We have fishing nets that need mending."

His face was still wet with perspiration. Was this the sort of challenge he was expected to embrace as a holy man? Was she waiting for some manner of spiritual boasting or perhaps, a mystical spell? Should he stand for himself and defend his honor? Perhaps he should levy a sinister curse of some manner, but he had no idea how to do that.

Linto left the wetu without a word.

The reality of events was slowly beginning to sink in. Although Metacomet was not present, he would certainly soon hear of the encounter. Should Linto be the first to approach him? How should he spin his meeting with the sisters and their crushing judgement? Would they tell Metacomet the prophecy has no validity?

Dejected, he staggered about the village aimlessly, and soon a powerful hand grabbed his shoulder from behind.

"Are you lost, skinny boy?"

Linto winced at the strength of the grip. He futilely wriggled and rushed forward in an effort to free himself. He then craned his neck to face his captor, and was relieved to be greeted by Annawon's legendary smile. "How do you stay so skinny in a village with so much food? Let's go. Metacomet wants to meet."

Could Metacomet have heard the news this quickly? Linto's mind raced as he pondered this meeting and what he could possibly tell Metacomet. They found the Sachem on the outskirts of the village, sitting alone and sharpening a long knife.

Linto knelt on the ground next to him. "Sachem, I..."

"Linto, is this our destiny?"

"Sachem?"

"Is this our destiny? Are we here to be subservient to Chogan and her witch of a sister? Is this why Mentayyup sacrificed himself? Is this why Nimrod was cut down?" Linto nervously played with his hands and tried to avoid eye contact. Was all of this even about him?

Metacomet continued. "Yes, we are well fed, and we are a thorn in the English side. But it is our destiny to liberate the nations from the oppressors. We are not meant to be meager underlings taking orders."

Annawon was nodding enthusiastically, but Linto did not respond. Frankly, these last few months had been a welcome respite after the nightmarish exodus from Pocasset. Additionally, Linto was relieved when he realized this urgent meeting almost certainly had nothing to do with his humiliation at the hands of the sisters.

Metacomet stood and extended his massive hand. Linto grasped it and Metacomet hoisted him to his feet. "Think, Linto. You are supposed to be an advisor. Think. Who do the Plimoth English despise even more than the Wampanoag?"

Linto did think, and he was too puzzled to reply. The fancy Boston men? No, that would be a silly answer. The Dutch? No, that didn't make any sense either. The Nipmuc? No that, would just inflame the Sachem's jealousy. Linto knew time was passing quickly, and his lack of a response was making him seem foolish. He had to say something.

"The Quaker men? Plimoth hates Governor Easton and his Quaker friends?"

"That's not a bad answer, Linto. But think harder. Think what Tobias told you years ago."

As commanded, Linto concentrated even harder, and he could picture the day he attended his first council of the Wampanoag. He remembered how intimidated he was by Tobias, but he also remembered his words.

"They fear the Quakers in Plimoth even more than us. But not as much as the French Catholics. Oh, how the Plimoth English despise the Catholics. Sometimes for fun I like to tell a farmer we've had Catholics in our village for a feast. Just to watch their heads spin."

Linto's face finally lit up with comprehension. "The French Catholics. Plimoth despises the French Catholics. But where are they, Sachem? Aren't they far, far away?"

"They are west of here. Perhaps a journey of seven sunrises. But they are there. We will go west and find the French Catholic men. They will trust us, and they will give us an army to make the English pay. And my father's people will no longer have to pay homage to the ugly sisters and their witchcraft."

That evening, Metacomet conveyed the news to the two sisters. He was grateful for their alliance, he was grateful for their hospitality, and he was impressed by all the destruction they had wrought upon their enemy. But if they were to truly alter the balance of power in these lands, they needed an ally from across the sea. Specifically, an ally that could manufacture muskets and supply powder.

The two sisters did not seem particularly disappointed or saddened at the departure of the Wampanoag, and they provisioned them with a generous ration of food. Although they did their best to conceal it, the notion of a new European ally greatly intrigued them. The two sisters knew the French had thousands of allies among the Huron people of the giant lakes. If a few dozen Wampanoag could march west and return with hundreds of well-armed warriors, this war would be very different, indeed. Consequently, she dispatched guides to help them navigate through the unfamiliar terrain west of the Nipmuc lands.

After the next day's sunrise, Metacomet led his warriors west. His son, healthier and happier after several moons of eating well, never left his side. The expedition had to remain vigilant, as the war was raging even as far west as the Connecticut River valley. During the autumn, vicious battles were waged throughout the valley, with the English settlers usually the vanquished party. Additionally, the wrath of winter was descending, and their journey was slow. They stopped to build fires and warm themselves four or five times per day. The hunting, however, was plentiful, and no one hungered during the journey.

The terrain rose sharply as they proceeded in the direction of the setting sun. Their Nipmuc guides were tremendously valuable, as they wove through the valleys and avoided the daunting elevations. Still, the journey took at least ten sunrises, much more than their previous estimates.

Four days after their Nipmuc guides returned to the east, the expedition reached the valley of the river the English called the Hudson. They encountered a fishing party of four Indians. When they explained the nature of their journey, the men became cordial and enthusiastic. Their people were greatly excited by the news of King Philip's rebellion, and they could scarcely believe they were in Metacomet's presence. They soon arranged a rendezvous with their French trading partners.

They were led to an enormous cabin with a stone chimney and a roaring fire in the village of Schaghticoke. Metacomet brought Annawon and Linto, and after a prolonged but comfortable wait, they were greeted by four Frenchmen.

"Bonjour! Mes amis de l'est! Je suis Colonel Richaud!"

The three Wampanoag eagerly rose and bowed politely to the short, balding colonel, who seemed disappointed by their perplexed silence.

"Parlez-vouz Francais? Non? C'est triste. Alain?"

A tall, gaunt subordinate stepped forward. His English was slow and labored, and the Wampanoag were not acclimated to his accent. "Forgeeve my cuhl-uh-nel, our new friends, no? I am Cap-ee-tehn Alain Fontaine of Marseilles. Cahn you understahn me? Anglaish ees good, no?"

Metacomet's vacant stare compelled Linto to speak. "Yes, we can understand English. We have traveled far, Cap-ee-tehn Alain. Thank you for seeing us."

"You are King Phillipe, no?"

"My name is Linto. This is the Sachem of the Wampanoag nation, Metacomet, whom you may know as Philip. This is Annawon, our captain of war."

Captain Fontaine whispered excitedly in French to Colonel Richaud. The colonel's eyes lit up, and he could not refrain from staring at Metacomet. Linto, however, could not stop staring at what seemed to be a French holy man. He wore what Linto would normally construe as an English woman's dress. It was a loose gown that was solid black in color, and accentuated with a prominent belt. In addition to a peculiar cap, he wore a large wooden cross around his belt.

Linto was surprised when the holy man addressed him in an Algonquin language. The language barrier was just too much, however, and he reverted to English, speaking it much better than Captain Fontaine.

"Hello, Linto. I am Father Jacques and I am delighted to meet you. I see you are fascinated by my attire."

Linto was taken aback. "Your English is so good! Are you a holy man among your people?"

"Thank you for the compliment. I also speak Spanish. And of course, French and Latin. I am a Jesuit priest. We are missionaries in the service of our Lord, Jesus Christ. Are you saved, Linto? Have your people heard the good news?"

Linto was non-committal. "We have received quite a few missionaries, Father Jacques."

"Oh, my. The English." He then made a rapid four-point motion across his chest that was unfamiliar to Linto.

"Father Jacques, if I may?" Captain Fontaine was clearly ready to discuss military matters. Utilizing Linto and Father Jacques to eradicate any language barriers, they quickly arrived at the heart of the matter. Colonel Richaud was the assistant military governor of the region, and he was delighted to hear of the rebellion against the English tyranny. Reliable intelligence reports were rare, but news of Indian victories and English setbacks was sweeping New France. Richaud's government had a very vested interest in a positive outcome for the Wampanoag, and they were ready to provide over two hundred warriors from the Huron nation. Additionally, if his government deemed the situation strategically favorable, they would almost certainly supply muskets and powder, and there conceivably could be a naval blockade of New England in the summer.

Metacomet and Annawon grinned with delight. Captain Fontaine said the warriors of the Wampanoag could remain at the village of Schaghticoke while the Huron expeditionary force was assembled. The Frenchmen subsequently sent their young underling to procure tea and port wine to commemorate the occasion, and Linto couldn't resist the opportunity to converse more with Father Jacques.

"Father Jacques, are you not fond of the English missionaries? Are they not Jesuits like you?"

"Oh heavens, no, my son. The English missionaries are very wicked men, and you must take care to avoid them. They are heretics."

Linto was baffled. *"They are heretics?* But they say everybody else is a heretic. How can they be heretics if they are Christians?"

Father Jacques looked downcast. "But they are not Christians, Linto. They are, in fact, wicked men. Our holy

Savior established one and only one eternal church. But the men of England decided they know better than God, and they turned their back on the Holy Catholic Church. They violate every precept of worship. In New England, there is no true priesthood, there is no confession, and there is no belief in the sacraments. Their clergy lie with women, and most can't even speak Latin. They are condemned, Linto. The Englishmen of New England are condemned to judgement and eternal damnation."

Linto was so astounded by all of this he could scarcely reply. Could any of this really be true? Could it explain why the English were so difficult to live with? Were they actually evil, wicked men who only pretended to be holy? Was the Gentle Son unhappy with them?

During the next two days, Linto spent every moment that he could with Father Jacques, while Annawon and Metacomet discussed military matters with Cap-ee-tehn Alain. Father Jacques taught Linto some French phrases, they discussed Latin, and they discussed England, both old and new. Linto was learning many new and inconceivable things.

On a bright and chilly morning, they strolled together by a stream. The snow was not deep at all, and it would be another beautiful day. They were feasting on crisp, warm bread, and Linto was full of questions.

"Father Jacques, how did all of these things come to be? Why did the English decide they didn't want to be Catholic anymore?"

"Because the King of England fell in love with a whore, Linto."

Linto nearly spit out his bread, and he assumed he misheard. "I'm afraid I don't understand."

Father Jacques delicately nibbled on his bread. "Sometimes, Linto, all men, especially men of power, like to pretend that they are serving God, but they are only serving themselves. They yearn to adhere to God's eternal law, until they find it inconvenient. A hundred years before the English landed at *Plee-mooth*, there was a king in England. The Lord blessed him with the most wonderful of wives, Queen Catherine of Aragon. She was devout and pious, Linto, and beloved by all."

Father Jacques had finished his bread. He came across a tremendous stone, and for sheer amusement, he threw it high in the air, and watched it plummet into the icy stream with a satisfying kerplunk. He continued. "Marriage between a man and a woman is forever, Linto. It is a sacrament, and a promise to God. But this king, King Henry, struggled to sire a child with his wife, the lawful Queen of England. After he lustfully eyed a wicked temptress, he cruelly dismissed his queen. Naturally, the Holy Father in Rome told him he could do no such thing, but King Henry decided he didn't need to obey God's law. He decided he would simply create his own church, and he would be in charge of it. Can you imagine such arrogance?"

Linto was doing his best to savor his bread, but his willpower faded and he quickly devoured it. He hung on every word as Father Jacques continued.

"Of course, the foul temptress soon received her own comeuppance. But, what did our blessed Savior say, Linto? *Upon this rock, I will build my church.* And yet, King Henry thought he knew better. King Henry thought he could be the rock. And that, in addition to a few other mentally ill heretics such as *Loo-thair*, is the reason New England is damned, Linto. Once a man decides he knows better than the Holy Catholic Church, there can be nothing but confusion, discord, and turmoil."

Linto nodded politely, and he tried to process what he was hearing. There was so much he wanted to ask. "Father Jacques, who lives in Israel now? Is it the Catholics, or the Hebrews?"

"Oh, my, Linto. There is so much to discuss there. That is now the Ottoman Empire and ruled by the sultan. They are our enemy."

"So, they are also Puritans?"

Father Jacques could not restrain his chuckle. "Oh, my, no. No, Linto. They are an entirely different religion. They are very different, indeed. They are called Moslems. They pray five times a day, and once a year, they will fast for an entire month. They even forbid alcohol! Imagine, no wine and no brandy!"

Linto silently imagined a world without alcohol, and the more he thought about it, the more he liked it. Here was an entirely new kingdom with an entirely new religion he had never even heard of. This was all so unbelievable. How many people lived across the ocean? Where was the Ottoman Empire? How many other kingdoms were there besides England and France?

They stopped walking, and Father Jacques appeared somber. "Linto, I must take my leave tomorrow morning. I am charged to go west, and spread the light of Christ among the Oneida people."

Linto was crestfallen. Father Jacques seemed to have all the wisdom that Linto had been so hungrily seeking, and now he was suddenly leaving. "You're leaving? The Oneida? That is so far west!"

"Indeed, but it is where I have been directed to go. I look forward to the journey, and the opportunity to serve Christ."

"Isn't that through Mohawk territory? Aren't you afraid?"

"The Lord guides my path, Linto. *"Ne timeas quia tecum sum ego ne declines quia ego Deus tuus confortavi te et auxiliatus sum tui et suscepi te dextera iusti mei. So, do not fear, for I am with you; do not be dismayed, for I am your God."*

Father Jacques reached into his satchel. "Before I go, however, I do have a gift for you, Linto." He pulled out a marvelous, ornamental hatchet with a captivating design. "Do you like it? It is called the fleur-de-lis. It is a lily, the symbol of my nation."

Linto had never received such a gift and was overwhelmed. "Father, I..."

"There is no need for thanks. You have taught me much these past few days, and I hope I have been able to teach you.

Please be well, and I wish you blessings as you liberate your lands from English oppression. You will be in my prayers, Linto."

And while Linto slept, Father Jacques disappeared.

Linto rose the next morning, and meditated before breakfast. It had been another week of remarkable events, and he ruminated on their journey to the west. There was much that troubled him, yet so much that encouraged him.

He was still troubled by the probability that the Blackbird's contemptuous judgement of him would eventually reach Metacomet, if it hadn't done so already. Should he directly address the issue with his Sachem, or was the matter best ignored?

If he was troubled by the Blackbird, he was delighted by their new French friends and this wonderful village. The Wampanoag were treated like conquering heroes, and the warriors of the Huron soon began arriving to pledge their allegiance to Metacomet.

If Linto was troubled by the Blackbird, and delighted by their new military alliance, he was completely transfixed by Father Jacques. Who could imagine a world in which the men of Plimoth were the heretics? Who could envision their holy and righteous men standing before government authorities to answer for their blasphemy, and plead for their lives? Linto tried to picture the men who sentenced Tobias to death being escorted to the gallows, because they believed the wrong things about God.

In a life spent seeking certainty, Linto could only seem to find more uncertainty. His time with Father Jacques, however, reinforced one simple fact: Throughout all his days, the more Linto thought he truly understood the strange white men from across the sea and their baffling faith, the more mistaken he was.

CHAPTER TWENTY-FOUR

ENROUTE TO RHODE ISLAND

"COMPANY! CARTRIDGES!"

Brewster's hand was trembling slightly as he procured a cartridge from his leather bag. His movements were deliberate but timely.

"TEETH!"

Brewster, along with every man to his right and left, tore open their cartridges with their teeth, and all were greeted with the gritty, burnt metallic taste.

"WAIT FOR IT!"

Some of the inexperienced men almost began pouring, but Brewster would do absolutely nothing until commanded.

"FRISSENS FORWARD! AND POUR! NOT TOO MUCH, YOU SCOUNDRELS! FRISSENS BACK!"

Brewster felt like there was frost forming on his brow, but he didn't take his hands from his flintlock.

"MUSKETS VERTICAL! POWDER IN! MUSKETBALL IN! WADDING...IN! DON'T YOU WASTE THE GOVERNOR'S POWDER, YOU DEVILS! PAY HEED!"

A cold wind from the north was gaining force. Brewster wanted to blow on his hands but didn't want to appear weak.

"RAMRODS! GENTLE, YOU SAVAGES! TREAT THE COLONIES' MUSKETS WITH RESPECT! THAT'S BETTER. RAMRODS...STOWED! GOOD, GOOD. RAISE MUSKETS...HOLD IT STRAIGHT, LAD, BE A MAN. HAMMERS BACK...AIM LIKE YOU MEAN IT, LADS. AND...FIRE!"

The sound was deafening as the flintlocks roared to life. Every weapon fired perfectly, and Brewster breathed a sigh of relief.

"MUSKETS...LEFT HAND. SABERS, FORWARD!"

The military drills continued throughout the frigid afternoon. After Brewster's brief service with the Providence militia, the situation was a welcome change. There were over a thousand men assembled and ready for combat. They were equipped with flintlocks, sabers, coats, boots, and food. This army was ready for any adversary.

But who was their adversary? Where were they going?

The camp was rife with rumors that they would be marching west tomorrow morning. Of course, they would be marching west. But what then? North to Nipmuc country? West to Springfield? Could they possibly be going south?

That evening, after a dinner of beans, dried bread, and salt pork, Cornet Barnstrom arrived with the news. They were to march west at daybreak tomorrow morning. Captain Church and Captain Moseley would sail together to prepare the next garrison, and General Winslow would personally lead the magnificent army to its destination. Brewster silently pondered who would control Moseley's pirates while he was sailing off, but these things were not his concern. He was a private in this militia.

The company was assembled after dinner, and Barnstrom quietly addressed Brewster. "Reverend Brewster. Would you bless us with evening prayers?"

Brewster hesitated. "Umm…I'm not certain I'm authorized to do so, Cornet Barnstrom. I don't think I'm even a minister anymore. Besides, you heard Governor Winslow. I'm not a chaplain. I'm just a…"

"Governor Winslow is not here, Reverend Brewster." Reddington was bold and direct. "Please take care of your flock."

Brewster's eyes darted to and fro, as if he was about to engage in some nefarious, forbidden activity. "Gentlemen. If you would bow your heads and be with me in prayer as I recite scripture."

"*The Lord is my light and my salvation; whom shall I fear? The Lord is the strength of my life; of whom shall I be afraid? When the wicked, even mine enemies and my foes, came upon me to eat up my flesh, they stumbled and fell. Though an enemy host should encamp against me, my heart shall not fear: though war should rise against me, in this will I be confident. One thing have I desired of the Lord, that will I seek after; that I may dwell in the house of the Lord all the days of my life, to behold the beauty of the Lord, and to enquire in his temple. For in the time of trouble he shall hide me in his pavilion: in the secret of his tabernacle shall he hide me; he shall set me up upon a rock. And now shall mine head be lifted up above mine enemies round about me: therefore will I offer in his tabernacle sacrifices of joy; I will sing, yea, I will sing praises unto the Lord. Hear, O Lord, when I cry with my voice: have mercy also upon me, and answer me. Amen."*

The company echoed "amen" in unison. Brewster tried not to smile. It felt right to be a spiritual leader once more, instead of a soul left adrift.

Morning brought no reprieve from the December cold. Flurries had begun to fall, but it was still a beautiful morning, and spirits were high as the army left Taunton. By midday, they were fording the Blackstone River, and after turning south toward Providence, the ranks buzzed with astonishment. The rumors were true. They really were marching on the Narragansett.

The southerly direction made Brewster's heart soar, yet filled him with dread. They would be marching remarkably close to Providence enroute to their next encampment, but the fact that the war was moving to a southern theater perplexed and alarmed him. Why were they assaulting the Narragansett? Brewster laid these thoughts aside, and he reconciled himself to the fact that he had been assembling barrels for these last four years. It was probably not his place to question the grand strategy of the United Colonies.

The mighty army continued on a southerly course, and soon they were skirting the outlying, western edges of Providence. The companies were anxious, but energetic. After weeks of incessant organizing and drilling, the men were excited to finally take the fight to the enemy. Governor

Winslow mixed readily with the ranks, and shouted words of encouragement.

Even Brownie seemed taken with a new sense of martial aplomb as she travelled with the company. As a private, it would have been unseemly for Brewster to be on horseback, so Brownie was quickly enlisted as a makeshift pack mule, toting food, blankets, and gunpowder. Brewster proudly strode beside her, and he encouragingly stroked her nose every half mile or so.

Brewster turned his gaze east, and he longed for his home. How he wished he could break ranks and be with his beloved. She was so very close, yet she may as well have been across the Atlantic. A few well-wishers had meandered out of the city to cheer and hand out warm bread. Brewster desperately longed to see his scarlet-haired beauty among the throngs, but it was not to be. The army was moving at a frantic clip, and there was no time for socializing.

The flurries were growing heavier with each hour, and the snow was now accumulating at a steady clip. Brownie seemed to spot something out of the corner of her eye, and the sight seemed to excite her. She loudly snorted, and Brewster spied an older civilian man running to and fro though the ranks.

"Brewster? Israel Brewster! Where are you, my boy?" It was Zeke!

Completely amazed, Brewster waved furiously, and a breathless Zeke caught up. "How are they treating you, son? Are they feeding you anything?"

"I'm well, Zeke. Is she..." Brewster scanned the surroundings and was soon crestfallen.

"No, son. Chasing down a militiaman in the December cold is no place for a woman in her condition, I'm afraid. She sent a letter, though."

"*Her condition! She is ill!*" A sense of panic overwhelmed him. "What malady plagues her, Zeke?"

"I'm afraid she's vomiting quite frequently. All is explained in the letter. Now take this food, and be well! Zeke handed Brewster a basket, full of bread and salted fish. He even found a carrot for Brownie.

"I can't keep up with the army, Israel. I'm headed back. Be well, son! The Lord keep and bless you!"

"But Constance! I must go to..."

"Read the letter! Farewell!" And the army pushed south, as Zeke returned east.

The snow was beginning to fall so intensely that Brewster questioned the wisdom of opening the letter, but he could not wait. He blew on his numb, icy hands, and tore away the ribbon.

My Dearest Israel,

It is difficult to find the words to convey the absence in my heart. I yearn for you to be back by my side, but I know I must yield to your Puritan sense of duty. I pray for your spirit daily, and I beseech the Almighty that soon this wicked violence will be a thing of the past, and husbands will be reunited with wives.

The Lord has indeed blessed us, husband, as I am now growing with child. Each morning brings a new sense of joy and devotion, but also brings a dreaded bout of nausea. To make matters worse, I fear I am growing averse to seafood during these child-bearing months. Imagine! The daughter of a Providence fisherman!

I plead that you will come home to me soonest so we can discuss Christian names. Father seems insistent upon yet another Ezekiel, but I seem to have my heart set on Daniel. Somehow, I just know it will be a boy.

When my thoughts drift to the separation of lovers, I wallow in my books, and I now lovingly transcribe this gem from Mister Giles Fletcher for you, my dear. It is, of course, one of his sonnets to Licia:

I wish sometimes, although a worthless thing,
Spurred by ambition, glad to aspire,
Myself a monarch, or some mighty king,
And then my thoughts do wish for to be higher.
But when I view what winds the cedars toss.

THE PROPHET AND THE WITCH

What storms men feels that covet for renown,
I blame myself that I have wished my loss,
And scorn a kingdom, though it give a crown.
Ah Licia, though the wonder of my thought,
My heart's content, procurer of my bliss,
For whom a crown I do esteem as naught,
As Asia's wealth, too mean to buy a kiss!
Kiss me, sweet love, this favor do for me;
Then crowns and kingdoms shall I scorn for thee.

Your Loving Wife,
Constance Brewster

A child! She was with child! Brewster read the letter three times, and as Barnstrom approached, he could sense his rapt joy.

"News from Providence, Reverend?" Brewster wished he would refer to him as "Private Brewster."

"A child, Jemmy! She is with child! A blessing from the Lord!"

"Indeed, Reverend. Say, what's in that basket? That seems too heavy to be lugging around."

Brewster was distractedly reading the letter for a fourth time. "Hmm? Basket? Oh, yes. Here, take it, take it. A child, Jemmy!"

Barnstrom couldn't bear to swindle the basket of food from Reverend Brewster, but soon Brewster was emerging from his reverie and was joyfully passing out Zeke's morsels. Barnstrom was growing increasingly concerned about the snow, but his men all had good stockings and shoes, and a well-fortified garrison house awaited them. He wondered how Captains Church and Moseley were faring on their journey.

Providence was soon a distant memory, and minutes turned to hours. Barnstrom considered asking Brewster to lead a prayer for more temperate weather, but upon further consideration, thought the better of it. He instead led his men in a marching ditty to hopefully pass the time and distract them from the brutal winter conditions.

Barnstrom bellowed forth: "*I knew a maid from Dedham...*" And the company answered in unison. "*She was the joy of the town!*"

I knew a maid from Dedham
She was the joy of the town!
The prettiest lass you'd ever meet
Dark hair and a velvet gown!

I knew a girl from Boston, west
She was the joy of the town!
Of all the gals, she was the best
Dark hair and a velvet gown!

Oh ladies, won't you wait for me
I wish I was by your side!
Oh ladies, we fight for your families
A New England man's filled with pride!

Dark hair and a velvet gown!
Dark hair and velvet gown!
Oh ladies, won't you wait for me,
Dark hair and a velvet gown!

I knew a daughter from Bridgewater...

Brewster was delighted as Barnstrom was able to lead and recite at least two dozen distinct verses. He wondered how much was from memory, and how much was improvised. From the time he was a child memorizing the Old Testament, Brewster could not hide his own otherworldly gift of memory, but even he was impressed by Barnstrom's fanciful list of New England lasses.

The ditties proved a pleasant distraction, and the hours passed. The sun was setting, and the countryside was now taking on a forlorn and desolate appearance. Chimney smoke beckoned in the distance, and the company was relieved when they arrived at their shelter for the night.

The army had moved an extraordinary distance through wintery conditions, and Brewster could not recall such a feeling of exhaustion. Sheltering at least a thousand men was indeed challenging, but everyone was provided for in one manner or another in a local settlement. Men were huddled in their blankets on wooden floors and sleeping twenty to a room, but there was nary a complaint. They were out of the elements, and sleep came easy.

The next morning, they were faced with another long, dreary march through the snow. The temperatures had dropped considerably, and the mood was somber. The army pressed south, ever south, enroute to their next garrison. General Winslow disseminated word through the ranks that they would be sheltered at Mister Jeremiah Bull's settlement, with even more generous accommodations than the previous night. The thought of the warm fires of Bull's garrison motivated the men during another frigid and exhausting day.

Brewster read his letter from Constance four more times that morning, despite the wintery conditions. By now, he had completely memorized Fletcher's sonnet to Licia, and he mentally recited it repeatedly. When that grew tiresome, he was sustained by psalmody, sung quietly and discreetly so only Brownie could hear.

As they veered east and approached the western shore of Narragansett Bay, Brewster was acutely aware that English settlements were growing few and far between. They were now deep into the wilderness. The snow was falling again, and he began daydreaming about Bull's garrison. The weather was already taking its toll on the men, and a chorus of sneezing and coughing followed them on their journey.

After the sun had set, the companies received word they were within a few miles of their destination. The wind, which had been a minor concern throughout the march, was now beginning to howl. The darkness was increasingly becoming a problem, but soon the comforting scent of wooden fires filled the air. The garrison was finally coming into view.

General Josiah Winslow had two problems on that snowy Saturday evening in December of 1675. First, he had more than one thousand men prepared to attack a heavily defended Narragansett fortress situated deep in a swamp somewhere, but he had no idea where it was, or how to find it. Of even greater concern, however, was the scene awaiting his freezing, exhausted army at the garrison.

There was no garrison. It had been burned to the ground, and all the inhabitants lay slaughtered in the snow.

CHAPTER TWENTY-FIVE

THE WILDERNESS OF RHODE ISLAND

Sometimes, there is absolutely nothing that can be done, except survive. Survive and pray.

After two brutal days of marching through winter's torment, General Josiah Winslow's glorious army had arrived at what was expected to be a well-fortified garrison for a night of peaceful and refreshing slumber. Instead, they found the snow soaked with the blood of at least a dozen slaughtered Englishmen, and at least twenty cabins reduced to ashes.

And there was not a scrap of food to be found.

Winslow feverishly conferred with his officers. Major Bradford, who had lost so much influence due to Cudworth's failings (and who ignominiously watched Benjamin Church rise in prominence), was struggling to even maintain consciousness. There were absolutely no options. A ten-hour nighttime march through the snow to return to their previous garrison was out of the question. They had no idea who destroyed the garrison, and what the enemy situation was. Church and Moseley were, blessedly, not among the dead, but they were nowhere to be found. They had no food, and they had no shelter. Even the humble act of lighting a fire would prove nearly impossible.

They had nothing but their faith, and their will to survive.

And survive they did. Over a thousand men slept in the open field as the snow continued to fall from the heavens. Hundreds stood watch, vigilantly awaiting an enemy that never returned. Men huddled in their coats and blankets, and tried to sleep without exposing their torsos to the snow-covered earth. They coughed. They shivered. They sang psalms. And they desperately prayed.

Somehow, the worst night imaginable came to a merciful conclusion. The sun rose. The snow stopped falling. And some of their fears somehow abated.

Their spirits were buoyed even more as Church and Moseley led a team of ten soldiers and one prisoner into the camp. They were unaware of the garrison's destruction, and they were appalled by the scene. Church promptly debriefed General Winslow. Church and Moseley had led their teams south on reconnaissance missions. They had engaged the enemy and had inflicted casualties. One young Narragansett, named Peter, had surrendered quite easily and was now their prisoner. They could not, however, get any inkling of where the fort might be.

They had left a well-armed contingent of fifteen men to guard the garrison, but they were obviously ambushed and taken completely by surprise. What's more, there was no sign of the supply ship that was supposed to be arriving from Boston, and they suspected it could not leave port due to the weather.

In the midst of the total catastrophe, Church and Moseley had one and only one piece of positive news. Their prisoner had offered his full cooperation, and pledged to guide them to the fort.

After the disastrous events of the last twenty-four hours, Winslow had good reason to be cynical. "Bring him forward."

Peter appeared to be about twenty years of age, and seemed much less nervous than one might expect from a man in his situation. "Well, young man? What do you have to say for yourself?"

The prisoner's eyes scanned his surroundings. He seemed to be marveling at the men, the horses, and the equipment. He cast his eyes downward, and was barely audible. His English was labored, and difficult to comprehend.

"Men never find."

Winslow was so exhausted and dejected he fought the temptation to just club the prisoner unconscious with the blunt end of his pistol. He took a deep breath. "I'm sorry? Speak up, lad."

"Horses and men no find fort. Hide too good. Far. Very far. I take men."

"You are offering to escort us to the Narragansett fort?"

"Yes. You follow me. Very far. I take men."

Winslow was silently marveling at Peter's tolerance for the elements. He wore deerskin leggings and a cotton tunic and seemed to only have the most meager of shoes. Yet he evinced no discomfort as he stated his case. "I ride. You follow. Roast pig?" Peter feverishly surveyed the scene in hopes of locating some nourishment.

"And why, pray tell, have you inexplicably expressed allegiance to the United Colonies and our noble cause?"

Peter blinked vacantly, and Church mercifully assisted. "Peter, tell great Winslow why Peter help English."

He instantly understood. "Peter hate Canochet. Canochet bad Sachem, very bad. Canochet take Peter's wife for himself. Canochet laugh at Peter. Canochet dumb to make English mad. Peter want to fight with English, like Mohegan. Peter hate Sachem. English give reward."

"A reward? What are you expecting?"

"English let Peter ride horse. Give warm coat. No put on boat, like Pequot. Peter stay with English. Give Peter good, long knife."

Winslow gestured at three of Moseley's men. "Stay with the prisoner. Church, Moseley, Bradley, with me."

They assembled out of earshot and kept their voices hushed. "A gift from the Almighty, gentlemen, or an agent of Satan?"

Church pondered the question. "He gave up with nary a fight. His cohorts fought to the death."

Bradford had experienced enough enemy subterfuge to be doubtful. "Too easy. Too perfect. How easy it will be to lead us into an ambush. I say we execute him."

It was very rare to see Josiah Winslow display any strain or emotion. Though his voice was steady, the adversity was beginning to show in his pink, wind-burnt face. "Moseley? What say you?"

Moseley's disdain for any Indian from any nation was well established. "I agree. Execute him. Certainly, a thousand men can find a fort. We can send six parties of thirty men each out. And then..."

"*And then we starve to death.*" Despite his new status in Winslow's service, Church would never lose his impulsive manner of speech. "General, we have to engage the enemy as soon as the Lord wills it. This army has nothing. The supply ships are not coming. I pray we can find this fort today and slay these heathens."

Winslow appeared conflicted, and Church pressed his case. "General, how can the prisoner lead us into an ambush? How can they ambush a thousand men? We have our own Indian scouts to secure our perimeter." Winslow nodded thoughtfully. Their army was reinforced with at least a hundred allied warriors from the Mohegan and Pequot nations.

"How far did he say it is?"

"Half a day's march. And we haven't even discussed the most important fact, General. He says the fort is normally impossible to assault, because the only entrance is via an enormous log crossing the swamp. But the entire swamp is frozen solid this week, and there is no need for the log bridge."

Winslow's eyes seemed to be growing wider, and Church was relentless. "General, I've personally surveyed the area in every direction. Unless we have help, this army will starve to death and freeze to death before we find that fort. We follow Peter and find it today, we slay our enemies, and then we have food and shelter. It's our only choice, General."

The assembly recognized the expression Josiah Winslow wore whenever he had made up his mind and was ready for action. His father frequently wore the exact same expression during the first catastrophic winter after the Mayflower arrived.

"Church, give the prisoner whatever he wants. Major Bradford, prepare the army to move."

CHAPTER TWENTY-SIX

SCHAGHTICOKE

Linto was failing dismally.

"Try it again. It's not difficult, Linto."

Linto's new Huron friends were lying to him. It was practically the most difficult thing he had ever experienced.

"Like this?" The ball dribbled pathetically out of his basket.

"Non, non. Regardez et apprenez."

"What?"

"Watch and learn. With your wrists, see?" His tutor effortlessly whisked the ball in a straight trajectory, and his cohort, positioned at least fifteen paces away, seemed to magically grab the wooden sphere out of the air with his own basket on a stick.

Linto tried again, and this effort was even worse. The Huron men could not contain their laughter. Linto smiled, and gave up. Tomorrow was another day to try and master their strange new game, and he went in search of Annawon.

When he finally found him, Linto burst into laughter. "You look absolutely ridiculous, Annawon."

Annawon tried his best to appear dejected. "Do you really think so? Well, what about this?" He removed his shiny English battle helmet, and replaced it with a floppy, wide-brimmed leather hat, the kind that the men of Plimoth were so fond of. He proudly pointed at it with both hands.

"Even worse. At least the first one will protect you when Metacomet smacks you in the head. As well he should."

"For a holy man, you can be awfully mean, Linto." Now it was Annawon who couldn't control his laughter.

"Where did you get those hideous things, anyway?"

"Our French friends gave them to me. You should get fitted for a helmet. Of course, you are the skinniest man I know with the fattest head."

Linto donned the helmet. "What do you think?"

"I think you should be first in the ranks. Our enemies will perish from laughter."

Metacomet and what remained of his army had been garrisoned at Schaghticoke near the Hudson River for several frigid, snowy weeks. The living was comfortable, however, as their new French friends ensured they were well provided for. Their Huron allies had been trickling in from afar, a few dozen at a time, but they had answered the call. They were loyal allies of New France, and Colonel Richaud's English enemy was now their enemy too.

"Metacomet has summoned us for lunch."

There were times during the last few weeks that Linto almost forgot there was a brutal, deadly war raging ten days east of them. He was usually warm by a fire, and now that Father Jacques was gone, Cahp-ee-tehn Alain was teaching him a few phrases of French, which he mastered very quickly. Unfortunately, he could not master the new game of the Huron, which the French called "the stick," or *la crosse*.

Lunch sounded very good to Linto. "Make sure you bring your hat, Annawon."

They found Metacomet warming himself by a large, stone fire pit. Wootonekanuske and Mendon were feasting on striped bass procured from that morning's ice fishing. They glumly took their leave when they saw Annawon and Linto approach.

"Where is *my* hat, Annawon? Shouldn't *King Philip* have a crown?"

"I brought you a belt, Sachem."

"I think I'd rather have the hat."

"I'm sorry. I look too good in it. Just ask Linto."

Metacomet had been in good spirits since sealing the alliance with French. He inspected and trained his new warriors, and his loyal Wampanoag warriors were infused with a new sense of optimism.

"And what news from the spirits, Linto? Do you have any signs for us?"

Linto had actually tried to inspect the entrails of a slain doe two days ago. Wantuk the powwas had shown him the auguries to look for when he was a teen-ager, but that was years ago, and he remembered little. He seemed to recall that if the lungs were darker than the liver, that did not bode well, but if the stomach was free of blood, then it would be a good moon for war, but if the heart was smaller than a fist...or was it the liver? Truthfully, Linto had no idea what he was looking at, and the entire endeavor made him a little queasy.

"No, Sachem. All is silent." Linto wondered if his status as a holy man was rapidly fading, and if it was, if that was such a bad thing. Perhaps the Blackbird was right about him. He wondered, however, if he was exhausting Metacomet's patience. "But all seems well, Sachem. The new warriors are fearsome, indeed."

Metacomet handed Linto a piece of bass with some dried corn. "It's not enough."

"Thank you, Sachem. It's more than enough."

"Not the fish, Linto. The warriors. They are not enough. One hundred and fifty? One hundred and eighty, with a half dozen Frenchman watching over them? We cannot control our destiny with such an army. We need more allies."

"More allies?"

"I cannot bear to see those foul witches elevated to be the Grand Sachems of the nations. Will we cast off the yoke of Skunk Genitals for the yoke of the Bluebird? Will she lord over us with her hundreds and hundreds of warriors after the English have given up, and sealed themselves away?"

Linto ruminated carefully on this. Frankly, he feared Metacomet was succumbing to foolish, destructive pride. On that summer day in Nipsachuck several months ago, their lives and the lives of all their loved ones were almost extinguished by a Mohegan ambush. They were lucky to be alive. They were still actively engaged in the war, and now they boasted an extremely formidable alliance. Metacomet and his followers were blessed.

Conversely, Linto understood and embraced his Sachem's feelings on the matter. The twin sisters of the Nipmuc were almost as haughty and obnoxious as the learned men of Plimoth. Their condescension was unbearable, and they personally humiliated both Metacomet and Linto in a public setting. Linto dreamed of a day when Metacomet could triumphantly lead five hundred, or eight hundred, or even a thousand warriors east to Boston while Chogan and her witch of a sister were relegated to a supporting role.

Linto realized how long he had been in thought, and cleared his throat. "But what allies, Sachem? Where are there more allies to be had?"

"West, Linto. To the west."

Linto was perplexed. "We *are* west, Sachem. If we go any further west, we will be in the big, deep lakes. Who is to be found to the west?"

Annawon and Metacomet exchanged knowing glances, and Annawon broke the news. "The Mohawks, Linto. The Mohawks. They are the strongest among us."

Linto was stunned. "*The Mohawks*? Our new friends hate the Mohawks. No one is more loyal to the English. What's more, they've never been friends of the Wampanoag, either."

Metacomet expected this response, and remained impassive. "They can be persuaded, Linto. We just need a...diplomatic mission."

"*You think they will receive us*?" Linto calibrated his words carefully, in order to maintain the proper respect. He lowered his voice and spoke slower. "Sachem, you really believe this is possible?"

"This is an enormous gamble, Linto. Our mission is extremely sensitive. Only we three will be going. It will be two long and difficult days through the snow. But the reward will be remarkable. Picture the look on the sisters' hideous faces when we return with an army of eight hundred warriors."

Annawon flashed his brilliant smile. "I'll bet the witch will be so shocked she'll actually say something."

Metacomet chuckled. "Perhaps she'll be so ecstatic she may even lie with a man. Perhaps you will be her first, Annawon."

Linto was getting into the spirit of things. "Make sure you wear your new, shiny helmet, Annawon. She'll be impressed."

"Oh, trust me, skinny boy. She's going to impressed."

The laughter subsided, and Metacomet made an odd request. "Linto, what passages do you know from the big, English book about slaughtering the enemies of God?"

Linto was surprised. It had been weeks since they'd discussed any English religion. "Umm…I would have to research that, Sachem."

"Find a good passage, and bring it. Tear it out."

"Tear it out?"

"Yes, there's no need to lug the big book on the journey. Leave it here with Wootonekanuske.

That evening, as Linto surveyed the book for an appropriate passage, he contemplated the act of removing a page. Was he desecrating the big book? Would anyone care? After an hour of research that strained his eyes, he was confident he found what Metacomet was looking for near the front of the book, in the section called Leviticus.

*If ye walk in my statutes, and keep my commandments, and do them; Then I will give you rain in due season, and the land shall yield her increase, and the trees of the field shall yield their fruit. And your threshing shall reach unto the vintage, and the vintage shall reach unto the sowing time: and ye shall eat your bread to the full, and dwell in your land safely. **And I will give peace in the land, and ye shall lie down, and none shall make you afraid: and I will rid evil beasts out of the land, neither shall the sword go through your land. And ye shall chase your enemies, and they shall fall before you by the sword. And five of you shall chase a hundred, and a hundred of you shall put ten thousand to flight: and your*** *enemies shall fall before you by the sword. For I will have respect unto you, and make you fruitful, and multiply you, and establish my covenant with you.*

The next morning, after Linto translated and explained the words, Metacomet seemed pleased. Linto was beginning to grasp his vision. They would present these words to the Mohawks, and remind them that the English believe that their God loves them and no one else, and it's just a matter of time before the English turn on the Mohawks, no matter how helpful and loyal they had been.

Metacomet had to convey a falsehood to their French allies, who would be extremely averse to any interaction with the Mohawks. He said he was proceeding south, in hopes of rendezvousing with a Nipmuc delegation in order to convey the good news about their new alliance.

They departed on their journey, and were well-supplied with food and warm clothing. The countryside by the vast river was glorious, even in winter, and at times Linto wished he could dwell here among the mountains and valleys. Of course, nothing could make him happier than to be reunited with Wawetseka and the children in their humble wetu at Montaup, overlooking the bay.

After a second day of rigorous travel, they made camp for the night. Annawon left to survey the area, and Linto quickly built the fire. Annawon returned after approximately an hour, and they settled into their evening meal. Annawon sang a very old song that Massasoit allegedly taught him, and the three of them warmed themselves contentedly. Linto noticed that Annawon had brought his funny English hat, but for whatever reason, had chosen not to wear it. Linto assumed it would be a gift for the Mohawk delegation.

Linto concluded this would be as good an opportunity as any to be forthright with Metacomet regarding the Blackbird. The situation had gnawed at him repeatedly in the preceding weeks, and he hated the fact he seemed to be withholding something so critical from his Sachem.

Why did he feel the need to be so candid about this, yet so deceptive about the prophecy?

"Sachem, there is something you need to know about the Blackbird. The day before we left Menameset, she said...well, her sister said..."

"I know, Linto."

"You know?"

"Of course. A Sachem has eyes everywhere, Linto."

"And you don't..."

"Care what she has to say? Of course not. She's a fraud, Linto. What kind of nonsense is that, remaining perfectly quiet all the time. I couldn't care less what she thinks about you, Linto. Or about me."

Linto was relieved, but there was the word again. *Fraud.*

Metacomet leaned into the roaring blaze, and drew closer to Linto. The shadows of the flames danced across his somber face. *"I was there, Linto.* I saw it with my own eyes. I saw my father lift you up, and sing to you. We pulled you out of that sea of death. Never forget what you mean to us, Linto. In this age of death and disease, the spirits of our ancestors have not abandoned us. They will never abandon us. That's what you mean to us."

Linto thought he might have a tear rolling down his face, but he assured himself his eyes were merely irritated by the smoke. Why couldn't he fulfill his destiny? Why wouldn't the spirit world speak to him? Why did he have to be an agent of fraud?

Metacomet put his hand on Linto's shoulder. "I have known you since you were a toddler, Linto. Wootonekanuske and I practically raised you." Linto nodded politely. "And I am your Sachem. I am the son of the greatest Sachem these lands have ever known. I have to know that you trust me implicitly, Linto, just as I have trusted you."

Linto could only nod apprehensively. Annawon was now leaning close to the fire as well. Metacomet's voice was scarcely a whisper. "This diplomatic mission to the Mohawks is not what you expected, Linto. Forgive the deception, but it is the only way."

"Sachem, what are you saying?"

Now Annawon had his arm around Linto's shoulder. "This is an extremely sensitive mission, Linto. That's why there's only the three of us. The Sachem needs men who love and trust him, and will obey his commands unquestionably."

Metacomet's eyes blazed with intensity. "We are increasingly desperate, Linto. The Huron warriors are adequate, but they have not sent their best fighting men. We need *warriors*, Linto, men who can fight and terrify the Mohegan. We *have* to have the Mohawks on our side."

Annawon revealed what he had been doing during the previous hour. "There is a Mohawk hunting camp, Linto, five hundred paces down the ridgeline. Almost all the men are away. There's only five or six men there, and they are drinking. They will be deep in slumber within hours. And then, Metacomet and I strike."

"You don't have to do anything, Linto, except stand watch. Alert us if anyone arrives unexpectedly. Annawon and I will do the rest."

Linto was too appalled to speak. Finally, he mustered his words and hoped his voice would not crack like a child's. "I...I don't understand any of this. What is happening? Sachem? Annawon?"

"Don't you see it, Linto? We leave all these English things at the scene, and the English will be blamed. The Mohawks will beg to join our fight."

"The English will be blamed? For what? Sachem, please. This can't be happening."

Annawon rested his hand on his knee. "Just stand watch, skinny boy. We will take care of everything."

The three of them rested in silence until the middle of the night. Linto prayed, and even contemplated another divine prophecy. It would have been foolishness. He knew he could not sell another ruse like that.

He would trust his Sachem. He didn't know what other choice he had.

Soon, the time for rest was over, and Metacomet approached. "One last thing, Linto. Give me the page from the book." Linto tentatively presented it, and Metacomet continued. "Point to the good words. About killing their enemies." Linto's hand quaked as he pointed out the passage.

"And ye shall chase your enemies, and they shall fall before you by the sword."

Metacomet unsheathed a dagger and carefully made an incision in his shin, drawing a discrete amount of blood. He soaked his finger in the blood, circled the passage, and hid the page away.

"Let's go."

They extinguished the fire and moved stealthily to their objective. Annawon's assessment was right. Not a man remained awake, and smoke wafted from a lone, makeshift cabin.

Annawon turned and faced Linto in the darkness. Nodding, he handed him an enormous dagger. He silently mouthed the words one last time. *"Keep watch."*

Linto crouched in the shadows of the cabin as Metacomet and Annawon surreptitiously infiltrated their objective. Linto expected they would accomplish their horrific work in less than a minute, but the minute would seem like a lifetime. He tried to breathe slowly, and he wallowed in a sense of disbelief that this could even be happening. In fact, the emotions of the moment were so overwhelming that they knocked Linto off of his feet, and into the snow. Shaking his head to rouse his senses, he gazed upward.

He couldn't believe it.

Metacomet and Annawon had been gone less than sixty seconds, and a tipsy Mohawk hunter had tripped over Linto on his way back from answering nature's call. Wide-eyed and terrified, the Mohawk stared at Linto and also tried to comprehend what was happening. Linto stared back, and they both stared at the dagger in Linto's hand. Linto was absolutely certain the stranger was inhaling, inhaling deeply in preparation to scream like a demon, and Linto did not know what to do.

Guided solely by instinct, he closed his eyes, gulped, and plunged the dagger into the Mohawk's abdomen with all his might.

Linto was so afraid he couldn't bear to open his eyes. He heard the nauseating "oomph" of his victim, and the warm blood oozed over Linto's hand. He anticipated a scream, but none came. With his eyes still closed, he withdrew the blade, and thought he heard the sound of retreat. He finally mustered the courage to open his eyes, and he saw the back of his victim as he staggered off into the wilderness, trailing a stream of blood.

He somehow managed to stand, and Metacomet and Annawon tore past him frantically. They had done it. They had furtively slaughtered five Mohawk hunters, and they left behind an English hat, belt buckle, and the page from scripture. In their hasty escape in the darkness, they did not notice the bloody snow, or the blood on Linto's hand and dagger.

For reasons unknown, Linto plunged his hand and dagger into the snow, and purged them of the blood. He was certain the wound was deep and fatal, and his victim was lying dead in the wilderness. He scurried after his Sachem.

The timing had been incomprehensible. In the mere sixty seconds it took them to carry out their foul deed, a stray hunter had stumbled over Linto, and Linto had no options. Linto was so troubled by his actions that he resigned himself to never speak of them. Metacomet and Annawon could never know what he had done.

But deep in his soul, Linto knew. Linto knew he had committed a horrible, unspeakable, vicious crime. And he knew that somehow, in some unknown way, he would one day pay dearly for his sins.

CHAPTER TWENTY-SEVEN

THE WILDERNESS OF RHODE ISLAND

"Well, we're alive, God be praised. What a night."

Cornet Jemmy Barnstrom could not keep still. If he constantly stayed in motion, he felt like the situation was almost bearable. Well, not bearable, but somehow survivable.

The sunlight on his face was a gift from heaven. He diligently inspected his company for hypothermia and frostbite. "Reddington, you don't even look cold."

"It was a little nippy, Cornet Barnstrom. After midnight, I had to unfurl my blanket."

Barnstrom decided long ago that if he ever had to storm the gates of hell, it would somehow be tolerable as long as he had Reddington by his side. "Reverend, you're still tied to this mortal coil, I pray?"

The night had clearly taken its toll on Israel Brewster. He was still not entirely reacclimated to the life of a New England militiaman, and he suffered horribly through the night. There were moments he genuinely believed he would perish, and the long, dark night was filled with prayer, memories, and regret. But he was alive. One way or another, he would do his duty for Middleborough and these colonies, and he would return whole in spirit to his beloved.

Almost inconceivably, the men were preparing for yet another grueling march through the most desolate of conditions. Rations had been depleted long ago, and the ceaseless suffering was beginning to devolve into a mood of numb resignation. The men increasingly believed there could be no torture that they could not grudgingly overcome through faith and sheer perseverance.

In the year 1675, the only thing in a militia that traveled faster than a musket ball was the wild rumors shooting through the ranks. As the companies assembled, every manner of story about their strange prisoner had made the rounds, sometimes even twice. Winslow had forced Peter at gunpoint to lead them to the fort. Winslow promised Peter a forty-foot sloop and an elegant home in Boston. Peter was the ghost of a young Massasoit, come to beg forgiveness for his son's treachery, and to lead his English friends to victory. Some had it on good authority that Peter demanded, and would be granted, five English wives, each with a different color of hair. The tales grew more outlandish by the hour.

No matter how desperate the situation or unbelievable the rumors, one thing was vividly clear. They were on the march again. They marched due west, with the December sunrise on their backs. The snow was now remarkably deep, and progress was painfully slow. Within an hour, the rumors started brewing again. Peter was evidently now the son of a Narragansett Sachem, and he was fiendishly luring them all to a certain death.

Regardless of his fear and exhaustion, Brewster marveled at the size and scope of the army. There were devout Puritans. There were Baptists. There were pirates and mercenaries. There were Pequot and Mohegan Indians. There were wealthy men and poor men, there were professional soldiers, and there were farmers. Men came from Connecticut, Massachusetts Bay, and Plimoth Colony. There were men like Brewster, Bradford, and Winslow, whose fathers and grandfathers sailed on the Mayflower, and there were men whose families had been settled in the New World for mere months. All had willingly enlisted for this holy and righteous mission, and they yearned to defend the United Colonies of New England from heathen aggression.

"Come on, you pompous, Puritan bastards! There's savages to kill! Vengeance for the men of the garrison! Vengeance for Swansea! Vengeance for Middleborough! Who's with me? Let's hear your voice, if your balls haven't frozen off!" Dutch Cornelius' voice was so loud, Brewster genuinely believed the entire thousand-man army could hear him.

Under normal circumstances, Major Bradford might direct Captain Moseley to reel in his band of crazed mercenaries, but at the moment, Bradford knew Dutch Cornelius' antics were just what they needed. Bradford contemplated exclaiming some bold hyperbole about his own anatomy, but even under these dire circumstances, his Puritan sensibilities wouldn't permit it. Additionally, after spending the last thirty-six hours exposed to the bitter winter elements, he knew any hyperbole about his private anatomy would be woefully inaccurate. For all he knew, his balls *had* frozen off. Instead, he raised his saber. "For Plimoth! Let's hear the Plimoth men!" He was greeted by a loud roar.

Brewster wondered if all the noisy encouragement was tactically sound, but then he discounted the notion as silly. A thousand-man army would not be sneaking up on anyone. He permitted himself an occasional "huzzah," and "God bless Middleborough!" If he was shouting and laughing, he reasoned, then he hadn't frozen to death yet.

Soon the midday sun had peaked, but little warmth was provided. An audible buzz throughout the army was discernible, however, and word quickly spread. They had arrived. They had found it. Peter the traitor had led them right to the inner sanctum of the Narragansett. And the men gasped as it came into view.

The fortress dwarfed anything Brewster could have imagined. It occupied at least five acres of dry land situated in the middle of a swamp. The palisades were enormous, and encircled the entire structure. Additionally, the palisades were augmented by massive walls of clay and mud. There were numerous blockhouses and towers, and under normal circumstances, there would only be one way to access the fort: An enormous log constituted a bridge, which would have to be traversed single-file, or at the very most, two abreast. Fortunately, due to the frozen conditions, they could pay no mind to the log-bridge. Overall, however, it was an absolutely magnificent defensive structure, and Brewster stood in awe.

The men of the United Colonies had spent months training and preparing for this moment. They had endured unspeakable hardships during their journey, and as such, there would be no lingering. There would be no speech, and there would be no sermon. General Winslow raised his saber, and the first company of Massachusetts Bay men prepared their flintlocks and darted across the frozen swamp.

It was a slaughter.

The virgin white snow and ice ran red with English blood as the Narragansett unleashed a wave of ferocious gunfire from their perfectly situated block towers. Undaunted, a wave of Connecticut militia followed suit, and quickly met the same fate. Despite the fact the men could run across the frozen swamp and bypass the treacherous log bridge, the fort was incredibly well-defended, and subsequent assaults would be equally brutal.

Brewster eyed the carnage from the ranks and was appalled. "Jemmy, this is madness. There's got to be another way."

"We're a thousand strong, Israel. There will be casualties, but we'll get through. Put your faith in Governor Winslow."

Brewster considered that sentiment, and he quickly assessed his faith in their commander. He was the man who humiliated Plimoth's Wampanoag allies four years ago with a despicable "peace treaty." He was the man who was ready to defrock and prosecute Brewster for ridiculous, imaginary crimes. And he was the man who led his massive army to the brink of death by starvation and hypothermia.

He would place his faith elsewhere.

"Jemmy, I'm breaking ranks. There's got to be a weakness in this fort somewhere."

"You're what?" The sounds of musket fire crackled sharply as another wave of New England militia were cut down.

"I'm headed around the fort. I'm off on a scouting mission." At that moment, Brewster swept Brownie's cargo and supplies from her back, and mounted his trusted companion. He broke north, and galloped away.

Reddington glared at his commander, awaiting some kind of directive. Barnstrom stood blinking in stunned silence, and the silence was quickly unbearable. "I'm going with him, Jemmy. Don't worry, I'll watch out for him." And without another word, Reddington was also gone.

Brewster furiously kicked and prodded his dark mare, but was quickly embarrassed to discover a sprinting Reddington easily keeping pace. This was a poor time indeed to be the master of the slowest horse in the colonies.

"Further north, Reverend! This way! We've got to stay hidden!" Not only was Reddington keeping pace, he was now leading the way, and Brewster wondered if a cold, starving Brownie would be able to keep up with the brawny corporal.

Their footing was difficult, and soon the terrain grew dense. They seemed to go undetected, however, and they proceeded cautiously. Even at midday, the swampland was dark and forbidding. They remained within visual range of the colossal fort, and Brewster continued to marvel. It was a testament to the diligence and will of the Narragansett.

"Anything, Reverend?"

"Nothing. It's like the fortress of Lachish."

"Excuse me?"

"The fortress of Lachish. In the second book of Kings, the Israelites were tasked to...Look! There, Thomas! Over there!"

Reddington peered around an enormous white pine tree. "Yes, I see it! What on earth happened there? The fortifications are collapsing."

Their impulsive scouting foray had paid huge dividends. Near the rear of the fort was a span of disarray. The palisades had collapsed, and the earthen walls were only two feet high. Additionally, the block towers seemed to be scarcely manned, if at all.

"Praise God, we have found it. Let's go, Thomas!"

The duo raced back to the company and found a scene of chaos. Englishmen had fallen by the dozens. Horses were shrieking, officers were shouting, and the Narragansett enemy was raining mockery down upon them. The army seemed no closer to infiltrating the fort than before, and Barnstrom was readying the company for the next assault.

"Jemmy, we've got it! Around back! It's barely defended, and the palisades have collapsed!"

"What? You're positive?"

Reddington knew his testimony would add the credibility Barnstrom was craving. "Absolutely! Send the men around back! We'll be slaughtered in a frontal assault."

Barnstrom stared vacantly in the distance. They would be the next company cast into another futile assault. He had, however, absolutely zero influence with General Winslow. But he knew who did.

"Wait here."

Barnstrom darted off and quickly found Church at Winslow's side. Church was frantically barking orders, but was desperately grasping for answers. After Barnstrom's report and some frenzied pleading with General Winslow, Church was given authorization to lead approximately three hundred men through the breach in the rear of the fortress.

Brewster tried to lead the way and direct the assault force to their destination, but he and his plodding mare were soon left far behind as hundreds of men furiously descended on their objective. Three hundred men could not move undetected, and the Narragansett were soon in position and waiting for them. The English and their Indian allies raced for the collapsed section of palisade, but were promptly cut down in a hail of gunfire and arrows.

Brownie finally conveyed Brewster to the scene, and he was horrified to discover a situation in the back of the fort tragically similar to the situation in the front. Soldiers maniacally and randomly rushed forth in the open field to infiltrate the fort, and their adversaries, secure in their blockhouses, rained death upon them.

Brewster was astounded at their inability to adapt. He was not a military tactician. He was a clergyman and a cooper, but the answer seemed glaringly obvious. Brewster shouted in as loud a voice as he ever had shouted before. *"Columns, Captain! Organize the men into columns! Two or three columns! Columns!"*

Church did not acknowledge hearing him, but as if the voice mysteriously came from the heavens, he complied. "Columns! Form up in two columns! Columns, lads!"

Reddington shot a knowing grin at Brewster as they assumed their places in the columns. Resistance was still fierce, and the first men in the columns paid a horrific price, but the tactic was vindicated. Soon ten Englishmen were inside the fort, then twenty, then fifty. Narragansett resistance began to unravel as the blockhouses were put to the torch. Soon hundreds of Englishmen and their Indian allies were inside the fort, and they unleashed a cruel and vindictive wave of violence.

More blockhouses and sentry towers went up in flames. Sabers were unleashed, and men, women, and children were indiscriminately cut down. The misery inflicted upon Winslow's army and all of New England would be avenged. Women and children fled the calamity and ran barefoot into the snowy wilderness. Men surrendered, but were mercilessly put to the sword. Soon, armed Narragansett warriors were few in number and difficult to spot.

If this was victory, it was being achieved at an appalling price. Plimoth men were still being gunned down at an alarming rate, and Brewster desperately surveyed the battlefield to see where the fierce resistance was coming from. He directed Brownie east, back toward the entry gate of the fort, and the answer was soon apparent. Winslow's men had finally breached the main gate, and were haphazardly shooting. Church's men were being mowed down by friendly fire.

Brewster knew he had to act immediately, and Brownie raced across the frozen snow into the heart of the malice and bloodshed. In the midst of the chaos, all sense of time was grossly distorted, and Brewster was uncertain if this was the slowest Brownie had ever run, or the fastest. After several hundred yards, Winslow and his glorious pacer were easy to spot.

"Stop shooting, General! Church is caught in the friendly fire! The fort is ours, the enemy is fleeing! Stop shooting!"

Winslow was highly reluctant to take orders or advice from the man he wanted incarcerated a mere six weeks ago, but he gave the order to cease fire. Afterward, no enemy gunfire could be discerned. Canochet's warriors had run out of powder, been fatally wounded, or had led the women and children into the wilderness. Brewster was absolutely correct. The fort was theirs, and Winslow gave his thanks to the Lord.

Brewster surveyed the scene, and he was greeted by madness and violence at every corner. Towers burned wildly, and the dark smoke rose into the cold December air. Muskets were fired indiscriminately, as enemy combatants were gunned down while fleeing, and mercilessly executed if too wounded to flee.

Benjamin Church finally came into view. He was mounted on horseback, and carefully assessing the scene. He directed men to inspect the wetus and longhouses for stores of food and weapons, and to ensure no warriors were lying in ambush. He seemed intensely fixated on the largest of the structures, as if wondering how many men it could accommodate, and he was momentarily oblivious to his surroundings. Brewster then observed a scene that made his heart race.

One of Moseley's pirates, Dutch Cornelius, had his flintlock pistol drawn and was preparing to fire. He was only ten yards behind Church, and he could only be aiming at one thing. Brewster leapt off Brownie, and screamed like the devil. "CHURCH!" Unsatisfied that he could be heard, he grabbed the nearest projectile he could find, a stone hatchet lying abandoned on the ground. He screamed, "STOP" as he let the hatchet fly through the bitterly cold, smoke-filled air.

Brewster finally caught Church's attention, and he turned his head just in time to see the hatchet land ten feet short of Cornelius' boots. The giant pirate lowered his pistol, and appearing almost amused, picked up the harmless projectile. He faced Brewster. "Was this yours, then? You throw like a tavern wench, laddie." He then expertly hurled the hatchet with remarkable speed and accuracy, and it sailed one foot above Brewster's head. Without pausing, he raised his pistol again and paced ten steps in Church's direction. "You really ought to be more careful, Captain."

He fired.

His aim was perfect, and he slaughtered a wounded Narragansett warrior who was crawling on the ground behind the longhouse, undetected by Church. Dutch Cornelius grinned a sickening, malicious grin. "You seem to have enemies everywhere, Captain Church. Beware." He sauntered away without another word, as Church tried to grasp what had just happened.

Brewster felt equally flummoxed, and he didn't know whether to seek Church's forgiveness or undying gratitude. Two hundred yards away, however, another horrific spectacle was unfolding, and he and Brownie rushed in the direction of the ear-piercing screams.

Cornelius' pirate comrades had found a secluded section of the fort where they could commit mayhem in relative privacy. They had found five or six of the most attractive women in the fort, and they were indulging their depraved, satanic lust. The women were stark naked, and were cruelly held face-down in the snow while being brutalized.

There were at least ten pirates in their midst, but Brewster would find a way to end this. He would end this, or he would willingly meet his eternal reward. He drew his saber. He looked in every direction for Church, Reddington, Barnstrom, or any other ally, but he was on his own. They were obscured by trees and longhouses, and if Winslow's men were aware of the criminal activity, they were seemingly oblivious to it.

Brewster was preparing to announce his incursion. He paused to consider his words. *Cease and desist? Unhand those women, you vile miscreants? Stop, or face my saber?* Just when he decided on a simple "stop," the situation became even more astounding.

A mere forty feet from the lustful depravity, a sentry tower was aflame. There were towers burning everywhere at that moment, but this one had three or four small children trapped within. They had fled the unfathomable terror and hidden themselves away, but now their lives were in imminent danger. The flames rose to consume them, and they helplessly wailed. What should he do? Should he provide aid to the women, or to the children?

As he dismounted Brownie and stood paralyzed with indecision, he was shocked as one of the Indian women boldly escaped her tormentor. She threw a sharp elbow into his temple, and as he reeled with pain, she turned over, flexed her leg at the knee, and drove her heel so deeply into his exposed manhood that Brewster would swear he could also feel the pain.

As the pirate howled with agony, she raced upwards into the inferno, oblivious to her nakedness. She emerged from the flames with two small toddlers in her arms, and an older child clinging to her back. As they reached the fleeting safety of the ground, the tower began to collapse.

"Run, children, run! The wilderness! Run!" The older child was able to pick up the youngest child, and they ran through the snow as the burning structure collapsed. A section of heavy, burning timber fell upon the heroine's head, disorienting her long enough for her assailant to recover from his excruciating pain and seek his vengeance.

Grabbing her by the hair, he kicked her legs away and pulled her to the ground. He then forced her face into the burning wooden debris, and he held it there as he relished the

252 | P a g e

screams. His diabolical pleasure was short-lived, however, as the flat of Brewster's saber instantly knocked him unconscious.

Brewster kicked him away and assisted the wretched victim out of the flames. He grieved he was too late to prevent the unspeakable damage inflicted upon her lovely face. Conversely, he was relieved the pirate's friends seemed preoccupied with their own malice, and were uninterested in his rescue attempt.

He cautiously evaluated the victim. The left half of her face and hair was grotesquely burned, and she would almost certainly lose an eye. Still disoriented from her head injury, she stared vacantly at him and tried to comprehend what was happening.

"*Two Ponds?*"

He was so frightened he fell backwards. His mouth fell open, but he couldn't utter a word.

"*Two Ponds? Why? Why, Two Ponds?*"

Four years ago, Israel Brewster had suffered through months of hideous night terrors, and Wawetseka was the one who cured him of them. Surely, this was all another nightmare. This had to be a bizarre, lingering side effect of the healing ritual, and he had to be in the midst of a shockingly realistic hallucination. Finally, the last twenty-four hours of his life made sense. The brutal cold, the hunger, the vicious slaughter. It was all a ghastly nightmare.

He forced his eyelids together as hard as he could, and held them shut. He opened them, and repeated the process two more times. He picked up snow, and rubbed it against his face in the pathetic hope that there would be no sensation of cold, thereby validating his suspicion that he was dreaming.

"*Why did you do this, Two Ponds? Linto loved you. I loved you.*"

Brewster was now slapping himself in an absolutely ridiculous attempt to wake up. With no other meaningful options, he prayed. "*Help me, Lord God. Relieve me of my terrors. Help me, Lord God. Take this all away.*"

Wawetseka could not comprehend any of his words, or any of his bizarre actions. She rose to her feet, and was clearly woozy and disoriented. She steadied herself, and seeing the depravity in her midst, she once again grasped what was transpiring.

Her hand found her face and, filled with dread, she caressed the smoldering flesh and her ruined, unseeing eye. Focusing again on the former friend that was now her most despised enemy, she hissed. *"I curse you, Two Ponds! You are not healed! You are cursed!"* She frantically tore away her unconscious tormentor's coat, and fled into the wilderness.

Israel Brewster remained kneeling in the frigid snow. A mere six weeks ago, he enlisted in the militia of the United Colonies of New England in the hopes that somehow, in some way, he could make a difference in this war. He prayed that if only men like him did their duty, there would be no more Middleboroughs.

He had done his duty. He had risked his life by marching at least twenty-four hours through the brutal, unforgiving countryside in the dead of winter. He found the lone weakness in the fortress, and saved the English army from certain slaughter. He redirected the assault into columns, ensuring their triumphant entry into the heavily-defended stronghold. He found General Winslow, and he stopped the withering friendly fire that was murdering so many Englishmen. And no matter what Cornelius would ever say, Brewster had no doubt he had saved Captain Church from a cruel murder. Israel Brewster was a hero.

And at that moment, kneeling alone in the December snow, Israel Brewster, the hero of the great swamp fight that vanquished the enemies of New England, wished that he were dead.

CHAPTER TWENTY-EIGHT

THE SMITH GARRISON

Bitter. Cruel. Relentless. It was increasingly difficult to describe the intensity of the cold.

Yet everywhere, fire raged. Flames rose and fell, and with a sickening crackling sound, their thirst for destruction was unquenchable.

Brewster remained oblivious to the flames, and almost derived solace from them. Any source of heat was welcome, but he felt like he was maniacally alternating between hypothermia and the fires of hell. Babies wailed, mothers moaned with grief, and through it all, Brewster held the hand of his beloved.

How exhausted she seemed. She stared at him with her probing, gentle dark eyes as if she expected him to somehow alleviate her agony. He stroked her hair, and he waited for their newborn to make a sound. None came. Yet, the cries of the other children were incessant and deafening.

Sarah slowly opened her mouth as if she was going to speak, but she was too weak. Her bed was surrounded by flames, and the entire home seemed to be an inferno. Brewster peered out the window, and saw the meeting house of Middleborough was crashing to the ground in a torrent of flame.

He wiped the sweat away. Even in these most brutal winter conditions, he could not stop sweating. He tried to grin to comfort Sarah, but his mouth was frozen. The shrieking persisted, however. The cacophonous, fearsome shrieking of infants trapped in the flames.

Brewster took the hand of his beloved. Somehow, it was ice cold. He gazed in her intoxicating hazel eyes, and he delighted in stroking her vivid, red hair. She was so full with child it looked like the blessed event could come at any moment. Constance gazed back at him, and gently guiding his hand, placed it carefully on her enormous belly. She shook her head with grim resignation, and Brewster began weeping as he now understood. There would be no child.

The wails and moans grew louder outside the window. Constance beckoned for him to come closer, and after his ear was almost touching her lips, she whispered her innermost thoughts.

"I don't think Jemmy's going to make it, Reverend."

Why was she telling him this? Nothing made any sense. Brewster was crushed by the news, and he placed his face in his hands. After composing himself, he was able to formulate his thoughts, and he stared intently at her beautiful, forlorn face and her soft, brown eyes.

"How do you know that? Don't say that, Sarah! You can't know that!"

And Sarah gave him the same look he had seen a hundred times before. It was the look of utter weariness, the look of utter acceptance that she was about to join their stillborn child in death. Brewster braced himself to hear the words once again. At this moment, she would inevitably gaze upon him, melt his soul with her dark brown eyes and whisper, *"How blessed I have been."*

She looked up at him. She then glanced hopelessly at their stillborn child and refocused her attention on him.

"I curse you, Two Ponds. You are cursed."

Stunned and bewildered, Brewster slowly backed away from her bed. He could feel the flames singeing his shirt now. This was not how this was supposed to go.

Sarah continued with her bizarre rants. *"It's bad, Reverend. I'm really scared. Wake up, Israel."* She reached across the room and grabbed him by his shirt. She shook him like a man possessed, and then she somehow commandeered Thomas Reddington's thundering voice while choking back tears.

"Please, Israel, wake up. I don't know what to do."

Brewster finally awoke and was greeted by Reddington's ruddy, tear-streaked face. As he struggled to comprehend reality and break free of his nightmare, one thing had become painfully clear.

Wawetseka did not dawdle with her curses.

During the first night after what history would call the Great Swamp Fight of 1675, Israel Brewster's night terrors were back, and they were more intense than ever. He was not surprised. Under the circumstances, he was not surprised Wawetseka would find a way to revoke the healing ceremony, and condemn him to a life of ceaseless, terrifying agony.

Brewster breathed deeply and surveyed his surroundings. He felt feverish, but he knew that on several counts, he was very lucky to still be alive.

After Wawetseka had conveyed her total contempt for him and escaped the fortress, Brewster remained kneeling in the snow, consumed by numb oblivion. Soon, some of the pirates had finished their cruel, barbarous deeds, and were preparing to engage the Puritan who knocked their comrade unconscious with the flat of his blade. Unbeknownst to Brewster, two had approached from behind with daggers at the ready.

And then, there was Reddington.

In his trance-like state, Brewster missed all of it, and Reddington was too modest to recount it. Jemmy and Captain Church, however, said it was unlike anything seen before in New England, as Reddington promptly disabled five pirates. Two suffered broken jaws, two suffered broken arms, and one suffered a crushed fibula. Immediately afterwards, Church and Barnstrom arrived via horseback with pistols drawn. The remaining pirates wisely surrendered, and the violated women quickly fled.

Meanwhile, the entire fortress of the Narragansett was going up in flames. In addition to sentry towers and block houses, wetus and longhouses were now being torched by fevered, violent maniacs. Church, however, pleaded with General Winslow to stop the madness. The men were sick, starving, hypothermic, and on the brink of collapse, yet here they were incinerating perfectly good shelters, and perfectly good storehouses of food.

Moseley stood at Winslow's other side, and offered a contrary opinion. "I'll sleep in the Atlantic Ocean before I sleep in a damned den of heathen blasphemy. I'm still furious so many escaped. Torch it, General! Make them pay for what they've done! I'm sure the supply ships will arrive soon and we'll have a perfectly good garrison over at Mister Smith's settlement, fifteen miles north of here. Burn this den of iniquity! Wipe this wicked sanctuary from the earth!"

It took Jemmy Barnstrom's company twelve hours to march through another brutal winter night to Smith's garrison, where nothing was awaiting them except a roof and a cold dirt floor. Even worse, Jemmy did not reveal to anyone that he had taken a musket ball to the leg earlier in the day, and he wavered in and out of consciousness atop Brownie during the journey. Reddington carried two casualties through the snow via a makeshift sled, and Brewster wondered if Reddington genuinely was stronger than Brownie.

Brewster was now fully awake. He crawled across the frozen dirt floor, and found Barnstrom in a state of semi-consciousness. His fever was excruciating, and the men attending him were still having difficulty managing the wound in his leg.

He opened one eye and recognized Brewster. His voice was barely audible. "You're a hero, Israel."

"Don't say things like that, Jemmy. I just made a few good suggestions. I've been fighting this war for scarcely a month. You've been at it for six."

Jemmy tried to smile. "Alright, then. Your horse is the hero."

"She doesn't expect much in reward. Her own apple tree would be nice."

"Count on it. I'll plant it in Middleborough. Would you...can you get me some water, Reverend?"

Brewster promptly fetched a drinking vessel. "You need to sleep, Jemmy."

"I fear I'm going to have a great deal of time to sleep very soon, Israel." He tried to smirk, and was then deep in thought. He suddenly wore a pained expression. "I hope you'll forgive me Israel, for I'm such a coward."

"Forgive you? Coward? The fever is making you mad, Jemmy. Here, take some more water. Are you taking food? I have some dried beans…"

"After Phelps and Winslow chased you out of Middleborough, I never said a word, Israel. I never questioned a thing. When you ran away, I assumed they were right. I assumed you did…" Barnstrom was coughing now, and couldn't finish the sentence.

"I didn't know what to think at the time, either. I was the real coward, Jemmy. I ran away and tried to drink myself to death. But don't think about such things. Preserve your strength."

"But look at you now. The hero of the great swamp fight."

"Please stop saying that. What have we done, Jemmy? We have at least two hundred casualties. The Narragansett weren't even in this war. How many women and children did we kill today? And we're the ones who enlisted those…those bastards in Moseley's company. They're not even men. They should be strung up."

Jemmy was growing weaker and did his best to nod. "How is Captain Church doing?"

"He's here. He has a terrible fever, too. And Major Bradford is in pretty bad shape."

He laid quietly for a prolonged period, and Brewster wondered if he had drifted to sleep. He woke suddenly, as if he had an urgent question.

"Can you believe it's all gone?"

"Gone?"

"Middleborough. Our homes. The meeting house. Burned to ashes." He softly coughed, and he lay silent. Slowly, he turned to face Brewster. "Did we do it? Did we avenge Middleborough?" Brewster was uncertain if he was being sardonic, as his voice was growing very faint.

Jemmy now had a faraway, vacant look in his eyes. "Do you remember Middleborough, Israel? Do you remember building my home?"

Reddington had been hunting for more nourishment, but to no avail. Returning, he joined the conversation. "I'll never forget that week. I lugged the timber, but my father built the house. And of course, Reverend Brewster helped as well. When he wasn't charming the ladies."

Jemmy actually chuckled, and seemed momentarily energized. "I remember. Oh, what a carpenter you were, Israel! I think Thomas' father secretly re-did everything you touched! How did you ever become a cooper? There must be barrels leaking all over New England!"

Brewster smiled and hoped some of Jemmy's strength was returning. "With God, all things are possible."

The thought was pleasing to Jemmy. "Thomas, you'll make sure Hope and the children are kept in good spirits, won't you? Make sure they know I did my duty. They must know that I did my duty for God and New England."

"Where are you going to be? You tell her. I'll be too busy rebuilding your home with my father. Maybe Reverend Brewster can even build a bucket for your privy. It shouldn't leak too badly."

Jemmy managed another smile. "Reverend, will you recite scripture for me? Did you bring that memory of yours?"

Brewster tried to ensure his eyes were dry as he meditated on an appropriate verse. He remembered the passage Easton cited when be brought news of Middleborough. "Gentlemen, the words of our savior, from the Gospel of John."

*"Verily, verily, I say unto you, that **ye shall weep and lament, but the world shall rejoice: and ye shall be sorrowful, but your sorrow shall be turned into joy**. A woman, when she is in travail hath sorrow, because her hour is come: but as soon as she is delivered*

of the child, she remembereth no more the anguish, for joy that a man is born into the world."

Brewster's voice was cracking, and he spoke slowly. *"**And ye now therefore have sorrow: but I will see you again, and your heart shall rejoice, and your joy no man taketh from you.** And in that day ye shall ask me nothing. Verily, verily, I say unto you, whatsoever ye shall ask the Father in my name, he will give it you. Hitherto have ye asked nothing in my name: ask, and ye shall receive, that your joy may be full. **These things I have spoken unto you, that in me ye might have peace. In the world ye shall have tribulation: but be of good cheer; for I have overcome the world."***

Cornet James "Jemmy" Barnstrom met his eternal reward shortly before sunrise on that December morning. He lapsed into unconsciousness after midnight, and he died in the arms of Thomas Reddington. Brewster prayed throughout the night, and he wept like a child when the moment arrived.

In addition to all the pillars of his Christian faith in which Israel Brewster believed so fervently, he now had another article of faith which he would not question until his dying day. He hoped the Lord would forgive him for it.

Israel Brewster now believed with all of his heart and soul that Josiah Winslow was the stupidest man in all of New England.

CHAPTER TWENTY-NINE

SCHAGHTICOKE

"Vous êtes malheureux?"

Linto morosely drew another card, and ignored Captain Alain Fontaine.

"Qu'est-ce qui ne va pas?"

Linto should have been using the opportunity, as Captain Fontaine expected, to study the language of their new allies. As the captain repeatedly conveyed, within a few years New England would merely be an extension of New France, and a working knowledge of French would be vital.

"Are you unhappy, Linto?"

The shift back to English stirred Linto from his dull torpor. He briefly made eye contact, played his card, and sighed. They were playing "one and thirty," and this would certainly be the fourth consecutive hand Linto would lose. His three cards currently added up to a paltry seventeen points, and he knew Fontaine would capitalize on his discard.

"I will take your three, and...voila. I have thirty-one. Or better yet, I have *trente et un.*" Linto stared vacantly into space.

"Linto, speak to me. You miss your family, no? I miss my family as well. My daughter is named Madeline. She is with her grandmother in Lyons. Tell me, what are the names of your children?"

Linto blinked and stared at the table. "Will Father Jacques ever come back, Cahp-ee-tehn Alain?"

Fontaine remained cordial. "I do not believe so. I have told you before. He will spend the spring to the west of here, on the shores of the ocean lake. It is very far, but he will save many souls. But I can answer all of your questions. You wish to know more about the English heresies? How they revile the Holy Father?"

Linto reached absent-mindedly for the cards, and lethargically shuffled them, much to Fontaine's surprise. "A fifth hand, Linto? Surely, your luck must be ready to change?"

Linto briefly ruminated on the concept of luck. "Cahp-ee-tehn Alain, do you confess your sins?"

"Excusez-moi?"

"Father Jacques told me true Christians will tell a holy man all the things they have done wrong, and they will ask to be forgiven. Do you think people are punished if they don't tell a holy man all the things they have done wrong?"

"You think of such serious matters all the time, Linto. The sky is clear, the English are on the run all over the land, and we are roasting ducks today. There will be a big lacrosse game to watch in the afternoon. I think we will also see at least thirty more warriors arrive this week, and they will bring muskets."

Linto continued his ineffective shuffling. "How often do you tell the holy man your sins? What if you do bad things every day?"

Fontaine reached for the cards and took them. "Linto, you have been moping like a sad Puritan ever since you went to see the Nipmuc. Weren't they overjoyed at the news? Aren't they making preparations for two hundred new warriors?"

The reminder of deception and falsehood triggered an even deeper gloom in Linto. He sat silently, and was relieved when one of Cahp-ee-tehn Alain's attendants came in with cheese and brandy. Linto hoped the subject would now quickly change.

The attendant respectfully set down the tray. He discreetly whispered in Fontaine's ear, and Fontaine's face went ashen. The attendant bowed and left the room.

"Brandy, Linto? It is marvelous to have on a cold winter's day?"

Linto had been persistently clear on the subject, yet the French never seemed to grasp his revulsion for alcohol.

"Then some cheese, perhaps?" Fontaine poured himself a brandy, and impulsively gulped it down. He poured another.

"Something is wrong, Cahp-ee-tehn?"

"Mohawks, Linto. At least two dozen have been spotted by our sentries. They seem to be enroute here."

Now Linto's face went ashen, and he wondered if the brandy could provide solace. The day of reckoning had finally arrived. He knew he had to feign ignorance. "Why would Mohawks come here?" He hoped his voice had not assumed a syrupy, insincere tone.

"Hopefully, it is no matter. They will want to know why we are assembling such a force. Their loyalty to the English has always been...problematic. I must go and find Colonel Richaud. Forgive me, we will resume the game at a more opportune time."

The next morning, a delegation of Mohawks arrived. The stern-faced men were diplomatically greeted and welcomed by Richaud, and were brought indoors for refreshments. They were led by a fierce war captain who, encouraged by the English, used the name "Ares," to commemorate the Greek god of war.

The meeting was attended by Richaud and Fontaine, along with Metacomet, Annawon, and Linto. Additionally, three senior warriors from the Huron were in attendance.

Ares thanked their hosts for the cordial welcome, and for the food and drink. He said they had travelled three days, and appreciated their hospitality. As expected, he inquired why hundreds of Huron warriors were assembling, and Metacomet took the lead.

"We are here to assemble friends and allies for our rebellion against English tyranny. Our French and Huron allies are ready to join the fight, and soon we will be marching east."

Ares was noticeably unenthused. "East. But not west?"

Fontaine interjected. "Certainly, not. Together, we are focused on bringing justice to the east, and putting an end to the arrogant English ways."

Ares pensively drank his tea. "That is indeed interesting, for the English have asked us to help put an end to the arrogant ways of the French. I see you have at least two hundred warriors assembled?"

"Oui. But many, many more are on their way. Hundreds." Fontaine hoped his deception would help deter any aggressive Mohawk schemes.

"I see, I see. Metacomet, I must confess this entire unfortunate affair perplexes the Mohawks. Haven't you been the most reliable of English allies among all the nations? Was not Massasoit beloved by Winslow the father?"

Metacomet was uncertain if he detected sarcasm or derision in Ares' tone, but he assumed the question to be a fair one. "Like the Mohawks, the Wampanoag have been trusted friends of Winslow and the English for generations. But Winslow the father is in his English heaven, and Winslow the son is scurrilous and rotten. They take the land, they lie, they take away our firearms, they put my people on trial and then murder them. They are no longer friends of the Wampanoag, and together with the Nipmuc, the Abenaki, and now the Huron, we will avenge the wrongs. Just as the English have betrayed us, Ares, they will deceive and betray the Mohawks. Your nation should join the rebellion."

Ares solemnly nodded. "It is interesting you speak of deception and betrayal. I am saddened to say we have very recently seen the murder of five of our warriors, who were slumbering after a day of hunting. Our Sachem is furious and demands answers."

They had prepared for this moment, and now it was time to elevate the gambit. Annawon's face became contorted with rage. *"The English! That is their way! They will turn on their closest friends! They think their God makes them superior to us, and we are less than animals! They have assaulted and betrayed our people, and now they are doing the same to the Mohawks! Join our fight, my brother! Imagine! Huron, Wampanoag, Nipmuc, Abenaki, and Mohawk! The ancient peoples united against the English disease!"*

Ares seemed surprised at the intensity of Annawon's outburst, and Metacomet quietly agonized that Annawon was overacting. He hoped they weren't overplaying their hand. Fontaine seemed intrigued by this new development, and gently probed for further details.

"Did these men have any enemies? Who would do such a thing?"

Ares remained calm as he signaled for more tea. "We have our suspicions. The assassins left evidence at the scene. Annawon clearly believes it was the English, but we will not, however, jump to conclusions."

The Mohawk war captain promptly changed the subject. "Annawon, you did not mention the biggest prize of the east. What does Sachem Canochet say? Where are the Narragansett warriors during all this upheaval?"

Metacomet addressed the question. "Canochet has been far too cautious in my estimation. The Narragansett have the luxury of living among the Quaker men, and the Quaker men are not full of hatred like Plimoth. Canochet signed a treaty with the English last year, but he has been good enough to safeguard our women and children from English brutality in his mighty fortress."

More tea was brought, and Ares seemed pleased. "I find that interesting, because our English allies are spreading word of a great victory. They say Winslow the son led his huge army to Canochet's fortress, and burned it down. They slaughtered hundreds, and chased the rest into the wilderness. Many were burned to death. Did you not know this?"

Fontaine appeared troubled, and he was embarrassed that his military intelligence reports were so lacking. "Any reports of such a thing are unverified. Such things are not to be believed without evidence. It is, however, just like the English to incinerate women and children, Ares. They did the same thing to the Pequot before I was even born."

If Fontaine appeared troubled and embarrassed, Linto now appeared as if his soul had left his body. He sat wide-eyed and numb, and he was now quaking. Wawetseka. The children. Linto knew he would be divinely punished for his vile transgression, but he never dreamt it could happen this quickly and this intensely.

Metacomet was also shaken to his core by the news. He was the Sachem. He was responsible for their women, children, sick, and elderly. This had to be a lie. This was Mohawk trickery. Canochet's fortress was impregnable. Ares was lying.

Annawon was also appalled by the news, and he feared their opportunity with the Mohawks was slipping away. He had to find a way to use the news to his advantage. He repressed his grief, and pressed his case with Ares. "The captain is right. It is just like Skunk Genitals Winslow to attack women and children. How can you be allied with such men? It is just a matter of time before they come for your women and children."

Clearly unmoved, Ares sipped his tea. "Our English alliance has served us very well, thank you. We believe any unrest and mayhem in these lands emanate from another source." He overtly glared at Richaud so there would be no misinterpreting his words. "Still, we have not resolved the first matter. This senseless murder of our young men is extremely unsettling."

"You said there was evidence at the scene?" A nervous Fontaine hoped to alleviate any tensions with the Mohawks as soon as possible.

Ares seemed to have had his fill of tea, and was now devouring a sample of winter sausage. "A big, ugly hat was left behind. We found a belt buckle as well. There was also a single page from a book written in English. I think it is from their Bible. Frankly, we suspect it was all a very clumsy attempt to frame our allies, but considering the turmoil of the past year, we cannot rule anything out."

Linto's eyes remained fixed on the ground. He could not make eye contact with anyone, and consequently, he was oblivious to the stares from one of the Mohawks. The staring grew more intense, and Metacomet and Annawon were unnerved as the pale and sickly stranger whispered in his leader's ear and pointed.

Ares squinted. "Who is that man? The skinny one, staring at the floor." Linto was now rocking in place with his arms wrapped around himself. He seemed to be softly muttering a prayer, and tears were welling in his eyes.

Metacomet remained composed. "He is my counselor. Linto, stand and be recognized." Linto ignored him, and his prayers were growing in volume and intensity. His eyes were now closed.

Ares did his best to mask his thoughts, but his teeth were overtly clenching, and his manner of speech was slower and deeper. "Gentlemen, you ask about the evidence of this unforgivable crime. There is, actually, more information to share. The most interesting fact is one of the victims survived." Since his dramatic words could not muster a reaction from Linto, Ares turned his attention to Annawon, who was now reluctant to make eye contact as well. "Uhntwissel, show these men your wounds."

Uhntwissel lifted his winter tunic and revealed a wound to his abdomen. Though serious, it was relatively superficial and in the process of healing. *"It was him."* He lowered his tunic and pointed at Linto. "I have no doubt. I swear it on my honor. That is the man who stabbed me."

Ares jumped to his feet. Richaud followed suit, and Fontaine suspected it was time to put away the tea and fetch the brandy. Metacomet frantically glared at Annawon, then Linto, then Annawon once again. Linto remained lost in his grief, and was unaware they were even speaking about him.

"You are mistaken!" Metacomet had to defuse this somehow. It didn't make any sense. Linto didn't stab anyone. "Linto has not left my side in months! Why would he be attacking complete strangers?"

Uhntwissel was not deterred. "I have never been more certain of anything, Ares. That is the man! See how guilty he looks!" Linto seemed to be lapsing into a trance of some kind, and tears were raining down his cheeks.

Although Ares was pleased the mystery was on the verge of being solved, he still did not have the absolute certainty he craved. He resumed his seat and pondered the situation. If Metacomet's man was guilty, the consequences would be astronomical. The Mohawks could not let such a crime go unavenged, and if vengeance dictated slaughtering the enemies of the English, so much the better. Still, he knew Uhntwissel had been drinking on the evening in question, and the crimes transpired in the dark of night. No matter how confident Uhntwissel was, and no matter what mania had suddenly befallen Metacomet's accused counselor, there was still an element of doubt.

Annawon felt compelled to discredit the accusation. He did his best to remain stoic and persuasive. "Ares, your man is clearly mistaken. It was the dark of night. You have our deepest sympathies, but it sounds to me like more English malice. They were sending a message. Look at the things they left. Their hat, their belt buckle. They even left a page from their big book, circled in blood. They were absolutely sending a message. You are their enemy now."

Ares did not reply, and Metacomet took a deep breath. The situation seemed to be defused for the moment. Even if the Mohawks would not be flocking to his cause, there certainly would be enough lingering doubt about the perpetrators. He just wished Linto could compose himself and say something. He was not helping the situation.

Metacomet faced Ares. "Annawon's words are indeed wise. This is the English way. They will use Indians to kill other Indians, but in the end, we are but unholy savages to them. Their big book tells them to kill us. And your accusations about my counselor are indeed hurtful and false. He is grieving at the news of the Narragansett fortress, and thinking of his family. Linto, we're not even sure the news is

JAMES W. GEORGE

real. Linto, stand up. Stand up, and tell the Mohawk people you did not stab anyone in the belly. Speak the truth."

Linto finally seemed to acknowledge that he wasn't alone in the room. His arms were now folded in his lap, and he was hunched over as if in agony. He peered through his moist eyes at his Sachem, but no words came. He tried to speak, but could only utter pathetic, indecipherable sobs.

"Tell them, Linto."

He was now bawling uncontrollably. He was a wretched, evil creature and deserved no solace in this world. He was guilty. He tried to murder a stranger, and it was little wonder Wawetseka and the children bore the brunt of his evil crime. Where were they? Were they even alive? His eyes returned to the floor.

Ares had heard enough. He gently set down his tea cup, and rose to his feet. "Colonel Richaud, we do thank you for your hospitality. Before we take our leave, however, I do have one last, thorny question." All eyes in the room turned to face him.

"Annawon, how did you know the page left at the scene was circled in blood?"

Annawon looked shocked and confused. "Because you told us! You said it was so!"

Ares was now smiling. "I certainly did not. I said there was a hat, a belt buckle, and a page from a book written in English. I never mentioned blood."

Metacomet could see the panic in Annawon's face. Annawon's mind was racing, but he was unable to concoct a reply. Metacomet desperately intervened. "But that is their way! That's what the English do! They leave pages from their book, circled in blood! They've done it to us. Many times! Always, circled in blood! *That is how we knew!*"

The room was now silent, save for Linto's wailing. Uhntwissel was now glaring at him with contempt. Before departing, Ares turned to face Colonel Richaud.

"Cul-uh-nel, let this not be farewell, but, how do you say…" One of his henchmen whispered in his ear. "Yes, of course. *À bientôt.* See you soon, gentlemen. **We will see you very soon**."

CHAPTER THIRTY

BOSTON

From the desk of Reverend Increase Mather, Boston
March 14, 1676

I pray these random and humble notations of mine may someday be put to good use. Although I am blessed to be a most prolific writer, the decision to dedicate myself to a journal documenting the grave events tormenting the English Israel and its holy inhabitants during the past year was a spontaneous and recent decision. If the Almighty deigns to keep me alive and well in the midst of this pagan violence, I pray I will be healthy enough to one day write a complete and accurate history of these wretched troubles and the miseries inflicted upon the saints of New England.

It has now been fifty and six years since our holy Puritan undertaking commenced on these blessed shores. The saints of God have, through His divine providence, built a holy society from a hostile wilderness. The elect have suffered plagues, hunger, blizzards, and all manner of torment. The mother country during this time has seemingly endured all manner of spasm and cataclysm as well. Lord Protector Cromwell unseated the wicked popish monarchy and instilled a proper, pious republic, only to see the righteous undertaking deteriorate in a sea of worldly squabbling and insidious papist conspiracy. We are indeed blessed to be so very far from those ancient shores, as afflicted as they are with wickedness and tyranny.

Alas, all eyes of the saints turn to the New World and this glorious undertaking. Will God's chosen people survive in this hostile, forbidding land? Will our righteous society, dedicated exclusively to His divine will, perish or prosper?

THE PROPHET AND THE WITCH

For years, I have been a voice crying out in the wilderness. God's chosen people have catastrophically mired themselves in a morass of rum, lust, adultery, laziness, and greed. Just as the fearsome and persecuted prophet Jeremiah, I have confronted our government on every occasion. I have conveyed in no uncertain terms that the Lord will not be idle in the face of wickedness, and He will inevitably unleash his wrath in one manner or another. Just as the kingdoms of Israel and Judah fell prey to barbaric, heathen hordes mere centuries ago, I fear the United Colonies of New England may now share a similar fate.

This grueling, tortuous conflict has gone on for nine long months. Although men like Winslow, Bradford, and Barron were convinced the victory of the Lord's chosen people would be relatively quick and easy, I, through the power of scripture and prayer, knew better. I knew Philip of the Wampanoag was an instrument of God, sent to punish the United Colonies for their transgressions. I knew we would be punished for our sinful nature with battlefield casualties, abducted women and children, decimated villages, hunger, and misery. Even I, however, failed to predict the duration and intensity of these events.

During these months, we have humbled ourselves and beseeched the Almighty incessantly for His blessing. We have pledged ourselves to multiple days of fasting and humiliation. I fear our sinful nature has been so grave, however, that the Lord has chosen not to hear our supplications.

It grieves me to note that Lancaster was assaulted last month, with many of God's saints carried off to captivity. The town's minister, John Rowlandson, was away imploring the authorities for additional security when, ironically, Lancaster fell prey to the fury of the heathen. Rowlandson's beloved, Goodwife Mary Rowlandson, was inhumanely abducted along with so many others.

I can scarcely keep track of Christians slaughtered, and towns devastated during this grave time. Lancaster.

Middleborough. Swansea. Brookfield. Springfield. Each and every one is a testament to our enemy's power and vile hatred. English Christians throughout these colonies have been brutalized and tortured, and I shudder to imagine how it will all end.

The have been, however, some blessed developments to speak of. In December, General Winslow heroically led an army of more than a thousand men south to Narragansett country. These savages were offering sanctuary to the enemies of New England and the enemies of our Lord, and were almost certainly conspiring to join Philip's treasonous rebellion. Praise God, the governor was able to infiltrate the seemingly impregnable fortress and vanquish the enemy. In a remarkable development, William Brewster's grandson, Israel, was said to show commendable devotion to duty on that day.

What an odd duck this Reverend Brewster character is. I recall his visit to Boston a mere four years ago, where I provided counseling and mentoring. He subsequently ingratiated himself with the heathen, and engaged in all manner of bizarre and unseemly behavior. He fled from Plimoth, and built a new life amidst the Quaker heretics of Providence. When duty called, however, he seemed to fight for Plimoth Colony like none other. The Almighty works in mysterious ways, indeed.

Unfortunately, sustaining an army of the Lord of that magnitude proved far too difficult. The army endured all manner of deprivation throughout the winter, including disease and hunger. Despite their momentous and historic victory at the Narragansett swamp fortress, Governor Winslow had no option but to subsequently disband the army. I, however, praise him for his courage and vision.

Perhaps the brightest news in many dark days has been the developments along the Hudson River, far to the west in Mohawk Country. It would seem King Philip, the treasonous malefactor who triggered this conflict, had allied himself with a despicable band of conniving French papists. Philip, forever plagued with delusions of his own royal grandeur, thought he could deceive the stalwart Mohawks into joining his cause. Our Mohawk allies report he engaged in all manner of murderous slander in an effort to deceive them. Thankfully, the pitiful and desperate ruse was uncovered fairly easily.

I shudder to imagine the terror the Mohawks unleashed once they were privy to Philip's hideous machinations. Reports from the region convey that more than five hundred Mohawk warriors descended upon the French encampment, and swiftly brought justice. Dozens of savage French lackeys fell to the Mohawk onslaught before scurrying off to the north (I believe they were Huron people, but these faraway Iroquois nations are most confusing.) Several papist French officers were captured and held for ransom, but alas, the wily King Philip and his depraved underlings escaped back to the east.

There is another unsettling development I unfortunately must record here. I increasingly fear much of the recent heathen military success can be directly attributed to witchcraft. Tales are sweeping through Massachusetts Bay of a hideous female witch who leads the heathen assaults among the Nipmuc. All manners of magical powers have been ascribed to her, and far too many brave and stalwart Englishmen are fleeing in her presence. Some report she has the power to paralyze her victims, whereas others report temporary loss of sight and hearing. She has undertaken the name *mother of evil*, and is also known as "the battle witch." I pray I may one day soon witness in her capture and execution, for as scripture attests, *"thou shalt not suffer a witch to live."* I shall counsel our chaplains to manifest greater vigilance and faith in the face of Satan's minions, no matter what form they take.

Closer to home, the Reverend Eliot and Captain Gookin have been interminable regarding the incarceration of the Praying Indians on Deer Island. It is indeed a difficult issue, but I am inclined to concur with the authorities of Plimoth and Massachusetts Bay. Although these be Christian men and women, it is increasingly difficult to ascertain which Indians can be trusted and which cannot. No matter their devotion, Indians residing in our very midst is a fearsome thing, indeed. Eliot protests relentlessly regarding the hunger and deprivation on Deer Island, but misery and suffering are pervasive during these dark times, and I fear his remonstrations on the topic have become excessive.

I pray this journal and subsequent summation of the conflict may one day serve future generations of New England men. I hope my thoughts and deeds may provide insight into these horrific times, and provide inspiration for God's chosen elect. It is now time for my mid-day meal, so I will conclude this entry with a short passage from the book of Isaiah.

Fear thou not; for I am with thee: be not dismayed; for I am thy God: I will strengthen thee; yea, I will help thee; yea, I will uphold thee with the right hand of my righteousness.

In Christ,
Increase Mather, Reverend
March 1676

CHAPTER THIRTY-ONE

MENAMESET

"Is he awake?"

"Yes. If you could call it that."

"He slept a very long time."

"I don't know what to say. I guess he's exhausted, Linto."

Linto surveyed the gray sky. There seemed to be no inkling of spring's arrival, and it was just as well. The weather was desolate, Metacomet's mood was desolate, and Linto's soul was desolate.

As promised, Ares the Mohawk war captain did return, and he was accompanied by five hundred crazed warriors. Linto wished he could say he truly witnessed a genuine battle on that day, but he knew better. It was not a battle. The Huron scarcely offered any resistance, and the slaughter was appalling. Their sentries were well aware of the invading Mohawk army, but yet, they were no match for their historical adversary.

Metacomet and his family, Annawon, Linto, and the four dozen Wampanoag warriors still loyal to the Sachem subsequently did what they had done so often: They ran, they hid, and they plotted for another day.

With almost no other options, the Wampanoag slinked backed to Menameset and the Nipmuc sisters. They were constantly on guard for Mohawk ambushes, and consequently, it had been a grueling, fifteen-day journey. They knew they were lucky to be alive.

Linto almost wished he had been the victim of a righteous Mohawk war club. He was responsible for this travesty, and he had brought nothing but failure and misery to the Wampanoag. By now, Wawetseka and the children were almost certainly frozen to death, starved to death, burned to death, or huddled somewhere in English chains.

And then there was the humiliation. The sardonic, mirthful cackling of the Bluebird when they presented themselves. Metacomet had two hundred loyal Huron warriors at his disposal. He had a European ally that could provide supplies, muskets, warriors, and even ships. And he had squandered all of it. Due to his egotistical posturing and obsessive ambition, it was all gone.

If Metacomet and the Wampanoag were the picture of shame and defeat, spirits among the Nipmuc could not be higher. Week after week, another English village, supply caravan, farm, or military unit fell into their lap. Their sanctum at Menameset was now teeming with sorrowful English prisoners, most of whom would be held for ransom. And throughout the land, all seemed to speak of the battle witch's mystical power. It was the witch of battle who made the English drop their muskets and run. The witch made the Nipmuc arrows straight and deadly. She instilled terror in the enemy's holy men. The witch of battle, also known as *Nitka-Wendigo,* made the Nipmuc invulnerable.

Conversely, there were the three leaders of the Wampanoag. The broken, dispirited Sachem who started this war, and had led his people from one disaster to another. The war captain, who was now captain of fewer than forty men, who despised himself for completely failing his people. And the shattered, useless counselor. He was the pathetic false prophet who even failed at deception. He was a crushed shell of a man who had lost his wife, his home, his children, and now just wanted it all to somehow end.

"Will he see me, Annawon?"

"I don't think so."

Linto bit his lower lip and looked away. The day had finally come. Metacomet had finally lost faith in him. He nodded vacantly, and wrapped his arms around himself for warmth. Pensively rocking, he was finally prepared to say the words he should have said weeks ago. "I'm sorry, Annawon."

"For what?"

"For what? For the French. I'm sorry for the Mohawks."

Annawon was restlessly sharpening a hatchet, and seemed lost in thought. He evaluated the blade, and when he seemed satisfied with its lethality, he stowed it and faced Linto. "You're not to blame. I'm the war captain. I should have dissuaded Metacomet from the entire scheme, but..." Annawon turned away. "I genuinely thought it would work."

"I'm supposed to be his counselor, and I never tried to dissuade him either. But I was the one who..." Linto's voice was cracking. "I was the one who left a witness."

"Bah. It was all my fault. My stupid comment about the bloody page. Those Mohawks are tricky bastards. They get it from the English. Still, you should have told us about the witness, Linto."

"I was so ashamed."

"Of what? Linto, look around. The spirits have given us a very cruel world. The English hate the French, the French hate the Mohawks, the Mohawks hate the Huron..."

"And we hate the Bluebird."

Annawon actually managed a smile. "It's a cruel world, Linto, and men need to kill for what they believe in. Men need to kill and die for the things and people they love."

Linto thought about that sentiment, and he thought about what he believed in. Linto believed in a world where men didn't have to kill each other in the name of love. He thought it childish, however, and would not utter such nonsense to Annawon.

"What have you heard about this witch of battle, Linto? What does she call herself now? Nitka-Wendigo? Mother of evil?" Annawon casually gestured for Linto to hand him his fleur-de-lis hatchet. Linto cautiously handed it to him, and Annawon curiously inspected it. "I guess calling herself the *Blackbird* wasn't fearsome enough. The prisoners say all the English are terrified of her, Linto. I thought she never left her sister's side. Where does she get her powers?"

Linto considered the question. Was it her uncompromising devotion to the spirit world? Father Jacques said the French holy men refrained from romance and sex, so they could dedicate themselves totally to God. He also mentioned that there were holy men in Europe who took vows of silence. Was that how the witch got her power?

Linto dejectedly replied. "I wish I knew."

"You have to try harder, Linto. You have to pray harder. You've got to find another miracle somewhere."

The words made Linto hang his head. What was the point? He was cursed forever.

Annawon was now balancing the hatchet in his hand. "This is beautiful work. You say it's supposed to be a lily?" Annawon looked at it inquisitively, failing to see a flower. "Do you want me to sharpen it for you?" Linto dejectedly shook his head, and Annawon returned the weapon. "Oh, I almost forgot. Metacomet does have a task for you, Linto."

Linto excitedly replied. "Really? What is it?"

"It's about the English prisoners. One of the ladies. He noticed her earlier today. You have to persuade her to do something for Metacomet. He wants this very badly."

Linto listened intently and immediately was on his way. "Tell the Sachem it will be done."

Linto scoured the village. Menameset had grown even larger over the winter, and continued to burst with warriors, families, and prisoners. An Englishwoman is difficult to conceal, however, and he soon found her sitting outdoors on a bench in front of a fire. She was using long metal nails to craft fabric, and she was guarded by two sour-looking Nipmuc.

Linto approached, and her guards seemed to pay no mind. They eyed him suspiciously as he sat on the bench and warmed himself, but they did not seem to object.

Mary Rowlandson was a thirty-eight-year-old prisoner abducted during the siege of Lancaster a few weeks ago. She peered at Linto, then resumed her knitting. "Another savage, come to leer and stare at the tormented Englishwoman? Here I am, young man. I hope I give amusement."

"I am not here to stare, madam." Rowlandson was so shocked that she dropped a needle on the cold ground. Linto rushed to retrieve it for her. He handed it to her and continued. "I am here on behalf of my Sachem."

"My word. How on earth do you speak with such eloquence? What manner of native are you?"

"My name is Linto. I am of the Wampanoag. I am pleased to meet you."

"Are you a Praying Indian? How is it you speak in this manner, Linto?"

"No madam, I am not a baptized Christian. I have certainly learned much from the good Christian men, however. John Eliot..."

"Eliot! The Reverend Eliot?"

"Oh, yes. I've attended many of his missionary services. And Sassamon. John Sassamon. He was not, however...very good. I'm afraid he was a wicked Christian."

"He was a *murdered* Christian. Such a vile, dastardly deed."

"He was very wicked to my people, madam. I am not sure he deserved to die like that, however."

"I pray that whatever malfeasance he embraced, his sins are forgiven."

There was an awkward silence. Linto exchanged words with a guard, who was unsettled that Linto came unannounced and conversing in English, but when Linto explained the purpose of his visit, he seemed placated. The guard resumed his sour glowering.

"Are you well, madam?"

"Am I *well*? That is certainly a fascinating question, Mister Linto. My home and community have been ransacked and destroyed by pagans. I cannot count the friends and family members who perished in the attack. My beloved daughter perished in my arms not ten days ago. I am scarcely fed, and I doubt I will ever see my husband again. So, no, Mister Linto, I am not well."

Rowlandson somehow managed to persist with her knitting while she continued. "But my faith in the Lord is not shaken, Mister Linto. No matter our earthly torments, He is with us. He has a plan for us, and He will never forsake us."

Linto was increasingly fascinated by this prisoner. She briefly continued her knitting, but then set her needles down as she continued. "I am reminded of the Book of Romans, Mister Linto. *The sufferings of this present time are not worthy to be compared with the glory which shall be revealed in us.*"

The notion of the *Romans* perplexed Linto. "The Book of Romans? Madam, I fear this business of Rome causes me nothing but confusion. Is Rome good or bad? I thought they were bad. I thought Rome was the enemy of the Hebrews and the Gentle Son, but Father Jacques told me God's chosen representative on earth lives in Rome, and that…"

"Father Jacques?" Rowlandson almost dropped another knitting needle. "Oh my. What blasphemy has he filled your head with, Mister Linto? Heaven preserve us. The Bishop of Rome. He presides over a throne of hypocrisy and falsehood."

Linto sighed and considered her reply. Why was there a Book of Romans? Why were the months named after Roman kings? How could the English and French be Christians but be consumed with such contempt for one another? He decided the issue did not merit further thought, and changed the subject to more important matters.

"I am saddened for you and your family, madam." Linto thought about Mary Rowlandson helplessly clutching her daughter in the merciless cold as she breathed her final breath, and he thought he might weep. "I too, have lost so very much. I have no idea where my family is, and I fear they have perished."

"Then, it is indeed a tragedy that King Philip has instigated this violence." Rowlandson saw the look in Linto's eyes, and she silently reprimanded herself for her unchristian remark.

"Forgive me, Mister Linto." She set aside her knitting, and took his frigid hand in her own. "Will you pray with me, Mister Linto?"

Before Linto could convey his consent or decline her overture, her head was bowed, and she eloquently spoke. *"Heavenly Father, all honor and glory is yours. We are humble creatures, lost and frightened in a wicked world of hatred and violence. We beseech thee for strength. We beseech thee for courage. We humbly pray for families and children, and we pray that the light of Christ may enter our hearts, and we may live our lives in accordance with the laws and scripture. Amen."*

She released Linto's hand, and resumed her knitting. The guards were still remarkably uninterested in the proceedings, and Linto almost forgot the purpose of his visit. "You are very kind, madam, and..."

"Please. Call me Missus Rowlandson."

"You are very kind Missus Rowlandson. But I have come for a reason. I have a very specific request from my Sachem."

"Your Sachem? And pray tell, who is your *Sachem*, Mister Linto?"

"I am here on behalf of Metacomet."

Rowlandson actually moved further along the bench, and further away from Linto. "Metacomet? *King Philip?* The madman who started all of this?"

"There is much I can tell you about my Sachem, Missus Rowlandson. Please rest assured he is no madman. He asked that I may persuade you."

Rowlandson rose and glared maliciously at Linto. Finally. Finally, the truth was revealed. Throughout her captivity, Rowlandson had been stunned that she had never been molested or sexually assaulted in any way by these savages. Now it all made sense. She was a rare prize, and a prize to be saved for the grand Sachem. She was to be given over to King Philip for his sinful, lustful pleasure.

She did her best to maintain her composure, and she scoffed. *"Persuade me?* Isn't it more appropriate to merely demand it? Isn't that how these things are done, Mister Linto?"

Linto seemed embarrassed. "I'm not so sure, madam. I suspect he thought things would turn out better if you would do this for him...willingly. He noticed you earlier."

"Willingly? Have you gone mad, Mister Linto? What manner of woman do you take me for?"

"I am sorry to have upset you. I did not realize this sort of thing was a matter of such gravity."

"Gravity? Mister Linto, you speak with such eloquence, and yet you are but a savage. *This sort of thing?* Does King Philip not have a wife for *this sort of thing*?"

"Oh yes. Wootonekanuske. But I have seen her try to do it. She is terrible at it, and it makes her feel very bad. The English ladies are so much better at it."

Rowlandson's face was crimson with rage. She was seething. "And if I refuse? Will you be the one to drag me away and force me, Mister Linto?"

Linto felt baffled and dejected that this was going so poorly. His Sachem had trusted him with this one simple task, and he couldn't even do this right. Was he using the wrong English words? *Persuade. Perrr-swayd.* He was almost certain that was correct. *I am here to persuade you.* Yes, that was right.

"I cannot stop you, Mister Linto, but please know as a Christian woman, I will resist you, and if I perish, then I will meet my savior willingly."

Linto was absolutely stunned. What was going on? He tried a different approach. "It is not even for Metacomet. It is for his son, Mendon. He is nine summers old."

Rowlandson was apoplectic. Her face grew ever more contorted and crimson. Linto was beginning to panic, as he feared for her health. He had to say something. "Wouldn't this be the Christian thing to do?"

His last remark seemed so shocking to her, Linto was genuinely worried she would lose consciousness and fall to the frosty ground. By now, even the guards had become interested, and they wondered what verbal torments Linto was unleashing in the wicked English tongue. What was he saying that could drive her to such madness?

"Try to understand, Missus Rowlandson. He is just a child. His ears get so cold in the winter. And perhaps a shirt. Would a nice, warm shirt be difficult to make?"

Rowlandson's eyes grew wide. She felt light-headed, and she resumed her seat on the bench. She gazed into the fire, inhaled deeply, and frantically replayed their conversation in her mind. What had Linto ever asked for? He never said what he wanted to persuade her to do. She merely assumed that...

Linto was increasingly concerned about Rowlandson's health. He always struggled to understand the unusual complexions of the English, and how easily they changed color. If they stood in the sun for half a day, they changed color. If they stood in the sun all day, they became another color. When they drank their rum all day, their faces were yet another color. Missus Rowlandson's delicate, fair skin now seemed to be taking on the color of an apple. And she had tears streaming down her cheeks. Was she giggling? Had she gone mad? How could he explain all of this to Metacomet?

He strained to understand her as she choked back tears of embarrassed laughter. "Mister Linto, I am mortified. You must think me the most bizarre woman in all Christendom. Forgive me, I pray." She wiped away the tears. "The child shall have a lovely, warm hat. And a shirt. But I must insist my kindness be repaid with more food for my children."

Before Linto could consider her request, another intimidating Nipmuc sentry hurriedly made his approach. "You are Linto? You are Metacomet's counselor?"

Linto apprehensively nodded. "Come with me. Nitka-Wendigo will see you now."

Linto wanted to bid an elegant farewell to Missus Rowlandson, but his heart sank at the news. The sentry seized him by the arm, and violently pulled him away. This could not be a good development.

While enroute, Linto imagined every possible scenario. Why would the Blackbird wish to see him? She was convinced he was a nobody, and Linto had certainly done nothing to dissuade her. She was now the most feared weapon of the rebellion, and her exploits as the battle-witch were becoming legendary.

Linto tried to conceive of the worst thing that could happen. Perhaps, as a peace offering, he would be shipped off to the Mohawks, and they could reap their terrible vengeance. Perhaps he was being too pessimistic. Perhaps she merely wanted to ensure he was being useful, and she would assign him duties appropriate to his station. Perhaps he could serve her, and scour the wilderness for roots and herbs.

He was surprised when the sentry led him to a modest wetu. It was certainly not the colossal, impressive structure the Blackbird shared with her sister. It was cramped and dark inside, and he could scarcely discern his host. When he did, he was startled by how she seemed to have altered her appearance. Instead of her dark, blackened face, she now seemed to boast a hideous mask of some manner. More importantly, where was her sister? How would the Blackbird communicate?

Of all the possible scenarios that Linto could imagine, absolutely none included what would happen next. Linto never would have envisioned the words that he would now hear in the confines of the dim, smoky wetu.

"Hello, my love. Where have you been?"

CHAPTER THIRTY-TWO

PROVIDENCE

Mister Barlow was deep in thought.

It was a splendid April day in Providence. Although elements of winter were still menacing and lurking, the promise of spring was increasingly evident. Despite the several layers of cirrus clouds that obscured the blue sky, the temperature was comfortable, and it was a beautiful day for hard, productive work.

Unfortunately for Barlow, there was no labor transpiring at the cooperage at that moment. He was quietly resting on a simple pine chair, and he nostalgically surveyed the expanse of his treasured place of business. He was thinking about the cooperage, he was thinking about retirement, and he was thinking about life.

Phineas Barlow had migrated to Providence from New Haven in 1644. He was a restless young man and never felt particularly drawn to the religious sphere of life. He was content to let the Almighty take care of His holy business, and Phineas Barlow wanted nothing more than to take care of his own business.

As such, Providence was an easy choice. Roger Williams had settled it a mere eight years prior, and it beckoned to him as a place where a man could be left to his own devices, provided he simply let his neighbor be. *Do unto others...*wasn't that what it was all about?

And a focused, diligent worker like Barlow quickly found it rather easy to turn wood into money. Wood quickly became his life. Pine. Oak. Maple. Barlow was obsessed with all of it, and craved nothing more than the invigorating aroma of woodworking, which delightfully evolved into the even more invigorating aroma of money. It had been a good life.

As he approached his sixty-third year on this earth, he certainly felt his share of regrets. He regretted never remarrying after his beloved fell ill with typhoid twenty-eight years ago. He sometimes regretted that his son had no interest in learning his father's trade, but on this particular day, Barlow was pleased that his son was faraway in Europe. Barlow regretted that Israel Brewster would certainly never assume the cooperage, because Barlow thought he was a wonderful young man who would quickly reap the benefits of his tremendous work ethic.

He was indeed filled with regret, but as he surveyed the cooperage, he delighted in the things that brought him so much joy over the decades. He could picture so many satisfied customers, but ultimately, he pictured the products. The barrels. The firkins. The tierces, puncheons, and the tiny, adorable rundlets. The white oak staves split from the densest part of the tree. The hickory hoops. How he loved it all. He even felt a grudging admiration for the smooth, birch arrow he was clutching.

As much as it pained him, Barlow had to admit that, unsurprisingly, the aroma was delightful. The flames crackled and danced, and grew in a monstrous fashion as they consumed everything in their path. He knew he should stand up and run, but he was too afraid. The birch arrow had pierced his chest, but it had missed his heart and lungs. He knew it was a fatal wound, and he suspected he lacked the strength to stand and run. As such, he expected to be consumed by the hideous, unforgiving flames, but he did not want to be certain of that. He wanted to live his final moments with the misguided hope that he still had the ability to flee the inferno that was his cooperage.

Barlow was now eyeing a quartet of Narragansett warriors as they sauntered through the apocalyptic scene. He opened his mouth to speak, but merely gurgled blood. He gazed helplessly and pathetically at them. He tried to identify the leader, and his eyes rested on the one who seemed eldest. He hoped his expression alone could convey his last request, since words were not an option. He couldn't even be certain they spoke English.

Please end this. Please don't make me watch my life go up in flames. Please kill me before I burn to death.

Barlow was relieved that the warrior he set sights on somehow acknowledged his silent plea, and sympathetically nodded. He understood completely. But before he would deliver the final, fatal blow, he conferred with his comrades.

The Narragansett warrior felt it vital to leave their victim with one final word. They wished to ensure Mister Barlow understood their actions, but their English skills were lacking. He thought the proper word was *angry,* but his three compatriots weren't sure that was quite right. The shortest of the quartet suggested *hate,* but still, there was doubt. A lanky teen-ager with a shaven head suggested *smelly,* but was told he was a buffoon and was not allowed to speak anymore. Finally, the fourth member of their assault team recalled his English lessons well enough to choose the right word. He hoped he could pronounce it convincingly.

"REEE-VEHN-JA!" And mercifully, the death blow came.

Two miles west of the cooperage, a mournful and defeated Roger Williams leaned on his enormous cane. He stared across a shallow stream at his former friend and now adversary, Canochet. Canochet stood proudly on the opposite side, surrounded by equally proud and imposing underlings. The city burned behind Williams, and the Narragansett were delighted. Standing by Williams' side was Ezekiel "Zeke" Wilder. Zeke had blessedly used his fishing vessels to evacuate most of Providence's population to the safety of Aquidneck Island, including his very pregnant daughter.

Canochet felt a genuine inkling of sympathy as he listened to a tearful, elderly Williams. Canochet had recently vanquished a company of English soldiers, and his warriors had destroyed the town of Rehoboth. He was conflicted about putting Williams' beloved city to the torch, but there could be no more accommodation of any kind for the English, no matter their religious persuasions.

Williams yelled across the stream, as loudly as a man of his advanced years could. "My own house burns, Sachem! My home! How many Narragansett have I housed there? How many friends have I fed under my roof? What has driven you to this madness? Were we not always civil and fair?"

Canochet was impressed by Williams' fortitude. "I am saddened to see you suffer, Friend Williams! You are advanced in years and deserve rest. You have been fair and right with the Narragansett. But English wickedness will not go unpunished! Plimoth betrayed us! Women and children were burnt to death before my very eyes!"

"We are Providence! These are not the United Colonies! We have no quarrel with you, Sachem! Withdraw your warriors, and break bread with us!"

"Aye, Netop! Your words may be true, but the time for those thoughts are long gone. Providence sends food, Providence sends guns, and Providence sends clothing! And you even send men! Will you tell me no Providence men attacked us, Friend Williams? Woe be unto your city, Williams! There can be no kinship! All that is built is lost!"

Zeke was increasingly concerned for Williams' health and safety. He turned and watched the sickening flames devour the city. The smoke could be seen for miles, but there was little sound to discern. Few residents remained, and those who did were certainly cut down by now. Even the invaders seemed increasingly lethargic, and they tired of their cries of war. Zeke was uncertain if his home could be saved, but he was intent on preserving his boats. "Come, Captain Williams. We should be taking our leave. There is nothing more to be done."

Williams finally abandoned his calm, stoic demeanor, and the emotions began to rise. *"Scoundrels! You make war by hiding and skulking! You make terror, and prey on the innocent! Meet an English army in the open field, Canochet! Then you will have your just desserts!"*

Canochet's voice was equally charged with emotion. *"We prey on the innocent? Friend Williams, your old mind has betrayed you. Look to Plimoth if you wish to see the scoundrels! Look to Winslow, if you wish to find terror!"*

Williams grasped the futility of his outbursts, and was growing calmer. His face was wet with tears. "I shall pray for you, Canochet. I shall pray that this evil in your heart be purged."

It was difficult to tell from across the stream, but Zeke thought he could discern tears on Canochet's cheeks as well. *"Do not leave by the main roads, Friend Williams! Take the back roads, down the hill. No one shall accost you there. Take your boats and leave, and be well, Friend Williams."*

Williams prepared to take his leave. "I shall leave you with a proverb from scripture, Sachem Canochet. *"Faithful are the wounds of a friend; but the kisses of an enemy are deceitful."*

There was no longer any doubt about the tears on Canochet's face. "I thank you for your words. Please remember, Friend Williams, you English are not the only ones with wisdom and verses. We also have a Narragansett proverb for you to remember." Canochet stepped forward to ensure he could be heard.

"Remember, Friend Williams, the cruel rain falls on both the wicked and the righteous."

CHAPTER THIRTY-THREE

MENAMESET

Linto did not recall making a deliberate decision to sit down, but he was now awkwardly splayed on the cold ground inside the dark wetu. All manner of perception had become absurdly distorted. His hostess, the witch, seemed to be bizarrely small, and at least fifty paces away. Time itself seemed to be standing still, and each second seemed an hour. His surroundings were slowly revolving.

He had experienced similar phenomena when he served as Tobias' counselor in Plimoth approximately twelve months ago. When Linto was absolutely certain he had convinced the jury that they did not have enough evidence to convict Tobias, but Tobias was sentenced to die anyway, Linto learned of the remarkable physiological effects that can be rendered by complete and total shock.

Just like that moment in Plimoth, Linto's ears were now ringing. He wasn't sure if he could breathe, and he had to focus all of his attention on the simple process of drawing air into his lungs. What's more, he was still uncertain if his vision was properly functioning. The wetu, despite a dim fire, was considerably dark, but Wawetseka appeared to be a revulsive stranger. Even her voice was different.

What could be happening? Was Wawetseka the Blackbird all along? No, that made absolutely no sense. How could he hold Wawetseka's hand for a prolonged period and not recognize her? Just like his vision and hearing, Linto's mind now seemed to be failing him.

"Aren't you going to give me a kiss, my love?"

Linto felt like he was finally composed enough to stand. His breathing was more natural, and the ringing in his ears had abated. He was slowly beginning to comprehend. As the tales of the fearsome battle-witch of the Nipmuc swept the land,

Metacomet, Annawon, and Linto always assumed they were hearing tales of the Blackbird. Now he understood. Nitka-Wendigo, the mother of evil. The battle-witch was never the Blackbird. The Blackbird hardly ever left her furs and her luxurious wetu. Somehow, Wawetseka was now the mother of evil.

In the midst of his mental paralysis, Linto was failing to appreciate the most significant issue of all. *She was alive!* Through all of his suffering and mental torture, *she survived!* Wawetseka survived the despicable assault on the Narragansett fortress, and somehow, through the divine blessings of the spirits, they were united again.

Despite his newfound joy, he approached with caution. They had only been apart for less than eight moons, but everything about her seemed unfamiliar and alien to him. He wasn't sure he could speak, and his voice seemed an octave higher than usual. "My love…where? How? Are you…"

She cackled with delight. "So many questions, lost, innocent, Linto. Perhaps I shall call you, *Linto the Lost.* Come, and bring me pleasure, husband of mine. Come, and pay homage to *Wendigo,* the spirit of all evil."

Linto approached with trepidation. The grim reality was soon revealed. Wawetseka was hideous. Her face had been mangled and burnt into a terrifying spectacle, and she appeared to be blind in one eye. He was uncertain if her entire face was equally deformed, as half her face was obscured by a grotesque mask fabricated from leather and bone.

"Will you not kiss me, Linto the Lost?"

Apprehensive and confused, Linto stepped forward. He was still not completely convinced this was real, and he held out hope that this was merely a mystical journey attributable to her supernatural powers. He closed his eyes, and kissed her.

"I thought you would be more enthusiastic, husband. Sit! Sit and tell me of your journeys! Have you slayed many English rodents with Metacomet?"

Linto meekly told of their journey to the west, the all-too-brief alliance, and the wrath of the Mohawks. He could scarcely speak, and did not discuss the real reason for the Mohawk wrath.

Wawetseka laughed and stood. Linto noticed she was completely naked, but covered in bear grease. She marched through the wetu, and excitedly regaled Linto with all manner of events. She was blessed to be chosen by Wendigo to unleash evil and hatred upon their vile enemy. Every day, her powers grew stronger. She personally had cut open at least a half-dozen living, breathing Englishmen, and evaluated their beating hearts for portents of future victories. And it was just a matter of time before she would hold Skunk Genitals Winslow's heart in her hands. Skunk Genitals killed her father. Skunk Genitals unleashed war on her people. Skunk Genitals led the invasion that brought her such suffering and humiliation.

Her pacing grew more frantic, and her manner of speech grew more menacing. She obsessively rubbed her hands together. She violently pulled her own hair. She caressed the skull of an English infantry captain that she kept in her wetu. She relieved herself in the fire, and tried to discern auguries from the smoke.

Linto was horrified, and he dreaded the answer to his next question. "Wawetseka…"

She hissed like a deranged cat. *"Do not call me such a name! You know what that name means! Pretty Woman! Am I a…PRETTY WOMAN, husband? I am NITKA WENDIGO! I am the MOTHER OF EVIL, and you will address me as such."* She kissed the skull and rubbed it against her cheek.

"Where are the children?"

She seemed aghast he would even ask such a thing. *"The children? Tsk, tsk. It is of no matter. I have cast a protective spell, and Wendigo shall provide. They are far away, but they shall triumph. And if they perish, then Wendigo will call them into the spirit world."*

She noticed the tears welling in Linto's eyes. "Oh, Linto the Lost. Oh, what a cowardly soul you are. You know so little of the world, Linto. I have so much to teach you. Do you know the proper way to curse the English muskets so they become too wet to fire? Do you know how to instill nightmares and hallucinations in their holy men? Linto, when the north star reaches its zenith tonight, I am to disembowel a breathing prisoner. Do you know how to properly do it, in order to inflict the maximum suffering? Let me show you what can be done with a terrified, screaming prisoner's manhood..."

Linto could bear no more, and he turned away. What had happened? How was this possible? She was the kindest, most beautiful woman among the nations. Her healing powers and love of all were without peer. She was the most wonderful mother, and the most devoted wife. What on earth happened to her soul? What had happened to her face?

And now, as he watched her set aside the skull and pick up an enormous, writhing snake, he stepped away in fear. He now understood. Wawetseka was completely deranged. Every last bit of her humanity, every last bit of her compassion, and every last bit of her sanity were casualties of war.

"Think not of the lost children, husband. Come, let us make a new child. Let us dedicate the conception to Wendigo." She removed her mask, revealing the half of her face that was still beautiful and unscathed. "I will turn to the side, and you can pretend my name is Wawetseka!" Her laughter chilled Linto to the bone.

He did not say another word. Linto turned and left the wetu, and gazed up at the March sky. There was to be a full worm moon that night, and while staring at the clouds, Linto tried to process everything happening around him.

Metacomet was humiliated and despondent, and would not speak with Linto. At least Mendon would have his hat and shirt. Linto's young children, far too young to care for themselves, were missing and most likely dead. The war still raged on with no sign of peace. And Linto was finally reunited with his wife. United with Wawetseka. What a couple they were.

He was a disgraced, false prophet. And she was a witch.

PART THREE
SUMMER
1676

"There is no work, however vile or sordid, that does not glisten before God."
John Calvin

CHAPTER THIRTY-FOUR

BOSTON

Jeremiah Barron could not fathom that another summer was upon them.

There simply was no denying it. When he referenced the calendar, it attested to the fact that this was indeed the last day of June in the year 1676. Whether he noted the bountiful quantity of daylight hours, or the excruciatingly warm temperatures, the result was the same. It was summer in New England, and that meant that the United Colonies had been fighting this war for an entire year.

As Barron scratched his shins, he ruminated upon the cosmic irony that a land cursed with brutal, deadly winters could be plagued by such stifling summer humidity. There were times Barron secretly contemplated abandoning this holy Puritan experiment in New England, and absconding back to the mother country. He would gladly barter a bit of theological righteousness for a more tolerable climate.

But Barron's grandparents immigrated to these shores, and he had a responsibility. In his wildest dreams, he could never have imagined this infernal uprising would still be raging a year after it began, but here they were. Here they were, painfully enduring yet another War Council of the United Colonies of New England.

The treasurer of Plimoth Colony sighed and stared out the window. The room was awash in beautiful sunlight, but Barron was pensively contemplating the loss and misery of the previous year. He shuddered to imagine the desolate English villages, the hunger and disease, and the combat deaths. As treasurer, he was equipped to objectively assign a monetary value to each and every disaster, but with each passing month, it increasingly pained him to do so.

Yet, the mood of the room was relatively buoyant. In the preceding weeks, new developments had emerged in this conflict, and the war council of the United Colonies had just spent the better part of an hour evaluating them. These developments were so startling and unexpected, the United Colonies could scarcely believe they were actually transpiring.

They were somehow winning the war.

The thought was almost inconceivable a mere two or three months ago. Canochet of the Narragansett was terrorizing the south. He had put Providence to the torch (a development Barron harbored mixed feelings about), and could not be stopped in combat. The Nipmuc to the west seemed undefeatable. They were energized by a hideous witch of some kind, who claimed to be the mother of evil, and Massachusetts Bay felt their wrath. Although Philip was hardly a warlord of any repute, the fact that he lived and continued to rally combatants to his cause was absolutely humiliating.

The United Colonies has spent the better part of the winter orchestrating contingency plans. How many villages could they abandon? Was the Connecticut River valley lost? Should they build a massive palisade around Boston's outlying communities? And, perhaps most repugnant of all, should they commence overtures to the various Sachems about their peace terms?

And yet, on this last day in June, the sun was shining, and God's chosen people were winning. The tide had turned. How was this possible?

The illustrious Reverend Increase Mather certainly knew the answer. (It seemed as if his opening prayers had grown even longer as the news of the war improved.) Mather's thoughts and prayers conveyed in no uncertain terms that this rebellion of the savages was part of the Lord's divine plan to discipline New England. His people had suffered grievously for their transgressions during this past year, but the Lord Jehovah, in all of his blessed mercies, had decided that the people had been punished enough, and the people had shown acceptable remorse and humility. It was the Lord's will that the United Colonies were winning.

The colony of Connecticut had sent a new representative to this War Council of the United Colonies. He brought news that their previous representative, Edward Elmer from Hartford, had met his grim demise at the hands of the Indians during the previous week. Like the desolation of Providence, Barron had mixed feelings about this tragedy. Elmer certainly seemed competent enough, but over the previous months Barron increasingly began to suspect Elmer was mimicking and ridiculing Barron's speaking voice when he thought Barron was out of earshot.

Elmer's replacement, Major Nathan V. Quill, was not reticent with his opinion regarding the tides of war. He attributed their recent successes to the death of Canochet at the hands of Connecticut militia. In early April, in concert with their Indian allies, the militia cornered Canochet north of Providence. After a proud, grandiose speech, he was summarily executed.

Daniel Gookin and the Reverend Eliot nodded appreciatively at the mention of Indian allies. They knew why the war had turned so rapidly in their favor. It was attributable to the Praying Indians.

By May, after months of Gookin and Eliot hectoring the authorities, vehemently protesting, and devoutly praying, the United Colonies finally acknowledged their misguided ways and liberated the Praying Indians from their cruel internment at Deer Island. Additionally, throughout the militia companies of New England, the indispensable asset of embedded Indian warriors was now unquestionable. Their stealthy tactics were increasingly adopted, and the men of New England were finally learning to match wits with their adversaries in the wilderness.

Samuel Symonds, the deputy governor of Massachusetts Bay, shared his assessment as to why victory was now within their grasp. In May, Captain William Turner, a Massachusetts

Bay man from Dorchester (and a non-conformist Baptist!) led a regiment of men to Peskeompscut on the Connecticut River. They came across hundreds of unsuspecting Nipmuc working a fishing camp.

The ambush was so overwhelming and the carnage so total, the Nipmuc subsequently sued for peace. There was even word that one of the Nipmuc Sachems (the Redbird, or Bluebird, or some such thing) perished as well. Captain Turner gave his life in the battle, but there was no doubt of the result. The Nipmuc, perhaps the most formidable of New England's adversaries, were out of the war.

Governor Winslow was delighted with each subsequent report. Although he was the hero of the great swamp battle in which his army overcame fearsome obstacles to vanquish their Narragansett foe, the subsequent weeks had been a disaster. Feeding and equipping and army of that magnitude in the dead of winter was a dismal failure.

But now summer had arrived, and Winslow had unleashed his most prized weapon. He had unleashed Benjamin Church to lead nimble, tactical companies through the Swansea area to track down and incarcerate King Philip's followers. Church was renowned for his unconventional tactics, and the enemies of New England were being mercilessly hunted.

Ultimately, however, Treasurer Barron knew the real reason their fortunes had changed so radically. He did not dispute the influence of the Almighty, or the ferocity of Benjamin Church and their Indian allies. He understood the importance of killing enemy Sachems, but ultimately, Barron knew what was important in war.

War was about adequately supplying your forces, and hoping the enemy was not capable of doing the same. War was about money and munitions. It was about muskets, gunpowder, and dried biscuit. War was about coats, blankets, and boots. The successful prosecution of any armed conflict meant providing for your warriors, and the enemies of New England simply could not do it. Across all the Indian nations, crops went unplanted, and families went hungry. Gunpowder was depleted, and muskets went silent. Clothing wasn't fabricated, and children went cold. War was about bravery, it was about honor, but ultimately, it was about things.

And Elijah MacTavish stood aloofly in the corner with his rakish grin. After a very grim year, his investments were finally paying off.

MacTavish knew very well how this conflict was destined to end.

CHAPTER THIRTY-FIVE

WACHUSETT MOUNTAIN

"Hear my voice, Great Spirit, for I am as a son."
Silence.

The month was July, and Linto had left Menameset on a spiritual journey. He would fast, he would pray, and he would deliberate about the events of the last three months.

Linto left everything and everyone in Menameset, and he wandered fifteen miles to the northeast. He scaled Wachusett Mountain, and made camp at the summit. The view was breathtaking. Linto had fallen in love with the gently rolling terrain of Nipmuc country, and he wondered if he was divinely preordained to be among the Abenaki and the mountains instead of the Wampanoag and their coastal dwellings.

Once again, July was upon him. The thunder moon. The month named for King Julius of Rome. It had been an entire year of war. An entire year of running, fighting, hiding, suffering, lying. Everything was horrifically worse than it was a year ago. His conviction from twelve months ago had been validated. Going to war with the English had been a catastrophe.

Linto turned his gaze to the northwest and earnestly prayed. The northwest. Approximately three days away by foot was the Abenaki village of Squawkeag, which the English now knew as Northfield. Situated another day's journey to the north was the village of Ossinak. It was Linto's Abenaki home. He peered to the northwest and wondered if he could see it.

What would his life have been like if Massasoit and Metacomet never discovered him there as an abandoned toddler? He almost certainly would have perished within days from hunger and dehydration. Why was such a miraculous, but cruel fate foisted upon him? He knew there would be no answer forthcoming, and he focused on the sound of his breathing.

He then turned and faced directly west. Far to the west was the Hudson River and Mohawk country. How could Linto atone for what he had done? Was the fate of his family a divine punishment for his sins? Linto wondered if Father Jacques was out there somewhere, and if he was in harm's way. Was he really as fearless as he claimed to be? Once again, Linto prayed for forgiveness for stabbing an innocent man.

The hunger pangs were beginning to consume him, but he would be strong. The process of fasting would impart renewal and clarity. He turned and faced directly east. Boston. The Puritan men. Linto could almost feel their hatred and anger radiating toward him. Would this war ever be over? Were any of the Boston men grieving as intensely as Linto was?

Linto knew Mary Rowlandson's home of Lancaster was very close to the east. She had recently been ransomed for a sum of money, and Linto missed her terribly. Throughout the winter, he took every opportunity he could to sit and speak with her. These opportunities were sadly limited, as her captors rarely permitted her to reside in one camp. No matter how intense her misery and fear, however, she always assured Linto she was praying earnestly for his family. When she was ridiculed and abused by her captors, Linto felt nothing but revulsion, and he surreptitiously provided dried peas and bear meat for her and her children.

And then Linto faced southeast. Montaup. His former home. The home he made with Wawetseka, and the birthplace of his children. Would he ever live to see it again? Was it now covered with wooden English homes? Which direction should he look to find his children? Were they still alive?

He lay on his back and peered at the sky. He tried to grasp all of the events that had transpired during the last three moons.

The most daunting issue that tormented Linto during these months was, of course, the children. He agonized about leaving Metacomet, leaving Wawetseka, and leaving Menameset to search for them. They must be out there somewhere. But then he recognized the futility of such an endeavor. They could be anywhere. They could be deceased. Additionally, he was sworn to be Metacomet's counselor. As Nimrod drew his last breaths, Linto promised him he would somehow take care of Metacomet. Finally, Linto hoped that if he stayed with Wawetseka, he could somehow undo the bizarre madness that had consumed her, and one day she would be back in his arms. On that day, she would be Wawetseka, and not Nitka-Wendigo.

Wawetseka's mother, Weetamoo, had found her way to Menameset as well. She was as vain and lustful as ever, and she had taken a fifth husband, Quinnapin of the Narragansett. She had even given birth this year.

Although Weetamoo was not with Wawetseka during the calamity in December, she generally understood the ghastly traumas that had befallen her, and was convinced her treasured daughter was lost to Wendigo. Linto pleaded relentlessly with Weetamoo to do something. He reminded her that she was Wawetseka's mother, but she merely reminded Linto that he was her husband. There was nothing to be done by either of them. Wawetseka was Nitka-Wendigo now.

As Nitka-Wendigo, her antics had grown even more appalling as the weeks went by. She became more manic, more distant, and somehow, even more hateful. It grieved Linto to see her in this manner, and he avoided her to the best of his abilities.

Nitka-Wendigo did manage to accomplish something, however, that Linto did not view as possible three moons ago: She completely reinvigorated Metacomet's spirit.

During the peak of the full pink moon, Nitka-Wendigo engaged in a ritual so revulsive to Linto he could scarcely fathom it. After torturing a chained English prisoner for days, she mercifully cut his throat. With assistance from a Nipmuc powwas, she then removed his heart while it was beating, and threw it into a fire. She inhaled the smoke and barked like a dog. She thrust the burnt side of her face into the fire, and pulled it out. She howled, and fell to the ground as if dead. After an insufferable lapse of time, she stood and made her announcement.

She had received a divine vision: No Englishman could ever kill Metacomet.

Metacomet seemed delighted by the revelation. If he had any misgivings or regrets about Wawetseka's new persona, he certainly did not express them. Day by day, the situation was becoming clearer. Nitka-Wendigo was now Metacomet's divine oracle of the spirit world, and Linto was nobody.

Also during the full pink moon, the strategic landscape of the war changed so quickly, Linto could scarcely believe it. First, the Mohegan unexpectedly cornered the great Sachem Canochet, and brutally executed him. After suffering the treachery of the English, and seeing the desecration of his seemingly impenetrable fortress, few if any fought the English with as much ferocity and passion as Canochet. He had invaded the English city of Providence a mere week prior, and his sudden demise sent reverberations of despair throughout the rebellion.

Next, in the midst of the full flower moon, an enormous contingent of Nipmuc warriors were gathered west of Menameset, along the Connecticut River. Desperately trying to combat the hunger that was now plaguing them, they had established a colossal fishing camp. They were not as vigilant as they should have been, and a regiment of English militia ambushed them. The slaughter was vicious, and the river ran red with the blood of the fallen.

Despite the successful counterattack, the day was a complete disaster for the Nipmuc. The situation, however, became even more catastrophic when another tragedy became apparent: The Bluebird was among those killed along the river. Blame and recriminations were rampant as the appalling failure to protect her became evident. Rumors abounded that she was distracted by a romantic escapade at the time of the assault, and had been caught *in flagrante* with a handsome lover when the English arrived.

When the Nipmuc concluded things could not get any worse, they learned how wrong they could be. As the Bluebird met her demise, so did her sister. The elders and powwas of the Nipmuc were devastated, and refused to discuss the issue. Conflicting rumors abounded. Many said that upon receiving the news, the Blackbird took a dagger to her abdomen. Others said this was malicious and false, and the spirit world called the Blackbird home at the exact moment her twin sister and soulmate perished.

Regardless of the Blackbird's circumstances, the Nipmuc were physically and emotionally decimated. Unlike the previous summer and fall, food was now an extremely scarce commodity. They could not dedicate themselves to planting and tending crops, and the chaos of the war rendered the hunting both dangerous and unproductive. They were starving. They had lost more than a third of their warriors in one battle. Their beloved and holy Sachems, blessed and gifted by the spirits, were no more, and there was no viable successor. They were running out of gunpowder, and had no viable means of replenishing their supply. The Nipmuc had been fighting this war for a year, and although they had inflicted terrible pain upon the English, they were realistically nowhere near victory. Every week seemed to bring more English militia, more English allies, and fewer positive developments.

The Nipmuc were done with this war. They would beg the English for peace.

When Nitka-Wendigo got word of the Nipmuc capitulation, Linto feared she might literally fall dead as well. She shrieked. She caked her torso in blood. She threatened to curse their children, and demanded that she be appointed Sachem. She called them cowards, weasels, and slaves of Skunk Genitals. She attempted to bring the Blackbird back from the dead. The entire episode merely reinforced what the

Nipmuc had come to believe about his wife. In fact, Linto had known and believed it for months.

Wawetseka was absolutely insane.

Linto then contemplated his Sachem's reaction to all of this. Metacomet obviously had mixed emotions regarding these developments. He was reenergized by Nitka-Wendigo's prophecy. If no Englishman could kill him, he would indeed be a fearsome leader. Now that Canochet and the sisters had perished, there could once again be no question who was the leader of this rebellion. Metacomet boasted a new prestige and status that he hadn't seen in almost a year.

Although he was elated by his new status, however, he recognized the grim reality. The human cost of this war was already horrific, and now they must fight on without the Nipmuc. Metacomet, however, would passionately lead the remaining loyal warriors. There were still Wampanoag, Narragansett, and Nipmuc who would never abandon the rebellion, no matter what fate befell them or their Sachems.

During that time, Metacomet assessed his forces. He could probably muster four or five hundred loyal warriors from across all the nations. They were desperate and starving, but Metacomet would lead them. These would be the most trusted and dedicated of all the warriors. And he would have Nitka-Wendigo at his side.

Metacomet informed his forces there was nothing left in Menameset or the outlying region for them. He had heard enough of places like Northfield and Lancaster. This new, desperate offensive would strike at the soft underbelly of Plimoth itself. They would return to Montaup and liberate their home. They would destroy Swansea and Taunton once and for all. They would drive east, ever east, until they burned down the inner sanctum of Plimoth and hung Skunk Genitals Winslow by his thumbs. Metacomet boisterously wondered whether he or Nitka-Wendigo could inflict the most pain on Winslow once they had him.

THE PROPHET AND THE WITCH

Linto had finally finished ruminating about the last three months. He had finished meditating, and he had prayed enough. He broke his fast with a meager ration of ground nuts. He slowly rose from the ground and stared at the sky blanketing Wachusett Mountain.

He almost wished he could just stay on the mountaintop forever. It was such a beautiful world, yet mankind was destined to suffer. He felt like he was destined to suffer. He rotated his body so he could absorb the view from every direction once more, and he came to rest while facing the southeast.

The prophet and the witch were finally going home.

CHAPTER THIRTY-SIX

SWANSEA

The assembled crowd jeered and shouted at the condemned heretic.

With no speech and seemingly little remorse, she was led to the gallows. An unusually icy north wind invaded the idyllic summer day, and the young, coatless militia-man shivered. The noose was tightened, and the doomed woman stared helplessly at the young man. He tried to turn away, but he could not. He actually smiled as the support was kicked away, and the criminal gasped and writhed. The wind now began to howl, and he noticed the condemned woman was pathetically clutching a deformed, stillborn child. The militiaman pointed and laughed at Mary Dyer as she violently swung and died.

Standing alone among the throng of hecklers was Wamsutta, the Sachem of the Wampanoag. The militiaman watched curiously as Major Josiah Winslow handed him a refreshment of some kind. Wamsutta devoured the drink, and heartily extended his gratitude.

Immediately thereafter, a second heretic was led to her execution. The wind was so noisy it was drowning out the contemptuous mockery of the crowd. The second condemned blasphemer was a young woman with attractive, dark eyes, and she also cradled a stillborn infant in her arms as the noose was tightened. Winslow kicked away the support, the crowd gasped, and another enemy of Plimoth Colony met her fate. The militiaman looked away, and noticed Wamsutta had fallen to the ground and was having some kind of seizure. He considered running to his aid, but by now it was time for a third female heretic to meet her just reward.

The militiaman was surprised to find himself upon the platform and tightening the noose, as he had no recollection of ascending the steps. This particular condemned woman was cradling two small infants, both of whom were wailing. He kicked away the support, and the young Indian woman quietly perished but continued to clutch the children. Meanwhile the mad, deranged crowd of spectators fell upon the seemingly dead Wamsutta, and began tearing him apart.

There was a fourth and final prisoner to be executed that day, and Winslow gave the militiaman a knowing nod. The wind was now deafening. The final prisoner was clearly with child, and he diligently tightened the noose around her neck, which was obscured by cascading locks of red hair. She was trying to scream her last words, but he could not hear anything due to the wind. Why was it so cold on a summer day? Why was the wind so loud?

He listened closely and thought he could barely distinguish her words. *"It's time to go. You've got to wake up now. Wake up, Reverend."* Wamsutta had now mysteriously reappeared, and was on the platform and shaking him violently.

Brewster opened his eyes and glared at Thomas Reddington's anxious face. "You've got to wake up now. We're moving out."

It had been another night of terror, and one thing was indisputable: Israel Brewster was on the verge of irrevocably losing his sanity. The nightmares had been ceaseless for six months.

Brewster found a bowl of water and vigorously soaked his face. He desperately hoped for a seamless transition back to reality, and far from the torments of the prior night. How long could he go on like this?

It was now July, and Brewster was part of Captain Church's regiment. King Philip had returned to his homeland near Swansea, and Church's unit would track him down once and for all. And on this day, like almost every other day, Brewster agonized with a fundamental question.

What was he still doing here?

Why was he still serving in this war? He was a sick man. If he had conflicting feelings about this war previously, the great swamp fight had reinforced his loathing and disgust. He missed his wife terribly. Why was he here?

And the answers were always the same. He had enlisted for a year, and he felt duty-bound. After Jemmy Barnstrom passed away, a tearful Reddington begged Brewster to stay on. He was now a renowned hero of the great swamp fight, and Church personally asked him to be a part of his newly formed regiment. Ultimately, the more Brewster fought alongside Benjamin Church, the greater his sense of profound awe. His sense of duty was infectious, and it was very difficult to decline a request from him.

But were those the only reasons? Brewster knew in his heart they were not. First, he did not wish to return to Constance in his broken, anguished state, and he hoped to stay on until he found a way to end the nightmares. While this rationale seemed logical five months ago, with each passing day he feared the torments were permanent. Secondly, he prayed that if he stayed, he might find...something. Perhaps he could find Wawetseka or even Linto, and beg their forgiveness. If only he could find her, he could explain what had happened. If only he could find Metacomet, he could...what? Beg him to end the war? Beg him to surrender?

If nothing else, it was remarkable to be a part of Benjamin Church's hand-picked unit. The winter after the victory over the Narragansett was truly horrific. Men died relentlessly of disease and malnutrition. Conditions grew so desperate some of the men muttered about slaying Brownie and consuming her. They probably would have acted on their desperation, had Reddington not pledged to slay the first man to harm Brownie.

Brewster had prayed constantly that winter. Despite his night terrors, he recited scripture, he counseled the fearful, and provided words of Christian comfort at funeral services. If anyone still recalled Governor Winslow's prohibition of Brewster engaging in chaplain duties, they seemed to be ignoring it. The suffering among the ranks was unbearable. By late winter, it became apparent there was no way to house and feed an army of such magnitude, and Governor Winslow disbanded it.

By spring, however, Benjamin Church finally got what he had desired for so long. He had Plimoth's authorization to raise, equip, and train a unit in any way he desired, and he had the authorization to do battle in any manner he deemed fit. No longer would he be moored to cautious, plodding men like Cudworth and Bradford. No longer would he be at Winslow's beck and call while they oversaw an unresponsive, leviathan army. Church's force would be agile, nimble, and lethal.

Church knew from the outset of the conflict that the key to success would be embracing the native way of warfare. As such, he leveraged the reputation and friendships he had established before the war near his frontier homestead. He wisely filled his ranks with disillusioned refugees from the forces of Metacomet and Weetamoo. These were deadly Sakonnet and Pocasset warriors who knew the ways of camouflage, ambush, and unconventional tactics. Foremost among them was John Alderman, a Praying Indian who seemed to harbor an especially intense hatred of King Philip. Alderman was adamant that Philip was somehow responsible for the death of his brother, and he would have his vengeance. He pledged to teach Church and his men the ways of Philip's swamps.

It was almost difficult to believe it was now July. During the month of April, the brutality of winter was gradually subsiding, but the sudden, cruel news of Providence's destruction had a horrific impact on morale. Church and Reddington engaged in pathetic and futile attempts to keep the news from Brewster. They feared the news would genuinely be the end of him, and they would have to confine him to an asylum of some manner.

In hindsight, it was indeed fortuitous that Church's connections to Aquidneck Island were so strong. Due to the fearsome enemy threats pervading Duxbury and Plimoth Colony, he had recently moved his pregnant wife and child there. She had developed a quick kinship with Constance, and Church gave Brewster his word of honor that Constance was safe. He was even able to provide what Brewster so desperately needed: A letter from home.

April 10th, 1676

My Dearest Husband,

What manner of terror and deprivation is upon us all during these dark times. Fear and hatred stalk every man, woman, and child, and Christian love seems so very alien and far away.

I have conveyed this letter to Alice Church, in hopes that she may be able to route it to you via her husband. I pray this letter will find you healthy and resolute, my dear Israel. How I yearn to hold your hand and kiss your handsome face. I am but a lonesome, childish woman who desperately longs for the strong arms and blue eyes of her husband.

Rest assured, your child grows and grows! I suspect he will be an August arrival. I hope you will forgive me if I am mistaken, but I am so confident it will be a bouncing boy with big blue eyes! Praise heaven I have outgrown the nausea and the seafood aversion. I (we) are so very hungry at times and food frequently seems to be such a scarce commodity. When we do have food, I eat so much scrod and scallops that I fear I may give birth to a sea creature of some sort!

I am certain word has reached you pertaining to the desecration of Providence. Perhaps it is the righteous judgement of the Almighty. We maintain that the good and humble people of the city did not deserve such a fate, but alas, 'tis the nature of violence and war. An eye for an eye for an eye... For as Holy Scripture dictates: "Recompense to no man evil for evil. Provide things honest in the sight of all men. If it be possible, as much as lieth in you, live peaceably with all men."

I am proud to report, dear husband, as you manifested every manner of bravery among the Narragansett and their fortress, so too, my father was so very courageous in the face of danger. With the help of the Lord, he did not tire or falter as he conveyed so many citizens to safety on Aquidneck Island. As his vessels procure the bounty of the sea, now they have saved so very many lives, including my own. Father sends his love, and prays you return soon with Brownie. There will be so very much to do.

I am sharing a hovel with two other families here on the island. We are all safe, but we certainly lack in material comfort. I am well enough to tend the children and nurse the sick, but oh, how I miss my books. Father believes our home was miraculously unmolested, and I pray he is correct. I was able to carry two volumes of the Bard of Avon, and I will lovingly transcribe sonnet number one hundred and sixteen as I dream of you with each stroke of the quill.

Your Loving wife
Constance Brewster
Aquidneck Island

Let me not to the marriage of true minds
Admit impediments. Love is not love
Which alters when it alteration finds,
Or bends with the remover to remove:
O no; it is an ever-fixed mark,
That looks on tempests, and is never shaken;
It is the star to every wandering bark,
Whose worth's unknown, although his height be taken.
Love's not Time's fool, though rosy lips and cheeks
Within his bending sickle's compass come;
Love alters not with his brief hours and weeks,
But bears it out even to the edge of doom.
If this be error and upon me proved,
I never writ, nor no man ever loved.

Armed with the testimony of Benjamin Church, armed with a letter from Constance, and armed with his faith, Israel Brewster would persevere. He would fight, he would pray, and he would serve. He would do his duty for New England, and he would implore the Almighty to not let the madness and night terrors consume him.

Israel Brewster would fight on.

CHAPTER THIRTY-SEVEN

SWANSEA

Although Linto knew very little about the art and history of warfare, he did know one thing. In war, the seemingly unthinkable becomes commonplace very quickly.

Metacomet and his lieutenants were passionate and confident as they led hundreds of warriors south to Swansea. These were the most devoted of the warriors, men and women who would not submit to English tyranny. And Metacomet was as awe-inspiring and ferocious as Linto had ever seen him. He was now the sole, uncontested leader of the rebellion. He had Annawon at his side, he had his wife and son with him, and he had Linto's prophecy. The fact that they were once again fighting in Swansea, in the very place where the first shot was fired, seemed to only intensify the prophecy.

What's more, he now had Nitka-Wendigo at his side, the bane of the English and their loathsome, false righteousness. She was the witch of battle, and they were rightfully terrified of her. Metacomet knew she spoke the unquestionable truth: No Englishman could possibly kill him. He and his army would be unstoppable.

And once again, the towns of Swansea and Taunton felt their wrath. Garrisons were burned, families were slaughtered, and the wicked English were tormented. The Wampanoag and their allies were on the attack once again, and soon their sacrifices would be rewarded.

But in war, passion, confidence, and virtue are frequently no match for the cruel reality of the enemy. The English had changed their tactics, and they were now a completely different adversary. Whereas the English of last summer could be counted on to noisily stumble through the wilderness with shiny metal helmets, horses, and enormous, useless pikes, these Englishmen had learned and adapted. With the help of their

Indian allies, they were mobile, silent, and lethal. Conversely, Metacomet's forces were literally starving to death, and they frequently resembled emaciated, disoriented corpses trying to wield weapons.

Metacomet strategically split his forces into agile bands of fifty to seventy men, and yet, the English were everywhere. When Metacomet's forces took refuge in a swamp, the English, led by their treacherous Indian guides, pursued. When they went deeper into the swamps, deeper than any Englishman had ever been, the English followed. Metacomet's warriors fell behind, they collapsed from starvation and fatigue, and they were ruthlessly rounded up and sent to the slavers' wharves.

Metacomet pleaded for answers. He implored Linto and Nitka-Wendigo to bring forth a plague upon the English. They prayed for supernatural strength from the spirit world. They prayed for storms and violent rains to drown their enemies. Nitka-Wendigo hissed and screeched throughout the day and night, but her mania merely reinforced the reality that she had completely lost her faculties. And then the unthinkable happened.

During one of the hottest nights of the summer, Metacomet and seventy trusted warriors were camped in a forbidding, remote swamp. In the darkest hour of the night, they were somehow found. Inconceivably, they were found by the English and their reprehensible, unrelenting Indian guides. Even with warning from their vigilant sentries, the English assault was so swift and so unexpected, the entire company was scattered into the darkness. They fought, they resisted, but they ultimately fled. When they reassembled the next morning, approximately two dozen were missing.

Among them were Wootonekanuske and Mendon.

Linto feared the loss of his wife and son might destroy Metacomet, but he fought on. He privately sobbed, he prayed in solitude, and he stopped eating. But the Sachem of the Wampanoag fought on.

THE PROPHET AND THE WITCH

Throughout the heat of the summer, the fortunes of the Metacomet and the rebellion grew more desperate. They continued to terrorize and assault the southern periphery of Plimoth Colony, but their numbers dimmed with each passing day. English forces were everywhere, and it seemed there was nowhere left to run.

If the loss of his wife and son did not completely destroy Metacomet, perhaps the subsequent loss of Weetamoo was the final blow. She had drowned while desperately trying to cross a river in the face of English pursuit. Metacomet had known and loved his sister-in-law for decades. Together they had endured the loss of Wamsutta, the humiliation at the hands of the English, hardship, suffering, and war. Linto could once again sense the pitiful desolation of Metacomet's soul, as well as his own broken spirit.

Linto wished they could be experiencing this anguish on some strange foreign soil, but the fact that they were facing the end in such close proximity to Montaup seemed to cruelly reinforce their shared fate. The Sachem now seemed to stagger through his days in an impaired, dream-like state, and Linto tried to resign himself to the irrevocable truth: The rebellion was ending, the war was ending, and life as they knew it was ending. And they were so close to home that they could almost see the throne of quartz rock.

During an evening filled with sudden and violent thunderstorms, they huddled in a swamp south of Montaup, unable to even enjoy the quiet dignity of a fire. The thunder roared, and Nitka-Wendigo removed her paltry clothing and danced. She said she would mate with Moshup the Giant on this evening, and the otherworldly beast was now summoning her with his thunder. Linto had tried relentlessly to find some sign or inkling of Wawetseka in the preceding weeks, but there was none to be found. His lovely wife was no more, and he tried to stay as far away as possible from the deranged monstrosity she had become.

It was time for what should have been an evening meal but was, as usual, nothing more than ground nuts, grasshoppers, and earthworms. Linto was thankful for the unshakable presence of Annawon during these dismal weeks, and he sat next to him. Metacomet sat across from them, and stared at the drenched ground. The storm was growing in intensity.

"It was all a lie, wasn't it?"

The question was seemingly vague, and neither Annawon nor Linto seized the opportunity to reply. They remained silent as the rain poured down upon them.

"The prophecy, Linto. It was just a lie? Mentayyup stood helpless on that English farm, and the musket ball pierced his heart for...nothing? Nothing, Linto?"

Linto's face was so wet from the downpour that his tears were indistinguishable. He nodded without a word. He thought Annawon might be sobbing as well, but it was so difficult to tell.

"Why would you do that? Why would you do that to me?"

He hoped he could adequately repress his sobs in order to speak. The thunder and rain seemed deafening, and whether from fear or dampness, he was now quivering. "I thought I could prevent the war, Sachem. I thought if I could only delay the war for another five or ten sunrises I could...I could do something. I thought I could somehow stop this."

Nitka-Wendigo was cackling and writhing in close proximity, and Linto wondered if she was listening or able to comprehend. Metacomet finally raised his head and made eye contact. "Why? Why have you done this?"

Linto had to take a moment to compose himself, and the lull seemed to be an eternity. "I didn't believe we could win, Sachem. I thought war with Plimoth would be a disaster. But I promised..." Linto had to compose himself again. "I promised Tobias before he died I would never let you humiliate yourself before the English again. I thought it was the only way. Forgive me. Forgive me, but..." Linto cast his eyes on Nitka-Wendigo, who was now gleefully rolling on the muddy earth. "I believe the spirits have punished me for what I've done."

Metacomet was now visibly sobbing and shaking his head in disbelief. "But the spirits. The disease. My father said you were sent to us for…"

Linto abruptly stood and wailed. *"I am no one, Sachem! Can't you understand? I have never heard the spirits, and they have never heard me! I am a lone child who was immune to the plague for some reason! Nothing more! I am a cowardly, frightened child who is a useless liar! Everything I have ever done or tried has failed horribly!"*

The din of the storm was a welcome relief as Metacomet sat silently. Annawon could bear no more. With tears in his eyes, he stood up and walked away. Metacomet finally stood, and placed his powerful hand on Linto's shoulder. Linto shuddered as he recalled the same gesture on the day Sassamon was dismissed.

"I have loved you like a son, Linto. I will never understand why these things have happened. But this falsehood has been the ultimate betrayal. I trusted Winslow and the English, and I was betrayed. I trusted Sassamon, and I was betrayed. All these years, I unquestionably trusted you, and now…" He couldn't finish the sentence, and tried to maintain his composure. "I must dismiss you from my service now. Please go, and know that I will always love you."

Linto opened his mouth to speak, but no words came. Instead, Metacomet continued. "It is well that it has come to this. My fate will soon be closed. Nitka-Wendigo has prepared a spirit tea for me tonight. She said it is the most potent thing she has ever prepared, and she does not know what the consequences will be. I will drink it after you depart, and I will embrace my destiny."

Metacomet released his grip and turned his back. His voice was low and somber, and Linto strained to hear. "I never dreamt I would see this moment. Leave me, Linto, for you are dismissed." The thunder burst so loudly even Metacomet seemed to wince.

"Farewell, my son. I pray that you find your path, somewhere."

CHAPTER THIRTY-EIGHT

MONTAUP

"That was the time, Sachem. That was the time to punish the English. We all knew."

Metacomet was surveying the assembled council. Everything and everyone appeared hazy, and the morning daylight was strange and otherworldly. Wootonekanuske stood by his side and seemed somber and cautious. The ceremonial throne of quartz rock was enveloped by mysterious shadows, and he struggled to maintain his bearing.

Tobias' face was wrenched with bitterness and rage. "That was the time, Sachem! Of course, your brother was poisoned. But the time should be now! Or it will be never! The English just buy and buy, and take and take. There is a new boatload every week! They are like mosquitos. Plimoth has betrayed us, and it is time to send the English back across the sea."

Metacomet wanted to reach out and touch Tobias, but he seemed so far away. "I have done it, Tobias! We have done it! We have made war on the English and avenged all their treachery. But the tide has turned against us. What have we done? Why did I wait? We should have attacked when you told me. Why did I wait? But we were brave, Tobias. We have made them pay dearly. Can you hear me, Tobias? Speak to me! Tell me we have done right!"

Time seemed to be distorted as Metacomet waited an eternity for someone to speak. He finally heard the unwelcome voice of Sassamon. "Lunacy! Blasphemy! Look at what the English have brought us. A whole new world of understanding, and the light of Christ. Look at their shipbuilding, their firearms, and their iron tools. And you wish to reject that? You wish to fight them? It would be a disaster."

Metacomet turned away and hunched over. The mere sound of Sassamon's treasonous voice filled him with convulsive rage. The sky seemed to be spinning, and he thought he would be ill. Tobias now had his hands around Sassamon's throat, and the world was now wet and bitterly cold.

Sassamon's face transformed into a hideous purple hue as Tobias violently clutched his neck. His eyes were large with terror, and Metacomet was submersed in icy water up to his chest. He had to do something. *"Stop it! Stop it, Tobias! I never wanted this! I told you not to do this!"* Tobias was oblivious to his Sachem's command, and the rage swelled in his eyes as his hands tightened around his victim's windpipe. Sassamon pathetically cast his glazed, fading eyes upon Metacomet, and Metacomet could not bear to look.

"This started it all! Stop it, Tobias! Stop it!" Metacomet was now struggling to stay afloat, and he sank deeper into the bitterly cold pond. Soon he was underneath the ice, and no one could hear his anguished cries for help. *"No, Tobias, no! Not this!"* He pounded on the ice above his head, but it was suddenly imposing and unbreakable. He was entombed, and surrendering to his fate, he sank deeper and deeper until he lost consciousness.

"Breathing has become very difficult. The end is near, my Sachem."

Metacomet blinked and inhaled the warm, dry air. He was inside Mentayyup's wetu, and Wawetseka was addressing him.

"He struggles for breath, and the coughing is worse. I fear we have to make preparations." A tear streamed down Wawetseka's face.

"Mentayyup. My bravest warrior. You are the most noble among us." Metacomet's voice was breaking with emotion. "Do not do this. Do not sacrifice your life on the English farm for me. I was wrong. There is no prophecy. I was wrong."

Mentayyup slowly and painfully rose from his bench. He nodded with comprehension, and he stood. He seemed barely able to stand as he surveyed his collection of war hatchets and chose the most imposing.

"No, Mentayyup. Stay on your bench and die in peace. Die with dignity. Do not do this, Mentayyup. I was wrong. I was betrayed, I was lied to. Do not die for me, Mentayyup." The light in the wetu was mysteriously fading, and Mentayyup strode for the exit. Metacomet was becoming hysterical. "*Stop it! Won't you speak to me? Mentayyup, can't you hear me? Why won't you speak? Do not do this!*" Mentayyup slowly and wordlessly left the wetu, and Metacomet collapsed on the ground, shrieking in agony. He remained on his knees with his tear-filled eyes tightly closed. Suddenly, he was pushed to the ground from behind, and he landed in a stream.

"Sleepy boy, tiny boy, time for your nap."

Soaked and befuddled, Metacomet stormed to his feet. He was now much shorter, and he felt like a child. He was outdoors, and the sky was burnt purple. His inability to distinguish reality from hallucination was tormenting him. He was now lost in a vision within a vision, and did not know what to do. He felt paralyzed, and was uncertain if he should attempt to move. Who pushed him?

Wamsutta!

Childlike and excited, Metacomet chased after his older brother. "Come back! Wamsutta! I have so much to ask you!" Wamsutta ran like a panther, and Metacomet struggled to keep pace. "Did Skunk Genitals poison you? Why did you die? Speak to me, brother!"

"Sleepy boy, tiny boy, time for your nap."

"Stop it, Wamsutta! Speak to me! Was I a good Sachem? Would you have gone to war? What else could I have done? Please, stop. I beg you, brother. Please, come back to me."

"Sleepy boy, tiny boy, time for your nap."

"*Wamsutta! Tell me that you're proud of me! Say something!*" Metacomet felt panic because he knew what was coming. The cliff was upon them, and still he could not get a meaningful word from his brother. "*Wamsutta!*"

And once again, Wamsutta ran for the cliff. Once again, he took to the air and soared away like an eagle. And tiny Metacomet, pathetically attempting to follow, plummeted to earth after losing consciousness.

Suddenly all was black, and Metacomet was certain he was dead. He slowly became aware of his breathing, however, and wondered if he was merely blind. He felt larger than the tiny boy who chased Wamsutta, but he still felt as a child. Then he heard the singing.

"Linto, Linto, Linto."

The stench of death filled his nostrils, and he was afraid to open his eyes. But then he heard the voice. The voice he last heard fifteen summers ago. The deep, confident, but compassionate voice. The voice of his father.

"It is a miracle! It is a divine gift from the spirit world!"

Metacomet could scarcely believe he was in the presence of Massasoit once more. He yearned to hug his father, but he remained stunned and motionless.

"Linto, Linto, Linto! What a man you shall be!"

He was finally able to find his voice. "No, Father. It is not a miracle. He was just lucky, that is all. There is nothing special about him."

"Can you see him, Metacomet? A gift to our people! He was delivered to us for a reason!"

"No, Father. No, no, no! He is not a gift! He is a betrayer! He will bring me pain! He will make me suffer!"

Massasoit resumed singing. *"Linto, Linto, Linto! What a man you shall be!"* He was swinging the filthy, starving toddler through the air, and it cooed with delight.

"Can't you see, Father? We wanted to believe in something. We needed to believe. Can't you see, father? *Father? Can't you see me? Speak to me!"* Metacomet had collapsed to the ground. "I loved him, Father. But he is gone now. He is lost to me."

Massasoit remained oblivious to his son's pleas, and hummed merrily as he cradled Linto the toddler.

Metacomet's voice was plaintive and immature. "Say something, Father. Please. Say anything. Was I a good son? Was I a good Sachem? Did I destroy everything you built? Did I squander our friendship with Plimoth?" Metacomet rose to his knees and tried to get his father's attention. "Are you ashamed of me? I tried to avoid the war for so long, but we were so humiliated. Winslow the Son. He is not like Winslow the Father. His heart is black, Father. Poison. Their hearts are as poison. *I did not want this, Father, but we are finished. The Wampanoag are finished, and it is all my fault. Forgive me, I beg you, Father. Say something!*"

Massasoit, the greatest Sachem among all the nations, focused his tender, dark eyes on his son, and finally addressed him.

"Come with me, my son. It is time to come home."

CHAPTER THIRTY-NINE

SOUTH OF MONTAUP

Linto staggered to the waterfront in a daze.

Since his Sachem had dismissed him, he had done nothing but aimlessly wander. He simply had nowhere to go. Starved and alone, he beat a path to the west. He beat a path to the south. He was so ashamed and heartbroken, he didn't even say farewell to Annawon or his former wife.

He knew the English were all over the peninsula, and he cared little. His soul was dead. He had lost his wife. He had lost his children. He had lost the trust and affection of the man who raised him. Soon, the Wampanoag nation would be little more than a memory. He didn't even have a scrap of food.

Linto was desolate.

Linto still had one solitary possession. He still had the beautiful fleur-de-lis hatchet that Father Jacques had given him. He didn't even have the English Bible anymore, and could scarcely remember where he left it. While pondering this fact, he removed the hatchet from his belt and held it aloft in the morning sunlight. It truly was magnificent. The blade was dull, however, and he wished he simply let Annawon sharpen it back in Menameset. Linto sighed and replaced it in his belt.

He peered south across the water as the sun rose to his left. He was facing the body of water now known as Mount Hope Bay. Little by little, every village, river, and puddle of water had been bought, taken, settled, and renamed in his lifetime. He remembered merrily swimming in this bay with Wawetseka when they were children. Now, everything around him seemed alien and revulsive.

He knelt and leaned into the clear water. He splashed it across his face, but nothing could invigorate him. The thunder and rain had ceased long ago, but the skies still seemed eerie and forbidding. He inhaled deeply.

THE PROPHET AND THE WITCH

Linto was ready to die.

He stood and closed his eyes. He turned around and embraced the heat of the rising sun on his face. He did not want to die. He was still young, and somehow, he was still healthy. He was exhausted, emaciated, and broken, but somehow, he was still healthy.

Where could he run? Could he make it north, back to the Abenaki? He would never make it. The English warriors were everywhere. Could he go west? South? Where could he go? There was nothing but Mohegan, Pequot, and Mohawks as far as the eye could see. Could he take a loyalty oath to the English, and be permitted to live among their Indian allies? He almost laughed when he reminisced about the loyalty oath the Wampanoag took five summers ago.

As he ruminated on the question, he winced at a deafening, powerful crack of thunder. The thunder was so intense, it knocked him to the ground. Then he heard the yelling, and the cries of the beasts. He saw the blood, and he felt the agonizing pain.

Linto was a fool. There was no thunder. He had been shot in his right knee.

The pain was excruciating, and he could not stand. He heard the whoops of the Englishmen, and he knew by their clothing and profanity that these were not the regular men of Plimoth. These were their vicious mercenaries, and they would show no mercy.

"He was just standing there! Why are they all so damned dumb, Diego?"

"The bastards are all crazy from hunger. Turn the dogs on him, he's got a hatchet."

And Linto heard the howling of the savage creatures. They were ferocious, gigantic monsters, and two of them were bearing down upon him. He tried to stand, but could not. The foul pirates were following, and he feared the end was near. In a final act of desperation, he unsheathed his hatchet, closed his eyes, and brought it down with all his might.

What followed were two shrieks of pain. One shriek came from a mastiff, as Linto's hatchet came crashing down upon its mighty snout. Linto watched as the wounded, humbled animal crawled away in pain. The second shriek was his own, as the other beast, drawn to Linto's bloody wound, locked his jaws below Linto's knee.

He desperately fought to maintain consciousness. He still had the hatchet in his right hand, and he swung it frantically, desperately making contact with any part of the beast he could. His efforts seemed to be making the beast angrier, and its powerful jaws seemed to clench tighter. On what must have been the seventh or eighth swing, he drew blood from the back of its enormous head, and with a mournful whimper, the creature seemed to loosen its grip and lapse into unconsciousness.

The two men were approaching, and Linto raised his hatchet in a defensive posture. They seemed unenthused at the notion of hand-to-hand combat, even if their lone opponent was mangled and weakened. They paused to prepare their muskets, and Linto knew what to do.

He crawled away.

He turned, and somehow crawled to the water's edge. He left his beautiful hatchet, for it would do him no good. He crawled into the water, and like he had done so many times before, he swam. He dove under the cool water, and heard the gunfire roaring above. He surfaced for breath, and somehow suppressed the cruel pain that radiated through his body.

Linto did not want to die. He wanted to live.

Somehow, he harnessed the energy to swim fifty yards to a small sandbar. He heard the blast of the musket two more times, but no gunfire came close. He could still hear the angry bellowing from the shore.

"That skinny bastard can swim with one leg!"

"He's got nowhere to go on that tiny island. I'm not swimming after him. They'll be by with the boat soon enough."

"Just look at these damn dogs. We'll have to put them out of their misery. He's going to be furious, you know."

"Let's at least give him this Frenchy hatchet, Diego. That might cheer him up."

"Just wait till he catches that skinny, water-loving bastard."

The sound of musket fire once again echoed through the morning calm, and a dog briefly whimpered its last.

"He'll get what he deserves. Trust me, he'll get what he deserves."

CHAPTER FORTY

SOUTH OF MONTAUP

Benjamin Church was growing tired of torrential summer rains.

His entire unit was equally tired of the incessant chill and discomfort. Powder seemed impossible to keep dry, and building a decent fire seemed to require divine intervention. But they were prepared to tolerate the unforgiving weather, because they were close. They were so very close.

Alderman seemed especially unfazed by the weather, as he was more confident than ever that they had the vile King Philip in their grasp. Soon he would have his vengeance. He could feel it in his soul.

Their accomplishments in the preceding weeks had been staggering. Yes, Major Bradford still led a large contingent of men to the north, and their results were noteworthy. Yes, Captain Moseley and his pirates still roamed Plimoth Colony like a serpent. They instilled terror in their enemy, and they sent prisoners to the slavers' wharves by the dozen.

But for sheer unmatched audacity, there was no comparison to Church's force. His native comrades like Alderman guided them deep into hostile, forbidding territory that no Englishman could have traversed alone. He detected their enemy from hundreds of yards, he anticipated their next movements, and he ensured they maintained the precious element of surprise with every encounter. They ruthlessly ambushed their demoralized and weary prey, efficiently inflicted casualties, and sent the survivors fleeing in chaos.

But each and every time, the elusive King Philip somehow slipped through their grasp.

Benjamin Church, however, would not tolerate any despondent sentiments. They were winning every conflict, their own casualties were minimal, and their reputation was renowned throughout the land among both allies and enemies. His passion was contagious, and his men would follow him anywhere.

Church led morning worship himself on that morning. The rain had finally stopped, and everything seemed oddly still after the violence of the storm. "The holy book of Deuteronomy, gentlemen. Book one, chapter twenty-one. *Behold, the Lord thy God hath set the land before thee: go up and possess it, as the Lord God of thy fathers hath said unto thee; fear not, neither be discouraged.*"

After a breakfast of dried bread and moldy peaches, they broke camp. Alderman moved like a man possessed, and only Reddington seemed able to keep pace. Alderman tried to slow his cadence in order to not completely lose his comrades, and he whispered menacingly to Reddington.

"They are close. I can feel their fear."

After half a mile of patrol, Alderman heard rustling in the distance, and he quickened his pace. Reddington struggled to keep up as the swamp water immersed his ankles, while Alderman seemed to carelessly soar across the muck.

And there he was.

Metacomet stood alone in a small clearing. He seemed disoriented, and he stared upward at the sun. Reddington had never seen Metacomet before, and Alderman's glee was palpable. He silently mouthed the words.

"It is him."

Alderman stealthily prepped and raised his flintlock, but Reddington was quicker. Reddington tried to ensure his hands were steady. The rest of the company was at least fifty yards behind. He, Thomas Reddington, the humble son of a Middleborough carpenter would end this war. With one shot, he would end the tyrant who started this madness and destroyed the Reddington home. The creature standing idle and unsuspecting before him was the reason Jemmy Barnstrom would never come home to his family. The anticipation was almost too much. Reddington fired.

Nothing happened. His powder was too damp.

Alderman, however, was fanatical about ensuring his powder was dry, and he would not let this opportunity slip away. He aimed his weapon and fired.

The prophecy was right. No Englishman would ever kill Metacomet.

The projectile clearly struck Metacomet in the chest, but he seemed unaware that anything had even transpired. Lost in a world of his own, he stared at the sky and seemed as if he was embracing it. Reddington lurched forward, and suspected the final blow would have to come from his own hands. Finally, like a mighty tree that had been standing perfectly upright until the final swing of the axe, Metacomet fell, rigid and silent, and landed in the mud.

Church, Brewster, and a half-dozen others had eagerly rushed forward after the musket blast, and had finally arrived at the scene. They all stood silently with their mouths agape. Brewster instantly recognized the dead man, and his mind spiraled back to their meeting at Montaup last year, and their deliberations with Easton.

"If I continue to live under the English, I will have no nation left to rule. Just as the English fight for their king, I will die fighting for my father's kingdom."

Brewster felt oddly morose as Church triumphantly propped one foot atop King Philip's lifeless head. Their comrades surveyed the perimeter, and were confident any of Philip's loyalists had fled.

Church raised his saber in triumph. "Brothers! I give you King Philip of the Wampanoag! The scoundrel that started all this madness! The wicked traitor who betrayed Plimoth Colony and made war on the Lord's chosen elect. Well done, Alderman! Vengeance is yours today, and you shall have his right hand! Now then. If any of you gentlemen will fetch me a sturdy axe, I will ensure this villain gets the burial he deserves!"

Brewster knew he had no desire to witness what would come next. He wandered south toward the bay, and Reddington followed. Church continued his victory tirade.

"Brothers! For Plimoth! For our fallen comrades!" The axe fell, and the noise was sickening.

CHAPTER FORTY-ONE

SOUTH OF MONTAUP

The celebratory whooping echoed behind him as Brewster made his way south.

Reddington quickly caught up. "It should have been my shot, Israel. Me. I should go down in history. I've never had a misfire like that. This entire bloody affair, and my musket has never failed to fire once. It's all this damned rain."

Brewster was pensive and slow to respond. "Ultimately, no Englishman killed him. Fourteen months of chasing him through these lands, and no Englishman laid a hand on him."

"Where are you going?"

"I don't know, Thomas. Somehow, I don't feel like celebrating. I remember my time spent with King Philip last year, and...I just wish things could have been different."

"He's the reason Middleborough and Providence are in ashes. He's the reason Alice perished in an inferno."

"I know, but it pains me. This entire affair fills me with such grief. I don't know if any of us have been righteous in the eyes of the Lord."

"He was an enemy of our Lord, Israel. He was a traitor and a coward. Bloody hell, most of the time he didn't even do his own fighting. I think your night terrors are beginning to wear your mind, Reverend."

Brewster could not dispute that statement, and they walked in silence. They had travelled at least half a mile, and were soon admiring the sunlight reflecting off of Mount Hope Bay.

"Will you be leaving us, Israel?"

"As soon as I can, Thomas. I suspect my child is to arrive any day now. I believe I have done my duty for these United Colonies. I..."

Brewster was interrupted by two of Moseley's pirates in the distance. "This one's ours! Keep your distance. You've been warned!"

They didn't reply, and they maintained a steady pace toward the water. As they closed within twenty yards, Reddington finally addressed them. "We've no concern with your shenanigans, pirate. We have just ended this ghastly affair, not a mile from here. King Philip is no more, praise the Lord. I pray we shall all be now reunited with our families, and perhaps you may be reunited with...well, whatever devious affairs command your time."

"Do not toy with us! Is it true? Has Philip been cut down? By Church?" The pirate seemed elated, yet disappointed they were not the ones to procure the ultimate prize.

Brewster ignored their conversation, and stared across the water at a tiny island that was practically a sandbar. He found the source of the pirates' attention, shielded his eyes from the sun with his hand, and squinted.

It was him.

He stood in stunned silence and refocused his vision in every manner possible. He curled both hands and, placing them together, tried to fashion a makeshift telescope. He walked closer, to the very edge of the water.

He was astonished. There was Linto.

In hindsight, he knew there was probably no need for such surprise. Wherever Metacomet roamed, it stood to reason Linto would be nearby. Yet, Brewster obsessed on the notion that this was somehow ordained by heaven.

He had to go see him.

As a man with no history of sea service, Brewster had no reason to trust his swimming abilities. Frantically scanning the beach, he quickly found an all-too-common scrap of timber board, most likely from an abandoned, rotted fishing vessel. Grasping the board across his chest, he waded into the water, dove forward, and began furiously kicking.

Brewster could barely hear the sound of the protests fading away. "What the devil are you doing? That's our property, he cost us two dogs!" The pirates quickly went silent, however, as Reddington stood closer and menacingly rolled up his sleeves.

If Brewster was afraid during his first saltwater swim, he was too distracted to notice. He emerged from the water, soaking wet, and found Linto barely conscious on his back.

Linto blinked repeatedly, and peered through the blinding sunlight. He quite rationally assumed he had perished, and he was surprised that Two Ponds would be the one to guide him to the spirit world. "You? You have come to take me? Well, I am glad, I suppose."

Brewster didn't answer, as he was horrified by the sight of Linto's leg. He was bleeding profusely, and Brewster was terrified he would perish within moments. Trying not to panic, he surveyed the scene. Using his foot for leverage, he was able to extract a shard of wood from his floating board, and he quickly removed his shirt.

Linto was slowly beginning to comprehend that he had not perished, at least not yet, and Brewster was not his spirit guide. His voice was weak. "Have you come to wrestle again, Two Ponds? You may have a chance today, but somehow I doubt it."

An enormous smile lit Brewster's face as he went about his work. Linto was still with him. He knew there would be no saving the leg, and he went to work fashioning a tourniquet. He silently prayed for help from the Almighty while he simultaneously wrapped his shirt just below Linto's knee. He wound the ends of the shirt around the scrap of wood, and rotated it until he was satisfied the bleeding was subsiding. It would hold. Linto's life was safe, for now, and he seemed to be regaining his faculties.

Linto craned his neck and evaluated the tourniquet. Fading backward with numb acceptance, he addressed Brewster. "Why, Two Ponds. Why? Why did this all have to happen to us?"

Brewster tried to think of something, anything to say to provide comfort. Nothing came to mind, and he wiped away the salty water from his face. "Are you in pain?"

Linto ignored the question, and grimaced. "I have done so many horrible things, Two Ponds. I am a liar. I am a fraud. I tried to kill an innocent man. I'm a disgrace in the eyes of my Sachem. He has dismissed me."

Brewster wondered if this was an appropriate time to break the news, and he could discern no reason to withhold it. "Linto, Metacomet is..." He couldn't bring himself to finish the sentence.

He had no need to, as Linto tightly closed his eyes with sad resignation. "Was it an Englishman?"

"No, it was Alderman. A Praying Indian."

Linto almost permitted himself to chuckle in disbelief. "She was right. Her prophecy was right."

"Prophecy?"

"Wawetseka. She said Metacomet could not be killed by an Englishman."

"*Wawetseka! She's alive? You've seen her?*"

"Oh, yes, Two Ponds. She is alive, but she is no longer Wawetseka. She is Nitka-Wendigo. She is the mother of evil now."

Brewster was horrified. "Mother of evil? What? What are you talking about?"

"She is possessed by demons now, Two Ponds. She is insane. Terrible things happened with the Narragansett, and she has lost her mind. Her face is mutilated, and she is a witch now. She is the witch of battle."

Brewster was devastated. He stood, and he tried to hide his expression from Linto. "Where are the children?"

"I don't know. Wawetseka doesn't seem to know or care. They are lost." Tears were welling in his eyes as he continued. "Two Ponds, I have lost everything. I have lost my wife and my children. I've lost my honor. I've lost my Sachem, I've lost my people, I've lost my leg. I suppose I will lose my life today as well."

Brewster could no longer contain himself and was openly sobbing. "It's all my fault, Linto. I went to war after Middleborough...I was there. I led us into the fortress. I led the damned pirates in..." His voice choked as he tried to continue. "Forgive me, I..."

"I know you could not have done wrong, Two Ponds. I know you walk with the Gentle Son." He tried to sit up, but could not. "Two Ponds, I will be dead soon. Please. Tell me more of the Gentle Son."

Brewster had to walk to the shore to compose himself. He washed his face with the cool saltwater, and he let the water run across his shirtless chest and arms. He peered into the sunlight and thought he saw a boat in the distance. He quickly returned to Linto.

"In the Book of Matthew, in chapter seventeen, Jesus took three of his disciples to a high mountain. And there, he was transfigured, his face shined like the sun, and his raiment was as white as light. And behold, there appeared unto them Moses and Elias talking with him. Then answered Peter, and said unto Jesus, Lord, it is good for us to be here: if thou wilt, let us make here three tabernacles; one for thee, and one for Moses, and one for Elias."

"Two Ponds, my time is short."

Brewster was surprised by the interruption, and embarrassingly blinked. "I'm sorry, I just..."

"Two Ponds, don't recite the big book for me. Tell me. Use your own words. Tell me about the Gentle Son."

Brewster blinked again and forced his wet hair out of his eyes. He stammered a few, incoherent words. After a long, pensive silence, he spoke. "Jesus wept."

"What?"

"The Bible teaches us that Jesus Christ, the Gentle Son, wept."

"Of course. The King of Rome whipped him."

"No, long before that. He wept for Jerusalem. It was the holiest of cities for his people, and he cried when he thought about how pathetic they were, and how they would suffer. *"If thou hadst known, even thou, at least in this thy day, the things which belong unto thy peace! But now they are hid from thine eyes."* When I was a child, I often wondered why the Son of God would cry for mere humans, but I suppose that is how He loved us."

Brewster paused and turned his eyes to the sea. There was definitely a boat headed their way, and Brewster could not distinguish its crew. He turned to Linto and continued. "I often wonder if He would weep for us, Linto. I wonder if He would consider everything this land of New England was supposed to be, and what it actually has become. I wonder if He could see the hatred, the war, the slavery and famine, if He would weep for us, too."

Linto rolled to his side and curled up, as if he wished to be alone with his thoughts. The waves gently crashed in the distance, and he didn't make a sound. After a lengthy silence, he rolled on his back, and raised his head to look Brewster in the eyes. "Two Ponds, do you think the Gentle Son could forgive my sins? Because I've done so many wicked things, and I have lied so very often."

Brewster speechlessly nodded and struggled for the words. "Yes."

"Then perhaps, I can be baptized before I die. Maybe, He will hear me if I pray for Wawetseka and the children?"

Brewster seemed uncomfortable and hesitant. "We can get you back to shore and find a properly ordained minister, because I'm not certain…"

"Brewster, they are coming! Hurry! You are the one to do this. Hurry!" Linto had never referred to him by his proper name before.

Brewster rushed to the bay and scooped water into his trembling hands. The boat was now clearly in view, and Brewster was horrified when he recognized one of the passengers. He quickly knelt beside Linto. He briefly thought of asking Linto to kneel, or to move to the lapping waters, but he quickly dispelled any such notion.

He contemplated all of the scripture and liturgy associated with the Puritan baptism rituals. Brewster had not conducted a baptism in at least five years, and he knew time was of the essence.

"Linto, do you renounce sin and wickedness?"

"Yes."

"Do you repent of your sins?"

"Yes."

"Do you believe in God, the Father, Jesus the Gentle Son, and the Holy Spirit?"

"Yes."

"Do you believe Christ was crucified for your sins, and rose from the dead?"

"Yes."

Brewster hesitated before delivering the final question, as it seemingly contradicted the Calvinist doctrine he had embraced for most of his life. "Do you believe God has given you the power and the freedom to resist evil, and the power to fight wickedness and oppression?"

"Yes."

Brewster tenderly poured the water across Linto's scalp. "Then you are now Linto, my brother in Christ. Linto, I baptize you in the name of the Father, Son, and Holy Ghost."

Linto was disappointed to realize he didn't feel any different. Brewster tightened the tourniquet once more, and they saw the men wade through the ankle-deep water and come ashore. Linto began to panic. "Find them, Two Ponds! Promise me you'll find my children! *Don't let them take my children!* You remember what they look like! *YOU KNOW THEM!*"

Brewster proudly stood and confronted the largest man among them. "I am Private Israel Brewster of Captain Church's regiment! This man is my prisoner, and I will deliver him to the proper authorit..." Brewster could not finish the sentence before he was knocked unconscious by Dutch Cornelius' flintlock pistol.

Cornelius thought long and hard about eliminating the nuisance of Israel Brewster once and for all, but he suspected the vaguely familiar, hulking giant watching from the shore was his comrade. "Shut your damned mouth, you yammering preacher man. You're the blasted reason I lost my revenge on Church." As Brewster crumpled to the ground, Cornelius thought about a discreet kick to the eye as well, but he was uncertain how much the man across the water was able to witness.

He assessed his prize. "So, you're the bastard who killed my dogs, are you? Damn it to hell, would you look at that leg? He might not even live. All this work for nothing."

Cornelius sighed. "Get him in the boat. We'll build a fire on shore and amputate. I don't know what the Scotsman will pay for a one-legged bastard that's starved half-to-death. Maybe he's worth a pint of rum."

And at that moment, Linto closed his eyes and said his first prayer as a Christian. He prayed that he would lose consciousness before the slavers took his leg.

Mercifully, his prayer was answered.

CHAPTER FORTY-TWO

PROVIDENCE

Brewster wiped away the sweat, and wondered if there was some kind of cosmic irony at work. The situation seemed absolutely unbearable.

Israel Brewster had been on this earth for thirty-two years, and each and every one was spent in New England. He was now certain this August afternoon in Providence was the hottest day he had ever experienced. He poured water over his head, and he felt like the mere act of breathing was painfully difficult.

He had returned from the war a mere week ago. King Philip was dead, and the last of his loyalists were being steadily rounded up. The city of Providence, under the leadership of Roger Williams, was beginning to see signs of peace and prosperity once again. It had been four months since Canochet and the Narragansett raided their humble community, and now, with the horrific war subsiding, the citizens were exuberantly returning and rebuilding.

Brewster gazed across the room at Zeke. Ezekiel Wilder was a fortunate man. His pregnant daughter was healthy, safe, and about to give him a grandchild. He recently received correspondence from his sons, who were healthy and well in West Jersey. His son-in-law had finally and permanently returned from the war. And shockingly, neither his fishing fleet nor his home had sustained any damage during the March invasion. Brewster was now standing in that very home as his wife went into labor with their first child.

He could only grasp at the cosmological significance of the weather. When his wife Sarah lost her life delivering a stillborn child eight years ago, it was the most bitterly cold night in memory. Now that his beloved Constance was in labor, the weather was so bizarrely hot and unbearable that he could only give thanks that he was not the one giving birth.

When a woman was in labor, there was little to do but wait. Ponder, pace, and wait. And pray. Brewster prayed without ceasing, and when he wasn't praying, he was thinking. He was thinking about the war and all who fought it.

He thought about Thomas Reddington. After Cornelius and the slavers took Linto, Reddington swam to the sand bar to revive Brewster. Reddington's face bore the marks of punishing resistance, as he did everything in his power to stop the pirates. Soon, the guns and sabers were drawn, and Reddington knew that even he was outmatched. He helplessly watched them sail away.

Brewster thought about Benjamin Church. Their farewell had been brief and unceremonious. Church thanked him for his service, and said he would be praying for Constance. He would continue to lead a small contingent of men, as they swept through the colonies seeking the last of Metacomet's rebellion. He was especially anxious to find the next great prize, Annawon.

He thought about Winslow. The war was won, and history would record him as a hero of New England. Governor Josiah Winslow, the proud son of the famed Edward Winslow. The noble and brave commander during the great swamp fight of 1675. How would he go down in history if Brewster, Reddington, and Church didn't win the battle for him?

He had also spent an inordinate amount of time thinking about Mister Barlow. Would Brewster be alive today if five years ago, Barlow didn't take a chance on a mysterious, troubled stranger with no discernible skills? Someone would probably have found his corpse behind a tavern with his hand still clutching an empty bottle of rum. Was Brewster responsible for Barlow's death as well? Would Providence have been assaulted if Winslow's magnificent army didn't destroy the Narragansett fortress?

And of course, he could not stop thinking about Linto, his new brother in Christ. Reddington and Brewster gave chase after Linto was taken away, but they soon realized the futility of pursuing men in a boat. Brewster wondered if Linto would have even survived another day due to his leg wound.

As if the thought of Linto wasn't painful enough, the thought of Wawetseka was equally agonizing. She was among the most beautiful, gentle people he had ever met. She took it upon herself to heal him of his nightmares. And now she was an enemy. Now she was a deranged, evil sorceress who had nothing but contempt for all of the English, and perhaps, rightfully so. What would become of her? His nightmares had subsided in intensity now that the war was over, but he was still a sick man.

And the children. Linto begged him to somehow find the children. How on earth would he find two small children in this war-torn land? Brewster assumed they almost certainly would have frozen to death after the swamp fight. He came very close himself.

Finally, he thought about Brownie. She had survived the cold, the hunger, the disease, and the bloodshed. She had transported countless supplies and wounded men. Through it all, she was at his side, and he would spoil her for the rest of her days as no animal had been spoiled before.

And now, today was the day. Today, he feared, he would once again be judged. Once again, all of his joy could easily be taken away by the unfathomable ritual of childbirth. Everything, he thought, seemed so different this time. The first time was a dark, bitterly cold night, and this was a bright, appallingly hot day. Yet everything seemed so eerily familiar. The look of trepidation on the expectant mother's face. The expression of anxiety on the mid-wife. His own frantic, unrelenting energy. And the hope. The never-failing, unyielding hope.

Zeke and Brewster sat in the front room as Constance endured the agonies of childbirth in the bedroom. There was little they could do, except to find more and more cool water to soothe her forehead. The hours felt like days, and the sun would soon be setting. Brewster retrieved her letters from the war, and re-read them for what seemed to be a millionth time.

He had mustered every last scintilla of self-discipline in order to not fearfully drink himself into a stupor. He feared that if he lost Constance or the child, it would simply be the end of him. He had survived so much, but his mental health was still so frail. Israel Brewster had endured every manner of loss and hardship, and somehow, he had survived.

As the shadows of evening began to fill the room, the terrifying shrieks of childbirth were almost unbearable. He yearned to burst into the room to comfort her, but Zeke knowingly shook his head. He had been through all of this three times before, and he knew childbirth was no place for a man.

Brewster now sat with his head cradled in his hands. He was drenched in perspiration, and wasn't sure how much more he could bear. He consistently engaged in silly but reassuring gestures in order to convince himself he was not dreaming, and this was not another night terror. He drank water. He touched anything and everything. He babbled with Zeke and read scripture. He wandered outside to stare at the sky, and he stroked Brownie's head. This was no dream.

Sunset was now upon them, but the heat was unrelenting. He feared he might sob, and even Zeke seemed to be unraveling. At last, they heard a loud cry, and it was not Constance or the midwife. The cry grew louder, and Brewster did not whether to smile or panic.

When he thought he could endure no more, the midwife opened the door a crack and peeked through. She had been in the New World for two years, and still boasted a thick Yorkshire accent. "A boy! Healthy as a horse, with a mat of dark hair! Praise the Lord! Give us a minute, won't you, gentlemen?"

Zeke did not restrain his tears and he embraced Brewster. The room was growing increasingly dark, and candles were lit. Brewster still could not escape his feeling of dread, and he felt dizzy. Soon enough, the Yorkshire accent filled his ears with the words he longed to hear.

"Well, get in here, come along. Stop standing about like a big oaf. The both of you, now. Come along."

The bedroom was somehow even hotter than the front room, and Constance was drenched. Her flawless, pale skin was inflamed and ruddy, and it appeared as if sitting upright was a struggle. "He has arrived, Israel. A boy. I just knew. Look at his dark hair. And his eyes are so big. Will they be blue?"

The sobbing had ceased, and the child appeared quite comfortable in his mother's arms. The joyous and peaceful quiet seemed odd after a day of shrieks and tears. Zeke touched his daughter's shoulder. "A big, strong fisherman! Little Zeke! We'll get him out on the boat tomorrow!"

Constance proudly smiled. "His name is Daniel. Daniel Ezekiel Brewster."

Numb with fatigue and joy, Israel Brewster turned to his ceaseless source of comfort. He recited scripture. *"Train up a child in the way he should go: and when he is old, he will not depart from it."*

"Ahh, the twenty-second Proverb. Shall you hold him, husband?"

Brewster's blue eyes grew wide as she extended her arms. The child was so beautiful and delicate. Brewster's life was starting anew.

Israel Brewster was once again a creature of joy.

CHAPTER FORTY-THREE

PROVIDENCE

Brewster distractedly examined the charred, mangled stave. He could not be certain where his shaving horse was, but he knew exactly where it had been. The merciless August sun bore down upon him, and he morosely cast aside the stave.

He searched for somewhere to sit, and almost wanted to laugh when he found the first bench he made. When he considered all the precious things and people destroyed in this cooperage, he could not grasp the absurdity that his ridiculous little bench had somehow survived the blaze.

The scene was one of total desolation. Mister Barlow had been buried in the cemetery on the north side of town, and Brewster was unaware if the news had reached his son across the sea.

Like Phineas Barlow, Brewster also had a son. Daniel was born two days ago, and was the picture of health. Constance had somehow recovered her health and stamina, and their home had been bursting with well-wishers. Zeke was anxious to get back to sea, as a rebuilding city was a hungry city. And Brewster finally found the courage to visit the cooperage.

How would he make a living now? How would he support his son? Zeke would obviously be delighted to bring him aboard the family business, but he could not picture himself as a fisherman. Of course, five years ago he could not picture himself as a cooper, and a year ago he could not picture himself as a militiaman. After the last decade of his life, he genuinely wondered if anything could cause him any surprise. At that instant, however, he was surprised.

"You there!"

He was absolutely delighted to see Easton, and they shared a long embrace.

"A war hero and a father! When will you be appointed governor?"

"I think you would enjoy working for me, John. You could brush Brownie in the mornings, fetch ale in the afternoons..."

"I could do worse, Israel. A deputy governor's life is a tiresome one." He took his seat on the bench and seemed aware of the absurdity. "I suppose some things are not worth burning."

Brewster wasn't amused, and he wished Easton would stick with his horse jokes. He mournfully surveyed the scene, and turned to Easton. "I guess I should be thankful I didn't purchase all of this."

Easton stared at the ground and grew somber. "I'm sorry, Israel. I know Mister Barlow was not a Christian man, but I miss him immensely. I've personally notified his son."

Brewster nodded earnestly. "What should I do, John? Should I rebuild it? Should I become a minister? Perhaps the world needs more fishermen?"

"Well, the Gospel of Matthew. Chapter four..."

"Verse nineteen. *And he saith unto them, follow me, and I will make you fishers of men.*" He smiled broadly. It was good to see Easton again.

"I was by the house. What a healthy child. I fear he may resemble you, however. Such a cruel handicap for one so young."

"You'll regret these jokes when I'm governor."

Easton grinned. "Israel, how is your soul these days? The birth must have given you great joy."

The change in subject matter was dramatic and abrupt, and Brewster wasn't certain how to respond. "My joy is profound, John. My family is so wonderful and the Lord has poured out His blessing. But inside, I'm tormented. I'm plagued by memories of the war, and I have nightmares. I close my eyes and picture all the death and cruelty. Do you remember Linto the Wampanoag?"

"King Philip's remarkable translator? How could I forget him?"

Brewster could not bring himself to pursue the conversation he started. Where to begin?

"Did something happen to him, Israel?"

Brewster sighed and tried to contain his emotion. "I think I saved his life. He was bleeding to death, so I applied a tourniquet, and then he asked to be baptized. Then the slavers took him away."

Easton tried to imagine his friend's agony. "These colonies have embraced a shameful enthusiasm for slavery. It's a despicable state of affairs in this allegedly holy land."

Brewster sat silently and could not seem to shake his misery. Downcast and sullen, he thought he might weep.

Easton leapt to his feet. "Come, Israel, come. There is only one solution for misery, and that is to do the Lord's work. Saddle Brownie up, and ride with me west of town. The congregation is bringing a wagon to the orphanage. There may even be an apple for your creature, provided she behaves and doesn't frighten the children."

Brewster nodded his assent. He knew Easton was absolutely right. He stopped at home to extend a loving farewell, and after Zeke filled his saddle bags with crab and dried fish, they were on their way.

The city was bustling with activity of all manner. Houses were being built, peddlers were back on the street, and the taverns were once again thriving. Soon, they were almost three miles west of town.

Brownie seemed invigorated by the summer air, and she seemed to perceive she was on a journey free of wartime violence and stress. She was starting to put her weight back on, and Brewster hoped they would be together for many more years.

"Why is the orphanage so far out of town, John?"

"It's a special place, Israel. Some may not approve, so we've established it on a remote farm."

"Not approve? Who would disapprove of an orphanage?"

"You'd be surprised, Israel. Mankind is fallen and wicked. Evil pervades these colonies."

The farmhouse was spacious but unremarkable. The crops seemed healthy and well maintained. The corn was tall and was weathering the August heat nicely. Two rows of mature apple trees could be seen in the distance. The beans were unimpressive, but would hopefully yield a good harvest.

Brewster noticed many of the workers tending the corn were children. As they grew closer, despite their baggy linen shirts and floppy hats, he noticed how swarthy they were.

These children were Indians.

Easton could see Brewster's stunned expression. "This is Providence, Israel, so Plimoth's influence is limited. Still, we like to be discreet about these things."

"How many are here?"

"At least three dozen as of last week. We can certainly take more."

Brewster seemed to ignore the answer, and he guided Brownie to the porch of the farmhouse. There were several young toddlers playing happily on the porch, and the merriment was a welcome contrast to the suffering and misery of the previous months.

When Brewster saw them, he almost fell off of Brownie. It had been a year since he met them, but there could be no mistake.

The power of the Almighty would always seem awesome and mysterious, and Brewster had spent a lifetime struggling to comprehend it. His faith had taught him that the will of God is apparent in every aspect of our lives, and yet he agonized throughout his days about what was divinely ordained, and what was mere coincidence. Consequently, Brewster would spend the rest of his days marveling and wondering about the significance of this moment.

Forty-eight hours ago, Israel and Constance Brewster had no children. Now they had three.

THE PROPHET AND THE WITCH

And suddenly, there were no more night terrors.

CHAPTER FORTY-FOUR

PLIMOTH

Linto could not bear the expression on Metacomet's face.

He turned away, and tightly closed his eyes. He desperately hoped that when he opened them, his Sachem would be lively and smiling. Cautiously, he opened one eye and peeked. Nothing had changed.

Metacomet appeared morose and defeated. His eyes were vacant, and his mouth was drooping. Linto stared and tried to recollect happier times. He tried to remember the serious but devoted Sachem who raised him from a child.

"I have told you for years what you mean to have meant to me and our people. Embrace your destiny, Linto."

Linto had tried to embrace his destiny, but he had failed. He had utterly failed his Sachem, and it pained him to look upon his countenance. He stared directly into his face, and cried out, "Forgive me, Sachem. I am so sorry for the grief I have caused." Metacomet remained expressionless, and did not reply.

"No talking, peg-leg. Keep moving."

Linto sadly gazed down at the pathetic wooden leg the slavers had fashioned for him. It was difficult to maintain his balance with his wrists tightly secured in manacles, and he had fallen three times while being marched across the wharf, much to the amusement of his captors. He looked at his Sachem's face one final time, and silently mouthed the words.

"I love you, Sachem."

He did not expect Metacomet to reply, as his lifeless head was mounted on a stake like a grotesque trophy. The slavers ensured all their captives were marched past it twice while enroute to the ships awaiting them at Plimoth's waterfront.

Linto tried to imagine his destination. Would it be hot or cold there? Were they being sent all the way across the sea to be marched through England? Maybe they were being sent to France to fight the Catholics. How long would it take to sail to France? Linto kept hearing the Englishmen on the pier say a funny word he had never heard before. Bur-mood-ah. Bur-mah-yoou-dah. He wondered if that was in England.

The cadence of the chained men marching across the pier echoed with a haunting rhythm. Linto scanned the faces to see if any were familiar, but none were. All had shackles on their wrists and ankles, whereas Linto's ankle remained untethered. He would not be running away.

His leg had healed remarkably well. The angry pirate had meticulously cauterized the wound after the amputation, and Linto's life was no longer in jeopardy. Linto subsequently prayed that Two Ponds had not been injured too badly. He also prayed for Two Ponds' friend, the enormous Englishman who fought so hard for Linto.

Linto had spent the previous twenty sunrises on small boats, in prison cells, in wagons, and on more boats. He could see by the size of the ship awaiting him that he was being prepared for a distant journey, and he knew he would never see home again.

As he was marched forward and inspected at every opportunity, he overhead a man in fancy clothing speak in a manner he had never heard before. He wasn't quite sure it was even English.

"Mister Barron, what am I to do with this? A scrawny peg-leg? He won't survive a week on a sugar plantation."

The next voice was also odd, but it was very familiar to Linto. It was the screechy voice of the man with the bulbous eyes who presided over Tobias' murder trial.

"Mister MacTavish. Elijah. Be reasonable. We are contracted for sixty healthy men this week. As the term *healthy* is so poorly defined, this man clearly meets the requirements. He is free of disease, he is standing upright, and...and..." Jeremiah Barron's jowly jaw fell wide open as he surveyed the man in question. "It's…this is…this is the troublesome Indian from the murder trial. My Lord, this is most extraordinary."

"Murder trial? Jeremiah, what are you on about? Just put him on the damned boat and I suppose I'll suffer the financial loss when he perishes in a week."

If Jeremiah Barron was unpleasant-looking when he was angrily scowling, he was absolutely hideous when he was smiling. Elijah MacTavish had never seen his business associate look so happy. He feared he may have lost his faculties in the summer heat.

"Mister MacTavish, this is perhaps the most articulate and intelligent savage in all of New England. He stood as counsel in a murder trial and was a terrible thorn in our side. I am uncertain I can permit a man of his talents to go to Bermuda to boil sugar cane."

MacTavish rubbed his chin but appeared unimpressed. "Oh, balderdash, Jeremiah. Not a cent more. You are lucky I'm even letting you fill your quota with him. He doesn't even have a proper wooden leg. It's more like a twig."

"Oh, no. No, indeed, my friend. I have a mind to keep him myself to assist with the unbearable drudgery of my paperwork, but I can't stand the sight of these traitorous savages. He would be a remarkable asset in a Bermuda trading house."

MacTavish was still unconvinced. "What is your name, prisoner? Say something intelligent for me."

Linto remained silent and did not raise his eyes. MacTavish was quick to rage, and he easily pushed Linto to the pier while kicking aside his wooden leg.

"WHAT…IS…NAME?"

Barron quickly intervened before MacTavish ruined his prize. "His name is Mister Linto! Mister Linto, do stand up!" Barron even assisted Linto to his feet. "Mister Linto, please show our good friend how intelligent you are. Please say something in English. I do beg you."

Linto faced MacTavish. "Me good man. Me talk good for you. Me name Linto."

MacTavish roared with delight. "Very amusing. On the boat with you, now. Jeremiah, I do suspect you are trying to swindle me for another African serving girl. Try not to sire another child with her, won't you? I fear even Plimoth Colony is running out of heretics to take the blame."

Perhaps it was the oppressive heat, or perhaps MacTavish's taunt had cut too deeply. Perhaps it was the strain of the war, or perhaps it was even was the memory of Linto and the murder trial, but for whatever reason, Barron became apoplectic with rage. His unpleasant face was turning purple. *"Very well, Mister Linto! Off with you, then! You foul, vile, filthy savage! Burn with the sugar cane!"* In a fit of vicious anger, Barron pushed Linto over, and back to the filthy wooden planks of the pier.

MacTavish was laughing harder than ever. "Oh dear, I do love my time in these Puritan colonies. Such holiness. Such piety. Come, Linto. There's a lad."

Linto slowly picked himself off the pier, and dusted himself off. He stepped forward, until he was only mere feet away from Barron.

Linto inhaled slowly, and began speaking. "Do you believe you are righteous and I am a savage, Mister Barron? Do you believe the Lord has looked in the hearts of all men, and has chosen you? Are you truly a saint, Mister Barron? Are you among the *elect*?"

Linto took a step closer. "For I know the words and deeds of the Lord, sir, and I pray for you. You are wicked, and your heart is filled with malice. For truly, the Gentle Son did say, *love your enemies, bless them that curse you, do good to them that hate you, and pray for them which despitefully use you and persecute you.* And I shall pray for you, Mister Barron. And I pray one day, you will come to understand which one of us is the true savage."

Linto turned away and began hobbling toward the boat. MacTavish roared with laughter yet again, and Barron raised his fist while preparing to assault Linto from behind. MacTavish intervened, and tightly seized Barron's wrist.

"Oh, no, Jeremiah. This is my property now. I have special plans for this one." When it was apparent Barron had regained his composure, he released his grip. "You shall have another servant girl, Jeremiah. Mister Linto is going to be a boon to my enterprise. An enormous boon, indeed."

Linto hobbled onboard the ship. He took a final look at the land of his birth, and the land of the Wampanoag. He knew that sixty summers ago, when Annawon was a child, this was not Plimoth. This was Patuxet and there was not an Englishman to be found. And now it was a hostile, foreign land.

He was led below deck, and in the fetid, sweltering darkness, he contemplated his destiny. He had lost everything. He had absolutely nothing in this world except his faith in the Gentle Son. But he would persevere.

Linto would persevere in this hostile, depraved world. Just as Father Jacques would show no fear wherever the Lord sent him, Linto would also show no fear. As Missus Rowlandson placed her trust in the Lord no matter what manner of horrific tragedy she encountered, Linto would also trust. And just as Two Ponds lost everything that mattered to him but somehow persevered, Linto would persevere as well.

He would not merely persevere. Linto would triumph. He would use his gifts to fight wickedness and oppression, no matter where this life took him. As a man who truly had nothing, he would have nothing to fear.

Linto now sat chained and despised in the foul, cramped darkness. He had been on this world for twenty-seven summers, and his very life was the result of a miracle.

And deep in his soul, Linto knew that somehow, for some reason, his journey was only beginning.

EPILOGUE

EAST OF REHOBOTH

The two grizzled warriors cast steely glares at one another through the firelight.

Church evaluated his adversary. He had known previously that he was advanced in years, but he did not truly comprehend his age until meeting him face-to-face. His wizened countenance was a curious mixture of joy and intense sadness. Of all the remarkable moments Benjamin Church had experienced during this war, this was perhaps the most astounding.

It had now been approximately two weeks since King Philip had been cornered and killed. Church himself ensured the body was properly decapitated and quartered in a manner befitting a scoundrel and a traitor. Subsequently, most of Church's company had gone home to their families. Still, there were some of Philip's loyalists still making war, and Church could not rest until the threat to the colonies was finally extinguished.

His adversary sat perfectly still as Church feasted on a late dinner of fire-roasted beef. He still seemed utterly amazed that Church and his men had captured him in the manner they did. The native warrior was encamped with approximately three dozen warriors at the bottom of a formidable cliff face. Rather than attempt to storm the well-guarded frontal approach, Church and his men audaciously scaled down the cliff face under cover of darkness. Although the native contingent completely outnumbered Church's men, they had had enough. It was two deserters who led Church to their encampment, and any further bloodshed was pointless. They surrendered and invited the English invaders to share in their meager rations. They even had beef from a purloined cow, their first real food in weeks.

Church warily eyed his prisoner. It was late, and everyone else in the encampment had fallen asleep except for the two opposing leaders. Church could not seem to turn away, and the two men stared and stared. He wished his prisoner could speak English, as there was so much he wanted to ask him.

Suddenly, without a word, the grizzled yet distinguished prisoner rose. Church tensed, and vigilantly watched his every movement. Was this an escape attempt? Church wanted to maintain the current tranquility, so he made no overt moves. He cautiously set down his beef and kept his right hand near his saber.

The prisoner seemed oblivious to his captor's suspicion, and he sauntered behind a tree. Church assumed nature was calling, but instead, he returned with a red jacket laced with an extraordinary collection of wampum.

"I suppose this belongs to you now. Philip was Sachem, but you killed him. Then I became Sachem, yet here you are. Here you are, Church. The Sachem of the Wampanoag's coat."

Church felt absolutely mortified that Annawon could speak English, as they'd spent the last hour silently staring at one another.

"Why didn't you say you could speak English, Annawon?"

"You never asked me."

Church didn't know whether to laugh or be angry. "It is indeed a remarkable coat."

"He was a remarkable man." He resumed eating his beef.

"He did a terrible thing, Annawon. He brought nothing but misery and bloodshed."

"I don't know what choice he had. I would have done the same." A pained anguish consumed Annawon, and he tried to change the subject. "Captain, what kind of name is *Church*? Are you a holy man among your people?"

He tried not to laugh. "No, I suppose not. I'm a farmer and a soldier. And a passable carpenter. I am a God-fearing man, though."

Annawon understood and nodded. "I am not surprised it is you who has captured me. Everyone knows of you."

"Well, soon I hope to be a farmer again. I am glad your capture has gone so peacefully. There has been enough bloodshed."

"What will you do with an old man like me?"

"I will escort you to Plimoth of course, to face the authorities. You have been so gracious and cooperative, however, that I am compelled as a Christian man to recommend the utmost leniency."

"What is leniency?"

"I will tell Governor Winslow I don't think you should be executed or imprisoned. I'd like to think I have some sway with Governor Winslow."

"Winslow. Skunk Genitals."

"Who?"

"How we despise him, Church. He is the cause of all of this, not Philip. Winslow the father was kind, but Winslow the son is wicked."

"I'd thank you to keep such thoughts to yourself if I'm going to recommend leniency."

"Harrumph. I suppose we are but captains of war, Church. It is our duty to do as our Sachems command. We try to persuade them when we disagree, but in the end, we follow orders. I know Winslow is your Sachem."

"I suppose that is indeed the way of the world, Annawon. The captains of war prepare, they train, they fight, and they pray for victory. They do their duty. At least tonight, two tired war captains can share a helping of beef together. I suppose we have done our duty for our Sachems."

"Thank you, Church. Captain Church."

Off in the darkness, neither of them could hear the sound of hissing. Nitka-Wendigo lurked in the night, undetectable to all. She heard their talk, and she saw Annawon breaking bread with Skunk Genitals' lap dog. How easily they all surrendered. How they humiliated themselves before the English.

Hissing louder, she stroked the bracelet she had fashioned from the hair of dead English soldiers. She stared at the moon, and quietly chanted a mysterious incantation. Annawon the cowardly traitor was now cursed.

The next day, Church escorted Annawon and the prisoners to Plimoth. Adhering to his word, Church enthusiastically recommended leniency for Annawon and the prisoners who surrendered with him. Church subsequently had further business to attend to in Boston, but he promised to return as soon as he could.

Church returned a week later, and was greeted by a revulsive new development in Plimoth.

Perhaps this new development could have been attributed to Josiah Winslow's stern and unyielding sense of justice. Perhaps, unbeknownst to Church, it could have been attributed to Nitka-Wendigo's mysterious and fearful powers. Regardless of the cause, one thing was painfully clear.

Metacomet and Annawon had been reunited.

AUTHOR'S NOTES

This is my second novel. I hope you have enjoyed reading it as much as I've enjoyed researching and writing it.

If you have read my author's notes for "My Father's Kingdom," then these notes will sound very familiar. First, I would like to emphasize that it's astounding King Philip's War is not a topic of greater study and reflection. Secondly, I'd like to emphasize that even though this a novel, the events you just read about are historically accurate.

King Philip's War was one of the greatest tragedies in American history, and far too many of us have never even heard of it. As I mentioned in book one, there is a remarkable gap in popular American history between the Mayflower and the Boston Massacre. The gap spans over one hundred and fifty years, and yet the era is full of remarkable history.

Why are we especially so intent on forgetting King Philip's War? There are probably two fundamental and obvious reasons. First, it is extremely unpleasant. We shudder to accept the reality that, fifty years after celebrating their historic Thanksgiving, the Pilgrims and the Wampanoag Indians were slaughtering one another with reckless abandon. No warfare is ever pleasant, but by any historical standards, King Philip's War was extremely vicious. Both sides engaged in varying degrees of torture, both sides burned homes and villages, and both sides showed no mercy to non-combatants. The fact that a large proportion of the losing side was sold into slavery only adds to the revulsion.

Secondly, King Philip's War is confusing. Even the name initially causes confusion, as it implies a European conflict of some kind. Trying to comprehend the changing loyalties of the various Native American nations, such as Wampanoag, Pequot, Mohegan, Narragansett, Nipmuc, and Mohawk can be challenging, indeed. Understanding the root causes of the war is also quite difficult. Additionally, much of the original source material, such as the journals of Benjamin Church, William Hubbard, and Increase Mather, are written in the language of the era, and are quite laborious.

I'm not a historian, and I strongly encourage readers to further research and explore this era. I have tried very hard to stay true to historical events in this novel, with only minor deviations for literary purposes. A list of which characters were fictional was provided in the beginning of the book. Some of the places where I took fictional liberties and deviated from historical record are listed below.

James Cudworth is usually referred to as a captain or major in the history books, not a colonel. I thought he deserved a promotion.

Dutch Cornelius Anderson is a historical figure, but there is no evidence he and Benjamin Church were bitter adversaries.

The notion of the Wampanoag referring to Winslow as "Skunk Genitals" is fictional.

Nimrod is a historical figure, but there is no evidence he was responsible for the massacre at Kickemuit, or was as hateful as depicted.

Captain Fuller is a historical figure, but I have exaggerated his shortcomings.

Characters are depicted as drinking tea throughout the book, but tea as we understand it today would probably have been an extraordinary luxury in New England in 1675.

Middleborough was attacked on July 8, 1675, not in the autumn of the year.

Although John Alderman allegedly blamed Metacomet for the death of his brother, there is no evidence to suggest he was a mutineer at Nipsachuck.

Although some of the Sachems of the Nipmuc are recorded in history, I used the fictional Bluebird and Blackbird. There is no evidence Metacomet would have

THE PROPHET AND THE WITCH

received such an unwelcoming reception from the Nipmuc, but considering the circumstances, it is probable they harbored some resentment.

I have no idea how capable and prepared the militia of Providence really was in 1675.

The notion of Metacomet trying to deceive the Mohawks in the disturbing manner portrayed is debatable. It is mostly ascribed to Increase Mather's journal, but it is based in history.

I depicted the Nipmuc as being primarily stationary at Menameset throughout 1676, but this is grossly simplified. They were highly mobile, as Mary Rowlandson's journal attests.

I probably depicted Josiah Winslow more negatively than he deserves, but history will be (and is) his judge. The United Colonies' decision to attack the Narragansett and the subsequent results is a very controversial part of Colonial American history.

Edward Elmer, the representative of Connecticut, is a historical figure. He found his way into my book because, as my mother-in-law pointed out, he is an ancestor of my wife's family. *Hi Lois!* He really did perish during the war.

It's also worth noting that one of the many remarkable things about King Philip's War is how quickly the tide turned. During the opening months of 1676, things appeared absolutely dismal for the United Colonies. By summer, they were on the verge of winning the war. I hope my chapter in part three about the War Council provided a concise, consolidated explanation for the astounding turn of events.

"The Prophet and the Witch" is obviously a novel rife with very intense subject matter such as war, hatred, torture, insanity, slavery, and religious strife. I've done my best to accurately portray the people, events, and mindsets of the era. Ultimately, I hope it is also a tale of love, friendship, faith, and courage in the face of evil.

If you enjoyed the book, please feel free to write a quick review at Amazon or Goodreads.

I hope to reunite Israel Brewster, Linto, Wawetseka, and Captain Church in a third book very soon. Oh. And Brownie, too.

James W. George
August 2017

Made in the USA
Middletown, DE
20 June 2023

33057960R00217